# Like a Sister

## a

## Sister

## KELLYE
## GARRETT

**SIMON &
SCHUSTER**

London · New York · Sydney · Toronto · New Delhi

First published in the United States in 2022 by Mulholland Books,
an imprint of Little, Brown and Company, a division of Hachette Book Group, Inc., New York

First published in Great Britain by Simon & Schuster UK Ltd, 2022

3 5 7 9 10 8 6 4 2

Simon & Schuster UK Ltd
1st Floor
222 Gray's Inn Road
London WC1X 8HB

Simon & Schuster Australia, Sydney
Simon & Schuster India, New Delhi

www.simonandschuster.co.uk
www.simonandschuster.com.au
www.simonandschuster.co.in

A CIP catalogue record for this book
is available from the British Library

ISBN: 978-1-3985-1763-9
eBook ISBN: 978-1-3985-1764-6
Audio ISBN: 978-1-3985-1765-3

Printed and bound in Great Britain by
CPI Group (UK) Ltd, Croydon, CR0 4YY

MIX
Paper | Supporting
responsible forestry
FSC® C171272

## Praise for *Like a Sister*

'I tore through *Like a Sister* – a stand-out, propulsive thriller from such a fresh, original voice. Lena is an unforgettable heroine – vulnerable, witty, and relentless in her quest for justice. Suspenseful storytelling at its best. Loved it!' **Caz Frear**

'A wholly captivating novel, one that grows more complicated – and tense – as the story unfolds. Loaded with twists and turns, this book will keep you guessing until the last shocking page' **Samantha Downing**

'Kellye Garrett, a break-out star in crime fiction ... A traditional mystery set in the world of reality television and Instagram influencers, it is equal parts charm and heartbreak, with razor-sharp insights on class, race, and family' **Laura Lippman**

'A riveting, read-through-the-night thriller by a masterful storyteller. From the very first page to the jaw-dropping finish, this is one you need to put at the top of your reading list' **Liv Constantine**

'*Like a Sister* is a marvel and a must-read story for the current moment ... A gripping narrative of domestic suspense which delivers hard, essential truths about race, class, and makes us question why some women's stories are too often disbelieved' **Ivy Pochoda**

'A crackling domestic suspense that has you turning the pages to see what happens next ... *Like A Sister* is one of those books that's best prepared for ahead of time, because once you pick it up, it will be difficult to put down' **Alyssa Cole**

'Domestic suspense for the Instagram gen. #lovedit' **Lori Rader-Day**

'A stellar suspense novel. Kellye's book is sharp, poignant, and loaded with twists' **Alex Segura**

'While the plot has its fair share of twists and turns, Lena's voice makes the novel shine ... [her] wit plus a packed plot will grab and hold your attention' *Time*

'Garrett's taut novel dishes up the glitz of the haves and the struggles of the have-nots in a New York cleaved along lines of race and class, infusing classic noir storytelling with Big Apply glamour and buzzy texts and tweets' **Oprah Daily**

'Explores the intricacies of strained family relationships ... The gap between media personae and private lives is a running theme, allowing for an expose of how fame is constructed in the era of "finsta" accounts and personal brands ... [a] briskly plotted, socially astute new thriller' *Los Angeles Times*

'An intriguing set up; an absorbing storyline that kept me guessing; a satisfying ending; and most of all, incredibly well-developed characters that I kept thinking about long after I finished the book. I want everyone I know to read it so we can talk about it' **Jasmine Guillory**, recommended pick on the Today show

'The writing is sharp, the commentary wry, and Lena is irresistible ... [a] whip-smart, heart-hurt, very entertaining heroine' *Kirkus Review*

'With tight plotting, deep characterizations, and Chandler-esque metaphors, *Like a Sister* is bound to be one of the best psychological thrillers of the year' *CrimeReads*

'In addition to creating a satisfying, twisty mystery and eloquently depicting the complexity of family relationships, Garrett explores racial identity, privilege, and discrimination as an organic part of the novel, with a deft, often funny touch' *Library Journal*

'Sharp, smart, and heartbreaking' *Reader's Digest*

'Stylish ... noir for the media-struck generation ... these elements of character and voice mesh with *Like a Sister*'s explorations of race, class and family in an arresting combination' **NPR.org**

'Groundbreaking ... With its biting insight and wry dialogue, Garrett's story is propulsive, fierce and witty. Do not miss this' *BookTrib*

'Terrific ... pulses with a rich vein of sarcastic humor and explores ideas around fame, race, and celebrity' **Mystery Scene**

'Arresting ... this family-oriented thriller is anything but ordinary ... a twisty murder mystery with nuance and heart' *BookPage*

'One of [the] buzziest crime books ... timely, relevant, and gripping' **Goodreads**

*To my sisters, Doni and Nikki. I love you even when I hate you and I know the feeling is mutual.*

# Like a
## a
# Sister

# ONE

I found out my sister was back in New York from Instagram. I found
out she'd died from the New York *Daily News*.

Her post was just as attention seeking as their headline. Hers came at
midnight. Look back at it. #birthday #25 #grownfolksbusiness #home
#nyc—all over a behind-the-back shot of her in nothing more than a
black slip dress and no bra.

The article came less than twelve hours later. FORMER REALITY
STAR DESIREE PIERCE FOUND DEAD IN LINGERIE IN BRONX WITH
COCAINE AND NO SHOES.

I'd come straight here—to where they found her—as soon as I'd seen it.

Why? I don't know. Maybe to confirm it was real. Maybe to hope it
was not. Maybe to get one last glimpse of her even though I knew her
body was long gone. Whatever the reason, I'd arrived at this particular
playground in the Bronx on autopilot. The place my sister had come just
hours before. It looked how I felt—all reds and blues and worn down. It
would never be accused of being the happiest place on Earth.

FORMER REALITY STAR DESIREE PIERCE FOUND DEAD IN LINGERIE
IN BRONX WITH COCAINE AND NO SHOES.

I hated it. For what it said. For what it represented. For what it
really meant.

My left wrist itched. I rubbed it, desperate for the feeling—my feelings—to go away.

"You okay?"

The voice was male, melodic, and a stark reminder I only *felt* alone. I was not, surrounded by police and gawkers and at least one TV reporter—all standing on opposite sides of the crime tape like it was an eighth-grade dance.

Was I okay? Not in the slightest. I hadn't seen my little sister in two years. Now I never would. I wanted to ignore the question, just like I ignored the trickle of sweat rolling down my cheek. It felt better than tears.

"I'm fine," I finally said automatically, not even giving the man a glance.

FORMER REALITY STAR DESIREE PIERCE FOUND DEAD IN LINGERIE IN BRONX WITH COCAINE AND NO SHOES.

Desiree would have hated the headline too, the use of the word "former" as much as the use of the word "dead." And the mention of what she wore, but not *who,* would've annoyed her more than calling out the cocaine, though last time we'd actually spoken she claimed she'd stopped using. I hadn't believed her. This was probably the first time I wasn't happy to be proven right.

"You sure you're okay?" The same voice again. I finally looked up from my phone to see who was talking. He was Black. Tall. Smiling like he knew the effect his face had on women. Not me. At least not today, or for the last couple of years if I was being honest.

I nodded. Unfortunately, he took it as a sign to continue. "You know her?"

Only well enough to have predicted this scenario. Both in nightmares ("You're gonna overdose one day") and in daydreams ("You're gonna overdose one day—I'll be there when you wake up to say I told you so"). I'd played it out dozens of times, in dozens of ways, for years before I'd cut her off. And yet, despite telling her this was going to happen, I still wasn't the least bit prepared. Did I know her?

"Not as well as I should have."

"She was famous," he said. "Well, kinda. Mel Pierce's prized daughter. You know him? Notorious music exec. I'm sure you heard the story about the window."

I sure had.

I nodded again but didn't say anything, hoping he'd get the hint. *Prized daughter.* He looked just as out of place in this neighborhood as Desiree must've been, wearing a black-on-black suit in 90-degree weather while standing next to a jungle gym. "They found her about five a.m. Cops think it's an—"

"Overdose. I know." Cutting him off, I gestured to my phone. "I read the *Daily News*."

Five times, in fact. Once at the bodega. I'd stopped by on my way to class for a Snapple and instead got a Google Alert. Three more times on the trip over. Twice on the 1. Once more after my bike and I got off at 168th to finish the trip. The final time right before he'd interrupted me.

"You kinda look like her, you know," he said, then abruptly closed his mouth as if realizing his faux pas, comparing a stranger to someone who'd just died. "Maybe it's the freckles."

It wasn't the first time I'd heard it, but I never saw it myself. We were technically half sisters, after all. If anything, I was the barefaced Before to her perfectly made-over After. I didn't respond, just let him stare at me as a woman with box braids pushed past us, anxious to gawk and report back to her friends like an NBC 4 reporter. The crowd was surprising. A dead Black woman wasn't normally anything to crow about. Not here. Not anywhere, really. Except Desiree Pierce wasn't just any Black woman. She was Mel Pierce's *prized daughter*. Just like the man had said.

The man who now stuck out his hand. "Stuart Jones."

He'd said his name like I should recognize it. When I didn't respond, he spoke again. "I'm the crime reporter. For the *News*."

He gestured to my phone. And just like that, I wanted to talk to him. "Aww," I said. Then, raising both brows, "You write headlines as well as articles?"

His hazel eyes widened. "No. That one…was a bit much."

My phone rang. I recognized the number and ignored it.

"Yeah. Just a bit." I gave him a tight smile. "Wonder if they would have went the 'bit much' route if it was a Kardashian. Any white girl, really."

"I doubt it," he said, and for the first time his smile seemed genuine. "Can I quote you on that? For an article, Miss…"

I shook my head. He tried to step closer, but my Schwinn blocked his path. "Don't tell me you're a Mrs.…"

I was not. But still. I didn't answer the question, instead opting for "Lena. Lena Scott."

It was my turn to see if he recognized the name. He didn't. Thank God.

I smiled in relief, but he didn't know that. He assumed it was for him. "*Ms.* Scott"—another grin—"wondering if you can help me out. It's for a follow-up. I'm interested in what the natives have to say."

"I'm not native." I'd grown up in Jersey and only moved to the city a year ago, when I'd started classes at Columbia.

"That's okay." He flashed that smile again. "I'm still interested."

I pulled my bike closer, then crossed my arms to cover the hot-pink I USED TO BE A PEOPLE PERSON…THEN PEOPLE RUINED IT FOR ME written on my fitted black T-shirt. A double barrier. "I'm not."

Box Braids returned, practically pushing me out of the way. "You can talk to me, cutie. I'm Toni White. That's with an *i.*"

"I'd love to, Miss White." Guess he wasn't as concerned about her marital status as he'd been about mine. "Did you know Desiree Pierce?"

"Of course! I loved her. I watched her every week on that girl's show," Toni said. "*NYZ.* She didn't have any goddamn sense."

*Editing. It's called editing, Toni with an* i. But I swallowed my flip retort.

Toni continued. "But I loved that about her."

I'd loved other things: her humor, her ability to talk to anyone, her glass-half-full attitude. The problem was that it was usually a glass half full of vodka. It was why I had decided to love it all from a distance.

"She had so much potential," Toni said, and at least that was true. She sucked in a breath, as if trying to keep it together, and started sniffling. I looked up to see if she'd actually cry. Her eyes were as dry as my sex life. I looked back down. "She was beautiful. Too beautiful to die," Toni finally said through attempted sobs. As if ugly people got first dibs on tragedy. "Too beautiful to be assaulted like that."

My eyes jumped to Stuart, the throbbing in my wrist back with a vengeance. "She was raped?" I could barely get the words out.

Stuart shook his head and the throbbing stopped. "No signs of sexual trauma."

"No rape?" Toni sounded disappointed. "But I heard she didn't have on any panties."

I wasn't surprised. Desiree had been known to go commando, considering it a lifestyle choice.

"She didn't," Stuart said, casually, like he was discussing the weather. "My source at the precinct is saying there was bruising on her legs but nothing to indicate foul play. They don't know how she got here, but they're working on it. So am I."

He watched me as he spoke, his chest puffed out like he was Superman sent to save the day. But it was too late. My sister was already gone.

"She musta been really needing a hit to come all the way up here." That was Toni again, working my nerves like a street corner.

"You know that's some bullshit." I shook my head as I cut in. "There are better places to get coke in the city. So I've heard." From Desiree, in fact. "She didn't come up here to score drugs. Not if she had been in Manhattan."

I stared her down like a bully in fifth grade, and she didn't say anything. Just looked away. And for the first time that day, I wanted to smile. So I kept at it. "She was last seen in Manhattan?"

Stuart nodded. "SoHo. Omni hotel rooftop."

"Latest hot spot?" I said.

"Yeah. You haven't been?"

"As a rule, I don't travel below 110th. Look, if a reality star"—I made sure not to use the word "former"—"with a rich father is going to get her hands on some coke, it would be at the hottest spot in Manhattan. Right?"

A miffed Toni grabbed Stuart's arm. "Police said she overdosed," she said. "If she didn't come up here for drugs, then why? A girl like that don't belong in the Bronx."

"That's what I'm trying to figure out," said Stuart, star reporter. "How did a woman like Desiree Pierce end up dead in a park above the Major Deegan Expressway?"

I could have told them both. I'd known from the moment I saw the headline.

She'd been coming to see me.

---

The cell's camera turns on to find Desiree Pierce in selfie position, left arm fully extended and raised just enough to make her look up at the screen. She turns her face slightly to the left. Pauses, then faces right. All in search of the perfect light.

Her brown face is beautiful and freckled. Her hair is long and pitch-black, in the kind of beach waves that most Black women get from Bantu knots. Her diamond necklace catches the light.

Behind her are the tasteful yet stark decorations of a hotel suite that's littered with clothes, shoes, and cups. Desiree turns again, stops, then moves a few centimeters to the left.

She smiles, showing off perfectly aligned white teeth.

Someone unseen takes in a long sniffle. Desiree's too busy smiling to notice.

"Freck, can you get your beautiful-ass face out of the camera for once?" The voice is female and teasing. It's impossible to tell where it comes from.

Desiree pretends to roll her eyes. "Let the record show the birthday girl is the first one ready."

The voice again. "That's 'cause you don't have to do all the shit I do! Your skin is perfect."

9

Desiree shrugs, pretends to look demure. "Black don't crack."

A second later she's finally joined by Erin Ambrose. Blond hair. Blue eyes. Surgically enhanced lips. She crowds into the frame. "I don't crack either."

"Yeah, you just do everything else."

"No comment." Erin holds up a white mug with OMNI printed on it in thick black letters. She raises it in mock salute. "To Desiree Pierce on the occasion of her twenty-fifth birthday. A toast."

Desiree does the same with her free arm, holding another hotel mug. She tips it just enough to show what's inside. It's filled with a clear liquid. "A toast...with water."

Erin nods. "That's definitely water."

"It is!"

"Right." Erin nods double time. "We're good clean girls who don't drink, don't do drugs, and sure as hell don't fucking curse. So that is definitely *not* vodka."

"It's *not*." Desiree chugs it, then flashes the empty mug. "See!"

It takes just a moment for Erin to roll her eyes. "Like you've never done that with vodka."

They both laugh as Desiree speaks. "My family might be watching this!"

"I thought I was your family!"

"You are. Just like a sister."

They finally clink mugs. Erin talks to Desiree while looking dead at the lens. "Happy birthday, bitch."

# TWO

Gram died five years ago in February, a stroke as sudden as it was painful—for her and everyone who loved her. And that truly was everyone. Gram always lit up the room. Especially for me, as she was the only grandparent I knew. My mom's parents died when I was a baby, and my paternal grandfather was never in the picture.

But if you could have only one grandparent, Phyllis Pierce was perfect. I wouldn't have gotten through her funeral without Desiree. We moved in tandem all day, only separating to go to the bathroom and even then just long enough to flush. I remember her doing my makeup, loading us both up on waterproof mascara and a healthy dose of setting spray.

My mother, on the other hand, had let me cry for half a day before informing me I needed to get it together. Phyllis Pierce and Olivia Scott had never been close, but that wasn't why she told me that. It was just my mother's way. We'd even joke about it, say she was putting on the Super Black Woman cape. You handle your business, and only then do you turn back into the ordinary girl who's allowed to cry. And there was indeed work to be done, a funeral to help plan.

So when my mom lost her battle with breast cancer three months later, I knew what to do, how to behave.

My mom had known her diagnosis for a whole year but hadn't told me. She knew I was enjoying my first job—as a project coordinator in DC—and she didn't want her diagnosis to be the end of my new life. She planned to survive cancer like she'd survived everything else, waiting until she was on her literal deathbed to tell me.

Even once she passed, the tears didn't come right away. Scotts weren't criers. I hated it, how it made me feel, how it made me look, turning my nose as red as Rudolph's. Besides, I was too busy with arrangements.

I'd been surprised when Desiree told me Mel planned to pay for everything. He'd left my mom and me going on twenty years at that point. We hadn't even been in the same room since before I graduated high school. My mom hadn't wanted his money when she was alive and she sure as hell wouldn't want it now. So I politely begged off, pointing at her insurance, and hid behind my Super Black Woman cape.

Unlike the Angry Black Woman label so many tried to make us wear, Strong or Super Black Woman was one we often gave ourselves. We wore it as proudly as a designer brand. It protected us from a lot of shit—earning sixty-three cents for every dollar that went to our white, male counterparts, or raising children not able to step outside without risking their lives. I don't know if it was always a good thing, but it was most certainly *our* thing, passed down by both nurture and nature from generation to generation, like a recipe for sweet potato pie.

And I wore it proudly—until the night after my mom's funeral. I insisted I was okay, sent everyone home so I could barricade myself in the house where I grew up in South Orange. But Desiree refused to leave. I cried so hard and so long my sister almost called an ambulance. Instead, she held me as I got snot on her Chanel dress, wiped my red nose, and swore it would be okay.

And now she was gone too, leaving me nothing but questions.

Research depends on the five *w*'s. I had the *who, what,* and *when* of Desiree's death since I'd figured out we had very different definitions of casual drug use. It was the *where* that had me so shocked.

The Bronx was my home. Not *hers*. She hadn't liked coming here even when Gram was still alive. And yet she'd come up here in the middle of the night.

*Why?*

I needed to find out. Like my mother had said, there was work to do.

I left the playground with Stuart's question banging around in my head. My neighborhood is deceptively hilly so I walked home, pulling my bike next to me like a cranky toddler. I'd been well past drinking age before I knew this area had a name. Highbridge. Washington Heights was just across the Harlem River, and the Yankees played less than a mile south. Cushioned in between was everything I loved—bodegas and buildings and brown people.

Gram had left me the house when she died, but I still thought of it as hers, especially since Aunt E kept on living there. It actually was the first place I'd called home as a baby, before Mel left my mom when I was four and she moved us to the Jersey suburbs. But I didn't move back into Highbridge until I realized it was just a hop, skip, and a bridge away from Columbia, way closer than my place in Jersey City and my childhood home in South Orange, which my mom had left to me free and clear. I'd been renting it out since she died. Between that and what I'd saved from the three years I worked for an engineering company in Newark, I was able to go back to school full-time. It helped I was cheap. Another way I was more Scott than Pierce.

I'd been playing with starting a nonprofit to help Black families cope with cancer since my mom died but had only decided to get my master's in Nonprofit Management two years ago. I didn't want anyone to have to go through what we did.

So I'd come to Highbridge for the convenience and instead found a community. When I'd first moved back to the Bronx, it was hard to distinguish one building from the next. On the surface they all looked the same. Six-ish stories. Beige paint. Fire escapes and NO LOITERING signs that everyone ignored. But those were the things nonresidents noticed when they raced through, protected by locked car doors and a sense of entitlement. Now I saw the details that made this neighborhood so beautiful.

Like how one building had its fire escape painted a hot pink. Or how another's super was meticulous in placing their city-issued trash bins. Or the apartments with the Superman mural. According to urban legend, the landlord paid a graffiti artist to spray-paint it after getting fed up with his tagging.

The side streets were mostly one-ways. Just narrow enough that if someone double-parked—and someone always double-parked—you'd have to hold your breath and maneuver your car like a Cirque du Soleil performer.

I'd just passed Plimpton Avenue when my phone rang. An unsaved number. I was tempted to ignore it like I had the previous four times. But instead, I hit the red phone icon and brought it to my ear.

"Hey, Tam," I said.

There was a pause. "It's me."

*Me* was definitely not Tam yet still a voice that registered as automatically as the number. I'd heard it all through my childhood—in music videos and radio interviews and award acceptance speeches way more than I'd ever heard it in my house.

I didn't respond, which caused him to speak again. "Your father."

As if I didn't know. I finally exhaled the breath I'd been cradling like a baby. Which is how I felt, like I was still the kid waiting for Daddy to come back home. Luckily for me, we didn't talk often. "Hi, Mel."

"You heard?" His voice was rich, as he was. And he had a standing reservation on Forbes's wealthiest in hip-hop list.

"Yeah…"

Another awkward pause. This one even longer. He was the first family member I'd heard from since finding out about Desiree—the fact he'd called proof it was already a different world without her in it. I broke the silence nervously. "How's Veronika?"

His wife. Desiree's mother. *My* mother's mortal enemy.

My parents had been childhood sweethearts, but according to my mom, Mel had always claimed he wasn't the "marrying type." Until Veronika had proved that wrong. My mom had never forgiven him—or them, since Veronika had been her friend. My mom'd even gotten her the receptionist job at Mel's first record label.

After my parents split, I saw Gram often. Mel technically had custody every other weekend and for a month in the summer, but you couldn't take a six-year-old to a video set. And there was no way in hell my mother would let me stay with "that heifer" Veronika. So my time was usually spent at Gram's.

If my mother's parenting philosophy was Tough Love, then Mel's was No Love. Over the years, his visits became phone calls. Phone calls became nothing at all. I extended an olive branch when I invited him to my high school graduation. He didn't show up. So I didn't invite him to my University of Pennsylvania one. It wasn't until after my mom died that he made any effort to come back into my life, throwing money at me like a rapper at his first album-release party. But by then I had no interest in being bought back.

"She's been in bed since we got the call this morning."

Despite what my mother would want me to believe, Veronika had always been more fun aunt than evil stepmother. I liked her—often more than both my birth parents, which made me feel guilty. So I always tried to steer clear. That didn't stop Veronika from trying, more for Mel's sake than mine, because that's what Veronika always did.

"Ahh." I drew the *h* out as I crossed smack-dab in the middle of the street, not even bothering to look both ways. I reached the sidewalk still searching for something else to say. Something more appropriate. I had nothing.

Mel and I barely knew how to talk to each other on a normal day, much less this one. We communicated best when not communicating at all. Our relationship had always been conducted through one intermediary after another. My mom had first taken up the role. Then, once they were no longer on speaking terms, it was Gram. After she died, it became Desiree. And two years ago, we'd switched to Mel's executive assistant, Tam.

When you never really have to speak to someone, you never learn how. Normally that suited me fine. Just not today, not when there were so many things I wanted to ask.

*Did you too know this was going to happen? Does it still feel like someone sucked the air out of your lungs? Are you also kinda relieved you don't have to worry about her anymore? Do you feel guilty about it too?*

And things I *needed* to ask. The *why*.

*Why had she been coming to see me?*

But I didn't say any of that, just waited for him to take the lead, as usual. There was a voice in the background and then he spoke. "Look, I gotta get to the office. The police are stopping by at two. I want you there."

He hung up before I could tell him no thank you. I was not in the right mental space. He'd barely registered when Desiree and I had stopped talking, so I knew he couldn't tell me what I really wanted to know: if she'd been ready to make amends.

"Hey, mamí," a voice called. Wally, the stock guy at the market on the corner where I always turned to get home.

Usually I was happy to see him. He looked out for me, just like Hector, who knew my breakfast order at the deli, and Malika, who made sure to ring the doorbell when she dropped off an Amazon package.

I wasn't just in my neighborhood. I realized I was at my street. My body had gotten me there while my head swam.

"You good, mamí?"

I was not, but did Wally really need to know? Did he really care? Or was it just some automatic greeting tossed back and forth like a game of catch? I glanced down at my Jordans. For a moment, I wanted to tell him the truth. That I'd been an only child for two hours now. That I was not handling it well.

But that seemed like too much to yell across the street, especially with the Latin trap music blasting from the car at the light. I rubbed my left wrist and smiled while I lied. "I'm good."

The smile instantly disappeared, and I scrambled to bring it back, making sure the follow-up was brighter, better, longer—because that's really all he wanted. He went back to unpacking strawberries, and I continued the two blocks home.

Someone once told me you can tell how gentrified a neighborhood is by the supermarket. When you see the Tom's of Maine on the shelf, you know Becky of Midtown will soon follow. Shopping. Jogging. Waving at the men drinking nutcrackers on their front stoops.

We weren't there. Yet. No cabs. No food carts. No tourists. The only interloper was me, and I'd like to think, given my family history, that I didn't count.

One of ten and the bookend, Gram's place—*my* place—was yellow brick like in Oz and probably as narrow as Dorothy's favorite road too. Inside were twin two-bedroom apartments, each taking up a single floor—combined living room and kitchen and then bedrooms. Gram and Aunt E had lived on the first floor since Mel was a teenager. Even now I spent so much time in Aunt E's unit that she no longer bothered to lock the door, and I no longer bothered to knock. We also had a basement that wasn't good for anything more than storing things and forgetting where you'd put them.

Aunt E was sweeping the front step when I got to our gate, wearing her usual T-shirt and yoga pants. A preference for comfort over sophistication was one of the things she'd passed down to me even though we technically weren't related. She was only my aunt in the way so many other Black people have play aunts and play cousins. Family created from bonds rather than blood.

Aunt E and Gram had been "roommates." Another Black euphemism instead of calling them what they actually were. What they actually had been since Mel was a teenager and they'd met at his high school, where Aunt E had been in charge of the cafeteria. If she'd been born white and male, she'd have a Michelin star by now. Luckily for the thousands of us who've eaten her food, she was not.

Family legend had it that Aunt E moved in soon after Mel's basketball team lost the finals and then stayed. This was Aunt E's home as much as Gram's, even though Aunt E refused to let us put the house in her name—saying she was too old to be a homeowner and that she didn't need a deed to know it was hers.

She was family. Period. So it wasn't any surprise she immediately knew something was wrong. "What happened, baby?"

Seeing her, I couldn't even speak. I stopped and stared and scratched my wrist. *She doesn't know. She really doesn't know.* "Desiree," I said. "She finally did it."

Aunt E rolled her eyes. "What that girl do now?"

"Died." It was the first time I'd said the word aloud. It scared me to think one day I'd get used to it. "Killed herself. Accidental overdose. Coke."

Her mouth morphed into an O, the broom banging to the ground as she rubbed a deep brown hand through her short gray hair. She didn't notice the dust settling back. It was soon joined by her tears.

"What happened?" she finally said, transforming back to the pillar she'd always been.

"You heard about the body they found at Nelson Playground this morning?"

"No, I've been out since eight. Saw a message from Mel but didn't check it, figured I'd talk to him when I went there for dinner." She stopped for a moment. "Overdose."

Aunt E was as familiar with Desiree's drug issues as I was. She'd never judged her for it, though—she was the lone person in our family who accepted each and every one of our flaws. It was why we all flocked to her. I'm sure she had opinions—about Mel and my mom. Mel and me. Me and Desiree. But she kept them to herself.

"All the way up here? Why…" Aunt E said, then decided it didn't matter. "Come here, Lena."

I walked over and we stood, holding each other, for a good minute. Aunt E was barely five feet and a hundred pounds but hugged like someone twice her size. The type of woman who wasn't afraid to take up space. I suspected she'd been like that her entire seventy-plus years on this planet. She'd certainly been like that the entire twenty-eight years of mine.

"You hungry?" she said. "I can make you something."

Food was the last thing on my mind. "I think she was coming to see me," I said into Aunt E's right shoulder, for once not caring about our nosy next-door neighbor who watched us like a television.

There was no way Desiree had been coming to see Aunt E while high. There weren't enough drugs in the world to have convinced her that was a great idea.

Aunt E disengaged, pulling back to look me in my eye. "She didn't mention stopping by last time we spoke."

If there was one way Desiree was religious, it was calling Aunt E the first Sunday of the month like it was early service. And those Sunday calls always turned into my Monday briefings about what was going on in her life. Or at least what Desiree wanted Aunt E to think was going on. There was no doubt Aunt E passed my news to Desiree too, made more noteworthy because, unlike Desiree, (1) I didn't have a public Instagram to stalk and (2) I told Aunt E the truth. The selfish part of me always hoped I was part of why Desiree called. In reality, I knew she loved Aunt E just as much as I did.

"You hear anything this morning?" I said, even though I knew the answer. "Anyone?"

Sure enough, she shook her head. "The alarm didn't go off."

Mel had installed some fancy-schmancy system when he fixed up the house after Gram died and Aunt E refused to move to a "better neighborhood." It was as much of a pain in the ass as he was, going off if someone so much as looked in its general direction. We'd only just started using it regularly after a minor break-in a month ago. I'd even paired it with my Alexa.

"Let's go inside," Aunt E said. "I need to call Mel."

Five minutes later, I was at her kitchen table staring down a plate of leftovers. Aunt E and I were in our usual seats—her closest to the stove and me to her left. Aunt E'd rejected any and all attempts to get her a cell phone, making her calls from a landline older than I was. The phone hung on the tiny expanse of wall that separated the kitchen from the hallway, and its ultra-long cord stretched past me as Aunt E settled in to talk to Mel. She didn't have a speakerphone, but luckily she kept the volume high enough you didn't need it. I leaned forward. It picked up on the second ring. "Mel Pierce's office."

Tam sounded as professional as always. A first-time caller wouldn't suspect she was the least bit upset. But I knew better. For one, she hadn't checked the caller ID. Otherwise, she'd have known it was us. Plus, I could hear it in her voice, the rawness in her throat that could only be the result of extended crying. "You holding up, Tam?" Aunt E said.

"Aunt E!" For a moment Tam's perky timbre was back. The one that sounded like it was truly her pleasure to say three words: *Mel. Pierce's. Office.* Like life got no better than answering his phones, checking his emails, and helping him stick to keto. A joy right up there with playing with puppies and eating only pink Starbursts.

It had annoyed the shit out of me when I realized it wasn't an act. Tam had been promoted to Mel's EA right before my mom died. Whereas most execs have two, even three, assistants, Mel needed only Tam, as she'd taken to the role like it was her baby, managing each and every little thing in his life—from his calendar to his travel. She'd also taken to his newly motherless firstborn daughter, having counseled me through one and a half breakups. Yet I'd never heard her even mention dating. She seemed to have no life. Lucky for her, Mel had enough for both of them.

"Where's Mel?" Aunt E said.

"On a call. We've been trying to reach you and Lena all morning."

Aunt E looked at me. I still hadn't said a word.

"I had Zumba," Aunt E said. "Lena let me know."

"Good," Tam said. "We thought about sending someone to the house. We just didn't want you to find out through the news."

I sighed.

*We.*

That's how Tam talked. We *were just calling to check in. You get the Apple gift card* we *sent for your birthday? We* wanted to make sure you were coming to the holiday party. As if Mel gave a rat's ass about when my birthday was or that I was saving up for a new laptop or if I'd be one of the five hundred special guests in attendance at his annual White Christmas extravaganza.

"The police are stopping by the office this afternoon," she said. "We want Lena to come."

Aunt E looked at me, and I shook my head.

"I can hear her breathing," Tam said.

I finally spoke. "Did Desiree say anything about trying to reach me last night?"

Tam paused long enough for me to get my answer. Mel—Veronika by proxy—had responded to my and Desiree's estrangement just as I'd predicted: not at all. "You were obviously on her mind," she said.

At five in the morning when she was high on cocaine. And just like that I was pissed. At Tam. At myself. And, most of all, at Desiree. I gestured to Aunt E, who was reluctantly handing me the phone. It felt like a brick. "You know this was inevitable," I said immediately, ignoring Aunt E's look.

A pause. "I'm sorry you think that," Tam said. "She was doing so well. We sent her to rehab earlier this year." She had left out the word "again."

"Guess that didn't work. *Again*."

"Lena," Aunt E said, suddenly looking every one of her seventy-two years. "Don't you think you're being hard on Desiree?"

I thought I wasn't being hard enough. Just like always. Even in death, even when she was found with cocaine, *we* were the ones making excuses. I handed the phone back. Aunt E waited for me to say something, then just gave up. She knew how stubborn I was. How I substituted anger and sarcasm for hurt like a teacher always calling out sick. Sighing, Aunt E spoke to Tam instead. "When's the last time you heard from Desiree?"

"Yesterday. We wanted to see if she got the gift. I keep replaying our last conversation. She didn't seem like herself. Was distracted. Said she wasn't feeling well."

Not feeling well was straight out of Desiree's "I'm using again" playbook. It was her excuse for why she was late. For the nosebleeds. For the constant trips to the bathroom. Yet for someone who never felt great, she sure loved to stay up all night. To talk about men. To binge reality shows with "Love" in the title that I hated but watched with her anyway. To share secrets. Just not the biggest—and worst-kept—secret of all.

The first time I saw her using was at dinner right after my mom died. I can't remember the place. I can remember the single-stall bathroom. All stark and silver, like the latest model Terminator had morphed into a sink. She'd followed me in and casually whipped out the baggie of coke like it was lip balm, offering me some as I sat with my panties wrapped around my knees. All I could do was shake my head. It was a good year before I could say anything more.

But when I did start to bring it up, the excuse was that she just wanted to have fun, not caring that a good time for her most likely meant a bad time for everyone else. Not that I was always clean and sober, but if I had to piss in a cup, you'd find only weed and enough alcohol to get me tipsy—and even then only on special occasions. And the more time we spent together, the more I began to wish she hadn't moved on to the harder stuff. I'd once flushed an entire gram of coke down the toilet when she passed out. She just bought more with Mel's money when she woke up.

"We didn't notice any of the usual signs," Tam said.

"Did any of you want to?" I said back.

"Of course." Tam ignored my tone. When you worked with Mel Pierce you were used to being yelled at for things that weren't your fault. His temper was as famous as his artists.

It felt like she was reading from an official statement. Knowing Mel, she probably was. His version of a midlife crisis had struck soon after Gram died. It wasn't marked by a flashy car or a hot young wife but by a desire to finally be seen as a respected entrepreneur.

I instinctively twirled the cord between my fingers like I had as a kid. I went round and round and round as Tam kept going. "There're a lot of unanswered questions, which is why we're happy the police are stopping by. You should really come. It might offer you some closure. Desiree was obviously worse off than any of us imagined if she was doing heroin."

I stopped twirling, the cord wrapped so tight around my pointer finger that it cut off all circulation. *Heroin.* Stuart the Star Reporter hadn't shared that little tidbit. "They found heroin in her purse?" I said.

"They didn't have to, Lena. There were track marks."

I repeated that for posterity. "Track marks? They think Desiree was shooting up?"

"Unfortunately."

"Fresh ones?"

"I believe so."

My finger began to swell. I finally freed it. Desiree had tried almost every rich-people drug known to humankind. Weed. Coke. Molly. If a hip-hop song mentioned it, she'd sniffed it and inhaled it, chewed it and swallowed it down—with one lone exception.

Heroin.

"The police can tell you more," Tam said.

"What time again?"

"Two."

# THREE

Desiree's death was everywhere. Trending on Twitter. Liked on Facebook. Posted on Instagram. RIP after RIP after RIP. I scrolled the comments under her last Instagram pic. It had become a virtual memorial. Heart emojis and praying hands and promises she'd be missed. Other comment sections were nowhere near as nice. The responses on The Shade Room made me hate people. Cheap "poor little rich girl" jokes and theories from people who hadn't even known she'd existed ten minutes before yet could suddenly wax poetic on why she'd been in the Bronx, why she'd had drugs on her, why she'd been in lingerie.

Since it was Wednesday, I should've been just leaving my Strategic Management of Nonprofit Organizations class, trying to decide if I should swing by Target on my way home since I was almost out of Eco Styler gel and needed my two cornrows to last another two weeks. Instead, I sat on the subway to Mel's office, reading each and every Shade Room comment, restraining myself from responding to all of them with the same message: "Fuck off."

*Track marks.*

Desiree hated needles. She didn't even have her ears pierced. The *News* article hadn't mentioned anything about heroin. Just the cocaine found in her purse. So where had it come from? And where had it gone?

I didn't know the answer to either question. What I did know was if Desiree had resorted to shooting up heroin, then she was lost in something larger than the Bronx. Something major had changed in the two years since we'd spoken. Had her early morning trip uptown been a last-ditch effort to ask for help?

I wondered if the cops would give her cell back. Since I'd blocked Desiree's number and resorted to only stalking her social media accounts, it would be the only way to know if she'd tried contacting me.

I wanted to see everything. Texts that had never made it to me. Texts that had made it to everyone else. Not to mention the calls I hadn't picked up and the ones she had. Hopefully they'd bring the cell to the meeting.

I could've taken the D down to 42nd and been closer to where I needed to be. Instead, I took the 4 to Grand Central and walked over to Bryant Park, hoping the weather—high 80s, sunny, slightest of breezes—would cheer me up.

It didn't.

My mom and I used to hop on New Jersey Transit and go to Bryant Park every winter. We'd freeze our Black asses off integrating the ice-skating rink, then warm them back up again with hot chocolate from a holiday pop-up shop. I hadn't spent much time here since I was a kid. Too commercial—from the office buildings to the tourist attractions. Times Square and Rockefeller Center were both a subway stop away.

Kat texted me on the walk over. She'd read about Desiree. Wanted to see how I was holding up. Technically, Kat was my best friend, if you could still be best friends with someone you hadn't seen in a year. My fault. I'd blamed school enough times she'd finally stopped asking me to hang out. I sent a thank-you, told her I loved her and lied for the millionth time about how we should get together. She sent hearts in return and asked if we needed her to drop food off or anything.

Pierce Productions overlooked the park. A glass skyscraper next to a glass skyscraper across the street from a glass skyscraper. You didn't identify them by numbers as much as by names. Salesforce. Bank of America. Building next to Bank of America. But they were never just buildings. They were always "towers."

I gave my name to the security guard in the lobby, then followed his detailed instructions to the fifteenth floor, where Mel ran his media empire. Tam had been inviting me to "stop by" for two years now, claiming she'd put me in the system so I wouldn't have to call ahead.

I hadn't taken her up on it, but I'd seen enough pictures to know what to expect. The hallway lasted at least thirty feet. Everything was white—including the receptionist at the end. Music blasted. I immediately recognized the song. Mel's first artist and hit. The track was accompanied by the music video. Unseen devices projected it everywhere. On the walls, the floor, and the ceiling. But just as you were about to get into it, the song switched. I recognized the next one too. It was from the same period. I made my way to the receptionist as the songs—and videos—continued. It was a literal trip down the memory lane of Mel's greatest hits. It took everything I had not to sprint down the hall like I was escaping a haunted house.

Mel always knew good music, even if he didn't always produce it. One advantage to being Mel Pierce's daughter was his collection. He was old old-school, preferring twelve inches of vinyl over tapes, CDs, and streaming. Though he lived in a big-ass apartment, he continued to store his records in his mama's house in the Bronx. The same place he'd stored me.

The summer I turned eight and Desiree turned five, my mom was doing an internship at a law firm while Mel and Veronika were off accompanying Free Money artists on their first world tour. Instead of taking me to class with her, my mom let me stay at Gram's. I'd known I had a sister. We just hadn't spent time together. But Gram had mentioned her often. And I'd seen her in more than one "perfect family" photo in *Ebony, Jet,* and *Vibe*.

I'd thought I would hate Desiree, that I would be jealous, but it was an instant connection. Gram and Aunt E gave us free rein over the house, the yard, and the music collection. We'd pick an album at random, plop it on the record player, and just dance our asses off while laughing ourselves silly. Usher was a particular favorite.

Those were the things I had missed most after walking away two years ago. You'd think—maybe even hope—having already killed our relationship would make this all easier. I'd already sworn I would never talk to her again. But now that I *couldn't* ever talk to her again, I realized I'd always known I was lying. That I would've eventually picked up the phone. That even though we hadn't been talking, I'd known she was still just a call away.

The receptionist silently watched my approach with a smile that looked like she'd yanked off the Crest Whitestrip right before I'd gotten out of the elevator.

"Welcome to Pierce Productions!" she said when I finally made it. "Do you have an appointment?"

I paused then. A mistake. My hesitation was over her word choice. If we were being technical, I didn't have an appointment. The police did. But judging from her expression, Ms. Whitestrip took it to mean I'd snuck past the security guard downstairs, a flash drive of my new mixtape wedged between both boobs.

I decided not to drop Mel's name. "Tam's expecting me."

"And you are…"

Then decided to drop his name. "Mel's daughter." I took my sunglasses off as I spoke.

"Lena?" she said, but it wasn't my declaration that had changed her mind. It was my eyes.

I've been told I look "just like your daddy" going on twenty-eight years now. Not just the eyes but the medium-brown skin. The freckles. The lips. The 4A kinky hair. All ripped from Mel's face and placed on my own. I'd even had the same gap before Dr. Sutton worked his Invisalign magic. It was strange—to be told your whole life you look just like an über-masculine man. But I've also been told that Mel Pierce made a damn beautiful woman.

"Lena!" she said again with more confidence, and I nodded. "You know where you're going?"

"No, but I can figure it out. Just follow the screaming."

She laughed then like she was supposed to. Legend had it the Murder Mel nickname was due to his ability to "scream bloody murder." He joked he'd inherited this from Gram, whom he could hear yelling to come inside for dinner from halfway down the block.

"I don't think he's in yet, but you can head straight back."

I thanked her and walked over to the door to the inner sanctum. Just as she was about to buzz me in, I heard her behind me. "And Lena. I'm so sorry for your loss."

It'd been five years since someone last told me that. Turned out I didn't miss hearing it at all. "I appreciate it," I said, then went inside.

The entire office must have had Slack because it was clear everyone knew who I was and why I was there. The hallway felt like it stretched to eternity, as starkly white as a hospital. Row upon row upon row of white desks. I've never hated the open concept so much. The journey to find Mel's office felt more like a walk of shame.

The faces were more colorful than the décor. Black and white and everything in between. None of them friendly, all aware of the "daughter from a previous relationship" mentioned in Mel's profiles but never photographed. After Mel left us, my mother hadn't allowed me to be used as a pawn in his magazine puff pieces.

His office was easy to find. As one might expect, it was in a corner. It was guarded by a four-person cluster strategically gathered at the desk directly across from Mel's double doors. None of them was Tam. Their lack of eye contact and weak attempts to look disinterested were dead giveaways I was the Space Mountain in this Magic Kingdom.

I paused ever so slightly. I had a choice. Stand around, pretending not to notice people pretending not to notice me. Or hide. Since I didn't know where the bathroom was, my only other option was Mel's office. I opened one of the double doors and went in.

It was as dark as the rest of the office was bright. Black walls, carpet, and blinds, which were at half-mast. Even the spines of the hardcovers behind his desk were black. And what wasn't black was gold. The couch. The vases. The picture frames.

"Is this a vampire's lair?" I said.

"They say I like spilling blood."

The voice had come from somewhere to my left. I looked over just as something beeped and the blinds rose like a church choir standing, about to grace us with His benevolence.

Suddenly it was 2 p.m. again. Light enough for me to see Mel's full face before the sunglasses resumed their position on the bridge of his nose. I caught the red rims around his eyes—my eyes. It wasn't surprising. Mel had always loved anything shiny, and Desiree was nothing if not that. He'd walked out of my life and into hers like he was on a runway in Milan. And I knew it wasn't her fault. But still it'd hurt. She and I had gotten past it by not bringing it up. Not the healthiest way to handle things, but it's what we had done.

Mel was at a full bar drinking straight from a bottle of his own liquor. And I don't mean he owned the bottle. He owned the company.

Murder Mel Pierce had become a millionaire a hundred times over with this image. Sunglasses on indoors and hands grasped tight around a bottle of liquor. Pouring it in women's mouths. Pouring it on women's boobs. And in one instance, with over ten million YouTube views, pouring it on women's weaves.

Back then it was jerseys and Jordans. Now it was suits and Salvatore Ferragamos. The only hint of his former life, the tattoos peeking out from both sleeves of the suit jacket. The inked handcuffs matched the logo for his first—and most successful—record label, Free Money.

I stared at them—at him—as he walked toward the massive black desk, the only indication he was looking back at me the slight uptick of his lips.

I couldn't remember the last time we'd been in a room together. I'd made sure to *miss* the White Christmas party every year.

"Sit," he said. I did. The seat was the type that looked better than it felt, all hard backed and just low enough that your knees jutted up at odd angles. He joined me a second later—his chair thick and leather and positioned so that he looked down at whoever sat across the desk from him—and slid a large black envelope my way, the Pierce Productions graphic displayed proudly at its center. "For you."

The last time he'd done this had been *my* twenty-fifth birthday, and the *For you* had been a Visa White Card. Though I'd needed it, I didn't want it. I'd given it back to Desiree so she could give it back to him.

I opened the envelope. The piece of paper held extremely detailed information on a brownstone on West 126th Street up in Harlem with a $2,575,000 price tag, an elevator, and a completely redesigned roof deck.

That area of Harlem had long completed Gentrification 101 and was ready to graduate. Instead of just putting Tom's of Maine on the shelf, they'd put an entire Whole Foods on a corner. An area whose lone distinction had long been the Apollo Theater now boasted an H&M, an Old Navy, and a Staples for all your office needs. I had managed to avoid them all except for the multistory Magic Johnson AMC on Frederick Douglass and West 124th. I'd often sneak in and catch a matinee by myself instead of going to lunch with the rest of my classmates.

"I had my realtor pull some listings this morning," Mel said. "I like this one 'cause it's not too far from school. What do you think?"

I thought giving back a house would not be as easy as giving back a piece of plastic. "I don't want to move from Gram's."

"You're gonna have to. It's not safe up there. Never was." I thought about the break-in we'd had but knew it was likely some bad-ass kids with too much time on their hands. When I didn't say anything, he spoke. "You know I'm glad you're finally letting me help you."

His help felt like bribes—pathetic attempts to be a parent now that I was grown enough to no longer need one. He'd started small—a five-thousand-dollar bike that had served as real estate in my downstairs hall—then upgraded to the aforementioned hundred-thousand-dollar-limit credit card. Now he was giving me whole houses. I wanted none of it. I was too Black to say that, though, so I said nothing at all, figuring later I'd tell Tam to tell him I wasn't interested.

Thinking about her conjured her up because there was a knock on the door. Tam appeared as if I'd said "Abracadabra" and pulled her out of a hat. "Detective Green's here." She spoke as if we didn't notice the guy already lumbering in behind her.

I took a breath, mentally reviewing the things I needed to ask. *Why had she been up there? What had happened to the needle? When could we get her phone back?*

I glanced at Detective Green's hands first, hoping he'd be carrying her things. But they held nothing, not even his own cell. *Shitnuts.* I finally glanced at the rest of him.

He was at least six feet and looked over forty. I hadn't expected him to be Black, but he was. He looked like he'd played college football before some ill-timed injury forced him into this plan B.

I had a love-hate relationship with cops. I knew they weren't all bad, believed there were only a few bad apples in the bunch. But the problem was, you had to get up close to see which ones were rotten. You couldn't always tell until it was too late.

Tam stopped by the door as Green kept walking toward us. Mel got up and met him halfway. Green stuck out his hand. Mel took it. Shook. Green was about to pull away when Mel tightened his grip. Then Mel leaned in. Green hesitated, shocked at the informality, then leaned in himself so their opposite shoulders touched and—finally—they patted each other swiftly on the back with their free hands. It was the automatic Black male greeting.

When they eventually pulled away, I noticed Mel's smile. It was just an eighth of an inch, but it was enough. He'd done the routine on purpose, wanting Green to think they could be friends. I mentally shook my head as they both walked toward me. Mel thanked Tam over his shoulder, and just like that rabbit, she disappeared again. Back at his desk, Mel sat, not bothering to take off his sunglasses. "Have a seat. How's Jim?"

There was a pause while Green and I tried to figure out who he was talking about. The light bulb went off over the detective's head first. "I don't talk to Commissioner O'Neill on a regular basis, but I'm sure he's fine."

"You're not missing anything," Mel said. The previous commissioner once had condemned Mel's record label for encouraging violence against cops. Now Mel was on a first-name basis with his successor.

Mel motioned to me. "My oldest. Melina. Getting her master's from Columbia. She's moving to Harlem to be closer to school."

Two truths and a lie.

"I taught her everything she knows," Mel said.

Make that two lies.

"I love the shit out of her," Mel said.

Possibly three.

Instead of correcting him, I shook Green's hand and smiled. "Lena Scott." I glanced at Mel from the corner of my eye to see if he'd react.

I'd changed my last name right after Desiree, Gram, and Aunt E were the only ones who'd come to my high school graduation. Ten years later, Mel still hadn't mentioned it.

Green finally took a seat, pulling a notebook out of his back pocket. Very twentieth century. "Thanks for agreeing to see me on such short notice. Before we go too in-depth, I obviously want to extend my condolences."

Mel nodded but didn't say thank you. I followed suit.

Green continued. "I wanted to give you an update on our investigation and answer any questions. Although we'll wait for the medical report for final confirmation, we don't suspect foul play. We are looking into why your daughter would have been at that playground, and of course there is the matter of the car."

I hadn't thought much about how she would've gotten up there. It was bugging the hell out of me they hadn't found a needle. But maybe she'd shot up in her Tesla and left the needle there.

"Did you find—" I began.

But Mel spoke at the same time. "I trust you'll wrap this up as quickly as possible. Just like I trust everything will be confidential."

Green smiled like he wasn't offended. "With all due respect, Mr. Pierce, that's how we always operate."

I tried again. "Did—"

Mel beat me to it once more. "Then who called the *News*? They had their story up ten minutes after you guys called us. It's bad enough they know about the drugs."

"It wasn't me or my partner."

"I don't know about that, but what I do know is that if I see one more word about my daughter printed anywhere, *you and your partner* won't be saying another word about anything."

They stared at each other. "What exactly are you implying, Mr. Pierce?"

Mel didn't answer right away, continuing the pissing contest. Finally, he spoke. "I'm not implying anything. I'm saying that you both will be getting fired. And I'll personally be there when Jim calls you into his office."

"Understood." Green spoke slowly, and Mel nodded. His dominance was firmly established.

Now that they were done, I spoke again. "So the car…"

Green smiled at me while avoiding Mel. "Yes. I'll be happy to get to that in a second."

I gave him a tight smile. Green glanced at his notebook like a cheat sheet. "As you both know, Desiree was out last night with three friends celebrating her birthday at the Omni hotel. We're still looking for the third person present, an Erin Ambrose, but we've already spoken with Desiree's boyfriend, Neil Marks, and a friend, Zarah Turner. Neither knows where Ms. Ambrose is, but we're confident we'll talk to her today. Mr. Marks left at about one a.m. to deejay a party in Jersey. Ms. Turner remembers last seeing Desiree about that time. She herself left around one fifteen for another engagement."

I cleared my throat. Detective Green looked up, and Mel nodded for me to speak. "Did Zarah say Desiree was using?"

Green shook his head. "Just drinking heavily."

That wasn't the same. I didn't say that, though, just listened as Green continued.

"Ms. Turner assumed Desiree had gone to her hotel room and passed out."

Mel and Veronika lived in a fancy co-op on the Upper East Side. It didn't make sense for Desiree to stay at a hotel unless she wanted to be as close to the rooftop bar as possible.

"We know that if she did go to her room, she didn't stay long. The valet recalled getting Desiree her car at about two a.m."

"Did he say she seemed high?"

"She did appear intoxicated, yes."

So there was a chance Desiree had done something in her hotel room and then left. But why? "You think that's when she went up to the Bronx?"

He nodded. "Yes, after speaking to her friends, we think she may have been going to see you."

And there it was. "They mention why?" I said.

I thought of the last time I knew she'd driven intoxicated. Two years ago. She'd wrecked her car and gotten arrested. I'd gotten tired enough to finally walk away.

I held my breath as he consulted his notes before shaking his head. "No."

Was it no because he didn't know or because he hadn't asked? The little faith I had in Green was disappearing quicker than bottled water before a natural disaster.

"I'd appreciate any insights you have into why."

He glanced at Mel, and I did the same. But Mel said nothing, which wasn't like him. Either he didn't know or he didn't think it was any of Green's business.

Green turned back to me. I decided to stick with questions he should know the answers to. "And she went straight from the party to see me?"

"We can place her in the Bronx around four."

I did some quick math. Desiree's body was found at five. The Omni was in SoHo. Physically it was a dozen miles from where they had found

34

her body. Socioeconomically, it might as well have been Tatooine. Even if you factor in Big Apple miles—which take five times longer to travel—it still didn't add up. "She had to have stopped somewhere first," I said. "It doesn't take that long to get to my neighborhood. Not at that time of night."

I glanced at Mel, to see if he was as concerned as I was, but he remained uncharacteristically silent. He leaned back as Green continued stating just the facts. "We spoke to a few residents. Someone on Woodycrest and 165th heard a woman yell 'Hey' around four, but they didn't check to see what was going on." Green glanced at his notes again. "We do know that's about when someone stole her car."

"A carjacking?"

# FOUR

Did this mean Desiree's death was just a case of wrong place, wrong time? Did someone see her, inebriated, sitting in her fancy car? Was that "Hey" Desiree yelling as they drove off?

I rubbed my wrist and glanced at Mel, but he might as well have been facing off with Medusa. His expression was stone.

"We can't say for sure," Green said. "We don't think they broke in because she didn't have her key fob when we found her. But we—"

I interrupted. I needed things to be clear. "So someone robbed her? Took her keys right from her? They hurt her?"

Again he shook his head. I was frustrated as hell. At him. At myself. At the fact he was bringing up more questions instead of giving me the answers I'd come to find.

"We don't have reason to suspect the theft had anything to do with her death besides making her more upset and inclined to use," he said. "There's security footage of the car near Yankee Stadium around four fifteen a.m. when she was still alive."

"Who was driving?" I said.

"The footage wasn't clear enough to make that out. We can just tell it wasn't her."

"So where did she go? Why not call for help?" I said.

"She didn't have her phone. We believe it's in the car, which we're trying to find now. Did she know your address?"

"I mean, she's been there a thousand times, but not recently," I said. "Not for the last few years at least. I doubt she knew the actual address. It never seemed important." At least not before last night.

"We did find her shoes," Green said, as if that would make us feel better. "One of them. Outside a liquor store on 167th a few blocks from the playground. We don't know when she lost it or what happened to the other."

I knew that liquor store. It was where Aunt E bought her lotto tickets. "That's not far from my house. Just a bit south. It's the opposite direction from where they heard her yell."

Green nodded. "We're not sure when she passed by your house, but a cop patrolling the area found her on the playground at five a.m. Pure luck. We think she may have been dead a half hour."

That liquor store was a ten-minute walk from my house. Yet she never found it. Why not? Hadn't she recognized the bodega we used to always hit up—the one where she'd always gotten Sour Punch Straws and I'd gotten Twizzlers? Did she miss the grocery store because it was closed up for the night? Did that random-ass steakhouse that just opened a block away surprise the hell out of her like it still surprised the hell out of me? And how, how, *how* did she overshoot my house—Gram's house—and end up on a playground damn near a half mile away?

Green spoke again. "We think she went to see you, got scared when the car got stolen, frustrated when she still couldn't find the house, and then ended up in the park. Where she…"

He trailed off, expecting us to fill in the blank. Again making it clear her death was her fault and her fault alone. But I didn't buy it. It didn't make sense.

"Why would she go through all that just to go shoot up on a playground?"

He didn't have to look at his notes this time. "We don't know. I doubt

Desiree knew at that point. Frankly, I'm surprised she drove up there with no problems."

Frankly, I thought he was full of it.

Green continued. "Your assistant is working on contact info for Ms. Ambrose. And we'll be heading down to check Desiree's hotel room. The manager's assured us no one's been in or out, even housekeeping. We have an APB out for the car. We'll have it back to you in no time. Hopefully as good as new."

He made it seem so simple. Like returning a Tesla would return things to normal. It was complete and utter bullshit. Leaving a party before it even got started was not Desiree. Casually abandoning her car and taking a stroll in the hood was not Desiree. Doing heroin was not Desiree.

I broke into his *Law & Order* monologue. "And she didn't mention to anyone why she wanted to see me?" He started to shake his head, but I wouldn't let him. I kept going. "You don't know. Right. What exactly did they say, though?"

It took him a few seconds to go through his notes. I waited. "That's all that she told her boyfriend, Mr. Marks. Just abruptly said she had someone she had to go see, someone she hadn't seen in years. We can only assume it was you."

*Someone.* That was it. Someone. "Desiree's ears aren't pierced," I said.

Green just looked at Mel like he could translate girl talk.

"She hates needles," I said. "Hates, hates, hates them. It's why she's never used heroin."

He glanced at me, then back at Mel, then back to me again before scribbling something on his dinky little pad. "Good to know. We'll keep that in mind. We do want to know where she got the drugs. We're hoping the hotel room will provide a clue."

I spoke again. "Just to confirm, you didn't find any needles on her?"

He shook his head. "Just the cocaine in the purse."

"What about Zarah and her boyfriend? They say they saw her shooting heroin?"

"They did not." He checked his notes again, flipping a few pages back.

"They did say she wasn't in a good place. Mr. Marks said she was acting depressed. Ms. Turner said she'd been distant."

"What about her dealer? You talk to him?" A jackass named Alfie who'd once bragged about being like Amazon. Daily deals. Delivery. Suggestions related to items you'd already purchased.

"Melina," Mel said, but I wouldn't tear my eyes off Green.

"We'd love to talk to this dealer," Green said. "Bring in the feds. Charge him with conspiring to distribute controlled substances resulting in death."

Mel nodded. He liked that. Shifting the focus to the big bad drug dealer.

Green flipped back to a clean page. "You know his name?"

"Alfie."

Green paused ever so slightly before writing it down. "And last?"

I shook my head.

He tried again. "Contact info?"

I didn't have it. Didn't want to have it. "It'd be in her phone." I gazed at the skyscraper across the street. "What if she went up there with him? Her dealer?" I didn't check to see how they reacted, didn't want them to even respond. "There's a two-hour gap where no one knows what she was doing. Who she saw. Just that she was going to see *someone,* who you're *assuming* is me. Her car is gone. You're *assuming* it was stolen. There was only coke found on her, but you're *assuming* she was using heroin. You saw what she had on last night. There's no way she would've worn a sleeveless dress if she planned to have needle marks on her arm. They would not have gone with the outfit."

I had his full attention now. He'd even put down his pen on Mel's fancy-ass black desk. "They were on her thigh."

I hesitated and hoped he wouldn't notice. Thigh? "She was afraid of needles." Even I could hear the desperation in my voice. "Ask her friends."

"I'd be happy to do that," Green said. "I want you both to know that we are exploring every avenue. When we spoke to Ms. Turner and Mr. Marks, they both insisted Desiree took no drugs at all. They denied knowing about the coke in her purse."

Of course. They weren't going to admit drug use to a cop. I finally looked at him. "Desiree didn't pick her friends because they were George Washington."

"Understandable. People can be protective of those they love. Sometimes too protective."

That's when I realized he was humoring me. He thought I was in denial about my sister's extracurricular activities. Like I thought Desiree was some angel who baked brownies. And not the kind with weed in them.

I turned to Mel, desperate. "Mel, we both know that coke was Desiree's go-to. Coke and alcohol. Even if you take away the needle thing, she was way too vain to mark up her body. Even a thigh."

He stared at me. The silence felt longer than my last Netflix binge. Then he finally spoke. "He's right, Melina. Desiree had changed a lot since you last talked to her."

So I was finding out. Apparently, everyone thought she was different. Depressed. Moody. Doing drugs she'd never done before. In ways she'd never done before. But no one knew why. *Why hadn't anyone told me it had gotten this bad?*

Mel addressed Green. "Like I said, I want this wrapped up as quickly as possible."

They kept talking while I sat there fuming. I guess a daughter dying from a heroin overdose in the hood was at odds with Mel's new incarnation. One clearly concerned only with his own reputation.

There was no way Desiree would have been able to inject heroin into her own body. I didn't know who had helped her use—her dealer, a friend, a stranger she'd met at the party, a stranger she'd met in Highbridge. But someone must have, and it'd accidentally killed her. It was clear the police didn't give a shit. I did, though. Whoever they were, I was going to find them. They couldn't get away with it.

There were two things I needed to see: her friends and her phone. Either could tell me if she'd met with someone else last night. Since her cell was MIA, along with her car, I'd have to start with her friends. I was banking on them being *less protective* with me than they had been with

Green. I spoke again. "What time will you be at the hotel? I'll meet you there." It had come out like a threat. And maybe it was.

"I don't think—" Green said.

Mel cut him off this time. "That's a great idea. Melina can pack up Desiree's stuff, make sure everything is in order."

I got the implication. My family obligation would be cleaning up after Desiree one last time. I smiled, sat back in my chair even though it was uncomfortable as hell. Mel could think what he wanted about why I'd volunteered. They both could.

Desiree had been in the Bronx for a reason.

She'd needed me.

I was going to find out why.

* * *

Back on the subway, I wished I'd brought my bike with me. It wasn't much—a ten-year-old Schwinn—but it calmed me like nothing else could. Definitely more than mass transit. If you're a New Yorker, there are just certain things you *know* about the subway. When a pregnant woman gets on, men with seats suddenly become fascinated by their phones. Once underground, cell coverage is spotty at best. And one never, ever, ever gets into an empty subway car during rush hour. Your nose will immediately hate you for it.

Luckily, the coverage gods were with me the whole fifteen-minute ride to the hotel. I spent it crowded next to some manspreader desperate to convince the world—and himself—he was rich. Rolex. Fancy suit. Gold pinkie ring. It all looked good at first glance. But on second glance the problems started.

The Rolex ticked.

The suit had plastic, painted buttons.

The gold plating was wearing off the ring.

Normally I wouldn't have noticed, wouldn't have cared. Other than a serious sneaker addiction—the only good thing to come out of my first relationship during my freshman year at Penn—I wasn't much for material possessions. I only recognized the telltale signs of "Fake it till you make it" because of Desiree. She'd had the ability to tell a person's entire net worth with just a once-over. There were worse party tricks.

She had always been into *things,* another of her addictions. Another way to chase the high, being the first to wear this or purchase that. But like coke, it was all temporary. If she were here, no doubt whining about why we were taking the subway instead of an Uber, she would've pointed out his missteps one by one—to him and to me—from his overgrown hair down to the uneven seams on his shoes.

I, however, had more important things to do, like check social media. It would not be the first time I'd spent an entire subway ride on Instagram. I had an account. Technically. I'd caved and gotten one I kept on private after starting grad school. My posts were few and far between, and never included my face. I'm sure the few friends I still had had forgotten I even had an account. And whereas I only accepted follow requests from people I knew, I followed with abandon, fully embracing the twenty-first-century version of stalking. Natural-hair influencers. Cooking experts. Gossip gurus. A therapist would have a field day with how my behavior was a holdover from my childhood, the only time I spent with my family through the pages of magazines. But I had never followed Desiree's account. Never commented. Never liked. That didn't mean I hadn't seen every post—even though it'd meant continually having to search out her username. Like I did now.

The RIP comments were still coming fast and furious on her most recent post. But I didn't care about that one. I'd seen it already. Had analyzed it like a forensics expert. I cared more about the others. Instagram wasn't known for its honesty. It was filtered in more ways than one.

Though Desiree had technically celebrated the big twenty-five on the Omni hotel's rooftop, in reality she'd celebrated it on Instagram. Every moment had been properly captured, filtered, posted, or storied. While I'd checked out each post earlier, I'd been focused on Desiree. This time I wanted to see who had been around her, hovering in the background. If I just zoomed in enough, maybe I could use some warped Spidey sense to figure out who had given her the heroin.

My first thought was her dealer, Alfie. A skinny white guy who'd transitioned into this new "career track" after his acting career fell flat. The most stable relationship of Desiree's adult life. Needless to say, we hadn't gotten along, playing tug-of-war for Desiree's time. I doubted he'd missed me after she and I stopped speaking. The feeling was mutual. I hadn't seen him in any recent pics, but that didn't mean he wasn't playing the back like an outfielder. It's what he'd always been good at.

Though Detective Green didn't know about him, it was hard to believe Alfie hadn't brought the party favors for Desiree's birthday celebration. Or that he'd ever make an effort to talk to the police. I'd get his contact info from Zarah. She was my best bet.

Zarah had been Desiree's first friend. They'd met in first grade when they were the only two Black kids in their ritzy private school. They'd co-integrated for the next eleven years, and then even separate colleges couldn't keep them apart. Zarah had jumped on the influencer thing early, amassing enough Instagram followers with her lavish lifestyle for TV to take notice. When Zarah had gotten her own reality show, Desiree came on to play her kooky best friend. But audiences loved Desiree's antics a bit too much. Zarah claimed she wasn't jealous, but *her* antics told a whole different story. When Desiree's accident netted her a DUI and E! wanted to drop her from the cast, Zarah happily agreed. It proved to be a mistake; the ratings plummeted and the show had barely lasted one more season.

I'd heard via Aunt E they'd also stopped talking. They'd definitely stopped taking pics and tagging each other. I was one of Zarah's ten million followers. I hadn't seen Desiree on Zarah's IG in years, or Desiree posting about Zarah's new makeup line. Yet Desiree's photos confirmed Zarah had been there last night, which meant they'd made up. I sent Zarah a quick How are you? text—mentally cheering when it went through—then checked my other messages.

There weren't that many, but then not a lot of people had my phone number. I'd drifted away from the childhood friends over the years—

even I could admit I'd started pushing people away after Desiree and I had had our falling-out.

There was a text from Omar, the one classmate I spoke to on a regular basis. This paper is kicking my ass. You doing okay?

I sighed as I figured out how to answer.

No one at school even knew I had a sister, much less that I was related to *those* Pierces. Even with Omar, I kept things surface. I knew he had a husband named Todd, but I'd never met him. Our relationship was predicated on shared notes, complaining about professors, and who was more excited for the return of *Veronica Mars*!!!

It was easier to keep people at arm's length.

I decided to be honest. Kind of. No. Found out my baby sister died.

The response was instant. Oh no. I'm so sorry. What happened?

That one was easier to answer. I'm not sure yet.

That's horrible. Let me know if I can do anything. Again my condolences to you and your fam.

He followed it up with three red heart emojis.

Afterward, I emailed Professor White to let him know I might miss class Friday but still wanted to drop off my paper. Then I went back to more important research.

The last photo on Desiree's Instagram was a group shot from her party, Desiree crowded in with three others, all wearing varying smiles like they'd dressed for different occasions. Both Desiree and Zarah wore glassy expressions you'd normally find at a twenty-first-birthday party.

Next to Zarah, the cute white chick I only recognized from Desiree's IG had a plastic expression you'd find at a graduation. Erin. She was the one who'd made her page private yet had over forty thousand followers—a transparent attempt to boost her follower count by making you essentially sign up to see what she was up to. The one who the police couldn't find. She could be hiding on purpose. When Zarah responded, I'd see if she had her number as well.

Up next was the boyfriend, who wore the awkward look of a three-year-old at his first school picture day. He'd come around long after I'd blocked Desiree from my life and my phone. Their first posted pic was one of those cutesy "Oh look at me hugging the back of someone's head" posts. She'd tagged him. I had, of course, immediately followed his DJ Naut account, desperate to see what he actually looked like. I was disappointed. Not because of his looks but because he barely had any personal pics—and none showing his face. He even wore a designer version of an astronaut's helmet while performing. I only recognized him because I once Googled "DJ Naut real face." I needed to talk to him too. Another request for Zarah.

I scrolled down past Desiree's birthday selfie to the next pic, this one from earlier in the day, judging from the teal romper. It was one of her with Mel. Or rather, Mel's arm. Desiree had cut the rest of him off. I wasn't surprised. She'd gotten in the habit of doing it with the camera-shy boyfriend. Now she'd given Mel the same treatment. The only reason I recognized him was the handcuff tattoo.

What I didn't recognize were needle marks. There weren't any on her arms, but maybe they had a filter to eliminate that sort of thing. And her last bikini pics had been posted over a month ago. None to be seen in those either.

Next to me, Mr. Manspreader put in his headphones. Airbuds, of course. The volume so loud I wanted to ask why bother. Apparently, he was a fan of Whitney Houston. He wanted to dance with somebody. I just wanted him to be more considerate. My annoyance propelled me off the N, north on Broadway, and right through the doors of the Omni.

Some poor interior designer had gone to great lengths to make everything appear "cool and hip" with conversation clusters of stuffed red velvet couches and leather chairs. None were being used. The place was empty. Either I was early or the cops had started without me.

The check-in desk was to the right of the entrance, as far from the couches as physically possible. A lone attendant wore an expression more suited to the overnight shift. She was tired and she was over it. She was also wearing a tag that said SHERRY. I smiled when I reached her even though it hurt as much as when I'd broken my arm.

"Hi. I'm Desiree Pierce's sister. I'm here to meet the police and pack up her stuff."

"Why." It was more statement than question.

I looked her dead in the eye. She didn't blink first.

I finally spoke. "Because she died last night."

She didn't even pause, just perfectly deadpanned, "Well, that sucks."

And I laughed because it sure as hell did. I needed the sudden jolt of honesty after feeling like no one else wanted to face the truth.

"Ms. Scott, you beat us." Green was behind me, joined by a standard-issue young white guy. The type who looked like he made daily use of his Planet Fitness membership but never wiped the machines down after. "My partner, Detective Zizza."

I reached for a handshake and instead got an eye roll. "I'm so sick of you rich kids thinking rules don't apply to you," Zizza said. "I don't care what anyone says. You're not getting in that room until we're done."

I saw why Green had left him at home for the meeting with Mel.

"You're a dick, right?" Sherry smiled innocently. "That's what they call cops? Dicks? Like in those old movies."

I smiled. She'd just made a friend for life. Based on Zizza's expression, an enemy too. "I think you're confusing them with private detectives," I said.

"Really? I would've sworn he was a dick," she said, and even Green had to laugh. She held up a key card. "Desiree's suite is on fourteen."

Zizza reached out to snatch the key card but missed. She slowly put it on the counter, as far from him as possible. There was a mini standoff, then he finally grabbed it. Sherry smiled again. "Have a great day!"

He ignored that, turning to me instead. "You can wait here."

Zizza took off toward the elevator bank, Green trailing him. I turned to follow when Sherry spoke. "I'm sorry to hear about your sister. She was always nice to me."

*Always?* I'd assumed Desiree had been here only for the night. I wanted to ask how long she had been staying but didn't want to get left. So I just thanked her and followed the detectives into the elevator.

Zizza fumed the entire ride up, then stomped out toward Desiree's suite when the doors opened. I was right behind him, just as anxious to get inside for different reasons. Because this suite might answer the question no one else could: Why had she been coming to see me? Or the question no one seemed to want to ask: What if she hadn't been by herself?

When we all got to 1407, I stared the door down like it owed me money. Green turned to me. "We *will* need you to wait outside."

"For how long?" I said.

"For however long it takes," Zizza said.

We glared at each other while Green put the card in the entry slot. "I'm not expecting longer than a half hour. We'll come get you if we need help identifying anything."

I spoke as he opened the door. "I really think I should come in with—"

I stopped abruptly. There was someone passed out on the couch inside. About the only thing covering her was vomit.

Desiree Pierce's face fills the screen. She's filming herself. The filter includes sunglasses and bunny ears.

Desiree speaks loud enough to be heard over a buzzing sound off camera. "It's midnight and someone has dragged me to a tattoo parlor."

A voice. "Freck, you begged me to go."

The camera flips to show Erin Ambrose getting a tattoo. She tries to smile seductively, but it's a struggle even with the filter. It hurts.

"He's almost done. I definitely made the right choice to go smaller. Who says bigger is better…" She trails off. Desiree's not paying attention.

"Yeah," Desiree says, but it comes out distracted.

"I think I'm gonna jump off a cliff after this."

Desiree again. "Me too."

Erin says nothing, just stares until Desiree speaks again. "What? Oh. Sorry. I got a text."

Erin perks up. "From him?"

"Yep."

"And…"

"He's sorry and wants to talk."

Erin smiles, despite the pain. "Say it."

"Nope," Desiree's voice says.

Erin tries again. "Say it."

"Fine."

A pause as neither speaks. "I'm waiting," Erin says.

"Youwereright."

Erin cups her hand next to her ear. "Excuse me? I couldn't make that out. Can you be more clear?"

"You. Were. Right."

Erin smiles. "I'm so glad this moment has been captured for posterity. Now the entire world will know that one time on May something whatever year it is I was right and Desiree Pierce was wrong."

"If I'd known, I woulda got you a medal."

"No need. I brought my own."

"Congrats," Desiree's voice says. Then, "He's going to kill me when he finds out."

Erin rolls her eyes. "Like I'd let someone even stare at you the wrong way, Freck."

The tattoo artist, who's been ignoring the conversation, finally speaks. "All done."

The camera moves forward, only stopping when the completed tattoo is on screen. A trail of tiny broken hearts lines Erin's hip bone.

"It's cute," Desiree's voice says.

"Thanks." Erin reaches for the camera. "Your turn."

# FIVE

Green rushed in, moving faster than he probably had since the Police Academy. Zizza was close behind. They stopped a couple of feet away from the woman, the pool of dried vomit separating them like two landmasses. Neither spoke. Then Green finally said, "She's breathing."

I exhaled a breath of my own. In their rush to check on her, neither cop noticed I'd also come inside.

"You know her?" Zizza said. Green just shook his head.

I recognized her even if they didn't, since she took the barely-any-clothes approach on her Instagram too. I could tell you her handle quicker than the square root of eighty-one. Desiree had certainly tagged it enough, usually followed by #likeasister #happy #lifeisgood.

#gag.

This bra-and-pantied white girl was Erin Ambrose. I didn't share that, though, just watched as Green sidestepped rock-hard vomit to shake her shoulder. "Miss," he said.

But she didn't wake up. So he repeated the entire process, this time adding, "We need you to get up." He kept on like this, gently at first but after two straight minutes not so much. My own nerves returned. I felt guilty for thinking ill of someone who clearly wasn't okay. I took my cell out of my jeans pocket, ready to call for help, but she finally woke up, peering at him with eyes so red you could barely make out the blue of her irises. Then she looked behind him at me. "There you are, Freck."

The cops both turned around. Zizza's eyes narrowed at the sight of me so I chose to make eye contact with Green instead. I could see the question on his face. *You know her?*

I shook my head. Instagram stalking aside, I didn't.

Now that I knew she was okay, I took her in. This Erin. It felt weird to see her by herself when I'd only ever seen her in photos next to my sister. Standing in what used to be my place. And here she was, too hung over—or still intoxicated—to even remember last night.

Quite the friend.

Erin must have noticed my judgment because she spoke again, her voice affecting a whine like a posh French accent. "You can't be mad at me for leaving you last night. That guy was cute! And quick. I was back in, like, ten minutes, but you were gone. I knocked on the bedroom door when I got back. When you didn't answer, I figured you were asleep. Don't be mad, Desiree."

I stared back, realizing she hadn't forgotten what had happened. She really didn't know. I felt like an asshole. Again.

Green and Zizza went from looking at me to looking at each other, no doubt playing a mental round of Rock, Paper, Scissors to see who'd have to break the news.

Just like that, I wanted to leave the room I'd been so desperate to get into just a few minutes before, not wanting to be present when Erin learned the news. I did an about-face and quietly shut the door behind me. I leaned on the wall across from the suite, slowly making my way down to sit. I couldn't hear a word, but I knew the deed had been done when Erin wailed so loudly the housekeeper two doors down checked to make sure everything was okay. "Should I call the police?"

"They're already inside."

She nodded like the police being somewhere before you needed them

51

was an everyday thing, then went back to work. I closed my eyes and just listened. Inside suite 1407, Erin was still screaming. I compared our reactions. I hadn't yelled. I hadn't cried. I hadn't so much as frowned. Instead, I'd just paid for my Snapple, got on my bike, and headed to the playground, my Super Black Woman cape flapping behind me.

I needed a ride to clear my head. But my bike was miles away, and I was stuck here in this hallway, breathing stale air. If I couldn't do that, I could at least meditate. I'd read an article once on "mindfulness" while cycling. It'd taken me a while, but I'd gotten good at it, often craved it like a pint of Graeter's chocolate ice cream. The only problem was, I could never remember the chants they'd recommended. So I'd started using Biggie lyrics.

*It's all good, baby, baby.*

Now I repeated the words over and over until I convinced myself it was better to be proactive than depressed. The Super Black Woman in me needed to feel like she was *doing something*. I went over what I wanted to ask Erin about Alfie, about Desiree's drug use, and about why she had been in the Bronx. Once I felt prepared, I fired off another text to Zarah, waited all of 0.2 seconds, then did something I hadn't done for two years: called Desiree's phone.

That was how I spent the next hour, cross-legged on the floor, relentlessly calling in the hopes someone would answer. I'd give it four rings, hang up, and start again. If someone did have her cell, I wanted to annoy them so much they'd pick up just to demand I stop fucking calling.

But no one ever answered. After the kajillionth attempt, it was me who gave up. I finally let it go to voice mail as I stared at my Jordans and discovered Desiree had actually recorded an outgoing message. Hearing her voice was jarring.

It came with its own musical score, an Usher song from *8701*. The album was a classic, and I recognized the beat immediately. We'd both always loved Usher. Desiree had let the instrumental play for a good thirty seconds before she finally spoke. "You don't have to call. It's okay, girl. You can just send a text. I'm not checking this anyway."

I laughed. Sarcasm was as much a part of our genetics as freckles. Hanging up, I tried on the "Think positive" approach like it was a pair of yellow-toe Jordans. The phone hadn't gone straight to voice mail. That meant it was still on wherever it was—even if whoever it was with wasn't picking up. Maybe Zarah or someone had Desiree on Find My Friends.

I still hadn't heard back from Zarah. I was about to call her when my phone rang. Aunt E.

*Shitnuts.* I hit the ANSWER button. "I'm sorry," I said instead of hello. "I should've called as soon as I left the meeting."

"No need to apologize. I spoke with Mel. I just wanted to see what time you'd be home so I could have dinner ready. I have everything I need for chicken 'n' dumplings."

Desiree's favorite. I smiled. "Mel wanted me to pack up Desiree's hotel suite." I didn't want to get into my growing concerns. At least not yet. "I shouldn't be more than a couple of hours."

"I'll have dinner waiting."

I hadn't eaten all day and still wasn't the least bit hungry. Maybe I'd have an appetite by the time I got home. "Love you."

"Love you too." She paused. "And Lena? Stay safe."

"I will." I meant it too.

I hung up and immediately went to text Zarah again. She was the type who either texted back within seconds or never at all.

You good?

The three dots appeared instantly, followed by two words.

No. You?

It took me longer to respond than it should have as I weighed telling the truth. I landed on not answering the question. Instead, I wrote: Was worried when you didn't hit me back.

She responded. Sorry!!!! Avoiding messages. Even canceled my event tonight. Been trying to see my doctor all day. Finally reached him!!!

I again couldn't help but contrast someone else's reaction to my own.

Me: Don't want to bug you but really need to chat.

She responded, Stop by anytime.

I thought of Aunt E's dinner plans. Tonight okay?

Another quick response. I'll be here.

She sent her addy in Tribeca and one final message. Love you, Lena!!!

We'd spent a lot of time together back when we both saw Desiree on a regular basis, but when I'd stopped speaking to Desiree, I'd inadvertently stopped speaking to Zarah as well. But still, I liked her.

Love you too, Z.

The door to the hotel suite opened. Finally.

Green stood there, surprised to see me still in the hall. I scrambled up or at least tried to. I'd been sitting so long my legs were asleep. Erin stood behind him, still dripping tears. They'd let her put on some clothes but not makeup. It would have been ruined anyway.

"All done?" I sounded hopeful. They had been in there so long they had to have questioned Erin about last night. I wondered what she'd told them.

He gave me what I'm sure he thought was a reassuring smile. "Not yet," he said, and I deflated. "I just finished speaking with Ms. Ambrose, but Zizza still needs to search the suite." Green glanced down the hall. "We need to check the safe, and the girl downstairs said she was on her way ten minutes ago."

"I'm sure Zizza can't wait," I said. Then, "I might be able to help."

He eyed me warily, like he knew I was just desperate to get inside. And I was, but I also really could help. "I know the code."

Green made me wait a full thirty seconds before he let me in.

This time I was actually able to survey the suite's living room. The interior decorator had gone with a less-is-more approach, though someone had done their damnedest to ruin the aesthetic. Stuff was everywhere. Clothes. Shoes. Cups. No food, though. No drugs either. As much as I wanted to blame it on Zizza's searching, I couldn't. Desiree had always treated her room like a pigsty. A side effect of growing up with a housekeeper. Meanwhile my mom had taught me to scrub a bath like it was a hard drive.

"It's in the bedroom closet."

Green was already heading over.

Erin immediately followed, leaving me to take up the rear. She kept glancing back at me, like an unsure eight-year-old encountering Santa Claus. I realized that just like I knew her, she knew me. That she'd probably heard Desiree talk about me. I could only imagine what was said.

Zizza was already going through the closet, holding up a little black dress like he was trying to decide if he needed a bigger size.

"Good news," Green said. "She knows the code."

Zizza took a step back and looked at Erin. "Great."

"He meant me," I said. "*I'm* the one who knows Desiree's code."

At least I thought I did.

Desiree had told me her phone code about three years ago when she was too drunk to make out anything except the Lemon Drop in front of her. I'd had to read texts to her like I was Siri. She later told me she'd used the same numeric code for everything. Identity thieves be damned. It wasn't the only way she'd lived dangerously.

I leaned forward and said a little prayer. *Please let this work.*

It was followed by another. *And please don't let there be anything illegal in here. Like coke, weed, ecstasy, or any combination of the three. Or heroin. Definitely don't let there be a needle. Don't prove them right, Desiree. That you were just a poor little rich girl with too much time and money.*

I quickly adopted it as a mantra. Singing it in my head as I typed in each number.

1

*No coke.*

1

*No X.*

1

*No heroin.*

0

*No needles.*

9

*No coke.*

1

*No X.*

I rushed through two more mantras before I pressed the ENT button. It buzzed, and I let out the breath I'd been holding.

My sister still used my birthday as her passcode.

It surprised me how reassured I felt. My birthday. Not her boyfriend's. Not Mel's. And definitely not Erin's. I opened the safe door. We all looked to see what was inside, what Desiree had felt was important enough to lock up.

Nothing.

God definitely had a sense of humor. So did Desiree.

Ten minutes later, Green and Zizza were gone, leaving business cards and more false promises that they were exploring every avenue and would keep us updated. It made me think Erin hadn't told them anything new.

She'd stayed behind, offering to "help" me clean, which essentially meant getting snot all over Desiree's clothes as she attempted to pack them up. Desiree would've flipped and demanded Erin pay her dry cleaning. I just let her do it. Neither of us said anything at first, just coexisted like a pair of two-year-olds who hadn't mastered the art of playing with others yet.

As I continued clearing off the night table, I went over the questions I wanted to ask, deciding to start with Alfie. I turned to see her examining me from my Jordans on up to my ironic shirt. I hadn't changed since this morning. Hadn't thought to. But now I felt self-conscious.

"I like your hair." It was the first complete sentence she'd said since the cops had left. It threw me off.

"Thanks," I said.

White girls staring at my hair was nothing new, especially since I went to Columbia. I'd stopped by my favorite African braiding shop on 125th the day before. A woman named Sadie had put in two large cornrows for twenty bucks plus tip. Thanks to the hair she'd thoughtfully added, both braids hung down to my ass.

"Don't worry," Erin said. "I'm not gonna touch it."

I checked the night table drawer, but it was empty. Not even a Bible. "Desiree taught you well."

"I keep thinking about Freck, up there, by herself. She's lucky she didn't run into, like, some gang members."

I shut the drawer with more force than necessary. Rich people stole, raped, killed, and took drugs just as much as the rest of us. They just had better lawyers. "I wouldn't walk *anywhere* at night by myself," I said. "You could just as easily be tied up in some mansion wine cellar."

She thought it over. "There are worse places to end up than stuck with wine."

Was she joking? I changed the subject. "The police talk to you about last night?"

She nodded. "I wish I could've told them more. When I left with that guy she was still at the club. Still in a great mood."

"They ask about Alfie?"

She paused, then bent down to pick up a pair of stilettos. "Who?"

"Her dealer. Was he there last night?"

She laughed awkwardly. "Figures you'd know Alfie." She put the shoes in an open Louis Vuitton suitcase on the king bed. "No, Alfie's long gone."

So Desiree had replaced him too. There went that lead. "Who was her new guy?"

"She didn't have one."

*Yeah, right.* "The police said she wanted to meet someone in the Bronx?"

"Probably you," she said. "I wouldn't be surprised, honestly. She talked about you a lot. Especially recently. Guess it was the five-year anniversary of your mom passing."

Five years and twenty-one days. Aunt E hadn't noticed the day of, and I hadn't reminded her. My mother wasn't a topic we discussed much. Instead, I'd gone to class, knowing that would have been what my mother wanted, and came home to sit in the dark listening to the last voice mail she'd left me. But I wasn't going to tell this stranger that. Instead, I said, "Yeah."

"It's been five years since your grandmother died too?" she said, but this time I didn't answer. "Maybe that's why Freck went to see you. Because she was worried."

"I was fine." A lie.

Her eyes followed me as I walked to the other side of the bed to check the other nightstand. "What?" I finally said.

"She said you looked alike, but still."

I softened. "It's the freckles. Mel has them too." The next question was out of my mouth before I realized what I was saying. "She never showed you pictures?"

"No," she said, and I was disappointed. "She didn't have to. There was a pic of the three of you as her lock screen."

I knew exactly which one she was talking about. Mainly because only one such photo existed. *Would* exist now. Thinking about that made me pause. Then I shook my head and opened the nightstand drawer.

The photo was from three years ago, a brunch to celebrate *NYZ* being picked up by E! It wasn't my choice to sit next to Mel, but Desiree had insisted, and I actually ended up enjoying myself. Mel could be extremely charming when he wanted. And that day he did. I had been drunk off both mimosas and attention, and it showed in the pic. The three of us lined up, all freckled and, dare I say, happy. Mel smiling so much you could even see his gap.

That photo wasn't just her lock screen. For a long time, it'd been mine too.

Erin tried to fold a T-shirt. It looked like my attempts to fold a fitted sheet. "I shouldn't have left her," she said. "The cops asked me if she'd been depressed."

"That's what her boyfriend told them."

"Naut?" She used his DJ name. "Typical man. Always assuming you're depressed because you don't want to deal with their shit anymore."

My heart started beating faster, glad someone was dismissing the police's BS. Even if it was Erin. I threw another name out there. "Zarah told them too. Said she'd been distant."

"Yes. To her," Erin said, and I wanted to smile—until she kept going. "Zarah abandoned Freck when she needed her most and then came crawling back a few months ago. Freck was keeping her at arm's length. If it was me, I wouldn't have talked to that bitch ever again."

She kept on, not noticing me staring.

"Your sister was fine. I'd know more than anyone. I was her best friend. The one she talked to every day. She was fine. Happy. We wanted to start a members' club. Like Soho House. We were even looking at spaces. We had a good time last night…Too much of a one, obviously. That's all. And I wasn't there. I'll never forgive myself, you know?"

She looked at me then, obviously expecting me to tell her that it wasn't her fault. Instead, I stood. "I have to go to the bathroom."

I closed the door when I got in there and mentally replayed the convo, hoping to pick up on any shade. Erin had been talking about Zarah, but had she also been talking about me? No one could be that oblivious.

I slid down the bathroom door and willed my mind to go blank. I took in the room. It was gigantic, the tub alone bigger than the average male ego. A separate shower felt like it was in a different wing. A stainless-steel pink water bottle perched on the side of the tub right next to me. The counter was big and littered with Desiree's makeup. Lipstick. Blush. Foundation.

I was contemplating melodramatically banging my head against the wall when I accidentally knocked over the water bottle. It hit the ground, then rolled. Something clanged inside.

I wanted to kick myself for not recognizing the bottle immediately. She'd had it exactly three years, a birthday gift from me. It'd cost thirty-five dollars, pricey to hold something essentially free, but it was one of those fancy-schmancy ones that claimed to keep your cold water cold and your coffee hot for eons. It was pink and glittery and the perfect size to fit in Desiree's Givenchy satchel.

And I knew it had been worth it once Desiree started hauling that thing everywhere. Her place. My place. Everywhere in between. If she was there, so was that water bottle. It was only later I realized why. She had needed someplace to store her drugs.

Maybe some things hadn't changed after all.

As if forming a sign, the water bottle stopped right at my feet. I lightly kicked it. Another clang. Something was definitely inside. But what? Cocaine didn't sound like that. Neither did weed or pills. It was something bigger.

Like a needle.

*Shitnuts.*

I wanted to leave immediately, walk out the bathroom door, then the hotel-suite door, then the elevator door, then outside. To keep going until I got to *my* door, even if it was miles away. But I knew that bottle would follow me, haunt me for the rest of my life. So I stayed, picking it up gently as if that would make whatever was inside disappear. And once again, I stated my mantra.

*No coke.*

I twisted the cap.

*No X.*

I took it off.

*No heroin.*

I tipped the bottle.

*No needles.*

A flash of white jetted its way to freedom. Whatever it was had been wrapped in a torn piece of purple paper. As soon as it hit the tiled floor it shot out from its layer of protection.

I peered down. It was a positive pregnancy test.

# SIX

"Everything okay?"

It wasn't, but still. I answered Erin through the closed bathroom door. "Yep. I'll be right out."

I sat on the toilet, gripping the test in my hand as if I'd just taken it myself. It said PREGNANT in bold blue letters. Had to give them credit for being straight to the point. No old-school plus or minus. No one or two lines. No presumptuous smiley face. It said what it said, and you could take the result how you wanted.

Clearblue even took it upon itself to estimate how many weeks. My sister had been at four. The police hadn't mentioned anything about a pregnancy. I sure as hell didn't know enough to know if that was something they could tell that quickly.

I'd had my last pregnancy scare about a month or so before Desiree and I stopped speaking. The result of my last friends-with-benefits situation. A guy I didn't want to spend the night with, much less the rest of my life. But he had a dick bigger than his IQ, and he always answered the phone on those rare occasions when I was in the mood for company.

I've never been big on relationships. My mother didn't date much after Mel left. The only time I saw a healthy relationship up close and personal was Aunt E and Gram. And possible baby daddy was no Aunt E. Desiree was the first person I called. She showed up at my apartment in Jersey City within an hour and marched me straight to the supermarket. The morning-after pills were in aisle 9A.

I peered at the price tag. "Jeezus, forty-seven bucks."

"Trojan Ultra Thins are only thirteen dollars. Too late now," she said.

I turned to her. "The condom broke. I told you that."

"And I told you that you need to be on birth control."

"And I told you I don't have enough sex to warrant it."

She gave me her best infomercial voice. "All it takes is one time."

"I'm gonna smack you."

She pulled out a credit card. "Then who's gonna pay for your emergency contraceptive?"

"Like that bill doesn't go straight to your father."

"Of course. I'm sure not paying for your irresponsibility."

I ignored that to stare at the shelf. It figured there'd be more than one choice. "Which one should I take?"

"Doesn't matter." Desiree fingered the plastic. "As long as you take it within five days, you'll be fine. Of course, the longer you wait, the less effective it is. If you're super nervous, you can try Ella. But that requires a prescription." She noticed me staring. "What?"

"Why do you know all this?"

She stared at me for a beat. "WebMD."

I laughed. "I figured maybe you'd taken one."

"I don't have to."

"Right. Because you use birth control."

"And condoms. And I still make him pull out. I figure if his little swimmers can get past all that, it's meant to be. I'm keeping it. What?"

This time her "what" was because I was avoiding looking at her. "Nothing," I said. "It's just that pregnancy and partying don't exactly go together." *Partying.* My code word for her increasing drug intake. "You'd have to stop."

"Right. And I would."

She sounded way too confident. It instantly annoyed the crap out of me, but I played it cool. "The only pills you could take would be prenatal vitamins." I reached for the plan B. But instead her hand grabbed mine. "Hey!" I said, finally turning to her.

She looked me dead in the eye. "You don't believe me?"

"I do," I said. She sounded so certain. I was obviously the only one here who didn't believe a word she'd said. "If you *do* get pregnant, I better be the first person you tell. Even before the daddy."

Letting go of my hand, she stuck out hers as if offering some blood oath. "Deal."

I grabbed the box and giggled for a full five seconds before I realized she was serious. So we shook. Then I said, "Now that's settled, I need to find some water to wash this down."

I stared at the pregnancy test as questions came at me like darts. Was that why she had come to see me? To tell me I was going to be an aunt? Or to tell me she needed help because someone wasn't happy it was his? Or wasn't happy it wasn't? My blood ran colder than an Alpha Phi Alpha chant. Had he followed her up to the Bronx? Gotten her high on cocaine, shot her up? Had he intended for her to overdose, after all?

I leaned back so hard my head banged against the wall, but I didn't even feel it.

*Desiree, what did you get yourself into? And why did you die before you could tell me?*

"You sure everything's okay?"

Erin knocked this time. I'd forgotten she was there.

I stood up, gripping the test so hard I was surprised it didn't break. There was nothing to be accomplished hiding in here. I bent down, picked up the crumpled paper, wrapped it around the pregnancy test, and stuck the whole shebang in my back pocket. Then I washed my hands. Twice.

I came out to find Erin checking her phone. Even though she'd just knocked, she jumped when she saw me, like I was some manager who'd caught her slacking at work. She quickly shoved the phone into her back pocket and hurriedly finished putting a pair of Desiree's shoes in a suitcase.

Seeing her cell reminded me of Desiree's. "Did you and Desiree have Find My Friends set up?"

"Wish we did. The police said her phone was missing." She paused for a second. "What was that noise in the bathroom?"

She probably already knew about the pregnancy test, but still, I played it cool. "Something fell. What did you mean before when you said she didn't have a new dealer? Had she been using a lot lately?"

Erin grabbed the pile of clothes off the bed. "No, despite my best efforts."

"When did she stop?"

"Honestly, I don't remember. It was like one day we went to get margaritas and instead she got water."

"Two weeks ago? Two months ago?"

"We were in Cabo, whenever that was."

Three weeks ago. The secret social media stalking finally had been good for something.

"All I remember is that she didn't want to talk about it," Erin said. "Made a joke it was some 'mid-year's resolution.'"

I nodded like I was thinking it over when I was really thinking about how if Ms. Like a Sister hadn't known Desiree was with child, Desiree hadn't wanted anyone to know. The least I could do was keep her secret— while figuring out prospective fathers. Factor in the four weeks on the test and the Cabo trip, and I was looking at a point of conception seven weeks back. I just needed to figure out who she was having sex with at that time.

"Was it because of a guy?" She looked at me strange so I kept on. "You said she and Naut were off again. Thought maybe she'd already found a replacement, as part of her mid-year's resolution."

She shook her head. "They broke up a couple of months ago, but it was one of those long-drawn-out things, and she wasn't seeing anyone new yet."

*Shitnuts.* Figures it wouldn't be that easy. Desiree was not above an occasional one-night hookup.

"I was surprised she invited Naut last night," Erin said. "Surprised he came."

I wasn't sure how he factored into all this—ex-boyfriend, friend with benefits, baby daddy—but he was the one who'd told the police Desiree needed to see someone: *me.* That made him worth talking to as soon as I could. "You have his number?"

I motioned to the phone stuffed in her back pocket making her butt look as lumpy as an at-home Brazilian butt lift.

"I don't. I tried to stay out of their relationship. She dragged me up to his place in Harlem once. They were arguing so much I finally said I needed to run to the drugstore and instead went to see a movie across the street. I can get his number, though."

"That's okay." As soon as she'd mentioned the theater I knew exactly where he lived. "Let's keep in touch, though."

In case I had more questions. She rattled off a number with an area code I didn't recognize. I immediately keyed it into my contacts, then texted her. "Get it?"

She nodded. "My butt just buzzed."

"Great. I should get going." I wanted to talk to Naut ASAP.

"No prob. I can finish."

The place was still a mess. "Don't worry about it."

"You don't want to check out?"

"There's no rush." Mel was paying for it, and I wanted to be able to come back if need be. "I'll just put a privacy sign on the door."

We went back into the living room of the suite. She grabbed her bag but hesitated, as if remembering Desiree was gone. "You'll let me know about the funeral?"

"Of course."

"Great. Let me know how I can help. I'd be happy to come up and see your grandmother's town house. Desiree talked about it so much."

I flashed on Erin in my neighborhood. Staring slack-jawed at the corner boys and the titis, avoiding the "New York rain" dispensed from overworked window air conditioners, covering her ears as the bass boomed from each passing car.

"I'd love to have you stop by," I said.

\* \* \*

I called Green as soon as I left. He was the last person I wanted to speak with but the best person to ask if Desiree was pregnant when she died. When he didn't pick up, I left a quick message, asking him to call back.

Then I called Aunt E to tell her I'd be late and to eat without me. She was upset—I could hear it in her voice—but she wasn't the type to complain. Still, for a second, I thought about going home. But then I reasoned I'd be there for breakfast tomorrow. Maybe by then I'd have an appetite.

By the time I hung up, I was a block from the subway. I caught the A, making the best use of the twenty-minute-ish ride to 125th figuring out a plan of action. I didn't know Naut's apartment number, but I was sure the buzzer had a directory. He was probably listed under his real name: Neil Marks.

If he wanted to know who I was, I'd say I had a package. If he wasn't home, I'd wait until he was. If he asked how I'd known where he lived, I'd blame Erin. I'd blamed her for far worse since her photo first popped up on Desiree's Instagram. If he didn't ask, I'd act like I thought they were still together and gently ask about what had happened last night.

Satisfied I'd covered every possible scenario, I spent the rest of the trip searching out info on Desiree and Naut's relationship. I started simple: Desiree's name.

Google is like a mom who tries so hard to be helpful she just ends up being annoying and intrusive. Perhaps its worst offense is trying to predict the exact thing your nosy ass is trying to find. Pre–finally giving in to full stalker mode and setting up a Google Alert, I'd searched "Desiree Pierce" enough to know the top phrases related to her name.

"Reality show." "Net worth." "Instagram." "Father." "Dating." But a new suggestion had already been added: "Desiree Pierce dead."

I'd been so focused on how Desiree had died, I'd managed to not think about how she was actually gone. Looking at those three words made my wrist itch. Was this what it was going to be from now on? I was prepared to avoid Usher songs and Lemon Drops and all the other ten billion things I knew would make me instantly think of her. It also looked like I'd have to add Google to that list. I'd have to find another search engine.

Desiree and DJ Naut had gotten together after I was long gone. Their relationship had started with a few Sightings mentions of her at his gigs. A tagged photo credit confirmed they were a thing.

A Google search showed a ho-hum white guy with straight brown hair, sleepy brown eyes, and one day's worth of stubble all on top of a scrawny body. The type you'd pass on the street and never know he was one of the biggest names in music. He'd blown up in the time they'd been together—first as a DJ and more recently as a producer—peaking when he made the cover of *Rolling Stone*. It was a shot of him completely naked—besides some Calvin Klein tighty-whities and of course the helmet.

I skimmed the article for any mention of her. She got one line that didn't even include a name, just that his girlfriend had introduced him to a few party promoters. It was as close as he got to admitting how many hours, days, and months she'd put into his "overnight" success.

Disappointing.

I went to Instagram, which is as dependable as your period on the first day of vacation. Naut hadn't posted any tributes to Desiree. He hadn't posted anything at all. At least not for the last week or so. The few posts he did have this month were single covers and artsy-fartsy pics of studio and DJ equipment. Nary a selfie in sight, much less any Groupies—both the photo and the human kinds. His profile pic wasn't even him, just a shot of his helmet sitting next to a soundboard. He also used the familiar fuzzy transmission signal on all his music productions, sometimes at the beginning, sometimes at the end, sometimes buried between the chorus and a verse. Always letting you know you were listening to a DJ Naut production.

His Instagram was all work to Desiree's all play. Opposites attract and all that. She had no shots of him either, though she had once upon a time. But they were all gone now. Deleted. The twenty-first-century version of letting the world know you're over. Right up there with no longer following each other. She wasn't. He was.

I got off the subway, went up the stairs, and headed east. The last time I'd popped up on a guy had been an ex at Penn and it'd been three in the morning. Hopefully I wouldn't find Naut in bed with his engaged TA.

The walk down West 125th—aka Times Square above Central Park—went by quickly. Lifelong residents whose idea of a vacation was a day trip to Coney Island passed oodles of tourists observing the natives in their habitat like zoo animals. A few even paid tour guides to take them to Black churches on Sundays, relegated to the upper levels, though they were far from the cheap seats. The pastor made sure the donation plates made it up there.

The phone call came just as I was about to get to Frederick Douglass. I didn't recognize the number so I ignored it. The text came a few minutes later.

Hi Lena. This is Stuart from the Daily News. Wish you'd told me who you were when we talked this morning. I would have offered my condolences. I'm working on a follow-up about your sister. Would love to chat with you. Please call when you can.

How did he even get my number? Not that it mattered. There was no way in hell I was going to contribute to some hit piece with another shitty headline. I deleted it as I walked past the Magic Johnson theater. The apartment building across the street was big enough to house both a hotel and a lounge. The builders seemed to have realized rooftops topped people's Christmas lists more than chimneys. There were several different ones on several different floors. The end result was a building with more shapes than a game of Tetris.

I looked up, wondering which square housed DJ Naut, then realized there was no front buzzer. It meant one thing. He had a doorman.

*Shitnuts.*

I don't know why I was surprised. They weren't uncommon. But this wasn't in my plan. Part of me wanted to leave. The other part strong-armed me inside and up to the lobby counter, where the doorman waited. They hadn't forced him to wear a top hat and white gloves, but they had put him in a suit jacket. He looked nice in it.

"And who are you here to see, ma'am?"

At least I'd prepared for that. "Neil Marks."

He picked up the phone and I hit another snag.

"And who may I say is here to see him?" The doorman had the receiver mere centimeters from his ear, both he and the phone ready to be of service. More ready than I was to answer. I wasn't wearing a uniform. I clearly wasn't Uber Eats or Postmates. Grubhub or DoorDash. I should have anticipated this scenario, stopped by the Little Caesars a couple of blocks back. But I hadn't, which left me with one option: the truth.

"Desiree's sister."

He looked at me like I was a member of Beyoncé's original group. But this is New York, where the only things hood folks and rich folks have in common is a hatred of tourists and a love of creative baby names. Smiling, he finally dialed. "Yes, is this Mr. Marks? I have a Desiree's Sister here to see you."

There was a pause longer than in a reality competition. I felt like this week's eliminated contestant, waiting to be sent home. The doorman's eyes darted everywhere. The smile slowly dissipated from his face until he finally spoke. "Are you sure? It's just that I can't be responsible since it's not protocol." Another pause. More non-eye-contact. "I understand."

He hung up and smiled at me like he didn't really want to, reaching down to produce a white box with "MacBook Pro" displayed proudly in bold black letters. "Mr. Marks asked that you take this up with you."

It looked like I'd be a delivery person after all.

# SEVEN

It was only when I got to Naut's floor and heard the music that I realized how silly this was. Like horror-movie-white-girl-running-half-naked-up-the-stairs-instead-of-out-the-door silly. It was eight o'clock and I hadn't eaten since a nasty-ass protein bar for breakfast. I'd been subsisting on anger with a side of grief. Apparently, dessert was "Have you lost your mind?" topped with fear. I didn't know this man, yet here I was traipsing up to his apartment after-hours to grill him on his relationship with my sister.

I was about to do a whole 180 when Naut popped out of a door a few feet away. Even sans astronaut helmet, he was taller than his online pics had led me to believe. He was also skinny enough we probably wore the same size jeans. His eyes were his crowning feature, pools of chocolate you just wanted to dive into. It was too bad he always hid them behind a mask.

I stood up as straight as I could, plastering my face with the expression I used when walking by a stranger screaming at the top of their lungs. The one that said "I'm not scared" even if I was. He said nothing, just held up his hand. For a split second I thought *gun*. It was only after the music abruptly shut off that I realized it was a remote.

I exhaled as he walked toward me. He stopped a few feet away to give me a once-over that was anything but sexual. More like taking in art or clothes. Based on his expression, he was ready to leave me on the rack. But then he got to my feet.

I had on Jordan 1 retro high-tops in black with a crimson tint. Reissues, but I had an original pair locked up tight at home. I'd read once that Elizabeth Taylor kept her diamonds in a vault and instead wore replicas. I understood completely.

Feeling more confident, I handed him his new laptop.

"Nice Jordans," he said. "Take them off before you come inside."

He didn't wait to see if I did. Just padded in socks back into his apartment while I paused at the door under the guise of taking off my kicks. Then I swallowed down any lingering fear and went inside. The place was open concept. The kitchen looked more like a lounge than somewhere to make food. All blacks and dark woods with a bar in place of an island. The glass-fronted cabinets displayed top-shelf liquor.

Naut was already holding a cocktail shaker. Though alcohol was exactly what I needed to calm my nerves, there was no way in hell I'd drink anything from him.

I wanted to bolt, but when I turned around I saw it.

The living room aesthetic was comic book to the kitchen's dark noir. All bold colors and odd-shaped furniture that didn't look real. But what sealed it was the mural. Someone had painted a replica of one of Desiree's Instagram mirror selfies. The wall dimensions weren't Instagram friendly, which had forced the artist to stop at her boobs, the line of cleavage blocked by the back of her cell. The skin tone was perfect. So were the meticulously added freckles and the hair cascading in artificial waves down her back. But what got me were her eyes. They displayed the hint of mischief mixed with wonder that made Desiree's so memorable. The painting was beautiful, capturing Desiree perfectly because she'd always been so larger than life.

Too bad someone had painted over bits and pieces in blood red, paint careening down her chest, face, and bare shoulders.

What if Erin was right—they had broken up? Had Desiree gotten pregnant by someone else? Naut couldn't have been happy. Had he followed her to meet the new boyfriend up in the Bronx? Left her body on a playground? Harlem was just over the bridge. He could've been back in bed within a half hour.

I jumped when he came up beside me, but he didn't notice. Too busy staring at her.

"Who did the mural?" I said.

"Me."

"Who painted over it?"

"Me."

"When?"

"Hell if I know. Three breakups ago, maybe. I couldn't even bring myself to do the entire thing."

"It's beautiful." And creepy.

"*She* was beautiful. *That* was a painting I did when I was bored."

He handed me the drink. I hesitated before taking it.

"To Desiree," he said.

I just stared. He downed his in two gulps. "You want to know what happened last night." He noticed my expression. "You're not here to say hi."

"You told the police Desiree went to see me?" I paused, then swallowed, trying to make him feel comfortable. "I just wanted to know why. You know we hadn't spoken in years."

He shook his head. "I said she went to see *someone*. The cops filled in the blanks and said it was you."

"You don't know who?" When he shook his head, I pressed him. "You didn't ask?"

I wasn't buying it.

"Like I told the cops, I was late for my gig. When you have three thousand people waiting for you, it's not good to run behind schedule."

His gig. I'd forgotten. Green had said he'd been in Jersey. An alibi.

*Shitnuts.*

I brought the glass to my lips. It was a Lemon Drop. Her favorite. Unlike Desiree, I've never been a fan. So I wasn't sure if it was that I hadn't had so much as a glass of water all day or that I was just feeling sentimental, but this one tasted amazing. I downed it like a shot.

"Another round?" Naut said.

I just handed over my glass, and he headed back to the kitchen. I could sense him watching me as he made my next drink. It still wasn't sexual. He filled my glass. "You two look alike. More than in pictures."

I didn't want to go down that road again. Not with my emotions still boomeranging. Instead, I walked over to the wall and allowed myself to really take it in. He'd gotten every freckle.

"I was so pissed at her last night." He came up and handed over the drink. "And now our last conversation will always be a fight."

And all I could do was nod, because I got it. The guilt. "I'm sorry. Our last convo also was an argument. Two years ago. At least you got to see her before she died."

He looked at me. "I'm sorry too." It took him a bit to speak again. "I lied. I don't know who she went to see because I didn't ask. She spent the whole night acting all excited because some dude she was hooking up with wanted to stop by. He never came."

I stopped staring at her to stare at him. "And you think that's who she wanted to meet up with?"

It came out rushed, but he didn't seem to notice. Just let out half a laugh even though he clearly didn't think it was funny. "I hoped not. Still don't, honestly. She never said his name. I never asked. Knowing who it was wouldn't help either of us. Different reasons, of course." He stopped. Stared at her a bit more. "I wanted her to be the mother of my children."

I should've said something about the pregnancy, but I didn't. It just seemed cruel. And right now it was the only real clue I had. Instead, I downed the rest of my drink and went to get another refill, pouring out what was left in the shaker. She could be a selfish asshole. She didn't realize it half the time, and the other half she didn't care. Just like her father. "Forget painting over it, you should take a sledgehammer to that thing."

But he didn't laugh one bit. "I should've stayed. Not gone to that gig. I would've if I'd known she wanted to kill herself."

It was the first time someone had assumed she'd done it intentionally. I set my glass down hard, the contents sloshing over the sides. He needed to take it back even though we were both twenty years past backsies. "She wouldn't kill herself," I said. "Not on purpose."

"She was depressed."

I flashed on Erin and what she'd told me. "Why? Because you'd broken up again? Erin said Desiree was fine."

"Erin was too coked up to know."

I yanked my phone from my jeans pocket, typing just as fast as I talked. "Black women, we don't kill ourselves." Yes, we die just as much as the rest of the population. From childbirth. Heart disease. Cancer. From accidents and diabetes and HIV. But not from suicide. I paused long enough to find what I was looking for. Then walked back over to show him. "There were more than forty-five thousand suicides in the US in 2016. Five hundred sixty-four were Black women. We don't kill ourselves."

He took the phone but didn't glance at it. Didn't accept my proof. "Then that's five hundred sixty-four that prove otherwise."

"No. Desiree was too vain."

"To kill herself?"

"To kill herself like that. She'd check into the Four Seasons, run a bath, do her makeup, and down just enough pills so she looked gorgeous when you found her. She wouldn't shoot up on a playground like a cheap hooker, especially since she was afraid of needles."

He looked unfazed, used to upsetting members of my family tree. When he spoke, his voice was soft, almost convincing. "Does it matter if you're numb? She was upset she couldn't get cast on another show. Felt alone. We couldn't get our shit together. And she couldn't talk to her family."

I didn't think I could get more mad, and yet. "For good reason," I said.

"I doubt it." He picked up my glass and drank. I was glad I hadn't told him she was pregnant. He didn't deserve to know. "They weren't talking to each other," he said.

*They?* Said family tree had only a few branches left. I knew she spoke with Aunt E on the regular. And Veronika took her cues from her husband, which meant one thing. "Desiree and Mel?"

He nodded while I shook my head.

"She saw him yesterday, for her birthday."

"No, she didn't." His voice was emphatic, laboring over each syllable to make sure they came out perfect.

But he was lying. Desiree was a daddy's girl. Still, I decided to humor him. "Fine. Tell me what happened."

"Wish I knew."

"Well, whatever it was, they made up. There's a pic of them on her Instagram."

Of his arm, but still. Mel hadn't mentioned any falling-out when I was in his office.

Naut shrugged, took another drink. "The photo couldn't have been recent."

It had to have been. She was in that teal romper. Desiree didn't re-wear clothes when lounging around the house—much less leaving it. And there was no way Mel could stay mad at Desiree. They'd have made up.

But if they hadn't been talking, it was for a *reason*. One I'd never have the courage to ask Mel about. If Aunt E had known, she'd have told me. I could think of only one other person who might.

Zarah.

* * *

I took an Uber. It was late. I was tipsy, but I wasn't foolish. Before I left Naut, I asked him about Find My Friends, but he didn't have it enabled. He sent me off with a bottle of water and his phone number to make sure I made it to my destination safe and sound.

I left another message for Green, then mentally replayed my conversation with Naut during the entire ride downtown. Erin was right. Naut didn't know what happened after he'd left for his gig.

Uneasiness bubbled inside me. I'd started the day wanting to know one thing: Why had Desiree been coming to see me? And instead of getting an answer, now I had a million more questions.

Zarah's building was as tall and pristine as a wedding cake. There was no doorman this time. Just an intercom listing apartment numbers. I hit 301 and waved solemnly at the security camera. It took only a few seconds for her to buzz me in.

But when I finally got upstairs, I realized Zarah hadn't buzzed me in at all. Her assistant was cute and Black, with flawless makeup and a long, straight lace front in the same trendy platinum color I saw all over YouTube but would never dare try myself. She introduced herself as Felicia.

"She's been in bed since the doctor left," Felicia said.

I nodded, not surprised that he'd made a house call. When you're rich and famous, doctors come to you.

"I'll get her," Felicia said.

"No, I don't want to wake her. I can always come back another time."

But Felicia was already making her way down the lone hall. "No, she wanted me to get her when you stopped by."

I looked around. It wasn't only the outside of the building that resembled a wedding cake. Zarah's apartment was white on white on white. Flow through and open concept, with a glossy white kitchen squeezed into one corner. The floors were a light wood she tried to hide under an oversize furry white rug. I knew from browsing her Instagram that it looked way better in photos than in real life.

Truth was, my objections to Felicia were solely home training. I had no desire to come back later. I wanted to talk to Zarah now, so I was glad she was willing to talk to me.

Then I saw her.

It said a lot about Zarah that even in oversize sweats, no makeup, and with her hair in a bun, she outshined me, Felicia, and probably everyone in a ten-block radius. She'd wanted to be a model when we were kids but never made it past five foot four. It also said a lot that she had managed to do it anyway, by launching a new makeup line designed specifically for women of color after struggling for years to match shades to her deeper complexion. Not that she needed it. Her skin came with its own filter, only disturbed by dimples when she smiled.

There were no dimples today. Just tears, her eyes a red-rimmed puffy mess that would require an intricate cocktail of creams and patches to rectify. She shuffled straight to me, only stopping when she was close enough to envelop me in the fleece blanket she'd brought with her from the bedroom.

The top of my T-shirt was drenched within seconds. I held her while Felicia busied herself in the kitchen area. Zarah finally pulled away. "Let's sit."

She shuffled to a white couch that looked uncomfortable as hell, but then so did the kitchen chairs and every other piece of furniture in the place. We sat, then just took each other in. I hadn't seen myself in hours. I was sure I didn't look much better than she did—minus the red eyes, of course. I should've asked her about Mel, but I didn't. There was something else on my mind.

"Was Desiree suicidal?"

It was as if Zarah suddenly inflated. "No! Are the police saying..." She trailed off. I was losing her. *Shitnuts.*

"No," I said quickly. "They did say she was going to meet someone after she left the party. She mention anyone?"

She shook her head.

I pressed. "Not when you said goodbye."

Her eyes teared up again. "I had to rush to Abby's lip-kit launch before the red carpet closed. We didn't say goodbye. I'm sorry."

"It's okay. I'm not blaming you. Do you think maybe it was someone she was seeing?"

Zarah's eyes lit up, happy to be helpful. "Maybe! She definitely saw him earlier. She was wearing a necklace he got her. Kept fingering it all night."

"Who was it?"

She deflated again. "She wouldn't say, just that they had to keep things quiet because of the press. And I didn't want to ask since we'd just started talking again. I should've. I'm so sorry."

The tears came fast and furious. I pulled her close and held her again as I spoke to Felicia. "Can you get her some water?"

By the time she'd brought the glass over, Zarah was just dry heaving. "She was like this all morning," Felicia said, like Zarah wasn't there. Couldn't hear a word. "The meds were helping, though. I can call her doctor. See if he can come back."

I shook my head. I could ask Tam about Mel. "Let's just get her to bed. Maybe that'll help." I turned to Zarah, gently rubbed her back. "Felicia's gonna take you to your room."

She just nodded, letting me and Felicia help her up and then down the hall.

# EIGHT

I texted Tam from the Uber on the drive home, but I wasn't surprised when she didn't answer. It was late. Aunt E's light was on when the Uber dropped me off, but her apartment went dark as soon as I opened our front gate. Just like when I stayed over in college.

She didn't open her door when I walked past, and I didn't stop in to say good night. Instead, I went straight up to my apartment. She'd been inside. The aluminum-foil-wrapped plate on my kitchen counter was a dead giveaway. Still not hungry, I put it in my fridge and left a trail of clothes to my bathroom, where I hunted down an old bottle of melatonin I hadn't used since the month after Desiree and I had stopped speaking. It was long past its expiration. I was willing to risk it.

I added gel to my braids, tied them down with a scarf, and popped three gummies.

I dreamt that night. Desiree and me playing hide-and-seek, something we had loved as kids. Gram's apartment and backyard weren't big, so we both knew all the places to hide and all the places to look. But it wasn't like that in my dream. I looked for her all night, checked everywhere, including the cabinet she loved. I never found her.

I woke up to the sun shining. I'd forgotten to close the curtains. It was 8:30—late for me—but that was far from why I felt so out of sorts. First thing I did was check my texts. My message to Tam was marked as read. She hadn't responded. I sent her a quick Morning.

That too was read immediately and ignored. It took me less than a nanosecond to decide to go see her. I rushed through my morning routine, throwing on my YOU HAD ME AT STAY AT HOME T-shirt and Jordan retros before heading downstairs to apologize to Aunt E.

I opened her door without knocking and made my way through the patchwork of furniture that had crowded the main living area as far back as I could remember. Aunt E had always referred to Gram as an organized hoarder. Claimed to hate that about her. And yet she hadn't removed a single item, even Gram's aged black leather recliner, which none of us dared use.

Aunt E sat at the kitchen table in her pajamas, talking on her house line. I could tell from her expression she was speaking to Ms. Paterson from next door. "Let me go, Denise. Lena's here." She paused. "She's a grown woman. If she wants to get in that late, that's her own business." Another pause. "I'll definitely let you know as soon as arrangements are made."

She hung up. "That nosy heifer will probably know before you or me anyway."

We both laughed, and she kept the smile on, genuinely happy to see me.

"No Zumba?" I said. She did Gold at least three times a week.

"Not today." She gave me a thorough once-over as if looking for cracks and tears. "You okay?"

I was not but didn't want to get into details. Not until I knew more. "Sorry I missed dinner."

"I'm sure you enjoyed the leftovers."

I nodded even though I hadn't eaten them.

"Let me make breakfast. You can tell me what all you did yesterday. You musta been busy to miss my chicken 'n' dumplings."

"I need another rain check." I still wasn't hungry, but I didn't want her to worry, so I grabbed an apple from a bowl on her counter. My first bite tasted rotten, but when I looked at it, it was fine. "Gotta go to Mel's office."

She paused, surprised I'd voluntarily go see him. My relationship with Mel was the elephant in the room, around as long as her plastic-covered couch. We never spoke about how he'd left me. Instead, Gram and Aunt E had just tried to fill the hole. She opened her mouth to say something, then closed it again. Changing her mind.

"Good," she said. It wasn't the first time I was happy she wasn't the type to pry. "I love you, baby. Know that."

I would have taken my bike, but I wanted to catch Tam as soon as the office opened, so subway it was. Since I was in the system, I got up to the fifteenth floor with no problem—only to be greeted by locked glass doors. I could still make out Mel's greatest hits playing on repeat. The lone concession to the office's closed status was that the videos played on mute.

Mel had started Free Money in his junior year at Morgan State after meeting a wannabe rapper named Free. I'd read enough profiles to know that no record label would give Free the time of day. So they'd started one themselves using Mel's scholarship money. The rest was a classic Hollywood tale. Making it big by sheer will. Falling out over money before the new millennium. Never speaking again. Desiree had assured me it had not been a clean break, but I'd figured that out myself, since Free killed a freckle-faced Mel lookalike in a video from his new solo label. Mel responded by smashing Free's platinum records during a photo shoot for *Vibe*. Neither was known for his subtlety. But despite the beef, they'd still both gone on to bigger things—marriage, kids, Grammys. The usual.

Even after their falling-out, Free was part of the Hall of Hits. Murder Mel would never let anyone—especially Free himself—forget the integral role Mel'd played in his success. He hadn't just served as manager and label head when they'd started out. He'd done whatever was needed, even helming Free's first video, "Wasted," since they didn't have enough money to hire a real director. *Complex* magazine had done an oral history for the twenty-fifth anniversary. They'd dubbed it a hood classic, up there with "Nuthin' but a 'G' Thang" and "It Was a Good Day."

Watching it now, I could see why. They'd forsaken the "money, cash, hoes" vibe of other '90s-era videos to craft an actual storyline. Free'd played a neighborhood boy trying to do right by his little girl. After being rejected for job after job, he's forced to turn to a life of crime. With no budget, they'd shot without permits and cast people from around the way. Mel's high school basketball coach was a McDonald's manager who refused to hire Free. Aunt E was a nosy neighbor who didn't like him hanging out on her stoop. The label's first receptionist played the nagging baby mama looking for formula money. To hear my mom tell it, Veronika soon proved a much better actor in real life.

The climax looked like a deleted scene from *Scarface*. A minute straight of real guns and fake death, shot in front of Gram's house. His friends all killed, Free leaves with nothing but his Glock and the two bullets in his chest. Instead of going to the hospital, he goes home. The final scene shows Free walking in the door, blood covering his shirt like a bib, and immediately checking on his three-year-old daughter. She's awake, as if she's been waiting for him to finally come home. He picks her up and snuggles her close, getting blood on her cheek. Then the screen fades to black.

It was my first—and last—starring role.

Desiree had also made an appearance, though no one knew it at the time. Real life imitating art. Of course, *Complex* didn't include Veronika's pregnancy in the oral history.

After watching the same videos repeating for thirty minutes, I accepted that Pierce Productions was not opening anytime soon. I went back downstairs. The security guard told me he never saw anyone before 10:30. I rolled my eyes—that was when I was usually on break from my first class.

I messaged Omar as I went back up to fifteen. How's class?

It took him ten minutes to write back. You're missing out. Nothing as exciting as Financial Management. How you doing? Need me to send notes?

Me: Yes please. 😊 😊 😊

He wrote again: I got you. You get an extension on the paper?

Me: Don't need it. Already done. Emailed White to see if I could drop it off tomorrow.

I didn't have class tomorrow but knew I'd feel better after I turned in the essay. I'd worked on it long enough. I could email it, but unlike Omar, I actually *liked* going to class. And I needed that normalcy, even if it was just for ten minutes.

Omar responded. Shoulda known. Would love to see you if you're coming to campus. 😊

I hearted the message without thinking, then responded: I really appreciate you.

Of course. We're friends. You'd do it for me.

I hoped he was right.

Up next was a text from Kat. I'd never responded to her last one, but she'd sent another—about the funeral. I hadn't even thought about it. I wrote back promising to share details when I had them.

That taken care of, I checked in on Zarah. She didn't respond. I hoped it meant she was in a medically induced sleep. I checked for any messages from Green, who still hadn't called me back. Nothing. I didn't know if detectives worked 9 to 5, but I made a mental note to call him right before lunch.

"Lena. What a surprise."

Tam held a travel mug, no doubt filled with coffee, and an actual newspaper. She looked tired. I scrambled up and scurried behind her as she used her key card to open first the glass doors and then the door to the inner sanctum. She held it open for me. "Your father's not in yet."

*Good.*

We made small talk until we got to her desk and sat down. Her morning routine consisted of booting up her computer, changing into her heels, and pouring what was left of her coffee into a real mug. Once done, she finally spoke. "How was the hotel?"

"Drug-free."

I left it at that because I sure as hell wasn't telling her about the pregnancy test. Or that I thought someone might have been involved in Desiree's death. Mel would know it all before I could even pause to take a breath.

"Did that reporter contact you?" she said. "The guy from the *News*?"

Tam read gossip religiously, everything from Page Six to Instagram accounts like The Shade Room. It wasn't because she actually cared. Tam was more likely to watch real lions of the Sahara than *The Real Housewives of Atlanta*. She was monitoring them for mentions of Mel. Any negative stories would be sent to his publicist or his lawyer, depending on the severity. Tam had even been known to call a reporter herself to relay a choice message.

"He texted me. I ignored it."

"He covered your sister's car accident a couple of years ago. Had some source that knew too much. Even got some award for his reporting. Now he wants to do a longer, in-depth story on Desiree's life."

He'd mentioned it in the suck-up text he'd sent. The one I'd ignored.

Tam kept on. "Mel thinks it's a good idea. He's going to talk to Stuart this afternoon. We want you to as well."

Of course they did. Mel had always taken a "Keep your enemies close" approach to business, but I was still surprised he'd talk to the press.

What wasn't a surprise was that Mel assumed I'd go along with this new plan.

"We just hired a new publicity firm," Tam said. "They're working up some talking points."

Talking points. My sister had been dead for just over a day and she was already reduced to bullet points crafted by some publicist probably coming off her first internship. I wanted no part in any of this. I'd just forget to text Stuart Jones back until after the article ran.

Tam noticed my expression. "Stuart's going to do the profile no matter what, so we want to control the narrative. Focus more on positive things. How much she meant to the family. Her career successes. How excited she was to turn twenty-five."

That was my in. "Oh, so things were fine between Mel and Desiree." It was posed as a statement even though it was a question. "Because I've heard they weren't even speaking."

"I can set up the interview if you'd like. Have someone from the publicity firm staff you."

She sipped her coffee. Again, I wasn't surprised. Tam protected Mel from everyone, including his own kids. But I was still going to push the issue. I thought about the pregnancy test. "What started their argument? A boyfriend, maybe?"

Another sip. "I can send over the talking points as soon as they're ready."

"Will they cover why Mel and Desiree were mad at each other?"

She took another sip. Or tried to.

"It's empty," I said.

She set the mug down. "Families have disagreements all the time. Doesn't mean they don't love each other. You should know that better than anyone, Lena."

We took each other in for longer than needed. I finally spoke. "I do. You made sure to tell Mel any time I had an issue with Desiree. And to tell Desiree any time I had an issue with Mel. But I guess I don't get the same courtesy, huh?" It still hurt, even now that Desiree was dead. I took in a breath and stood up.

Her eyes didn't follow me. Too embarrassed. The human part of her was breaking through, the Terminator T-800 finally showing emotion. "Wait," she said softly. "You know it's not my place to talk about this, but I can share that it's really hurting Mel they weren't in a good place. That he wasn't able to see her on her last birthday. I'll have him call you when he gets in."

"Fabulous!" I said, though I didn't mean any of the three syllables. "I'll take my phone off vibrate."

And with that I was gone.

If Mel wanted to use me to "control the narrative," to push some perfect-family bullshit, then I could have "talking points" of my own. I banged out the door to reception, mumbled goodbye to the blonde now sitting behind the front desk, and stopped dead in the middle of the Hall of Hits to text Stuart Jones. When can you meet up?

After I hit SEND, I forced myself to breathe deeply, mentally reciting

Biggie even if it wasn't all good. Once I calmed down, I realized the trip wasn't a complete cluster. Tam had confirmed one thing Naut'd told me. Desiree and Mel hadn't seen each other before she died. So what about that Instagram photo? I pulled it up. It definitely wasn't a throwback. She'd had the same teal romper on in other posts that day.

The man in the photo wasn't Mel. But that tattoo…

I looked up just in time to see Free once again cradling baby me to his chest. His bare arms covered in blood—and a very familiar handcuff inked on his wrists.

---

Desiree Pierce stares at the screen. Comments scroll over her neck and chin before disappearing.

You one of those annoying people who look better without makeup, sis!

I've been wondering where you been.

Pull the camera back some, ma! Let's see what you rocking.

She laughs at the last one. "Pull the camera back? You just want to see my tits."

But she obliges, revealing a cleavage-less T-shirt. She's in bed, hair down and uncombed.

She pushes a button on her phone. Suddenly the screen divides into two squares stacked one on top of the other. Erin Ambrose appears in the bottom box. "Oh, Freck," she says. "You look like shit."

"That's 'cause I slept with my head in the toilet."

"You've been throwing up?"

"Yes," Desiree says. "Think it's food poisoning."

"Just you?"

She nods and flips the camera angle. "You guys have to see the view, though."

As she gets up, she knocks a man's watch off the nightstand. Desiree's hand picks it up and dismissively puts it back. She heads toward the window.

"Look at this!" She tips the camera down. She's on a high floor of a skyscraper.

She brings the camera back up. At this height only the tips of sleek silver buildings are in frame, contrasting with a clear sky that's a mix of purples and deep oranges.

More comments scroll by.

That Audemars Piguet is 50Gs at least. Sis is so rich she don't even care.

I would trade places with your sick ass in a heartbeat.

Definitely worth the trip. From the US. And from the bed!

Desiree reads that one and laughs. "And I can't even enjoy it!"

Erin's straight-faced. "I hope *someone* is taking good care of you."

"If you mean room service, then yes." Desiree flips the camera again to show her face as she walks back toward the bed. "And my driver will be making sure I get to the airport okay."

"You're going to the airport by yourself?"

"Apparently, *they* are expecting other guests. Tonight." Desiree gives the camera a look that's clearly meant just for Erin.

Erin shakes her head. "*They* aren't shit for that. They should have let you know before they flew you out there."

Desiree gets back in bed and balances her phone on her knees so she can put her hair in a sloppy topknot. "Oh, I already let them know I was not happy with the service. At all."

When she picks the phone back up, Erin gasps. "Where's your earring?"

Desiree's free hand immediately moves from hair to ear. She's wearing only one clip-on. She stares at the camera, again clearly staring at Erin, who stares back. They look at each other as comments come in double time now.

Girl I hope that earring wasn't expensive.

Check under the bed, sis!

At least u kno it's in the room since you aint left.

Erin speaks. "You should probably look for it."

Desiree smiles. She looks up to no good. "I probably should, huh? We don't want the next guest to find it." There's a knock on the door. Desiree's smile just gets bigger. "Gotta go."

# NINE

Mel and Free were about the same skin color. Desiree would've been able to name their exact foundation shade in MAC, Fenty, and NARS. I had to settle for saying medium-ish brown. A quick Google search showed Free's Free Money cuffs hadn't been lasered off or covered up either, displayed in recent pics a few inches from a wedding band as thick and bronze as an Instagram model. I'm sure his keeping them was a power move, like Mel still showing their old videos. His reminder to everyone that Free Money's success was just as much his as it was Mel's.

Another check of Desiree's IG post confirmed the ring definitely matched. If I'd been paying better attention earlier, it should have been a red flag. Mel never wore one. He and Veronika had matching ink on their ring fingers, Veronika wanting every assurance he couldn't take *that* off.

Unlike Mel, Free was still with his high school sweetheart. They'd had a rough patch a few years back when she'd filed divorce papers. TMZ had had a field day when they discovered there was no prenup. Either the filing was a wake-up call or Free decided it was cheaper to keep her, because his wife withdrew the petition a few months later. And like a true hustler, Free used his personal problems for professional gain. His

*Love & Marriage* album was twelve tracks insisting he was as new and improved as a box of Pampers. A man who didn't cheat.

So much for that.

Although their official bio claimed Mel's scholarship money had funded Free Money, hip-hop legend held there was more to it. Free, who had never gone to college, had indulged in a variety of extracurricular activities. He had ten LPs' worth of claims about drug deals, corner shoot-outs, and home invasions. That stuff had built the entire hip-hop industry, with its focus on driving fancy cars, screwing fancy models, selling fancy drugs. But hip-hop was nothing if not exaggeration. The Bentley gets repossessed. The hot girl goes home when the director says cut. And the only things most rappers have ever stolen are the stories about illegal exploits.

My mom always swore Free's backstory was pure bullshit, that the first time he'd held a gun was in the "Wasted" video. That Mel had had a rougher background than Free. But it didn't matter if Free had actually joined a gang in his previous life; there was too much money at stake in this one. He'd lose everything if his wife left him because he'd gotten another woman knocked up—even if that woman was Desiree Pierce.

I couldn't get out of that building fast enough. I ran straight into Bryant Park, New Yorkers instinctively sensing something was off and getting out of my way. The city had set up clumps of small, dark green tables that could barely fit their matching metal chairs. I sat in one anyway and scratched my wrist until it felt like I'd uncovered bone.

*Free.*

The few memories I had of him were good ones. Great ones. He was the reason I knew star quality wasn't something publicists made up for press releases. I'd picked up on it even as a kid. It helped he'd paid me more attention than Mel had, sneaking me candy, listening to my too-long tales of preschool, turning the studio into a makeshift bowling alley courtesy of alcohol-free red Solo cups and tennis balls.

I had to remind myself that I hadn't seen him in decades, didn't think of him unless he popped up on the radio or my YouTube suggestions. I doubted Desiree had known him at all. He and Mel had fallen out when she could barely walk.

I'd never expected him to factor back into any of our lives—especially not like this.

*It's all good, baby, baby.*

I said it over and over until my wrist stopped aching and the Super Black Woman returned. I didn't know what this meant. Not knowing was something I wasn't used to. I didn't like the feeling at all. If Free was involved—whether in Desiree's death or just in her life—I needed to know, which meant I needed to find him.

Confronting him was out of the question. This wasn't *Law & Order: Hip-Hop.* No, I just needed him to admit something—anything that I could take straight to Green to get him to see that Desiree's death hadn't been an accident. I pulled out my phone and searched to see where Free might be. He'd owned a SoHo loft BC—before cheating. But in what was probably an effort to prove how serious he was about a fresh start, Free had sold it and set up home base in Atlanta, which meant I didn't even know if he was still in New York, much less where in town he'd be. According to Wikipedia, which I used so much I actually gave them five bucks whenever they asked, New York City had 270 hotels and 75,000 rooms. And who knew how many Airbnbs? I couldn't knock on every door, no matter how much I wanted to.

Free was as private as he was old-school. No Instagram. No Twitter. Definitely no TikTok. Not even ones run by publicists and well-compensated social media strategists. I couldn't even use context clues like I'd done with Naut. Still, I checked Desiree's pic again anyway. Just as I suspected, she'd cut off more than Free's face. She'd also cut off any revealing details about where they had been. I moved on to the caption.

*Vibes.* It was followed by the camera emoji and a link to the photographer's IG handle.

Erin.

* * *

"Erin!" Someone called from across the room.

Erin waved, a queen addressing a loyal subject. She smiled too, but sitting across from her, I could see it didn't reach her perfectly made-up eyes. I glanced over to see who'd yelled. I couldn't tell you the woman's name, but I recognized her. I'd hit SKIP AD for her new TV show the last time I was on YouTube checking out natural hair tutorials.

Erin refocused on me. "I'm really glad you called. I still can't believe she's gone."

This time it was my smile that faltered. I just nodded and glanced at the menu.

She kept on. "What are you thinking of getting?"

"The gnocchi."

"Good choice."

"Great. Maybe I'll get two." Based on the plates at the table next to us, the portion size was minuscule.

Manhattan is known for its skylines, not its malls. There was a pitiful attempt at one down by the Macy's flagship in Herald Square. When the World Trade Center reopened, they'd thrown a mall in there too. One that looked more like the set of an overpriced neo-noir sci-fi action film than anywhere you'd actually want to shop. My lone excursion had been rushing through it to catch a 3 a.m. PATH train to Jersey. It had felt like I was running for my life. And then there was Columbus Circle, where we sat now.

We were on the fourth floor. A spot called Amico. Cheesecake Factory it was not. But you didn't come here for the food. You came to be seen, which is why I felt instantly invisible. The only thing salty in the place was me—still pissed from my chat with Tam. Central Park was across the street. Once again, it made me yearn for a bike ride. But it'd have to wait. I was doing lunch.

Stuart Jones had wanted to meet for lunch too, before his meeting with Mel, but I'd decided talking to Erin was more important. I'd gotten here early as usual, which gave the blond hostess fifteen minutes to straight ignore me without so much as a "Do you have a reservation?" For once, I didn't mind, too focused on getting Green on the phone. I'd tried every number listed on his card and some that weren't, but even the cop who answered the main line at his precinct couldn't find him. I left yet another message.

I'd just hung up when Erin came gliding in, heading for her "normal" table. I'd offered to come by Erin's town house, but she'd suggested this place, claiming she was starved.

The waiter dropped off waters and bread, then took our orders. I only went with one portion of gnocchi. Erin opted for Caesar salad, "dressing on the side." After he left, I looked around again. The décor was what an HGTV host would call rustic. Lots of deep woods on the walls, floors, and tables, all offset by sheer white curtains hung nowhere near windows. Everyone "eating" had dressed with a similar vibe. Artfully ripped jeans below flimsy white T-shirts that probably cost as much as the wine list.

When I focused back on Erin, she was staring at me as she absent-mindedly pulled apart a piece of bread. The same look she had given me at the hotel. Taking me in, no doubt comparing me to Desiree. Realizing I didn't stack up. She opened her mouth, and I said a quick prayer to the conversation gods that she wasn't going to talk about the weather in Cannes this time of year. We had nothing in common, and any more small talk would make the gulf between us feel as large as the Atlantic, even if you were flying on a private jet.

"I have a confession," I said quickly.

She leaned in, smiled. At the ready, like this was 1 a.m. at an eighth-grade sleepover.

"I texted you because I need to talk to you about something."

She stopped shredding but only for a second. "Of course. I'm happy to help. What do you need to talk about?"

*Free and him possibly fathering Desiree's unborn child.* But I wasn't ready to dive into that just yet. "About who Desiree was dating. You sure she wasn't seeing anyone?"

She deflated, obviously having expected something else. She recovered quickly, though, and started to shake her head. "She'd called it a sabbatical. I don't think she was even hooking up with Naut."

My phone was already on the table. I unlocked it to find the Instagram app just where I'd left it—open on Desiree's page. I showed Erin the pic. She smiled. "The Lark filter always did wonders for her. I think it was her skin tone. What would you call it? Peanut butter?"

"Who's the arm?"

She barely glanced at it. "Don't know."

"You took the picture."

"Yes, but I didn't take it sober." She finally put the bread down. It hadn't gone anywhere near her mouth. "It's probably some fan. I was always put on photographer duty. She got recognized a lot."

*Fuck it.* "It's Free. They were messing around."

Her expression clouded over. "You got all that from a picture?" I just stared her down until she finally spoke. "How'd you find out?"

"Not because you told me. How were they on her birthday? He seem mad about anything?"

"Don't know. Only stayed a few minutes, then left to get her gift. She seemed fine when we met up later that night." Erin pushed her plate away. "Look, I know things were weird between you guys. Desiree thought the world of you. She was always so hurt that you didn't think the same of her. She wouldn't want you to know she was dating a married guy, especially *that* married guy. And wherever she is right now, I know it's killing her all over again you know she died of an overdose."

I sat back, leaving my anger hunched over the table staring at its reflection in the fancy silverware. Desiree thought the world of me? Still? It felt like a gut punch. I *did* think the same of her—which was the only reason I had been so hard on her. Why I hadn't wanted her to snort her life away. I'd always wanted to protect her reputation—still did.

It turned out Erin and I had something in common after all.

"She was pregnant." At least I thought she was. Green hadn't called back yet. "I found a test yesterday in her stuff."

Her face collapsed. "And no one told me." She didn't have to tell me who she meant. She started to cry. Again. "We told each other everything."

I waited for my usual annoyance. But it never came. Instead, I felt myself feeling for *her*. I reached over, took Erin's hand. "Everyone's been saying she wasn't herself before she died," I said. "It seems like she wasn't telling a lot of people a lot of stuff. And we'll probably never know why." I thought back to the woman working at the hotel. "It sucks."

Erin didn't laugh.

I kept on. "And I didn't tell you for the same reason you didn't tell me about Free. Protecting her. But we both have it wrong. Desiree wouldn't have wanted us to remember some Instagram-filtered version of her. The rest of the world? Yes. But not us—"

"She was like a sister."

"She loved us unconditionally, and she'd want us to do the same. That means being honest with each other. No more lies or secrets."

As I said it, I realized I meant it. The whole "Like a Sister" thing wasn't just a cute hashtag or, worse, a personal attack against me. Desiree wrote it because she meant it. I felt horrible. My sister was gone and I had been jealous of the woman who'd filled the gap I'd left. I should have been happy all along that Desiree had had someone who loved her as much as I did.

Erin pulled her hand away to grab her napkin and clear the snot out of her nose. "Freck wasn't talking to your dad when she died."

I knew that. Erin didn't know that, though. It made me appreciate her sharing. "Yeah, Tam refuses to tell me why." Mel hadn't called yet, as she'd promised, but that was on-brand. "Was it because of Free?"

Erin shook her head. "She messed with Free because they weren't talking. Not the other way around. Payback. They'd stopped talking because of rehab. There was an intervention during Fashion Week in February. Mel said if she didn't go, he'd cut her off."

Desiree had also inherited the Pierce stubbornness. Unlike the freckles, it wasn't our best characteristic. "Let me guess. She got mad. Left."

"No."

"She stayed…"

"No, she left. Just not because she was mad. They put her in some uptight treatment facility in Connecticut." She made it sound like the third circle of hell. "She wanted to go to this place in Hawaii that half the cast of that MTV show got sent to. She even had me call to make sure they had space. But he refused to pay for it. Cut her off. Said she owed him the one hundred forty thousand he'd put down as a deposit in Connecticut. Father knows best."

Our waiter dropped off our plates. I didn't even pick up my fork. Too shocked to eat. Yes, Mel was a shitty father. To me. Always to me. Never to Desiree. I'd had Murder Mel. She'd had the guy with the fifteenth-floor office suite.

Even when Desiree'd gotten her DUI, Mel'd rushed in to clean things up. He wasn't afraid to get his hands dirty, especially if it meant keeping her record clean. Anyone else would have gotten jail time. Desiree got volunteer work.

When Naut told me they weren't talking, I had assumed it was because of a minor disagreement. That Mel had still been funding the lavish lifestyle I'd seen splashed all over the internet. But no, Murder Mel had cut her off, and she'd fucked his mortal enemy. A "Screw you" that was also a "Screw you." And that was screwed up, even for us.

Desiree had never had a proper job in her life, but she'd had money from the reality show and the occasional sponsored ad. Now I realized that couldn't have lasted long. Not with the purchases she put on Instagram and the drugs she didn't. Maybe Naut had been taking care of her? Or Free? And she'd screwed it all up by getting pregnant?

"Hate to be all rude, but your dad's a dick," Erin said.

I signaled our waiter. I needed a drink. "I'm well aware."

"Yeah, Desiree said he treated you like shit growing up. That she tried so hard to make him treat you like he treated her. But I'll tell you something I never had the courage to say to her. Living with Mel and getting all his attention didn't always make Desiree the lucky one. It was conditional. The rehab thing was the first time she didn't do exactly what he wanted. Look how that turned out. When she tried to contact him, he ignored her. She even tried going through Tam and her mother. I told her she was better off. That she could take care of herself."

I played with my gnocchi, my appetite shrinking with each word until it was as small as the portion size. Maybe Erin was right. I'd never thought of their relationship like that—too busy seeing it through my own broken lens. Like they say, hindsight is 20/20.

"When did she run into Free?"

"Party in Miami couple of months ago. We found out he was performing. She really wanted to see him. I got us into the party. She got us backstage."

"And what if I really want to see him too? Can you make that happen?"

"Why?" she said. "So you can tell him about the pregnancy? What would be the point—now?"

"Because I don't think Desiree's death was an accident."

There. I'd said the quiet part out loud. The quiet part that had been banging around in my head louder than the illegal fireworks set off in my neighborhood every Fourth of July.

Erin choked on air. "Of course it was an accident."

"Was it?" Saying it out loud made it feel real. Made me feel even more determined to figure out what the hell had happened. Not just what everyone else wanted me to believe. "You said yourself she'd stopped doing drugs. That she wasn't depressed. If she was going to use, wouldn't she have done it with you?" I could tell from her expression that she wasn't convinced. I kept on. "I think it had to do with her pregnancy."

I let that hang.

"And you think Free…?"

"I don't know what to think. If we had her phone, it'd be different. But it's gone, so the only option is talking to him."

Her eyes started to well up, and once again I watched her cry. "No. No one would kill Desiree. Not even Free."

I said nothing, did nothing—not even giving her the courtesy of looking away. Instead, I stared her dead in the eye. Even the waiter knew to stay away.

I understood Erin's denial. She'd been born with a silver spoon, one which she'd used to do coke. It was easier for her to buy Desiree dying of an accidental overdose than admit someone she'd trusted might have wanted her dead.

If Erin didn't want to help me, it was fine. I'd find another way.

Erin finally spoke. "You really think…"

I just nodded. After a few seconds, she wiped her tears away and grabbed her phone from the table. "I'm not convinced." She paused long enough for me to deflate. "I do know where to find Free, though."

# TEN

It was another three-melatonin night. Same dream. Me chasing after an elusive Desiree, still not able to find her. I woke up with a headache that rivaled my hangover after earning my bachelor's but still managed to be out the door in twenty minutes. Two of them I used to check for news. Even though I'd turned off my Google Alert for Desiree, I still did a quick search. There were a ton of articles, most rehashing what they'd already reported on her death. Thirteen I used to shower and put on my oversize Melanin T-shirt and leggings. Three were for forcing a granola bar down my throat. The final two to swallow down a Motrin and pray the lingering headache would disappear before I made it to Manhattan.

Aunt E and I had finally eaten the chicken 'n' dumplings last night in front of her TV watching a replay of *The Real Housewives of Potomac*. Well, she ate. I picked at my plate and then threw most of it away when she went to the bathroom. Neither of us brought up Desiree, the designer-clad elephant in the room. It was quiet and awkward, which wasn't our usual MO. But we were both lost in our own thoughts. Aunt E was the only family member left who knew me well enough to know something was wrong, and I didn't want to have to tell her anything I suspected. At least not until I had more info.

I had begged off breakfast, blaming it on having to stop by school to finally drop off my paper. I grabbed it from where it'd been sitting on my printer in the spare bedroom for the past week and a half and ignored the clothes still on the floor as I left my apartment. I barely remembered to set the alarm when I grabbed my bike from the downstairs hall.

I had things to do. Places to be. People to confront. But first I needed a bike ride.

If you really want to enjoy Central Park, get there at about 9:30 a.m. The early morning health nuts are long gone—shined and showered and strolling into work feeling damn good they exercised this morning and you didn't. The tourists are still enjoying overpriced breakfasts at places like Junior's and Roxy Diner. Those who can still exercise at 9:30— the stay-at-home moms, the trophy wives, the college kids—are dropping forty dollars per class to have some over-muscled, under-endowed instructor yell tenderly in their ear as they do burpees.

No thanks.

I was an avid biker, that rare mix who uses it for both transportation and exercise. I just don't look the part, forgoing aerodynamic attire for whatever's clean. I don't ride for speed. Considering I still use the ten-year-old Schwinn my mom had gotten me for my eighteenth birthday, I can't. It's more about taking my time, concentrating on the air blowing on my face like the Big Bad Wolf. More than once I've heard some rich white guy laugh as he sped past me on his $2,500 Liv Langma, or seen women in yoga pants give me a look as they slowly drove past in an Uber on their way to spin class, judging way too hard to see the irony of the situation.

Today I tried to let my mind go, but there was too much on it, and coming from so many directions that I felt gridlocked. Desiree being cut off. Being pregnant. Being with a married man. Free, at that. If the baby was his and he knew it, he couldn't have been happy. His wife definitely wouldn't have been. Maybe Free really had made sure she would never find out?

It was hard to reconcile the "Uncle Free" I knew as a kid with this person.

Our society loved to hold celebrities up to mythic proportions. Believe that because someone could make you cry, make you laugh, make you cheer, they couldn't possibly be evil. It was why so many were able to get away with so much. And though I was the last person to put any celebrity on a pedestal, I did find myself not wanting to believe it could be true.

Erin had claimed she knew Free's afternoon workout schedule because she'd once had a "thing" with his trainer. She'd told me about Billy right before insisting she pay for lunch. He and Erin were no longer speaking, but she was adamant that whenever Free was in town, he and Billy would work out at a gym in Midtown. There was never a set time, other than the afternoon. That was usually when Free woke up. My plan was to camp out in the gym lobby from noon until the end of time if need be. I'd promised to let Erin know how it went. I'd let Green know too, even though I still hadn't reached him.

*It's all good, baby, baby.*

I repeated the five simple words as I headed south past the reservoir.

* * *

Stuart Jones was waiting at the Starbucks across from campus when I finished dropping off my paper with Professor White and letting him know I needed a few days to deal with a death in the family. I'd taken my time on the walk over, just enjoying the familiarity of campus.

He sat at a table for two, the omnipresent black suit again a dead giveaway he didn't belong. I hesitated, then finally pulled up my big-girl panties. Always one to be prepared, I'd read up on him the night before.

Desiree's DUI had been his first byline in the *News*. His previous stories had all been for some small paper in Central Jersey. His coverage of the accident was extensive, and his bosses must've liked it because he began popping up consistently afterward, this time with "Staff Writer" under his name. It had changed to "Police Reporter" a year ago.

It made things tricky. And the whole interview made me wary because there was no way I planned to share my suspicions about Desiree's pregnancy. At least not yet. I'd come with a clear agenda, though now that I saw him, I was rethinking everything. But it was too late to back out.

He stood and spoke as we shook hands. "You okay?"

I gave him a toothless smile, then sat in the chair kitty-corner from him. His phone, notebook, and pen were already on the table along with a cup of coffee. "You want anything?"

I shook my head. "Thanks for meeting me up here."

"Wasn't a problem at all. You're still going to class?"

"Not this week. Just needed to drop off a paper." My smile stayed tight. Reserved. Both wanting and not wanting to keep up the small talk.

"Don't you think your professor would have understood if you emailed it? Considering the circumstances…"

I shifted. Now he wanted to turn our interview into a pity party. "It was fine. I needed air."

"You walked? From the Bronx?" I didn't know who was more surprised. Him for thinking I walked or me for realizing he'd looked up my address. But then I remembered he'd also found my phone number.

"Biked," I said.

"Nice. What do you ride?"

"Ten-year-old Schwinn." I didn't mention the fancy Liv Langma Mel had sent me. It was still collecting dust in my hallway. I braced, ready for him to mock my Schwinn. Make some joke.

"Classic," he said. "I like it."

He picked up his pen but didn't open his notebook. Just twirled the Uni-ball in his hand like he was the star majorette. "So you don't go by Pierce…" He let the question linger, as if expecting me to explain why.

"Nope."

When he realized I wasn't going to say more, he spoke again. "I need to apologize for trying to flirt when we first met. I didn't know who you were, what you were going through. Still, it was pretty clear you didn't want anyone bothering you. And I kept pushing. I'm sorry. It won't happen again."

I hadn't expected that one. But still, I appreciated it. He wasn't the first guy to try to hit on me when he sensed vulnerability. He was the first to apologize for it, though. "Thank you." I left it at that.

"So we can start over?" When I nodded, he smiled. And unlike on Wednesday, it seemed genuine. "Appreciate that, just like I appreciate you doing this. I know it's not easy. And I don't want you to think I'm trying to trick you. This is not an article about your sister's death. It's about her life. I'm sure you've seen the chatter online. The comments. The judgment. I want to remind people who Desiree Pierce really was."

I nodded, not about to thank the person who put my sister's lowest moment on the front page. I didn't care how fair he thought his coverage would be.

After a beat, he finally stopped twirling his pen and opened his notebook. "What should I say is your occupation? Grad student studying Nonprofit Management?"

Not sure why he even had posed it as a question. He'd clearly visited my LinkedIn profile, probably had done a full background check like he was renting me an apartment. I just nodded.

"You don't have any experience yet? Your background is corporate?"

I nodded again. Also on my LinkedIn.

He kept on like we were having an actual conversation. "It's amazing you made such a big change. Makes my dreams sound selfish as hell. Win a Pulitzer and a National Book Award. I mean, I volunteer, deliver meals for God's Love We Deliver. But only on Thanksgiving and Christmas. Have since my mother got cancer ten years ago. It's a great way to spend the holidays."

That's when I defrosted. I couldn't help it. "I'm sorry about your mom. Mine died of breast cancer five years ago."

"I'm sorry too. Shitty club to be in."

"The worst. It's actually why I went back to school. I want to help Black women dealing with breast cancer. Provide resources for them and their families."

"Yeah, there's no manual. Wish there had been. I was barely legal when she died." He put his pen to paper like he was ready to write down every word I said. "But this isn't an interview about me. Back to Desiree."

We spoke longer than I'd anticipated. I barely even noticed when he finally started taking notes. He made it easy to talk, delivering on his promise to focus on Desiree's life. I found myself forgetting why I was here, too busy recalling stories that had been long buried. Like the time she'd found a love letter at Gram's house I'd written to a member of 'NSYNC. How she couldn't ever remember what day it was but could always recite every line. She'd pick one at random, quote it at the most inopportune times. She had whispered one in my ear at my high school graduation. And how when she'd actually met him, she made him write me a joke proposal.

Remembering put me in such a good mood that I forgot why I'd wanted to speak with Stuart in the first place. My "talking points." I wondered if I should even bring up the other things I'd decided not to tell him. The pregnancy. Maybe he'd know more.

"Have you heard anything at all about her autopsy?" I said. "Did they do it yet?"

"Police didn't tell you?" He seemed surprised.

"I can't even get Detective Green to return my phone calls."

He nodded. "He's a decent guy. Just overworked. He'll get back to you as soon as he can. Let me know if you still don't hear from him and I can check with my source."

I was instantly suspicious. "That's nice of you."

"I owe you. You've really given me some amazing stuff. Between this and talking to your dad and stepmom yesterday, it's going to be an incredible profile. Hopefully it'll run Sunday."

"How was meeting Mel?"

"I won't lie. I was a bit nervous. Your dad has a rep."

"The window," I said.

He nodded, laughed. "The window. But I enjoyed talking to him. He and your stepmother invited me to their apartment. Wined and dined me, I suppose. But I appreciated how honest he was about Desiree and her past issues."

I wondered if Mel had mentioned their current ones.

"It must be nice to have a family as close as you all are," Stuart said.

*Yeah, it must be.*

"He mention how things had been between him and Desiree recently?" I said.

"He said things were going better, which was why he was so surprised by her overdose. Didn't understand why she'd started using again. Why do you ask?"

That was it. I didn't have to make a decision anymore. Mel had made it for me. "You mentioned your source earlier. How does that relationship work?"

He put his notebook in his bag. "It works however they want. They usually tell me something that they think is important but can't say on the record. So they're just a source. Source at the police station. Source at the mayor's office. Source at the—"

"Mel wouldn't know how Desiree was right before she died because he'd cut her off. Because he didn't approve of her choice of a rehab facility."

Stu paused a second, then immediately pulled his notebook back out.

I leaned forward. "You didn't hear that from me, though."

He looked at me as he put the notebook away a second time.

* * *

Stuart and I had spoken longer than I'd anticipated so I wasn't able to see Omar. I sent him a quick text, then checked my messages. Green had finally called. I'd kept my phone on vibrate. I couldn't tell you my ringtone if you offered me a free trip to Jamaica, so I'd missed it. And when I called him back, he didn't answer. At the rate we were going, he'd join Aunt E and Tam as the only numbers I had memorized. I left another message. He was back to being It.

It took about another half hour to bike down to Midtown. The temperature had topped 90 degrees. I was sweaty and gross, but I was also going to a gym so I doubted it mattered. The fitness center was in the Parker New York hotel. There were two Starbucks so close you could see one line from the other. New Yorkers love their chain restaurants as much as they hate their tourists—me included, since it usually makes deciding what to eat all the easier. And we don't just love McDonald's or Wendy's—though we have plenty of them too—but a whole subset of places known more for panini and salad than burgers and fries. Ask a New Yorker how to get to a fresh&co and they'll point you in two directions. Both will be correct.

I found a spot to chain my bike, then walked over to the hotel. My first mistake was assuming the gym was off the lobby. It wasn't. A guy at the front desk pointed me to an open doorway across the large room. It led to a hall that led to an elevator. There was just one button so I pushed it, prepared for wherever it might take me. Up, down, or even sideways. Gravity Fitness had been relegated to the basement. But since even New Yorkers don't want to drop two-hundred-plus bucks a month to work out in a cellar, the hotel had branded it "underground."

Gravity wasn't alone in its lower-level status. The gym shared space with a nail salon, a blow-dry bar, and a facial place that willingly had chosen the name Skin Laundry. I ignored the women getting pampered on both sides of the hallway to hit the gym in the back. I felt like I didn't belong. Again. It didn't help that the woman stationed behind the front desk barely paid me any mind. One would think I'd be glad to be ignored since I wasn't there to exercise, yet I still felt the need to speak. "Just waiting for a friend."

It was like she didn't hear me. I searched for where that waiting would take place. They'd forgone a couch for three armless brown leather chairs. Erin sat on the one closest to me.

"Surprise!"

Indeed it was. "You work out here?"

She shook her head. Offended. "My trainer has her own gym. Only charges five hundred a session too." She got up. "If what you're saying is true, there's no way I'd let you confront that asshole by yourself."

She gave me a hug, and I had to admit I was glad to see a familiar face.

I was starting to see why Desiree liked her. She was loyal. Not something I was used to.

"If it makes you feel better, this is just a fact-finding mission," I said. "Not a confrontation. I just want to ask him some questions." I reminded myself that I wasn't the police. I was a concerned sister.

She nodded and sat. "We can ask him what Desiree was like after I left. See if he knew about the baby."

"No matter what he says, we play it cool, then take that info straight to Green. I want to force him to take it seriously."

I settled in next to her.

"We should take a pic," Erin said. "Want to do a selfie?"

My growing goodwill didn't extend that far. "I think we're good." I could only imagine what she'd hashtag it.

I looked around nervously, as if Free would jump out any second like the guy from the Friday the 13th movies. The gym's main workout space was off to the left, hidden behind one of those cloudy white walls meant to let in light while also ensuring privacy. It worked too well. From my vantage point, only two machines were visible. Both empty.

"He'll be here soon," Erin said.

I hoped she was right. "I don't mind waiting."

"Me neither."

She lasted fifteen minutes, ten of which she spent staring at herself in her camera. It took me a sec to realize she was just as nervous as I was. This was her way of showing it. I let her be, channeling my own energy into my phone too. Stuart had texted. Checked with my source. Autopsy should take two weeks.

I sent a quick thank-you. Those two sentences were more than I'd gotten from the cops. Beside me, Erin abruptly stood up. "Gonna go chat with the girl at the front desk." She strolled over. "Hey, is Billy here? Tell him Erin wants to talk."

The chick at the front desk placed a call, and just like that, Billy magically appeared. He was one of those beautiful, deceptively skinny guys who used to be my type.

He gave Erin a once-over. "I hope you're here to work out."

Why did the pretty ones always ruin it by opening their mouths? I tore my eyes off him in time to see Erin freeze, confidence dripping out like water from a broken air conditioner. She pointed to me. "She wants to talk to you."

Speaking with Billy wasn't part of the plan. I thought quickly. "I'm a huge fan of Free, and Erin said you knew him. And we were in the area. And I was just hoping, like, maybe to get an autograph when he comes in." I smiled as innocently as I could.

He spoke to me while glaring at her. "As much as I would love to help out any friend of Erin, Free left an hour ago."

Erin glanced at me, then back at Billy. "I thought he worked out in the afternoons?"

"Mornings. He comes here straight from the studio. That was the problem with you. Too self-centered to listen."

I jumped in again. "It's cool. We'll be here tomorrow."

"He won't. After his show tonight, he's on a flight to England."

"And I don't suppose you'll tell us where we can find him now?" I said. "I really want that autograph."

He just laughed and turned to Erin. "I want my ring back," he said. "Now."

At that point I was over it. If he didn't want to help, I didn't want to kiss his ass any longer. He must've noticed me glaring because he smiled, probably thinking it came off as charming. "My apologies. I can be a dick."

"Probably to make up for the small one God gave you," I said.

Billy gaped, then looked at Erin.

"Don't look at her," I said. "Who do you think told me? Bye, Billy. It was a pleasure to meet you."

Erin spoke as soon as we walked down the hall. Neither of us looked back, though I'm sure Billy was just where we'd left him. "You. Are. Amazing. That's something your sister would have said."

"Billy mentioned Free has a show tonight." We got to the elevator and

I pushed the UP button. While we waited, I searched online. "I don't see any shows listed on his website."

Erin shrugged. "Maybe it's some surprise appearance."

Great. New York City had dozens of concert venues, from the massive Madison Square Garden to the more intimate Mercury Lounge. There was no way we'd be able to hit each one. I briefly considered calling them all but realized I could call someone else.

Naut picked up just as the elevator doors opened. Erin started to go inside, but I motioned for her to stay put.

"How you feeling?" Naut said.

"Better than you sound." I remembered I'd stopped after two Lemon Drops while he'd kept going. Judging from the clinking of glass in the background, *still* going even though it had been two days. "Quick question. Have you heard about Free doing any secret shows tonight?"

"Just PowerJam."

PowerJam was a big concert one of our hip-hop stations put on at Madison Square Garden. "You sure?" I said. "I don't remember hearing he was part of the lineup." I'd know. I followed the station's Instagram.

"Surprise guest. To celebrate the twenty-fifth anniversary of his first album."

"Give me a sec, Naut." I turned to Erin. "Think you can get us PowerJam tickets? I know it's sold out." The station had posted that tidbit too.

"I don't know," Erin said. "I have a ticket guy, but he's been acting kinda shady."

That wouldn't do. I spoke again to Naut. "Can you get us backstage?"

# ELEVEN

It took fifty minutes and two transfers to get to Erin's place. She'd texted me her address off Tenth Avenue in Chelsea. Not exactly a hop, skip, and jump from where we were going—or anywhere, really—but it didn't matter. The only walking most residents did in this neighborhood was from front door to waiting car.

When we first met, Erin had called Gram's place a town house, as if it had something in common with where she lived. Her version was different from anything you'd find in the Bronx, even putting the red-brick exterior and multiple levels aside. My place was missing about six thousand square feet, a multimillion-dollar price tag, and a set of front stairs long enough to land a plane. It took Erin forever to make the trek to answer her front door. I passed the time looking up her address on Zillow. It turned out she was walking on $2,533 per square foot. I'd take my time too. When the door finally opened, there was a gust of central AC colder than most windchill factors. Her electric bill probably cost more than most rents. Of course, Erin wasn't the least bit concerned with letting all that expensive air out.

She kept the door wide-open for five minutes of small talk between me, her, and someone who looked like her exact replica. Exact same weave. Exact same makeup. Exact same amount of store-bought cleavage. The overall effect was like one of those statues outside Madame Tussauds. It didn't help that Erin 2.0 had just as much forehead movement as a wax figurine. She had a name: Starr. Erin said she was the best "MUA"— makeup artist—east of Nashville. Since my own routine consisted of a dash of lip gloss and some eyeliner when I was going fancy, like today, I had to take Erin's word for it. We shook hands, and Starr got into a waiting Uber, probably off to create someone else in her image.

I watched her car head toward 23rd, then turned back to find Erin giving me a once-over. I'd forced myself to put some effort into my appearance, pairing my best sneakers with black jeans and an ironic gray T-shirt that read EQUAL RIGHTS FOR OTHERS DOESN'T MEAN LESS RIGHTS FOR YOU. IT'S NOT PIE. I'd even Googled "How to make your eyes look less tired" and done my best to get rid of the bags.

"You look cute," she said, because that's what women say to other women when they're going out together. It sits in the linguistic library next to saying "Fine" when asked how you're doing, even if you've just lost your dog and been diagnosed with pinkeye.

"You too," I said, because that was the only correct answer, with "You think?" a close second.

I wasn't lying either. She did look good. Amazing, even. A dark silver tank minidress that shimmered and shined more than a cartoon. She smiled. "You think?" She looked back down the street. "Where's your car?"

"I don't have one." Then I realized what she meant. An Uber. "I took the subway."

"That's, like, two whole blocks." She looked impressed.

When I glanced down, I got why. She was balancing on four-inch heels. There were no telltale red bottoms, but they were probably made by some trendy designer nonetheless. One who didn't have a marketing genius behind him like Mr. Louboutin. "It's not that bad in flats," I said.

"I don't own any."

I believed her. Desiree had been like that too. Their lifestyle was one that didn't require a pair of sneakers. You didn't need them for Pilates and yoga—or a trip to the plastic surgeon.

"We can get a cab, I'm sure," I said.

But Erin already had her phone out. "I'll take care of it."

Five minutes later we were in the back of a black SUV with a guy named Arjun pointing out USB ports and the bottles of water he'd thoughtfully left in the cup holders. Ten minutes later we were stuck in traffic on Eighth Avenue while Erin and Arjun swapped life stories. They'd both spent time in India. Only one of them was actually from there. Twenty minutes later we were finally at our destination.

As a proud Jersey girl, I've spent a lot of time in Penn Station, but I can't begin to tell you how to get into Madison Square Garden. I don't think out-of-towners realize the Garden and Penn Station are one and the same. Most commuters probably forget themselves, the onslaught of jersey-clad Knicks and Rangers fans so common they might as well be part of the architecture. A true case of *Upstairs, Downstairs*. Fans crowded into one space. Tired commuters heading to New Jersey and Long Island into the other. Both paying far too much, whether they're staring at Billy Joel or a departure board.

There is a reason why every movie set in New York City has a scene in Grand Central and why, in Hollywood, Penn Station doesn't exist. It has all the bullshit and none of the ornate architecture. No arched windows. No ceiling murals. No artwork. Instead it has chain restaurants, endless construction, and the occasional lost bird. The only thing it has going for it is Krispy Kreme, and that's only if you like donuts. It's not the first time New York has decided to shit on New Jersey. And it won't be the last.

When we got out of the car, I felt more lost than Gretel after she let Hansel convince her bread crumbs were a foolproof plan. Luckily, I had both Erin and an All Access pass. She'd wanted to come, and I'd realized having someone fluent in "rich and famous" would be a good thing. Once our credentials were picked up and placed around our necks, I followed her up and around and up again until we were gliding toward a Black woman security guard.

I double-fisted the pass, ready to present it like an ID to a bouncer. But she didn't stop us, barely even glancing our way as Erin glided by. I took more tentative steps until we were through a set of black curtains and into the "back of the house." It felt like more people were backstage than in the arena proper, and it was way more diverse than I'd expected. Gruff white guys in dirty jeans hauling instruments like furniture. Cute young blondes clutching walkie-talkies like pearls. Overdressed couples, the women in too-high heels and the men in too much cologne.

A music caste system, and I didn't fit in anywhere. Too female for the roadies. Too brown for the event staff. Too broke for the VIPs. Erin didn't have that problem. We could barely get two feet without someone stopping her to trade air kisses and promises to meet up in LA. Unfortunately, none were Free.

I'd been fine until we'd gone through the curtains. But then my nervousness kicked in. The plan had seemed foolproof. If you're going to ask one of the most powerful men in music if he had anything to do with your sister's premature death, a public place seemed the spot to do it. Now that I was here, however, backstage just felt full of secrets. Doors and curtains and people so self-involved they wouldn't notice someone getting shot right in front of their eyes. But I'd come this far. I needed to talk to Free, and I was going to talk to Free. Even if I had no clue where he was.

I had too many options. There were posters plastered on the walls with arrows pointing a million ways. PRODUCTION. DRESSING ROOM. BROADCAST ROOM. STAGE. Free could be in any of them. We kept walking, destination unknown, while a redhead as thin and pink as a Pocky stick blocked our path. "Erin, baby, I'm sorry to hear about Desiree. Feels like we just had drinks last week to discuss that club you two wanted to start. What was she doing up *there*?"

Erin didn't glance at her. She glanced at me. "Cassie, this is Lena." Cassie shook my hand, her fingers as limp as a male body part, eyes already searching for someone more exciting. "Lena is Desiree's sister."

Cassie turned back to me so fast you would have sworn she'd been slapped. "Oh, you poor thing." I noticed she didn't ask *me* what Desiree was doing up *there*. "You're so brave to be out and about so soon. You know Desiree was one of my favorite people."

*To gossip about.* I threw Erin a look. Even she rolled her eyes.

"Let me know if I can do anything to help," Cassie said. I could see her mentally composing the text she'd send to her yoga group chat. How I was at a concert instead of mourning. How we were both the same, loving to party too much.

"You can tell me where Free is," I said.

That stopped her. "Does this have to do with Desiree?"

"No, he's a family friend."

"Oh. Free Money. That's right. He's performing after one of the ASAPs so I doubt he's here yet."

"You know if he's doing press?" Erin said.

"Doubt it. It's not a coincidence his new artist is on the bill. It was the only way he'd agree to do the show. I'd try his dressing room." She took out her card, handed it to me. "Please let me know about the funeral."

With that she was off, leaving me glad she was gone.

"Okay, so we need to find the dressing rooms," I said more to myself than Erin.

Luckily, an arrow pointed to dressing rooms to our right. I took off, power walking like I was in Rockefeller Center the day the Christmas tree went up. The only indication Erin was following was the people calling her name as we passed. The hall curved past a table chock-full of snacks before hitting a dead end that would have forced us to go right. And I would have, except for the guard.

He stood smack-dab at the wall, about ten feet from an open area. Now that I had a plan, I had no fear. No nerves. An All Access pass was good for any impending anxiety.

"Lena." Erin was still behind me, but I ignored her. Too focused.

We'd run out of arrows, which meant this had to be Free's dressing room. I was all ready to breeze past the guard when he put up his hand. "I'm sorry, ladies, but this area is restricted."

I forced a smile and held up my pass. "We're credentialed."

"Lena." Erin again. I still paid her no mind.

The guard was white and old, with more hair on his chin than the top of his head. He made no bones about glancing at my chest, for once not checking out my boobs. I raised my credential higher. "Doesn't all access mean…all access?" I tried to hold my sarcasm in.

Security Santa smiled. "No, ma'am."

He sounded like he'd never been so happy to say two words in his life. I wanted to yank him by his beard.

Erin stepped forward. "I tried to tell you. We need a sticker."

She motioned to the wall at our left. Yet another poster. This one listing the types of credentials. There were at least ten in total, from "Working" to "Press" to "AAA." Erin pointed at the one that kept sending me invites to join their motor club, then spoke to the guard. "That's the God pass?"

He nodded.

She turned to me. "It's the only one that's truly all access."

*Shitnuts.* "What are we gonna do?"

I was talking to Erin, but Security Santa spoke. "Not wait here."

I really could do without the extra helping of attitude, even if I was the one who'd served it up first. My frustration was back full force.

Erin came to my rescue. Again. She gave Security Santa a smile that could melt margarine, which made sense since she was trying to butter him up. "We only need to get back there for a second. You can even come with us."

He looked dead at me while answering her. "Can't." He'd obviously heard that one before, from cuter girls than us.

"Can you at least tell us if Free's here?" I said, though I was sure he'd heard that one too.

"No."

He didn't bother to elaborate, and my pride refused to ask him to clarify. Instead, I gave him another smile. It was looking like the only chance I'd have to chat with Free would be if I jumped up onstage.

Erin and I retraced our steps. Me glowering. Her texting all the people she'd spoken to backstage, asking them to let us know when they saw him. We walked past a bathroom, and she stopped. "I gotta tinkle."

She left me standing by the snack table, scratching the inside of my wrist like I'd just taken off a set of too-tight cuffs. Things were not going how I'd envisioned. Maybe it was God's way of telling me this was not a good idea. I was about to go in to tell Erin we could leave when I saw the mass.

The energy is different when there's a celebrity in the room. There's this crackling undercurrent everyone feels even if they don't acknowledge it. Even if no one is looking directly at the star—and at events like these, they never are—everyone is aware of their presence. The air surrounding me suddenly felt rich. I was in the presence of fame and fortune.

The mass came toward me, a headsetted blonde up front playing Pied Piper to a group of Black men of all shapes and sizes. The tall, beefy one in the lead was constantly looking around—the bodyguard. The others weren't nearly as tall or as anxious, their energy directed not out but in, at a lone person I couldn't make out.

But I didn't have to. I knew who it was.

A skinny white kid confirmed it when he jumped in front of me, cell phone extended like a gun. "Can I get a selfie?"

The only indication anyone had heard him was the bodyguard. He tensed but didn't stop. Neither did the rest of the mass. The kid came forward anyway. The bodyguard stuck his hand out, but a voice stopped him.

"You're good, little man."

The seas parted, and there he was. I'd figured Desiree had screwed Free as payback. But now, up close and in person, I wasn't so sure. Free was one of those men who got better-looking as they aged. The type so pretty in their twenties that the gradual appearance of fine lines and gray hairs made them more accessible. It helped that Billy's workout sessions were paying off.

I'd caught snippets of his new album when I'd scrolled my favorite IG pages. Watched my YouTube tutorials. Put on Jimmy Kimmel to help me get to sleep. Despite his new, mature look, his lyrics were still the exact same. Still hit you so hard you got a concussion and needed to stay up all night listening on repeat.

I stared. It'd been twenty-five years since I'd seen him. I doubted he would recognize me, so I played out how I would introduce myself as he chatted the kid up and let him snap a smile-free selfie. Saying "Lena Scott" would get me ignored. Saying "Mel's daughter" or "Desiree's sister" would get me escorted out.

I was still deciding when he looked right at me. And I knew he'd seen me all along. I flashed on the man who'd bowled with me in the studio and listened to my three-year-old day. Then I smiled.

"Melina."

He moved toward me, so the mass did too. He pulled me in for a hug so hard he lifted me off my feet. He smelled like expensive cologne and good weed. I resisted the urge to tell him how I still hated that little girl who'd pushed me on the playground. I hadn't thought of her in years.

He was good memories. He was also the man who'd been fucking my sister behind his wife's back. Maybe got her pregnant. Maybe did much, much worse, even though it was hard to believe that now, seeing him in person. I had to remind myself that's what they always say about killers. I took a big step back. "We need to talk."

"I know."

I was immediately swept up in Team Free. Even with the cadre of men surrounding me, I could still feel people noticing us or pretending not to. That current.

We moved past the roadies, past the women in headsets, past Security Santa, into a hallway. The only inkling it was celeb central was the occasional big, bulky bodyguard posted outside a door. We didn't stop until we got to one with Free's name on it. It was only when we entered that I realized I'd left Erin behind.

# TWELVE

I t was a half hour before I actually got to speak to Free. There was a line. The blond escort from the station. His manager. Even his barber. Everyone wanted five minutes. To go over the schedule. To discuss logistics. To cut his hair. And we were all crowded into a space about the size of a bedroom with a couple of couches, a battered coffee table, and a credenza decked out with such an odd collection of things that they had to be straight off his rider. His boys had descended on the sofa, one rolling up a blunt with the utmost concentration.

I leaned against a wall, ignoring them ignoring me, reading the latest pep talk from Erin on my phone. Security Santa hadn't let her pass, and I was afraid if I left to get her, I'd never get back in. So I stayed, using the time to reevaluate how to bring Desiree up. This wasn't a pool. I wasn't going to jump right in. I'd start with the shallow stuff—baseball, kids, how great his new song was—before finally getting deeper. The plan still needed to be the same. Fact-finding mission. Not confrontation. Especially not here with his whole crew of lackeys.

They'd re-created a barbershop in the far corner. Clipper, brush, guy named Ralph making Free's hairline as crisp as a new dollar bill. Free nodded his satisfaction, and Ralph began to pack his stuff.

I was up.

The barber didn't so much as look at me, getting paid as much for keeping his mouth shut as for cutting hair. I wondered who he thought I was. *What* he thought I was. And if he'd seen Desiree and thought the same exact thing.

Free was ready and waiting. He sat back in his chair. I'd spent enough time in hair salons to know the seat wasn't comfortable, yet he looked at home. And he probably was. Backstage second only to the studio for him.

He smiled, maybe at my nervousness, maybe just at me. I stopped a full three feet away, scared to come any closer. Not even looking at him directly but via the mirror. Him in spotlight, me in shadow.

"She seemed fine last I saw her."

His voice was so matter-of-fact I immediately wanted to cut the bullshit to meet him halfway.

"Three days ago," I said.

"Yep. Had to drop off her gift even though she could only fit me in for a few minutes." He laughed. "She was a busy girl, but I wanted to see her. Twenty-five is a big deal."

"It is. Still young, though."

He laughed again, turned around to finally face me. "I liked her, you know."

He probably liked a lot of women. I didn't say that, though, just stared until he turned back and we were both looking in the mirror again. He spoke first. "You came here to ask questions. So ask them."

"How?"

"She showed up backstage one night. Just like you. Next."

"When?"

His eyes jumped to his crew. "Yo, Pee. When did Desiree start coming around?"

One who wasn't rolling weed spoke. "Miami."

The entourage all seemed to have some purpose. Bodyguard. Barber. Weed roller. Pee must've been the schedule keeper. Free looked back at me. "March."

"That was right after Mel cut her off."

"So I heard."

I wasn't surprised he knew. I was surprised by how blasé he was about it. Like he wouldn't have freaked if things were reversed and Mel was screwing his kid. "So she wanted revenge," I said.

"Maybe she just wanted a good fuck." He sounded as blunt as that spliff. I ignored it.

"She say what happened? Between her and Mel?"

"Mel raised her to be a princess. Always knew it'd be hell on any dude she messed with. I was right."

"But you liked her. What about Cyn?"

I'd said his wife's name but thought of my mother, how she never got over Mel leaving her. The cheating was annoying but forgivable. The abandonment was not. She and Cyn were one and the same.

"I'll tell her you said hi."

It wasn't what I meant. He knew it too. "TMZ has your divorce papers online," I said.

He didn't speak for long enough I thought maybe he wouldn't at all. But then he did. "That shit was a threat. An empty one. My wife and I have an understanding. I don't have to keep it in my pants, but I do have to keep it out of the news. I don't leave the house without an NDA, my man Bones outside, and a condom. Protected in every single way."

"'Only thing broke about me is the condom,'" I said. One of his lines. We just looked at each other's reflection.

"'But I pay for my mistakes,'" he said. The line after it. "Your sister cost me a quarter mil. She tried to get cute. Leave her earring at the hotel. I found it. Sent her home. She wasn't happy. Couple of weeks later, she texts me a photo of a pregnancy test. Nothing else. So I texted her the name of my doctor. Nothing else."

"Desiree wouldn't have an abortion." I thought of that day in the supermarket.

"Someone get my phone."

The timbre of his voice hadn't gone up at all, yet the crew—who had been acting like they couldn't hear a word—suddenly all looked at us. I, in turn, looked at the cell on the counter in front of him. "What's that?"

"Family phone."

By then, Pee had made his way over. He handed the non-family phone to Free, then went back to his assigned seat. I peered over Free's shoulder as he scrolled through his camera roll, quickly understanding the need for two phones. Lots of nudes. Nipple size and color indicating they weren't all the same person.

I had no clue what he wanted to show me, but it didn't matter. Desiree wouldn't get an abortion. I clung to that thought. It was my life raft, if only because I didn't want to think of the alternative. That she did and what it'd made her do after.

That would make Naut right. Prove I really didn't know her. Not anymore.

"Here we go."

He handed me the cell so I could get a closer look. The photo wasn't a selfie, but she'd never take a pic like this herself. Not looking like that. The clothes were hospital, not designer. Her face sans fancy filters. She looked worn down despite the perfectly made-up face, staring at the phone in her hand with eyes as vacant as a lot.

I handed the phone back. No need to look any longer. The photo was permanently burned into my brain. It had been for two years now—ever since I'd taken it.

That had been the last time I'd seen Desiree.

* * *

Twenty minutes later I was back in familiar commuter territory. If Free thought Desiree'd had an abortion, then there was no reason to believe he'd have met her in the Bronx. Part of me was relieved. The other part was just confused. The photo meant something. I just had no clue what. Just like I had no clue what to do next.

Free could tell the photo had me upset, but he assumed it was because I'd taken some pro-life stance. I didn't correct him. He didn't deserve it.

After I left Free's dressing room, I sent Erin a Got to go text, then hauled ass to the safety of the lower level of Penn Station. I wanted to go home. I needed to go home. But I didn't. Subway cell service was too spotty, and I was desperate to talk to Detective Green. He still hadn't called. This would've frustrated me on a normal day. At that moment, it had me homicidal.

I selected his number from Recent Calls. It was either the late hour or God taking pity on me because Green finally picked up.

"Ms. Scott. Sorry it's taken so long to connect, but we're making progress on the Tesla—"

"She was pregnant when she died. She was supposed to have an abortion, but she just pretended. Even sent a picture from her accident a couple of years ago as fake proof." I stopped to take a breath, and he didn't say anything. "She was pregnant," I said one last time.

Finally he answered me. "You're mistaken. We test for that sort of thing."

"She had a pregnancy test. A positive pregnancy test."

"I'm not saying she was never pregnant. I'm saying she wasn't pregnant when she died. When do you *think* she was pregnant?"

I chose to ignore his emphasis. "A few weeks ago."

"Okay. It can take a couple of weeks for the level of hCG in a woman's blood to return to normal. If she'd had an abortion—"

"She wouldn't."

"Or a miscarriage, say, last month, then we wouldn't know. It would explain a depression, though. A desire to be reckless. More so than usual."

A thought hit me so hard I damn near tripped.

What if Green was right?

* * *

"Thanks. I'll be right down."

I slipped the bellhop one of two bills I had on me—a five with a missing corner—then watched as he carted all three designer suitcases to the elevator. Desiree's belongings packed more neatly than her life had ever been. It was only when he turned the corner that I stepped back into the suite and closed the door.

I'd been at the Omni bright and early. I hadn't dreamed about hide-and-seek the night before, but only because I couldn't sleep, too busy trying to make sense of the possibility that maybe everyone else was right. That they knew my sister better than I had.

I'd hit up Google at four in the morning like I was making a booty call. Lying in bed in the dark, I studied how to overdose and ignored the first mention for the National Suicide Prevention hotline. Mixing cocaine and heroin increased the risk. Was that why she'd gotten over her fear of needles? Because she'd gotten over her fear of dying?

Did any of it even matter? It wasn't like it would bring her back.

By 5 a.m., I'd accepted that the only thing I could do for Desiree was pack up her stuff for real. Then I'd emailed Omar, thanking him for sending his notes and telling him I'd see him in Grant Writing on Monday. By habit, I checked for news stories on Desiree. There were fewer than the day before. Again, no one had had anything new to report. Not even Stuart.

Packing Desiree's things had taken longer than it should have. Blame my mother for being one of those a-place-for-everything-and-everything-in-its-place people. Beds were immediately made. Dishes immediately washed. Clothes placed in the properly color-coded hampers. It was no surprise that she'd taught packing as an art form. Everything had been rolled and grouped and placed together just so.

Though I'd rebelled against my mother in many ways—I didn't own a comforter, much less put one on my bed every morning—it turned out that when it came to organizing my dead sister's belongings, the familiarity of her rituals had been oddly comforting. It had been a brief respite, one that lasted just until I'd zipped up the last suitcase.

With the bellhop taking the final traces of Desiree to the lobby, there was nothing left to do. I should've left then. But I didn't. I couldn't. I found myself staring around the suite like it was Desiree's final resting place. I couldn't leave it like this. The place still resembled some white-boy frat house. Half-filled cups, dirty-ass plates, and so much trash that it had erupted from the bin and blanketed surrounding areas. Though I knew there were people who got paid—though not well—to tackle the mess, my home training kicked in.

Starting with the cups, I gathered as many as I could and lugged the whole lot to the bathroom. There, I dumped the liquids in the toilet, the colors combining to create a murky green much worse than anything that could come out of your body. I left the glasses in a neat line on the bathroom counter and then gathered plates as if on a scavenger hunt. The bed was made next, pillows plumped, wrinkles smoothed out.

That left the trash. The suite had come with several strategically placed trash cans. Desiree had elected to use just the one in the living room. I grabbed an empty one from the bedroom and brought it back to the mountain of mess. The excess of garbage appeared harmless. No gross food, no used tampons, nothing that would make you want to vomit. I still took no chances. I'd gotten a bottle of Poland Spring at the Duane Reade on my way over. I placed the plastic bag over my hand glove-style and picked up as much as I could.

One piece of purple paper was covered in Desiree's handwriting. It'd been haphazardly ripped in half so the bottom of the letters was missing. I could still make it out, having read secret notes from Desiree for years.

*Check Karma.*

The last line of the *a* extended to the paper's edge. She'd done the same thing when spelling my name. Her handwriting matched her personality. Melodramatic as hell.

*Check Karma.*

I just hoped it hadn't caught up to her.

I added the paper to the new can and kept going until everything was off the floor. Then, I grabbed my book bag, left the other five dollars from my wallet, and headed out the door. It was time to check out—in every way possible.

I finally glanced at my phone as I waited for the elevator. There were enough unanswered texts from Erin that she'd resorted to actually calling me. U ok?

I hit her back. Fine. Tell you more later. I just hoped I wasn't lying.

When I got into the elevator, I saw Stu had texted again too. Desiree's profile is running tomorrow in the Sunday edition. Hope I captured the woman you told me about.

I wrote back. Looking forward to it.

And I was. It was going to be bedlam at Pierce Productions when Mel found out Stuart knew he and Desiree hadn't been speaking. Part of me wanted to *happen* to call Tam just so I could hear him yelling in the background. He'd be even more pissed when he couldn't find out who Stuart's source was.

It was as close to a good mood as I'd been in since learning Desiree had died.

Stuart wrote again. Heard the police are still putting a lot of time into finding Desiree's car.

I hearted the message, not surprised they were still focused on her ride. It would be nice to have her stuff back. I still wanted to see her phone.

Sherry was at the registration desk. It was too early for checkout so the lobby was deserted. Bored, she stared me down as I approached, barely blinking until I was just a foot away. "You look like shit." She slapped something on the counter between us as she spoke.

The bill.

It was two full pages. Front *and* back. She eyed me as I turned it over, waiting, waiting, waiting. I glanced at it without really looking. At least until I got to the final page.

$38,873.13

I choked and glanced up. Sherry smiled. I'd given her exactly what she'd been waiting for. "You could buy a place for this much," I said.

Sherry blinked at me. "Where?"

I flipped the bill back over so I could start at the beginning, paying attention this time and seeing exactly what Desiree had gotten for Mel's money. "I don't know. Some red state that starts with an *A*."

She leaned forward so she could read upside down. "I doubt your average Alabama foreclosure comes with the Mystique spa package. Or a fifty-dollar Caesar salad."

I noticed the name in the top right corner. "Why does this say Melina Scott?"

"Because that's the name she used to check in."

"Like an alias?" I'd heard of celebs using them to hide from fans and paparazzi. I didn't think Desiree had been on that level. She'd obviously felt differently. Part of me was flattered she'd chosen me. Just like the passcode. Further proof I'd been on her mind.

"It's the name on the credit card," Sherry said.

"That's impossible. *I'm* Melina Scott."

"Oh? Then you probably should check your wallet."

I didn't have to. "She might have used my name, but she didn't use my card. My limit's nowhere near that high."

"Yeah, she did. I checked her in. Visa White Card. Best believe I paid attention to the name."

It hit me. "That heifer."

Sherry smiled. "Let me guess. It's your card."

"Technically. Mel—our father—gave it to me a few years ago. I didn't want it. So I gave it to Desiree to return."

Sherry stopped smiling solely so she could grin again. "Pity. She must've forgot."

I signed the bill, handed it back. "Well, I'll definitely make sure this gets paid. Since it's my credit and all."

I pulled out my Alexa app to set a reminder for when I got home. I'd ask Aunt E to tell Tam to cut it off.

"I'm sorry, you know, about Desiree," Sherry said. "I knew she'd been stressed, but she seemed okay the last time I saw her."

There it was again. Stressed. Depressed. Another person telling me

Desiree wasn't in a good place. *The baby.* I must've also said it out loud because Sherry spoke.

"Huh? No, her arrest."

"How do you know about her arrest?" It had to be her DUI two years ago. If there'd been a recent one, it would've made my Google Alerts.

"How I know about everything. I eavesdropped. She asked to use the phone in the office. Said her phone was out of juice. I let her. You know, 'cause she always tipped well. I couldn't hear much until she started crying hysterically about her accident. Something about she'd been looking for this person for a couple of years. They knew she wasn't driving. They needed to tell the police or she would. Said something about a video. She was pissed. She knew I heard her, but she didn't care. Rich people never do—no offense. A couple of days ago, when I asked how she was doing, she said she was feeling better. That the problem was taken care of."

*Shitnuts.*

She'd been just as insistent the last time we ever spoke.

# THIRTEEN

There are sixty-two emergency rooms in New York City, which meant sixty-two frantic calls in the three hours from when I thought my sister had died to when I wanted to kill her myself. It'd been two years since that night, but I remembered it like it was last week. Remembered it better than last week because I had no clue what I was doing last Saturday.

At the time I was still in my basement studio apartment in Jersey City. It was fate—not the phone—that woke me up that Friday night. My cell was on vibrate, as usual. Otherwise, I would've woken to my customary 7 a.m. alarm for my weekend bike ride, just in time to learn that Desiree wasn't dead. Instead, I had to pee. I was stumbling back to bed in the dark when I heard the familiar buzz of my phone on my nightstand. Only one person on Planet Earth had the gall to call me that late.

Desiree.

I picked it up. The photo that popped up proved me right. It was the one of her and me and Mel, all cheesing it up like the happy, functional family we could only be for the time it took to tap a button. I glared at the trio of matching faces as I sat on my bed. "If you want me to convince you not to go back to some random's house…"

But where Desiree normally would cut me off with a plaintive "Leeennnaaaaa," there was nothing but silence. I trailed off on my own, the dread bubbling up like boiling water. "Des? Everything good?"

A voice answered. One that didn't belong to my sister. I still don't know who she was—I never got her name. At the time, it didn't occur to me to ask. So I've given her my own nickname: Zor-El. Since she became my own personal superwoman.

"Is this Lena?" she said.

"Yeah…" I said a quick prayer that maybe Desiree had left her phone on the back of some dirty-ass public toilet. There was precedence.

"I couldn't reach her parents and you were her last call, so—" She stopped abruptly. And when she spoke again, it wasn't to me. "No! Keep your eyes open. The operator said you need to keep talking, Desiree. It is Desiree?"

"Yes," I said even though she wasn't addressing me. "Her name is Desiree Pierce. She's twenty-two. Has some allergies…"

And then Zor-El was talking over me so I shut up, hoping to piece together exactly what the fuck was going on. "Desiree, stay with me, okay? Help is coming." Another pause. And then, "Shit." And finally, "Shit."

"Is she okay?" I yelled it to be heard over my rapidly beating heart. "What's going on?"

But the only thing that answered was sirens.

Zor-El spoke to me again, breathless. "They're here. Meet us at the hospital."

She hung up before I could ask which. I called back immediately. She didn't answer. I never spoke to her again.

Desiree and I had FaceTimed earlier that night. I'd just come back from drinks with Kat. She was putting on her makeup, getting ready for her 3,334th night in a row of not staying in. Another night. Another event. Another outfit. It was why I couldn't remember where she had said she was going.

I scrambled to look it up on my cell, still sitting in the dark. Still sitting in my bed. Still sitting in my pajamas. Though she'd uploaded a pregame selfie earlier—complete with wineglass—there was no mention of exactly what she was pregaming for. I searched social media for any and all launches, events, and official after-parties in Manhattan. Places she'd *have* to make an appearance. If I knew where she'd been coming from, then I could narrow down where the ambulance was going to.

A few must-attend events littered Instagram but none with her tagged in pics. And much to her—and now my—dismay, she wasn't famous enough for any celeb sighting tweets. That's when I started cold-calling hospitals like I was trying to sell them a vacuum. The Upper East Side was first in case she had been on her way home. NewYork-Presbyterian. Then Lenox Hill and Mount Sinai.

No Desiree Pierces.

I expanded west, north, and south. Bellevue. Harlem Hospital. Beth Israel.

Googling. Calling. Hanging up dejected. Over and over and over again. Nothing.

I finally willed myself to get out of bed, as if that would change my luck, like trying a different table at a casino. The calls kept me busy, kept my mind off what it meant if Desiree wasn't at any hospital at all. When Gram died, the ambulance left without her. It was the morgue that picked her up, carting her off to who knows where to do who knows what. It was better to call hospitals than police stations.

I kept dialing as I did my laps around the apartment. St. Luke's. Mount Sinai West. Langone.

Finally, at 5:30, I called Aunt E, knowing she got up early and hoping she might have more info. Maybe she had spoken to Mel and Veronika. She picked up on the second ring. "Lena? Everything okay?"

I continued Googling the number for Bronx-Lebanon. "Someone called. Something happened to Desiree. I've been calling hospitals but no one…"

I trailed off, and Aunt E didn't rush to fill the gap. After a moment, she spoke. "We need to pray."

I didn't question it. Just dropped to the ground, my bare knees hitting decades-old carpet I'd only gotten around to cleaning once. I wore nothing but an extra-large T-shirt. We stayed on the phone and prayed. It felt longer than a Black preacher still going at 1 p.m. on a Sunday afternoon, but for once I didn't mind. I kept my eyes closed, my ears open, and my mind clear.

Prayer was soon replaced by Bible verses. The names were out of my head as soon as they were mentioned, but there's one I'll never forget. "But let all who take refuge in you be glad; let them ever sing for joy. Spread your protection over them, that those who love your name may rejoice in you."

Aunt E stopped only when her caller ID beeped. She put me on three-way.

Tam.

Desiree was at Lenox Hill Hospital. She'd been admitted after I'd called. They'd tried the house, but Mel and Veronika were out of town. Veronika's assistant was housesitting. Tam gave us the TL;DR version of what had happened. I put her on speaker while I added a bra and leggings to the T-shirt.

Desiree had been driving on West 64th Street when her car veered and hit a stoplight. She got out, took off on foot. The prosecution would say she fled the scene. The defense would say she was too dazed to realize what she was doing. Desiree would say nothing at all. A good Samaritan—my Zor-El—had found the car wrapped around a pole and followed a trail of blood to Desiree half a block up, passed out on the sidewalk from either the accident (her lawyer) or a mix of vodka and cocaine (the prosecution).

Zor-El indeed tried to reach both Mel and Veronika before she tried to reach me. She didn't have much luck. Veronika picked up only when she got a call from her assistant. Mel never answered his own phone. Tam claimed they were arranging for a private jet to take them back from Maryland as we spoke.

Our transportation was much less glamorous but got us where we needed to go. I took an Uber. Aunt E had Mr. Buck, a church friend, drive her in his Caddy. We got there almost at the same time. The walk through the building felt longer than the ride. We found Desiree still in an emergency room bed, looking tired but surprisingly good for someone who'd plowed into a stoplight at sixty miles an hour. Her lipstick was even still on. A deep red from NARS that was the only reason I knew semimatte was a thing. Desiree had dragged me past three other Sephoras before the Uber finally dropped us off at the one she'd wanted. She only bought lipstick from someone named Gee, and Gee only worked at the Sephora on Lexington. She'd purchased six tubes at twenty-six dollars a pop. Stocking up, she'd said. Gee had been pleased. Me, not so much.

So I wasn't surprised to see the lipstick. I just didn't expect it to match the color of the bandage on her left hand. It would've been white if not for the blood that had seeped through. Desiree didn't seem to notice, scrolling her phone with her good hand. She spoke as soon as Aunt E and I pulled the curtain back and squished in behind it. "I'm fine." She at least had the decency to sound embarrassed.

She didn't look up, which meant she didn't see my abrupt about-face.

The tears held until I got to a bathroom. It was empty. I went into a stall anyway and shut the door. And that's when I cried. Big juicy tears I didn't bother to wipe away, just letting them plop into the toilet a few feet down. My nose getting more and more red. Super Black Woman had flown away, leaving a scared-as-hell Lena Scott in her place.

I was gone six minutes—three minutes for tears, three more to make it look like they'd never showed up. By the time I got back to Desiree's bed, I looked as good as new. Better, considering I hadn't had makeup on when I'd come in. Aunt E stood over Desiree, their hands clasped, eyes closed, and chins jutting down. I didn't have to hear what they were saying to know what they were doing. Praying. Probably repeats of what I'd heard hours before.

I waited for the amen before I entered.

"Where's the bathroom, baby?" Aunt E said.

"Down the hall."

She took Desiree's face in both hands, then leaned in to kiss both her cheeks. Desiree and I watched her go, then stared long after she was out of sight. I looked at Desiree first. It took her a second to look back. We said nothing. Did nothing. Then I placed my bag on the bottom of the bed and hugged her so tight her collarbone almost drew blood. I pulled away to take inventory. Face. Hands. Body. Up close it all became clear. There was a reason she looked so damn good. The red lip hadn't survived the accident after all.

There was no doubt that if I ripped off the bedsheets, I'd find her beauty blender still holding telltale signs of the Fenty 350 shade we both shared. She'd bought that from Gee too. Two bottles. I wanted to suck my tears back into the ducts, rewind every phone call I'd made, remind her that paparazzi didn't make bedside visits.

Instead, I took a step back as if pushed and finally spoke. "How you feeling?"

She missed the edge in my voice and answered like I genuinely was asking. "I'd be better if this hospital offered VIP treatment." She laughed. I didn't. "Come on, that was funny. I'm fine. And I'm trending. #prayfordesiree. Twelve thousand tweets."

She showed me Twitter on her phone. I wanted to swat it out of her hand. "You scared the shit out of me," I said. I thought of Zor-El. "Did you even get that woman's name?"

Desiree was back looking at her cell, her thumb caressing the screen like it was someone's cheek. "The nurse?"

I paused. "Desiree…"

But she didn't respond.

"Can you just close Twitter for one second?" I said.

"Sure." She did, then opened Instagram. Clicked on her latest pic and caressed her phone some more.

"You drove your car into a light," I said. "If that isn't a literal sign for you to stop, I don't know what is."

"I'm not silly enough to drink and drive. And you know I stopped using coke."

I wasn't sure of that so I threw out a lie, wanting to see if she'd catch it. "That's not what you said when you called me a few hours ago."

She stopped scrolling her feed for a nanosecond, then regrouped. "You must've heard me wrong."

A fumble. I knew more about her accident than she did. Just as I suspected. "Desiree, you blacked out."

"Even if I did, it doesn't matter because I wouldn't drive drunk."

"Then who would?"

Her pause was so pregnant it was two weeks overdue. And that's about how long it took her to deliver an answer. "Not me."

"Do you even know how you got here?"

But she was back eyeing her phone. "Rihanna left me a comment. 'Get well, bitch.'" She shoved the phone in my face. "Ooh. Diddy did too. And two out of three Jonas brothers."

She kept on like that. Name-dropping celebs. After a minute, I took out my phone too and opened the camera function, stepping back so I could get everything. The bed. The hospital gown. The bracelet. The only thing I didn't catch was the bandage on her left hand. "Ugh," she said. "Some troll said he hoped I'd died."

Her face contorted. Desiree hated trolls more than she hated gluten. The moment was perfect. My finger pressed hard on the HOME button, capturing as much as I could until she finally smiled. "Blocked!"

I went with burst mode, selected the photo, hit Settings, and scrolled through my handiwork. There were seven total, each worse than the last. I went with number five. Desiree had never been one for candids, blaming her resting bitch face. I looked them over. Even with the Fenty and the NARS, she was not camera ready. I texted the shot to her. Call it speaking her native tongue.

It took a few seconds to make its way across the room. I waited. She was still mentioning celebs like she was hosting an award show. "Selena DMed. Says we need to do lunch as soon as I'm out the hospital."

She paused. My photo must've arrived. She finally looked up. Finally looked at me. It wasn't a staring contest, but she still looked away first, just like when we were kids. "Do I really look *that bad*?" she said.

I opened my mouth, glad I'd gotten through, ready to reassure her I'd help her as long as she wanted to help herself. That we could get through this together. That this was just a bump in the road. But she continued.

"I wasn't ready. Can you take another? Maybe while I'm still looking away. I'll post it. Tag E! This could be my season-two storyline."

My anger grew with each declaration. I yanked my bag off the bed. "I'm not going to sit around waiting for the next call from some stranger. I'm not going to rush to the hospital ever again to see you give more of a shit about your Instagram than your own life. I'm not going to let you lie about how bad your problem is. You could've killed yourself tonight. You could've hurt someone else. Because *you*—not anyone else—hit a fucking pole. And guess what? You're probably going to jail for it."

I stared her down until she looked at me. "I can't do this anymore," I said at last.

"Then don't." Desiree went back to her phone, made a point of ignoring me.

"Everything all right?"

I turned, found Aunt E standing at the curtain. "I'm going home," I said.

By the time I got out of the building, I'd blocked Desiree on everything. Phone and email. *I'll show her*—that was all I could think.

But as it turned out, I'd only showed myself.

A snowy New York sidewalk. Desiree Pierce stares straight at the camera, ignoring people streaming out of the club behind her. She's solemn as she addresses the camera. "Someone saved my life today. Want to meet them?"

Erin Ambrose crowds into the frame so they're cheek to cheek, their equally glassy eyes a few inches apart.

"This is Erin…" Desiree trails off, unsure of what comes next.

Erin speaks up. "Ambrose. Erin Nicole Ambrose."

"Pretty!" Desiree says, then remembers she is supposed to be stoic. "This is Erin Nicole Ambrose and she is my hero. Let me explain. I was expecting a really important delivery of cookies."

Erin chimes in. "I love cookies. I literally cannot function without them."

"Exactly. I usually keep enough around, but I was running low. And my friend—Alfie—was supposed to drop them off. At midnight. And midnight comes—"

Erin interrupts. "No Alfie."

"One a.m."

"No Alfie!"

"Two a.m."

They say it together. "No Alfie!"

They look at each other. Giggle. Then again remember this is supposed to be serious. Desiree turns back to the camera. "I call him. No answer. I keep calling because now I really want that cookie. And guess what? His car broke down. He wanted me to pick them up. But I'd been drinking, and I don't drink and drive. I really thought I'd have no cookies. I'm all sad. And then this one comes up to me and is all 'Why are you so sad?'"

Erin jumps in. "She explained to me what happened. And I felt so bad."

"But today turned out to be my lucky day because Erin had cookies."

"I was happy to share."

"And we ate cookies and danced our asses off and now we're going to eat."

"I'm starv—" Erin stops abruptly. When she speaks, she's panicked. "My purse. I left it in the club."

Desiree's eyes widen. "Crap. I remember seeing it in the bathroom. I'm sure we can get back in if we just explain." She looks at the camera. "Love you all. Talk later."

# FOURTEEN

"Get your skinny butt on up. It ain't even five o'clock."

Past Me should have changed the locks as soon as I moved into Gram's house so Aunt E couldn't just let herself into my apartment. As it was, she found Present Me in bed on my laptop. I'd been trying to hack into Desiree's Instagram since I'd gotten back from the hotel. The username wasn't the problem. The password was. I'd tried my birthday. Her birthday. Gram's birthday, which I had tatted on my inner right wrist. Mel's birthday, which I knew only because The Shade Room did a yearly post. Even Veronika's birthday, which I'd searched for online, noting that her age was off by about two years. All were Not It. Lisbeth Salander I was not.

I wasn't the only one who broke ties with Desiree after the accident. E! followed suit, dropping her from *NYZ*. The grapevine, by way of Aunt E, told me she'd been devastated. The network had wanted her to seek professional help. We *all* had wanted her to seek professional help. And she'd refused, parroting her new go-to line, that she'd never drink and drive.

Like the rest of us, the police had disagreed. Desiree had been charged. Just like I told her she'd be. But I hadn't accounted for Mel's money, which had gotten her a good lawyer, who in turn had gotten her off with just community service. She'd done an Instagram video in the car from the courthouse. A publicist must have been on the other side of the camera holding cue cards and a gun because Desiree went on and on about learning experiences and mistakes—all while not admitting any semblance of guilt.

There was no further mention of her blacking out or that she wasn't driving. I'd thought maybe she'd given up on that story, but what Sherry had overheard suggested otherwise. Could Desiree have been telling the truth all these years? It suddenly seemed like it wasn't BS at all, and that she'd found someone who could prove it. I could think of only one person who'd know if Desiree had been behind the wheel.

Zor-El.

But if Zor-El had been such a Good Samaritan, why wasn't she helping Desiree now? Sherry'd made it sound like Desiree was angry. If someone else really had been driving, Desiree obviously hadn't known who it was. If she had known, surely she'd have gone to them directly.

Had Desiree found someone else there that night too?

If another person had been involved, they'd clearly had something to lose, since they hadn't come forward. What had they been hiding? And how desperate would they have been to keep it secret?

Since Zor-El was the only witness I knew about, she seemed like my best chance to find out what Desiree had uncovered—and what it might have to do with her death.

I just needed to find Zor-El.

But it wouldn't be through Desiree's Instagram DMs. Or her missing phone. Or the hotel bill that listed calls but not numbers, in order to protect their guests' privacy.

So I'd gone through Desiree's stuff twice. There weren't any names, numbers, email addresses. Save for scouring her Instagram posts for an "I was there when you had your accident—LOL" comment, I wasn't sure what steps to take next.

Instead of getting up, I asked Aunt E, "Did Desiree ever talk to you about The Accident?"

Aunt E and I hadn't spoken much about it ourselves, but that's what we'd always called it when we did. *The Accident,* like it was some privileged-white-people-in-peril show on HBO.

"Not a once," Aunt E said.

She didn't expand, as usual, just zeroed in on my Warm Apple Pie candle and trudged over piles of dirty clothes to blow it out. "I hate these things," she said. "Always getting my hopes up that you finally cooked something."

One of the reasons Aunt E and Gram had worked so well was they'd complemented each other. Aunt E was TV and ten-minute showers. Gram, books and baths. Aunt E was color. Gram, classic black and white. Aunt E had a loud mouth. Gram had a sweet tooth. One she'd passed down to me. Her chocolate pie recipe had been my potluck go-to since Kat first invited me to friendsgiving freshman year at Penn. But then both Gram and my mom died back-to-back and even chocolate pie lost its taste.

Aunt E looked around. "This room is more of a mess than the last episode of *Real Housewives.*"

I couldn't argue. Aunt E loved her reality TV as much as her Bible. Once CBS canceled *Guiding Light,* she'd simply packed up and moved down the dial to Bravo and VH1. "Now get up, Lena. Buck's gonna be here any minute."

I closed my laptop, not bothering to ask where we were going. I didn't need to. Aunt E only took Mr. Buck up on his open-ended offer to play chauffeur to go to the doctor or over the bridge into Manhattan. And she would have told me if she had any checkups.

We were going to see Mel. The last place I wanted to go. I was too smart to say that, though. Just got up, got dressed, and got into Mr. Buck's car, riding in his back seat like Desiree and I used to as kids. He drove only Cadillac Sevilles, refusing to touch anything else, which meant he hadn't had a new car since the mid-2000s. At least this one was in pristine condition. Gram used to say he treated his cars better than he treated his women. Considering he was single, she must've been right.

My phone buzzed just as we got on the FDR. I felt like crap as soon as I saw the sender.

"Who's that?" Aunt E said.

"Desiree's friend. Erin."

"The white girl?"

The white girl I'd essentially blown off since I'd walked out of PowerJam. After she'd made a point to support me when everyone else was acting like I'd lost my mind. I felt horrible about that. I really did. I opened my texts, expecting to find Erin annoyed. Instead, she'd written: What's ur addy? Found something of Freck's I know she'd want u to have. LMK. It only made me feel worse, especially when I realized one thing.

I needed her again.

If Desiree had been looking into The Accident, there was a good chance Erin knew something about it. I wasn't even annoyed that she hadn't brought it up—as long as she was honest now. I needed to talk to her—but not with Aunt E and her super ears in the front seat. She was the only person I knew whose hearing had gotten better with age. She was chatting happily with Mr. Buck about the Yankees, but Aunt E was a master of doing two things at once, especially if one of those things was eavesdropping. I'd learned that the hard way.

So instead, I texted Erin excuses about being busy, followed by my address—adding that the delivery person shouldn't leave the package with our next-door neighbor, Ms. Paterson, if we weren't home. She'd "accidentally" opened one more than once. Then I finished it all off with a Thanks!!!!!!, crying emoji, *and* heart eyes. The text version of the Father, the Son, and the Holy Spirit.

I closed the app just as Mr. Buck pulled up to Mel and Veronika's building on Park Avenue. The Pierce family should've been downtown in Tribeca with the rest of the celebs, only traveling to the Upper East Side once a year for the Met Gala. But Mel loved going where he didn't belong. Urban legend had it that fresh off his first twenty million, Murder Mel attempted to purchase a Park Avenue co-op in the second most exclusive building on the UES. He'd been unanimously rejected by the building's board. It was a money thing as much as a color thing. He had enough of it. He just hadn't had it long enough.

But while they were rejecting Mel in their boardroom, their kids were blasting his artists in their bedrooms, part of the middle- and upper-class white-boy set consuming 80 percent of hip-hop. So the same year Free Money artists performed at a bar mitzvah for the head of the co-op board's son, Mel purchased an apartment in the most exclusive building on the Upper East Side. Once moved in, he'd stayed put for twenty years and counting.

Mr. Buck dropped us off, the doorman let us up, and Tam let us in. I was surprised to see her. The office was her domain. The apartment was all Veronika's. Yet here she was sans both Mr. and Mrs. Pierce. It threw me.

I hadn't spoken to her since our argument in the office two days before. For a split second, I wondered if that was why Aunt E had dragged me here. Maybe Tam wanted to apologize. But no. Aunt E got a hug. I got a question. "You talk to that reporter yet?" she said as she closed the front door.

I paused ever so briefly, not expecting it. "Yep."

"Great," Tam said. "Let's sit in the living room. There're a few things we need to discuss."

She didn't say where Mel or Veronika was. Neither of us asked, just followed her down the hallway. The apartment was a "classic six," as much an Upper East Side staple as the nannies and the 6 train. The living room was large, with floor-to-ceiling windows along one wall, hardwood floors, and an oversize gray rug that underscored two mismatched white couches.

I sat on one, smile ablaze. Tam did the same on the other, pulling out a notebook. She'd brought notes. *Great.* Lucky for me, I didn't need any. I'd placed first in debate championships senior year of high school. I ran through both my constructive and rebuttal speeches.

"Thank you for talking to the pastor," Tam said to Aunt E. "I spoke with the cemetery. There's a plot near Mrs. Pierce available."

Her words took forever to reach my brain, then slammed into my cerebral cortex like a runaway train. We weren't here to play nice. We were here to talk about the funeral.

My fingers flew to my wrist.

I'd spent a lot of time thinking about Desiree dying. Watching her life had been like watching a driverless car. You knew she was heading straight toward a brick wall at one hundred miles an hour. You knew you couldn't stop it. You knew it was going to be painful and messy and hurt like hell. But for all the minutes, hours, years I'd spent thinking about Desiree dying, I'd never thought about what would happen after she did.

She and I certainly had never discussed it. It hadn't even come up. Not after Gram's burial. Or my mother's homegoing. Or when her tutor got hit by that car. I had no clue what she'd want. I could only guess.

My gram had a plot. My mother did too. I'd gone to visit them both exactly once, and even that was at Aunt E's forced suggestion. I had no problem with cemeteries. I just didn't think my sister belonged in one.

The idea of her being stuck in a box for the rest of eternity—makeup eaten off by rats and slugs and whatever the hell else hung out underground—just didn't work. It couldn't work. Not for someone like Desiree, whose energy couldn't be contained. Even in photos she looked 3D, like you were viewing her through those cheap plastic IMAX glasses that always left you a bit discombobulated.

"It's not unreasonable that an entire restaurant doesn't want to close down so Veronika can host Desiree's repast there," Aunt E was saying as Tam scribbled like she'd be quizzed later. "What's wrong with the church basement? They just redid it."

"Cremation," I said.

Aunt E stopped talking, and they both looked at me. I spoke again once I had their full attention. "Desiree should be cremated. Ashes spread in Puerto Rico." She'd loved it there. "And you need to get her a dress. From one of the fall collections."

Tam didn't write any of that down. Instead, she glanced at Aunt E, then back at me. "We were going to pick out something from her closet," she said.

"When is it?"

"Right now the plan is to wait until the end of the month. Give people time to fly in."

That meant they had time to get her something designer. "When's the last time Desiree repeated an outfit?" It felt weird for something so silly to be so important. But still. "She needs two. A separate one for the viewing."

"This is a funeral, Lena," Tam said. "Not the Oscars."

"You're right," I said. "Make sure the designer knows they aren't getting it back."

I stared Tam dead in the eye until she looked away first. "I'm sure Veronika's stylist can make some calls," she finally said.

"Great." I stood up. "I'm going to get some water. Anyone else thirsty?"

But I was gone before either of them could answer. I smiled as soon as I got back to the hall. If Desiree had insisted she wear something from the Oscar de la Renta fall collection to her own funeral, I would have been sharing disgusted looks with Aunt E and Tam. But there's no doubt that she would have insisted. And I was happy that at least I was able to get that for her—silly as it may be.

The kitchen wasn't eat-in, but it was connected to the dining room so it didn't matter much. Veronika didn't cook but also didn't let that stop her from creating the ultimate chef's paradise every few years. When Aunt E'd first seen the latest iteration, she'd spent a good half hour caressing each and every appliance while the rest of us wondered if we should give them some space. Even I had to admit it was beautiful.

Stainless-steel appliances.

Sub-Zero refrigerator and freezer with a vacuum seal.

Gas range with a 20,000 BTU burner and a griddle.

Two ovens with something called warming trays.

Two sinks.

Two dishwashers.

One island.

Though it wouldn't take the place of my Magic Wand, I could see why it got Aunt E so hot and bothered. I got a bottle of water out of the humongous fridge, then leaned against an island big enough to film *Survivor*. I took a long drag, then almost choked when I heard the voice behind me. "Isn't it good? We get it shipped from Japan. Four hundred bucks a bottle."

Veronika.

I turned to face her. "Good thing I didn't spit it out."

She was as put together as the rest of the house. Nails done. Hair laid. Makeup precise, as if applied by X-Acto knife. You'd never be able to tell she'd lost her lone daughter. She said nothing, just walked up and pulled me into her. And I let her.

There's that saying. *How you got him is how you lose him.* Veronika had clearly taken it to heart because she was determined not to lose. She was a socialite who wasn't social. A stay-at-home mom who never stayed at home. A trophy wife who didn't think she was the prize. She'd chased Mel until she got him. Twenty-five years in and she was still in pursuit. She went with him everywhere—be it chauffeured car, private jet, or yacht—oftentimes with Desiree and a tutor also along for the ride.

Veronika broke the hug first but kept her arm around me as she too leaned on the island.

"How you doing?" I said.

"I've been better," she said. Super Black Woman. She smiled, laughed a bit, as if hoping to take the edge off. But that's when I noticed the lipstick on her teeth. She must've rushed to pull herself together when she heard us come in. I didn't tell her.

I couldn't bring her daughter back. I couldn't take away the pain. But I could let her at least think she was doing a good job hiding it.

Veronika was so seamless at playing Stepford Wife it was easy to forget she was an actual person. But even I had to admit she and Mel worked, both loyal as hell to each other in their own unique ways. I put my head on her shoulder as we leaned on the big fancy island in the big fancy apartment in the big fancy building. Each quiet, each lost in her own thoughts. For once, the silence felt comfortable, like we were actually family. Then she shifted and got back to our regularly scheduled programming.

"You need to do a better job of talking with your father, Melina. He'll never admit it, but he's been beating himself up. But he had to cut that girl off. He gave her everything. Gave all of us everything. And she was still acting like a child." Veronika always spoke like this. Like she was presenting Mel with a lifetime achievement award. "Still, he thinks it's his fault. He's not taking Desi's death well."

"I'm sure *none* of us are," I said.

"Of course not, but your father is taking it especially hard. You need to talk to him." She waited for me to respond.

"You have lipstick on your teeth."

Her eyes widened, perfectly painted pointer finger rushing to rub it away. We both said nothing until the nude brown was all but gone. Then I took a sip of four-hundred-dollar water and felt like shit so I changed the subject.

"When's the last time you saw her?"

"We were supposed to have a spa day, but Mel had that last-minute trip to Miami. I FaceTimed on her birthday. Sent her flowers. You wish her a happy birthday?"

"No," I said.

"You two really haven't spoken since the accident?"

"Unfortunately. It feels silly now." I couldn't think about it. "You know, someone called me that night. The person who found her."

"She called me too. We were at Morgan's graduation."

I'd forgotten Zor-El had said she'd tried to reach both Desiree's parents but couldn't. That's why she'd called me. "But you didn't talk to her?"

Maybe I'd remembered wrong. Maybe she had spoken with Veronika. Maybe that's how Desiree had found out who Zor-El was.

"Nope," Veronika said. "She left a message."

I perked up. "She leave her name?"

Veronika turned to face me. If she hadn't had Botox, she'd have probably raised her eyebrow. "If she did, the message is long gone." Her pause was brief. "Why are you asking all these questions?"

I didn't want to answer. Luckily, Tam came into the kitchen.

"The police are here. Should I call Mel?"

\* \* \*

No one offered Detective Zizza a four-hundred-dollar bottle of water. He stood in front of us awkward as hell, like he was giving a book report. Still, he had a rapt audience. Veronika, Tam, Aunt E, and I all sat around the room. Mel had been called but apparently had an important meeting. I was surprised. That was standard behavior when it came to me, but this was his prized Desiree. I was sure he'd have Tam give him a play-by-play. Detective Green was also noticeably absent.

"We found the car," Zizza said and then paused, as if waiting for a standing ovation.

We remained seated. Finding the car was what they were supposed to do.

He kept on. "It's what we thought. Two local thugs who wouldn't have passed a driver's test even if they were old enough. Like to steal cars but never bothered to get past the 145th Street Bridge. Didn't even think to ditch the car. Or sell it for parts. They were still joyriding when one of our guys caught them this morning."

I tore my eyes off his mini rant to read the room. Veronika and Tam were nodding like he was a catchy beat. Aunt E was side-eyeing him so hard I could barely see the browns of her eyes. She looked like I felt. Like there was more to the story than an episode of *World's Most Clueless Criminals*. I didn't care how rich and powerful Mel Pierce had become; NYPD wasn't making a house call just to rail about two kids who'd happened upon Desiree's Tesla.

I interrupted, ready to rip the Band-Aid off even though it had barely covered the gaping wound in the first place. "What did they say about Desiree? I know they had to say something."

"Yeah," he said. "They did. They said she met someone up there."

# FIFTEEN

He'd buried the lede so deep it would take a backhoe to find it. Tam and Veronika had stopped nodding, both staring at him, mouths all agape. Aunt E still looked unimpressed.

Desiree had been in the Bronx to meet someone. It took a moment for that to settle in. I should've been relieved. For the first time in four days someone was telling me what I'd suspected, what I'd eaten for breakfast, lunch, dinner. Even as a midnight freaking snack. Desiree hadn't been up there by herself. But all I could think about was one thing.

*Desiree hadn't been coming to see me.*

"Who?" Veronika said at last. "Who did she meet?"

She turned to Aunt E.

"You know I ain't leaving my house for nobody that early in the morning," Aunt E said.

Had this really never been about me at all? Two years ago I would have stopped right here and now. Washed my hands of all of this like I'd washed my hands of her. But I couldn't. The guilt still remained. She still needed me even if she'd been too stubborn to know it.

Veronika's eyes were back on Zizza.

"I'm assuming her dealer," he said. "It would explain the drugs."

"She didn't know anyone up there, besides us," Aunt E said. "Not even *dealers*."

She was right. Our neighbors weren't Desiree's people. They didn't tweet or post or filter the hell out of their selfies. They just lived. Sometimes barely.

Who was important enough to have made Desiree leave in the middle of her birthday party? It must have had something to do with the accident. What else could be that important? And if it was, there were just two people worth the trip: Zor-El or the other person who knew about the accident.

The missing driver.

Sherry had overheard Desiree arguing with someone—a witness—who Desiree thought could prove she hadn't been to blame. But a couple of days later she'd told Sherry everything was taken care of. That meant she'd gotten what she needed, right? Had Zor-El taken a video that night? Told Desiree something that'd helped her ID someone? Had Desiree confronted them only for things to go horribly wrong?

Of course, none of it made any sense. Why would someone want her dead? Why come all the way to the Bronx?

I finally spoke. "And the kids. They didn't give you a description?"

Slowly, he pulled out his phone, tapped the screen a few times, and started reading off notes in a monotone flatter than an Instagram model's ass pre–silicone shots. "They claim they only saw her get out of the car 'from a long distance.' By herself. Didn't even close her door. She walked up the street. When she turned the corner, she said 'Hey' to someone they never saw."

One of the first witnesses had heard Desiree say "Hey" too. I'd assumed she had been yelling it at the kids when they stole her car. Turns out I'd been wrong about that too.

Zizza was still going. "Kids claimed they politely waited five minutes, and when she didn't return, they took advantage of the key fob she'd left in the passenger seat, alongside some other belongings." He tapped his phone again and put it back in his pocket. "It's all bullshit. Desiree could've been yelling at them."

I'd thought the same thing, but it still annoyed me to hear him say it. It was clear how seriously he was taking my sister's death. "Why would they lie about that?" I said.

"Because carjacking is a Class C felony with a maximum fifteen-year sentence. We caught them with the key fob so we know they didn't just break in. These guys are smart."

A minute ago they were idiots. I didn't point that out, though. "What if they're telling the truth?" I said.

"They're not."

"But you'll still look into it," I said, then took a breath, ready to finally share what I'd found out. That this had something to do with her accident, even if I still wasn't sure why.

But then he rolled his eyes harder than a pair of dice. "Of course we will."

Sure. Right after they flew to LA and figured out who shot Biggie.

Zizza kept on. "But we have no reason to believe there was any foul play. *If* she did meet someone up there, we'll find them and talk to them about the narcotics we found in her purse. But we don't believe the carjackers were involved in her death."

That settled it. If I told him my news, he'd just smile and nod and not do shit about it. Zizza and his brethren didn't give a crap about any of this. Any of us.

Desiree was a crackhead.

The thieves were liars.

I was just over it.

"Bullshit," I said.

"Don't be rude, Lena," Aunt E said. I'd forgotten she was even in the room. "Act like you've got some home training."

Gram and Aunt E lived by the adage that if you don't have anything good to say, then don't say anything at all. Probably why they never brought up my mother. So I took a sip from my bottle of expensive-ass water and wished it was a glass of Cîroc. I needed to know who had been up there with Desiree. And there was one way left to find out. Her phone.

"When can we get Desiree's stuff back?" I glanced at Aunt E. "Please."

"We'll need to hold on to all her belongings for the time being since they're part of an active investigation," Zizza said. "Might take a while. We'll keep you updated if we find anything of note."

*Yeah, okay.*

My left wrist itched, but for once I ignored it. Because even if I didn't know why the person had come to the Bronx—to meet her, or to follow her?—I knew I wasn't wrong about the most important thing. They'd played a role in her death.

I just needed to figure out how to find them.

* * *

"Who's the white girl?" Mr. Buck's voice chopped through my thoughts.

I'd spent the entire ride back fantasizing *Black Panther*–esque methods of figuring out who had killed Desiree and why. Me breaking into the Omni hotel offices. Hacking their computer. Tapping their phone. I was doing it all. And not even wearing skintight vibranium to do it. In reality, I couldn't hack or tap or break anything, which didn't leave me much to hunt them down with. But I did have one lead. Zor-El. If I could find her, she could tell me exactly what she'd told Desiree.

If there was a video, she had it.

"Hope she's not a new neighbor," Aunt E said.

I finally glanced up.

We'd left the gate open because our neighbors knew not to park in front of our driveway. Aunt E and her broom would be out the front door before they'd be out of their front seat. This person hadn't gotten the memo. Yet.

The first thing I saw was a black coupe haphazardly pulled into our drive. I didn't need to know the make or model to know I couldn't afford it. The second thing I saw was a familiar set of blond extensions. "She's a family friend," I said.

We didn't have much of a front stoop, just one step leading to about two feet of standing space. Erin lounged on it like it was Malibu. She watched as Mr. Buck stopped at the curb and came around to help us out. By the time he pulled off, Erin was on her stilettoed feet and advancing toward us with her arms spread out. "Are you Aunt E? Can I give you a hug?"

Aunt E said nothing, just gave her the same look she gave Ms. Paterson's son whenever he walked his pit bull without a leash. I stepped in between them and walked into Erin's outstretched arms. Better me than Aunt E. For all of us.

"Erin, what a surprise." I'd wanted to talk to her but not now. Not right after our convo with Zizza. "What are you doing here?"

"You said you wanted to chat, and I've always wanted to see this place. Desiree talked about it like it was Disneyland."

She eyed Aunt E again. I stole a move from Veronika, keeping one arm around her. The better to herd her away from the cranky Black woman trailing behind us. It'd been a rough day. Plus, I could sense my neighbors watching from windows and stoops and front doors. Sometime over the next forty-eight hours Ms. Paterson would "happen" to run into me to find out who that had been. The quicker I got Erin happily on her way back to Chelsea, the less our nosy neighbor would have to share with the rest of the block.

"Now's not a great time," I said. "We were about to go inside and eat."

"Really?" She looked back at Aunt E as I unlocked the door. "Freck…I mean Desiree always said you had the best mac 'n' cheese she ever tasted. I'm from the South so you know I love some mac 'n' cheese. Do you use Velveeta?"

"Of course." Aunt E smiled. Food was not just a way to a man's heart. It was also the way to Aunt E's good side. "But the key is Muenster. You didn't hear that from me, though."

Erin zipped her lip while managing to say "Mmm" at the same time. "Sounds delicious. I'm starving."

"I was just about to whip some up," Aunt E said. "Why don't you keep me company? Lena's place is in no shape for guests."

I watched them both walk inside Aunt E's apartment. Erin slowly took in the living room, all the furniture spread out like Aunt E was twenty-five moves deep in a chess game. She went all around the room before stopping at Gram's recliner. Its black leather was cracked and fading. "Vintage. I love it." Then she followed Aunt E into the kitchen.

Guess she was staying.

Aunt E was right, though. I'd neglected any and all housework since Desiree had died. Clothes were spread out on my floor like a man on a subway. Cups sat around unwashed. Schoolbooks had been left abandoned on the living room floor. About the only place not junky as hell was my fridge. It housed expired milk and one extra-large egg.

There was no way I was going to talk to Erin about Desiree in front of Aunt E, which meant Erin had to come upstairs. I did a drive-by clean, which meant the books were thrown into my bedroom, hidden behind a closed door. Cups were congregated in the sink "to soak." And I grabbed my laundry bag and foraged for dirty clothes. The trip downstairs to the washing machine was quick, but I was still a bit wary. Despite what Karen in Middle America might have you believe, our street wasn't a hodgepodge of gangs, guns, and ganja. But still.

I hesitated going down the basement stairs even though it was still daytime. Making a production of turning on the light, talking loudly as I stomped down each step, giving would-be burglars time to make their escape or hide. The basement was one room that took up the entire length of the house, the whole shebang a maze of Gram's old stuff mixed with childhood toys and a few things I'd brought when I'd moved. Boxes upon suitcases upon books and bags. Lots of stuff I'd been "meaning" to go through for five years and counting. Aunt E refused to touch it.

The good news was that the washing machine was near the stairs. I started with the warm-cold mix. Panties and jeans and the like. I'd read somewhere that turning your jeans inside out reduced wear and tear. So far I had no proof this was true, but I always did it just in case. I was pulling one leg through itself when I found the pregnancy test.

It was still shoved in my back pocket, long forgotten. Still clumsily wrapped in the torn piece of purple paper I'd picked up from Desiree's hotel room. I hesitated, not sure what to do. It wasn't the type of memento I wanted to remember my sister by, but it still felt weird to just throw it away.

I was unwrapping it like a white elephant gift when I noticed Desiree's handwriting.

# SIXTEEN

Desiree's handwriting was impeccable. When she was five, she'd said it needed to be for future autographs. She'd already signed more than a few for people so desperate for a piece of Mel that they'd shove a pen at his daughter, who barely knew how to read.

Erin read it slowly. "'Dodson.' What's that mean?"

She handed the piece of paper back to me from across my kitchen table. After seeing Desiree's note, I'd rushed upstairs to find her acting as Aunt E's sous-chef, folding macaroni into the cheese mixture. I'd waited until they'd gotten it into the oven, then rushed Erin upstairs.

"Exactly. I found the other half in the hotel trash. It was clearly the same sheet. Same color and everything. There were two words written on it. 'Check Karma.' But that makes no sense. You can't check your karma. It's not a bank account. Unless you put it all together. Check Karma…" I trailed off.

"Dodson?"

"Yes!" If I'd had a gold star, I would've given it to her. "Check Karma doesn't make sense. Check Karma Dodson does. She was looking for someone. Karma Dodson."

Zor-El finally had a name.

I shared everything with Erin, partly because I figured—hoped—it would trigger something related that Desiree had told her. Partly because I owed her an update after ghosting her post-Free. And partly because I was excited as hell.

I started with the night of Desiree's accident, bypassing me freaking out—both at home and the hospital—and ending with my suspicions that Desiree may have agreed to meet her killer up here. And that Zor-El was the key to finding out who.

When I was done, Erin just stared at me. "You're wrong."

So much for Erin's help. She stood up, paced the small area between my table and fridge. "She would've shared this all with me." I opened my mouth, but she cut me off. "Don't even mention that damn pregnancy test. She would have told me, and I would've gone with her to meet Karma. And I definitely would've gone to meet the piece of shit who let her take the fall for the accident. Whoever his ass is."

"Didn't you hook up with some guy you didn't know?"

"And? Friends before mens. I would have brought him too."

I laughed and it felt good to do so, each chortle making me feel ten pounds lighter. That's when I realized it. I actually *liked* Erin. Yes, she was blond and rich, and she probably considered a broken nail an epic tragedy. But she was also funny and sweet and a damn good friend. Grinning too, she walked toward the hall. "All I know is that Karma is a horrible name to give a kid."

"Bathroom's to the right."

I used the opportunity to grab my cell from my book bag by the front door. It made me think of Desiree's phone—the one Zizza seemed to be in no rush to return—and how much easier this would all be if I could look at it. I didn't have the patience to wait until we finally got it back—not with Desiree's killer roaming free.

I'd just sat back down at the kitchen table when Erin returned. She'd left her bag on the table and now she made a whole production of reaching into it. She produced a jewelry box. Even I recognized the distinct robin's egg blue. It was square and flat. Perfect for a necklace.

I put my phone down on the table. "Are you proposing?" I said.

"Am I on one knee?"

She smiled as she handed it over. I wasn't much for jewelry. I opened it. Jelly bracelets. About ten. All different colors.

"That heifer."

The bracelets were mine. Or at least had been years ago. They'd disappeared the first summer I spent at Gram's. Desiree'd sworn she didn't take them. Sworn all summer. Then swore on birthdays. Swore on Christmas. Even swore on Easter. Year after year after year. It became a running joke. We'd be hanging out and I'd randomly find a way to mention my bracelets. She'd deny, deny, deny. But she couldn't do that anymore. They were here and she wasn't.

I rubbed my wrist. It took a minute, but I finally spoke. "Where'd you find them?"

"She left them at my place after a 2000s party. I got stuck with the Livestrong bracelets. Nowhere near as cute."

I put them on, twisting my wrist to fully examine them. "They still fit. Thank you."

"Of course. And that's not all I brought. This is from me, though."

She reached back into her Birkin purse, which could pay for eight $1,756 credits at Columbia, and brought out a bag of marshmallows.

"You making hot chocolate?" I said.

"Better. Honey, I can tell you're stressed AF over not making up with her before she died. You need to take your mind off this Karma person. Even take your mind off Freck."

Erin was right, but the only thing that would stop me from being stressed AF was finding Karma/Zor-El. I picked up my cell as Erin held back up the bag of marshmallows. "Best edibles in the Western Hemisphere."

"I'm assuming you didn't get them off those green Weed World vans camped out by Penn Station."

"Theirs don't even have any marijuana in them."

When I didn't respond immediately, she grabbed my cell out of my hands. I gave her the same look my mom gave me whenever I'd asked for McDonald's for dinner. Unlike me, Erin was undeterred. "We'll make a deal. You have a marshmallow, you get the phone back." I hesitated. "Just one. Whatever you have to do can wait a few minutes."

"Fine."

She handed me the bag. It turned out she wasn't lying. The marshmallow took my mind off any and every thing. My thoughts had parked and weren't even moving for street cleaning. One marshmallow turned into two. We started shooting the shit.

It felt nice to just talk as if I hadn't a care in the world. I hadn't done it since the last time I'd seen Kat. It made me think of school. And how I desperately wanted to be back in a classroom, bitching to Omar about first-world problems like having shitty cell service on the subway or a final coming up. I hoped I could get back to all of that soon.

I was telling Erin how I'd moved to the Bronx to be closer to school when Aunt E let herself in. I'd just taken a bite, so I almost choked. Erin didn't play it any cooler. We tried not to look at each other as Aunt E stopped a few feet in front of us. "I was coming up to tell you the food is ready, but I see you're doing dessert before dinner." She looked me dead in the eye. "Looks like you finally decided to eat something."

I forced myself to swallow. "Just a snack."

Aunt E held out her hand. "I love snacks."

This time Erin and I did share a look.

*Shitnuts.*

Erin spoke first. "These were my last two…"

A lie. Aunt E knew it too. She did an about-face, heading back to the door, talking over her shoulder as she crossed the room. "Your generation swears you're the first and only to do everything. Your gram was making pot brownies before you were even a thought." She finally stopped and looked back. "Now come down here, get yourself some food, and bring that bag. We can make s'mores."

We spent the evening high off marshmallows and stories about Desiree. It was exactly what I needed to stop thinking about Desiree's death and start appreciating her life. I wasn't the only one. We were all mourning Desiree in our own different ways.

But then midnight hit, and it was just like Cinderella. Everything was back to shit. Aunt E went to bed first. Erin tried to go home, but I wouldn't let her. Chelsea may have been just ten miles away, but it was late and I had a spare bedroom. Luckily, she had a Louis Vuitton weekend bag she kept in her car for "quick jaunts to Mexico or the South of France." She was asleep as soon as she hit my freshly washed sheets.

I should've gone to bed myself. But I couldn't have another useless dream about playing hide-and-seek. I stayed awake, sobering up, eyeing my cell phone like a drunk dude at a club. Then it was in my hand and I was searching Desiree's Instagram following list for Karmas. I came up empty.

Strike one.

I moved on to Desiree's followers. A much more extensive list. That one had three Karmas, none of whom listed a last name of Dodson. I screenshot them all anyway.

Strike two.

Up next was a general Karma Dodson IG search. Three Karma Dodson handles came up, a grand total of one post and five Instagram followers between them.

And strike three.

I moved on to Twitter, still hoping for a hit. Desiree had an account she'd used solely to link to Instagram posts. No Karmas followed. No Karmas following. I did find a Karma Dodson handle with no listed location and only a few posts from 2014.

I didn't even waste time with Snapchat. Desiree had never been into it. Something about some sponsored post gone awry. And she'd stayed off TikTok too, probably because she never had enough rhythm for dance challenges.

So Facebook it was. I wasn't much of a fan myself, and Desiree didn't even have a page. But the reasons I hated it were the same reasons it'd be helpful. It made it hard to be anonymous. Full names. Locations. Doing the utmost to tell everyone your business, from your birthday to your new job to your comment on that pic of your friend's cute new baby.

I typed in the name. Three people popped up. I clicked SEE ALL in the upper right corner. Facebook loved to make more assumptions than a Black grandmother: that you missed a letter, added a letter, got the word order wrong. It was too late at night and I was still too high to make much of the full list, but I tried, using my finger to scroll. One Karma listed Arizona as her current location even though she was wearing a knit scarf in her profile pic. It'd been two years. Could she have moved?

Number two had a dog for their profile pic and a Pennsylvania hometown. I doubted this Karma would drive two-plus hours to get to Manhattan. Not when Philly was so close. Number three bypassed both location and human profile pic, offering only the Knicks logo. I was about to click on the basketball fan when the guest bedroom door opened. Erin stumbled out, hand covering her mouth, and headed toward the bathroom.

I jumped up to make sure she remembered which door it was. Last thing I wanted was projectile vomit all over my coats. Erin made it in the nick of time. I stood outside feeling useless. Her hair was up in a pony so she didn't even need me to hold it back. She puked, then retched, then puked some more.

I took it as a sign. It was time to go to bed.

* * *

I was the last one up Sunday morning, but then I'd been the last to go to sleep. Same dream. Same result, never finding my sister. The guest room door was open, the bed unmade, the carefully curated pillows Aunt E had given me strewn across the floor like landmines. It was the only clue Erin had been there. She was nowhere to be found, but it was okay. I knew where she was.

Aunt E's kitchen.

I was surprised to find her actually eating, fork moving toward her mouth versus just around her plate. She stared at me in wonder. "I've never had grits before!"

I didn't tell her she'd never have grits like that again. Aunt E's grits could stop wars, at least long enough for both sides to eat. It took almost two decades of straight begging to get her to tell me the secret. Heavy cream and mascarpone. And according to generations of Black people, her foot in it.

Aunt E had my plate ready and waiting. It was part of our morning ritual, along with the hug, the kiss on the cheek, the waiting for me to take the first bite so I could properly compliment her and she could properly play shy.

"This is delicious," I said. And it was. It wasn't why I still struggled to eat. She beamed. "Not my best, but I'm glad you like it."

"What are you doing today?" Erin said. "Checking Karma?"

I gave her a look. Not in front of Aunt E. "No plans," I said. "You?"

She shook her head. "Desiree and I would usually do brunch at Balthazar. I can probably go with someone else, but it'd be weird. But I don't wanna go home either. It's been hard to be alone since she died."

Being alone was my happy place—at least over the last couple of years—but I still felt for Erin. She hadn't mentioned much about her family, and as usual, I hadn't asked—but it was clear they weren't close. I at least still had Aunt E. Even if we hadn't spent as much time together since Desiree had died, just knowing she was downstairs was comforting. Erin had nothing but a big, empty house.

Aunt E must've felt just as bad because she stood up, gently rubbed Erin's stick-thin arm. "Well, we definitely aren't kicking you out, baby." She smiled. "Especially not with those dishes in the sink. I'm gonna go get dressed. You two get to work."

She left, and we did as told. Aunt E had a dishwasher, thanks to Mel, but she considered that solely for extra storage and special occasions. I spent a lot of time standing in front of her side-by-side sinks, elbow deep in soapy dishwater. Sometimes Desiree had been next to me. Today it was Erin, but it took her just turning on the faucet for me to know she had never given much thought to how dishes were actually cleaned. She used cold water.

"It helps if the water is hot," I said.

"Great tip!"

She said it with so much enthusiasm, I wondered if we'd need to stop for her to write it down. Once we got the water to a suitable grease-killing temp, she made mistake number two. I grabbed her hand just as it was about to dive into the water and gave her a pair of rubber gloves. "This will preserve the mani."

"Another great tip! My manicurist is on set with Scarlett. I'm not flying out to see her until next week. Though I guess I could book a flight tomorrow if need be."

We couldn't have that. I handed her the dishrag. It'd been whiter than Erin once upon a time but now was a shoddy gray as depressing as New York in January. "How about I wash, you dry?"

That's how I'd done it with Desiree too, though Erin caught on quicker than my sister. Drying turned out to be her forte. We got into a groove, working in a silence so comfortable I was surprised when she spoke. "I'm going to help you." She must've noticed my look because she kept on. "Find Karma Dodson."

I smiled, then started washing even faster. We had the kitchen spotless in five minutes and were back in my place in seven, me showing her the three Karma Dodsons listed on Facebook. "We could definitely shell out for one of those people searches, but they're not the most accurate." I ignored her how-do-you-know-that look. "I figure we start here. If she was out that late at night, I bet she's young, and what person under thirty isn't all over social? Figure I could send them each a message."

"Let me do it. *I* actually have a Facebook account. We might have better luck if I friend each of them instead of just sending them a note that goes to their 'Creepy Stranger' list they don't check."

She had a point. I hovered while we went through each page on her cell. It was much easier to read while stone-cold sober.

"Let's not mention Desiree," I said. "Maybe ask if they helped out with a car accident a couple of years ago in New York."

Erin nodded. "I'll mention there's a reward."

"But there's not…"

"People respond better to stuff like that. And if they do want money, I'll take care of it."

That wouldn't have been my first choice, but I went with it. I was watching her type out a note to number two when my phone rang.

Mel, or rather his line.

*Not now.*

I ignored it, hoping it would go away. It just moved to text. Tam.

Mel wants to see you ASAP. When can you stop by?

*Never.* I wrote back: Today's not good. It's Sunday.

An immediate response: He's pissed about the profile in the News. Trying to calm him down but the longer you avoid him the worse it'll be.

I'd forgotten about Stuart's story. I pulled it up on my phone. Two paragraphs in and I could see why Mel was mad. I wasn't too happy myself.

"Everything good?" Erin said.

It wasn't, but I nodded. "I just need to go see Mel."

Then I texted Stuart Jones.

# SEVENTEEN

M el had gone viral a few months ago. I couldn't tell you when or where the original video came from, but I knew it was old. Because of the fuzzy quality that looked ripped from a VHS. Because no one in the video was glued to cell phones. Because Mel had twenty less pounds and one inch more hairline, only the handcuffs tatted on his wrists looking the same. It had to be mid-'90s, probably from one of those MTV shows where they follow you around as you pretend it's a normal day. Except back then, this *was* standard operating procedure for Murder Mel Pierce.

He was stomping around some conference room table like he was playing a round of Duck, Duck, Goose, walking past skinny blondes, old white men, and everything in between. He was screaming at the top of his lungs, his deep baritone reverberating like too-loud speakers. I counted seven creative uses of the word "fuck" in the first fifteen seconds.

All because the people in the conference room had decided to have a meeting about Free's next album without telling Mel. It later came out that Free was the one who hadn't wanted him there because he was signing a new deal sans Mel. But Mel hadn't known that then. When he found out, using just seven fucks would've sounded like a lullaby.

If Free was known for his in-your-face bars, then Mel was known for his in-your-face bravado. There wasn't an interview that didn't mention his "reputation." His quick fuse. His threats of ass beatings. His promises to end careers. I know because I read them all.

The video played on repeat in my head as I biked into Manhattan. Even though it was Sunday, Mel was at work. I'd taken a long shower and spent even longer laying my edges and deciding what to wear—a delay tactic more than anything else. In the end I'd just chosen my black Afroed Rosie the Riveter T-shirt and black jeans.

The walk to Mel's office felt like another walk of shame, somehow made worse by the empty desks. I sat outside his door like a kid in a time-out.

"He's ready for you," Tam finally said.

My cell rang again as I stood up, but I hit DECLINE like I'd done the other five times. I made my way over, looking down as if I could actually see the eggshells. It took me four steps to get there. Then I knocked.

Truth was, Mel had never used his infamous temper on me. And I had never given him a reason to, treating his presence like a field trip to a museum. *Don't touch anything. Don't run anywhere. Don't talk to strangers, even if they're your father.* Desiree had handled it differently. Doing everything short of screaming for attention. Not me. Never me.

He yelled, "Come in!" and I finally opened one of the double doors. I figured he'd be behind the big black desk, staring me down behind ever-present sunglasses. But he was pacing, eyes on full display and focused on his cell. He didn't look up when I walked in. Mel didn't use a computer much, but he stayed on his phone constantly. The only time I hadn't seen him on it was during our meeting with Green.

"Sit," he said, but he didn't stop moving himself.

"I'm okay."

"Sit." He'd put more bass in that one, and I did what I was told.

The next few minutes felt longer than a 10K, me sitting as Mel did laps. I didn't dare look back. Finally, he appeared next to me, leaning on his desk mere inches away.

"What the fuck is going on, Melina?" He didn't yell. Just spoke in an über-calm voice, which I took to mean the storm was inevitable.

"What do you mean?" I didn't know what else to say, and I couldn't stand another stretch of silence.

"You're not acting like yourself," he said.

I didn't say what I was thinking. That he wouldn't know.

"You're showing your ass with the police," he said. "You're being rude to Tam. You were backstage like some groupie looking for Free."

Of course, he'd know about that. I felt myself regressing like a New Year's countdown. I wanted to stamp my feet. Suck my thumb. Melodramatically throw my body on the floor and roll around. Instead, I swallowed back some smart-ass retort about how Desiree was the one acting like Free's groupie. Because, present circumstances excluded, I wasn't a snitch.

He kept on. "And then I see that article today. Some 'family member' being quoted that Desiree and I were estranged. I'll say it again. You're not acting like yourself. You're acting like your sister."

Again, the calm voice. I would've preferred he yell. That was the Mel I knew. The one on TV and in memes. Not the one acting like a father. Rubbing my wrist, I worked up the nerve to look at him.

"You don't feel guilty?" I said. "Because I feel like shit."

He stood up, took his time going to his office chair. "She'd changed since the last time you were in contact with her."

"Yeah, you've said that. But you didn't say how."

He finally looked at me. With *my* eyes. *Desiree's* eyes.

"What was going on with her?" I said. "Do you know who she was meeting up there?"

He did. I could tell by how quickly he looked away. For a moment, just one split second, I thought he was actually going to tell me. But then he put on the sunglasses at the ready on his big black desk. "It doesn't matter anymore."

"Maybe not to you."

He palmed his phone. "I have a call."

Just like that, I was dismissed, which put me back in familiar territory. His directness had been startling. Clearly Desiree and I weren't the only ones not acting like ourselves. It made me wonder if something more had happened between them.

I stood up, made my way to the door. He waited until I opened it before he spoke again. "And, Melina, no more quotes from family members."

\* \* \*

My lock screen was a string of missed notifications. Texts from Stuart Jones. Calls from Stuart Jones. Calls from an unknown number I assumed was Stuart Jones. I ignored them all—having already texted him a piece of my mind—instead focusing on the two missed calls from Aunt E. It had to be important for her to call me. Twice. But the last thing I needed was more bad news. The service was shit in the elevator, so I hit her back as soon as I got to the lobby. "Everything okay?"

"Some man's been calling here for you."

*Really, Stuart?* "He say what he wanted?" I said.

"To apologize. He didn't say what for, though. I told him you were going to see your father." She took in a breath. "Everything okay?"

"Yeah. He's a reporter from the *News*. That's all. If he calls again, just hang up."

There was a beep. I pulled the phone from my ear to check. Stuart again. A text. He was lucky I decided to ignore him. "Is Erin still there?" I said to Aunt E. I was glad she had someone to keep her company. And vice versa.

"Yeah. The way she's loitering, she wants to talk to you too."

Erin was on the phone within seconds. "So…"

I'd made it through the revolving door and was headed back to my bike. "He wasn't happy with the article." I contemplated telling her my new suspicion, that Mel knew something he wasn't saying, but I'd snitched enough for the week. "He told me to mind my business."

She sighed. "Of course he did. I hope you let him have it. So what now?"

"Please tell me you found Karma Dodson."

"Who's Karma Dodson?"

I always thought I could smell bullshit a mile away. I was wrong. Stuart was next to me, his smile tentative yet present.

"Let me call you back," I said to Erin and hung up. I looked at Stuart. He wore his usual black suit. "Stuart Jones."

"First and last name. Not good. You're mad about the article."

I kept walking. "You screwed me over."

"You didn't want to use your name. I didn't use your name. Not sure where I went wrong here."

I stopped dead in the middle of the sidewalk, a New York no-no, up there with standing on the left side of the escalator and rooting for the Red Sox. The man behind me grunted his displeasure as he huffed past us.

"You called me 'a family member.' We're not the royal family. There's no twentieth in line for the throne. There are four of us left. Mel. Veronika. Aunt E. Me." I counted us off on my fingers. Resisted giving him the middle one when I was done. "You might as well have published my name, social security number, and credit score."

I took off again and he followed. Stuart had half a foot on me at least, so he had to slow down to match my stride. I refused to run. This wasn't the climax of a rom-com.

"I hope I didn't get you grounded." He smiled again, and when I still didn't return it, he continued. More serious this time. "If it makes you feel better, you're not the only Pierce who reamed me out today."

"I'm not a Pierce."

I quickened my pace. He finally got the hint. I didn't need to look back to know he was standing there watching me.

I did two and a half loops around Central Park before I felt right enough to ride home. All I could think about was my convo with Mel. He knew something about why Desiree had been in the Bronx at four in the morning.

My stubbornness kick-started. I'd spent over twenty years without his help, and I sure as hell didn't need it now. I'd find Karma Dodson and then I'd find who killed my sister and then I'd tell him I'd handled it on my own.

I didn't look at my phone until I got stuck at the Shakespeare intersection.

Stuart had sent me another text.

\* \* \*

"I still can't believe you didn't tell him to shove it."

When I got home, Erin was back where I left her: on my couch, staring intently at her cell.

"And get knocked into next week?" I said. She obviously didn't grow up in a Black household. "You tell *your* dad to shove it growing up?"

"I didn't tell my dad anything. He wasn't around."

"Divorced?"

"Worse. Business trips. And vacays. Looked like fun from the photos." She flopped further on the sofa. "Even now I don't talk to my parents much. Not that they seem to notice. We're like planes passing in the night."

"Did you at least have a sibling?" I sat next to her.

"No. But I had a lot of nannies. My favorite was Altirice. She was French, lasted a good year before my mom found out my dad was fucking her. All my nannies after that were a lot older. And never wore makeup."

I laughed, then she laughed too, and we just stayed like that for a moment. It was much better than crying. It felt kind of nice to be reminded I didn't have a monopoly on shitty parents.

When we finally lost steam, Erin changed the subject. "I heard back from two Karmas. Neither of them had any clue what I was talking about."

It was disappointing, but it meant we could narrow it down. "Who's left?"

"Pennsylvania. I can message her again."

"No need." I held up my cell. "Mr. *Daily News* sent me contact info for her and her family. Well, all three of them, but you said the others aren't ours."

Erin thought it over. "That's one way to apologize. I prefer jewelry."

Laughing, I stood up. "I'm calling PA Karma now. Maybe she'll answer."

But she didn't. I got four rings before the voice mail kicked in saying I'd reached the Dodson residence. I left a message knowing damn well most people hadn't checked their voice mail since 2012. "Yes, hi. I'm looking for Karma Dodson…"

I trailed off, unsure what to say next. It felt too complicated. All the bits and pieces needed to be parsed out over a cup of coffee or a glass of wine, not contained after a beep. I settled for a *Law & Order* impression. "We believe she might have been at the scene of an accident a couple of years ago."

Erin's eyed widened and she shook her head. She was right, it sounded way too accusatory. I tried to reroute. "She was a Good Samaritan. Saved my sister's life. And I wanted to thank her." I paused, then added one additional thing. "With a reward."

When I hung up, Erin was giving me the kind of smile parents reserve for the participation medal winner.

"She's not going to call back," I said.

"I mean, she might."

She didn't. I kept trying. Unanswered call after unanswered call even though Erin pointed out that all Dodson residents may be at work, then at dinner, then in bed. I didn't get a hit until six the next morning. Erin had stayed over again, obviously not wanting to go back to her empty oversize town house. I was fine with it, especially since it'd been another night of s'mores and talking too loudly over a Netflix marathon of *Russian Doll*. I'd been the one to crash first, dreaming once again of hide-and-seek, and was only up because of my damn bladder. I balanced on the edge of my bed, my silk scarf barely holding on, while a woman's voice picked up on the second ring, sounding as sleepy as I felt. "Yeah."

"Karma Dodson?"

There was a pause. "Who is this?"

"I left a few messages. I—"

"Stop calling."

It was followed by a click. I immediately called back. Someone picked up, then hung up again. Fine. If she wanted to play it like that, I'd just reach out on Facebook. I pulled the app up on my phone and did the now familiar search. Only two Karma Dodsons popped up.

She'd deleted her profile.

A parking garage. Alyssa Myers is next to a sign advertising a $5.99 special in big black letters.

Alyssa leans into the camera and stage-whispers, "Y'all. You won't even believe this shit. So me and Jazz are at Marquee. We leave. 'Cause we both gotta work in the morning. Y'all. Guess. Who. We. See."

She flips the camera to show us a woman in a black minidress bent over like she might throw up. Another woman stands next to her.

Alyssa speaks again. "Y'all, that is Desiree Pierce. Let me tell you, sis is lit. Jazz has been trying to stop her from puking her guts out for five whole minutes. You know Jazz, always trying to help someone."

Alyssa pauses as we hear Desiree Pierce start to gag. Jazz Brown pats her back. Desiree throws up as Alyssa continues her play-by-play. "Y'all, she is gonna puke all over her Gianvito Rossis."

Jazz rushes to grab Desiree's hair, then yells back. "Alyssa, you gonna film or you gonna help?"

Alyssa opts for both, keeping the camera on as she rushes over. She zooms in on the vomit as Desiree finally straightens up, and Jazz lets go of her hair. Eyes glassy, Desiree wobbles. She notices the camera and attempts a smile. "Hey!"

Alyssa speaks from behind the camera. "You okay, sis?"

"Probably something I ate."

"Or drank." But Alyssa says it so low that Desiree doesn't hear her.

Desiree's too distracted by an incoming text. Her voice is singsongy as she dances. "Guess who might be getting some. Guess who might be getting some."

Alyssa quickly turns the camera, gives it a quick bugeye, then turns it back around. "Yeah?" Alyssa says. "What's his name, sis?"

But Desiree's not paying attention. She's looking off somewhere. Her eyes narrow, and she ignores the valet when he drives up in a Mercedes and stops a few feet away. He gets out, tries to hand her the keys.

Alyssa finally speaks again. "Your car's here."

Desiree snatches the keys out of the valet's hand.

# EIGHTEEN

I raced to the guest room like Pennywise was giving chase. I did manage to knock. I just didn't bother to wait for Erin to tell me to come in. "Where're your car keys?"

I stood at the foot of her bed, typing in a flurry on my phone while the tiny mass under the purple-flowered comforter spoke. "You doing a Starbucks run? I'd kill for a nonfat white mocha, no whip."

If she hadn't figured out by now this wasn't a Starbucks neighborhood, I wasn't going to break the bad news. "We can get it on the way," I said. "I'm sure there's one at a rest stop."

She sat up. No one should look that good first thing in the morning. "Where are we going?" she said. "Even clubs are closed at this hour."

"Northgate. There probably won't be much traffic heading west on the George Washington Bridge, but we should still leave as soon as possible. Waze says it takes only two hours."

"I have a meeting with a potential partner for the club Freck and I were working on. I'm not going to Pennsylvania," she said and must've seen the true intentions radiating off me like steam. "You're not either. Calling is bad enough. Going to someone's house is stalking."

"I won't be hiding in the bushes. I spoke to her."

Erin stared at me for a good minute. "And she invited you to stop by for tea?" She lay back down and pulled the comforter over her head.

"No, for a nonfat white mocha. No whip." I inhaled. "She hung up. Maybe suggested I stop calling."

The silence was heavier than she was. I spoke to the lump. "You've never done anything that you knew was ridiculous but you just had to do?"

I was two states and two hours away from finally coming face-to-face with Zor-El. The person who'd saved Desiree's life two years ago and the person who might know who'd taken it last week. I didn't just want to talk to her. I needed to. Though I knew it wouldn't bring Desiree back, my life would feel on pause until I knew what had happened. And Karma Dodson was holding the remote.

Erin lowered the covers enough that I could see her face. We locked eyes. "I'll even drive," I said.

She looked away. Shook her head.

"You can sleep in the passenger seat," I said.

Still nothing.

"I'll have you back for your meeting."

"You don't even know what time it is."

She reached a hand down the side of the bed, pulled that Birkin off the floor, and stuck one manicured hand inside it. She was proof that the old wives' tale about leaving your purse on the floor was complete BS. "You'll need to get gas."

She handed me her key fob.

I quickly washed up, threw on the same clothes I'd worn the day before, and twenty minutes later was on the road. One hundred twenty minutes later I was in Northgate. One hundred twenty-one minutes later I realized my first mistake. Erin's car. It probably cost more than Northgate's median property value, even accounting for the immediate deflation when it was driven off the lot. Its sole purpose was to attract attention—one thing I didn't want. Not at that moment. Not ever.

Northgate looked like the type of place where even the drug dealers were broke. It was all hills and red brick. The houses. The storefronts.

Even the converted laundromat on the corner. This little piggy was not happy.

It was a city but not the type I was used to. This was a place that had mini-marts versus bodegas and so little traffic the side roads didn't even bother with yellow lines. I stopped by the lone Rite Aid as soon as Waze told me I was five minutes from my destination. It was Monday morning. I didn't know if Karma would be home, but I was more than prepared to wait. I just needed water and maybe some chips to keep me company since I certainly wasn't paying an Uber driver to stand guard with me. I had Erin's car, not her bank account. I parked and headed into the Rite Aid. Of course it was red brick.

I have a theory that you can tell the number of Black people in a neighborhood by the number of ethnic hair care products in a drugstore. Judging by the selection here, I was not with my people. They were probably minding their business in their own neighborhood. One with Shea Moisture and a big vat of green Eco Styler gel.

First wrong car, now wrong skin color. This wasn't exactly a stealth mission, but I sure as hell wasn't driving back. I paid for my Deer Park and my salt-and-vinegar Lay's, promised the friendly cashier I'd have a good day, and went off to find Karma Dodson.

She lived in what was probably considered a nicer area. The houses duplexes and single families, all close enough you could see in your neighbors' windows if you squinted. The lawns mowed probably by owners, not gardeners. The cars clean, if not new. Her two-way street wasn't narrow but was clearly from a time pre-dating the cars that lined both sides. Now it was effectively one-way for whatever car was lucky enough to get there first.

I made it to her house without playing chicken, then counted three US flags and two FOR SALE signs on her block. The Dodson house had neither. What it did have was a bright red door to go with the red brick and white shutters—and it was a duplex, the entrances on opposite sides of the house like a couple in a fight. There was a car in both driveways, a Tercel that looked past its expiration date on the Dodson side. Their neighbor drove a late-model Buick.

Erin'd made me promise to reach out when I got there so I texted her as soon as I parked. Then I noticed the text from Omar. I'd blanked on even having Grant Writing today. A first. I texted back. Gonna miss class but should hopefully be at Strategic Management on Wednesday.

If things went like I hoped today, I could swing by campus tomorrow.

Text sent, I got out and walked up the slight incline to the door. I rang the bell but got nothing. It was still midmorning, which meant no telltale lamps or lights to let me know if someone was inside. Even if Karma wasn't home, her mother, the property owner, should be. Stu had also texted me her name. LinkedIn claimed she worked at a senior facility.

I decided to wait. Maybe she was asleep, but she'd have to get up sometime, even just to pee. I knocked again and heard rustling. Unfortunately, it wasn't from her side of the house. I was being watched. I just couldn't see by who.

Figured this neighborhood would have their own Ms. Paterson.

Both duplexes featured large bay windows. Karma and Co. had gone with vertical blinds. Their neighbor had picked a gauzy white curtain designed for maximum spying. I waved and prayed the person hiding behind the curtain didn't call the cops. I would have had better luck praying for world peace. The cop was behind me almost as soon as I'd gotten back into Erin's car.

Every Black parent has had The Talk with their kids, especially their baby boys. It's not about sex or drugs or why Mommy and Daddy will no longer live in the same house. It's about what to do if you're stopped by the police. I got The Talk at seventeen, the signature still fresh on my driver's license. Like most, mine had come with a strict set of rules. Keep your hands on the wheel or at least in plain sight. No sudden movements. No back talk. Do what they say and only what they say. And never, ever, ever resist arrest.

I'd been stopped before—one time for rolling through a red light—but had never had to use my training. My tickets had come in the safety net known as South Orange, where I'd grown up riding around in a car that had a MY KID IS A COLUMBIA HIGH SCHOOL HONOR STUDENT bumper sticker. My mom hadn't put it on because she was proud but because it let the cops know we were local.

I didn't have the bumper sticker here. This was an eighth-of-an-aisle hair-product area, stuck in the back of Rite Aid like it was the back of the bus. And I was in a car with no idea where the registration or insurance was located. I'd been too distracted to ask, and now I was paying for it.

Karma indeed.

I ran down the rules, then temporarily replaced Super Black Woman with Perky Black Girl and hoped for the best. The cop took his time getting to me. If it was an intimidation tactic, it worked. I spied him in the rearview mirror, all white and bald but with the ruddy complexion of a redhead. I sucked at guessing people's ages, but I pegged him for a well-kept white forty-five. (Black forty-five was a completely different thing.) He looked like he belonged to the Anytime Fitness I'd passed on my way in and viewed the name as a personal challenge.

My hands on the steering wheel, I counted Mississippis until he finally sauntered over. My window was already down so I heard the whistle. It was not directed at me.

"Santorini black."

I said nothing, just pasted on that Perky smile while I wondered if I should be offended.

Another whistle. "A 2019 Jaguar F-Type First Edition R-Dynamic. Only comes in three colors. Zero to sixty in four point nine seconds. I've never seen one in person before."

He finally bent down and smiled like he was expecting me to congratulate him. He had a slight gap and pretty pink gums.

"I'm going to assume I'm not arrested," I said, still smiling.

"Disappointed?" He looked at the car, whistling again. One more time and I'd suggest he switch careers to construction. Satisfied, he nodded to the Dodsons' duplex. "Them two got some sort of old-lady turf war going on. Wanna spend their last days trying to get the other arrested. Last call was reporting the Dodson lady for whistling. Apparently that's illegal here."

"So you just broke the law." I smiled, still in Perky Black Girl mode. "Should I make a citizen's arrest?"

"If you're gonna haul me in with this car, I might consider it." He waited a beat before speaking again. I could practically see him putting on his official cop hat. "You lost?"

"Not at all. I just left the Dodson house. I'm looking for Karma."

He smiled again. More gums this time though same amount of gap. "Of course you are. Can't even say you're the first person in a fancy car looking for that girl. She ain't in there. A good thing. Trust me."

"She doesn't live here anymore?"

"Haven't seen her," he said. Then, "You should probably go. Maybe not come back."

I gestured back at the house, at the neighbor who hated whistling. "I'm sure you'll know if I do."

He took a step back as I turned the car on and pulled away. I waited until I was in motion to wave. I waited a bit longer to flick the middle finger at the snitch next door.

Erin's car had Bluetooth—for a First Edition, I wouldn't expect anything less—so I called her as soon as I turned off the block. "They called the cops."

"Karma?"

"Her neighbor. The mother's probably asleep inside."

"How high is your bail? I can have my finance guy wire it to the police station."

For once I understood why rich people had so many friends. "I'm not in jail," I said. Yet. "He let me go. I'm on my way back."

"Great. I should be done soon."

"I'll drop the car off at your place in Chelsea."

"Cool. Text me when you're on your way. Just park it on the street if I'm not there. I'll move it to my garage when I get home. You can give me the keys later. I have another set."

*Of course.*

After we hung up, I had every intention of getting back on I-78. But I wasn't ready to go. Not when I was literally twenty-five feet from the answers I needed.

I decided to waste a few hours in town, then risk trying my luck again. Though I still had no appetite, a restaurant felt like my best bet. I pulled out my phone and found the Jersey girl version of comfort food. A diner.

The Tick Tock diner was the same glossy silver as an Airstream. It had the look of a place that claimed "World Famous Burgers" without sharing any definitive proof. Their array of oversize desserts should come with an expiration date.

When I got inside, all I saw was mauve. Mauve walls. Mauve tabletops. Even mauve name tags. My waitress was named Sophia. White with dark brown hair and black-rimmed green eyes, she looked like she subsisted on a steady diet of salads and YouTube makeup tutorials. She had the disposition of someone who still believed the world could be theirs.

It was a bit too early for the lunch crowd so I practically had the place to myself save for two trucker types minding their own business at the counter. Perfect. I took a four-top by a window in the back. Sophia waited patiently as I sat and checked a menu so thick it could rival a Cheesecake Factory's.

"I'll take a burger," I said.

"No."

"Okay, then." I chose the next photo I saw. "Spaghetti."

"Uh-uh."

"Salad…?"

"Definitely not."

Finally, I closed the menu. "What would you suggest?"

"Grilled cheese."

"Works for me."

She smiled then, flashing her Invisalign and taking my menu. "You the one camping outside the Dodson place?"

I had been, but still. "Nosy Neighbor called you too?"

"That old bat? Nope. Try Broadcastify. It's got police feeds. Someone reported a sports car."

"Santorini black," I said. She just looked at me.

Sophia sure was a nosy one. I decided to make that a good thing, especially since I was in no rush to get my plate. "You know Karma?"

She had to. Even with the makeup pancaked on and just missing syrup, her face looked young. According to the DOB Stu had sent over, they were probably the same age. "We went to school together," she said.

"Friends?"

"Ha. *No one* was Karma's friend. Closest she had was Lisa, and she slept with Lisa's boyfriend during prom. Not before. Not after. During."

Not exactly the work of a Good Samaritan in the making, but still. "The cop made it sound like she'd moved."

"Yeah," Sophia said. "I mean, I woulda been surprised if she hadn't. She talked about it enough. I figured she'd lead a ticker-tape parade out of town as soon as graduation was over. But she stayed a couple of years, pretending to go to classes at LCCC. Then one day, like a year or so ago, she just disappeared. Poof. Vamoose. Gone off the face of the Earth."

It was the last thing I wanted to hear. "New York?" I said, hopeful.

She thought it over. "Maybe. Bev over there thinks she's someplace exotic, like Paris. I'm thinking LA. Miami. Someplace you can rock cleavage all four seasons. But maybe you're right. She'd go to the city every weekend. Someone swore she had a boyfriend in the Village."

I perked up. Desiree's accident had been in the early hours of a Saturday. Maybe Karma was Zor-El after all. "She ever mention seeing a bad car accident while there? It'd be a couple of years ago." Sophia shook her head. I went a different track. "What about a celeb sighting? She ever mention meeting Desiree Pierce?"

"The dead girl?"

I rubbed my left wrist, surprised at how hearing that made me feel. There had been no malice in Sophia's words. She'd said it like she was stating a fact, like two plus two equals four. And it was a fact.

"The reality star," I said.

Sophia thought it over. "I don't think so. Why?"

No way was I going to tell her so she could share every detail with her next set of diners. So I changed the subject. "What's the name of that police-feed site again?"

# NINETEEN

"Twelve, code five, go ahead."

Broadcastify had its own app. One that immediately pushed a premium membership with no ads. I passed on that, hedging my bets Nosy Neighbor wouldn't call the cops while I listened to toothpaste shill. Once the app was downloaded and the Northgate police feed pulled up, I left both my food and a good tip for Sophia.

It took the first voice to realize there was a problem—I didn't speak one iota of Cop. Between the static and the codes, I had flashbacks to high school French. I desperately tried to catch stray words, like "black car," "Black woman," "whistling." At least not understanding wouldn't tank my GPA.

It would just land me in jail.

Officer Whistle While You Work had implied the Dodson duplex wasn't a high priority, but who's to say the occupants hadn't made a few more calls in the half hour I'd gone to eat?

But the coast was clear when I pulled up in front of the duplex. I'd barely gotten the car in park before I was out of it.

I walked back up the stairs. I pushed the doorbell. I watched as a door opened. Of course, it belonged to the neighbor. She was white with hair dyed the same deep black as a Sharpie and skin the texture of a walnut. I pegged her for white-people seventies.

She stepped onto the porch, holding a cordless phone. It took everything I had not to put my hands up in surrender. She met my eyes. "She's not there."

It took me a second to realize she wasn't saying *I'm calling the police.* "Karma?" I said.

"Her mom. Nicole. Been gone since early this morning. I was trying to get your attention earlier to tell you, but then that cop showed up."

So she hadn't called the cops, which meant someone else had. I chewed on that for a second, then realized it didn't matter. As long as they didn't call them again. I smiled. "Can we go inside?"

Five minutes later, I was sitting on a couch older than I was while *The Young and the Restless* played on mute. A portable air conditioner gathered dust in a lone window. The room was a mess of knickknacks, family pics, and doilies. It felt like I was seven again at Gram's. Not a bad thing.

The neighbor, Ms. Stocking, regaled me with Karma's life story, as told by someone who'd watched it from her front window. It matched what the waitress had said. Karma had a penchant for stealing things. Clothes. Money. Boyfriends.

"Nicole hasn't had many visitors since that girl left," Ms. Stocking said. "Some woman's been over a few times, but that's about it, and even she ain't shown up for months. Can't say I blame either of them. Nicole Dodson is pure evil."

I nodded. "And you don't know where Karma went?"

"No. I just hope she stays wherever she is. And her mam—" She stopped short at a noise. "What was that?"

"Garage. Maybe one of your neighbors is going somewhere."

"Sweetie, you see a garage anywhere around here? Somebody's car is getting towed."

I rushed to the front door. Sure enough, the Jaguar was being loaded onto a truck. I was expecting to see the stereotypical gruff, bearded white dude, someone who could've been a defendant on *Judge Judy*. Instead, I got a white woman young enough to make me think she must be paying for college.

*Shitnuts.*

I ran out, waving my arms. "What are you doing?" But I already knew the answer to that one. So I tried something new. "I'm calling the police."

She smiled when she saw me but didn't stop moving. "Great. I was going to swing by. Let them know that Capital One—the lender on the car—has authorized me to take repossession. You'll save me the trouble."

"You have the wrong car."

"Really?" She stopped what she was doing to pull a piece of paper out of a back pocket. "License plate's the exact same."

She read it off. Indeed it was. *Double shitnuts.*

"This has to be a mistake," I said, though Erin definitely seemed the type to forget to pay something as "unimportant" as a car note. "I can clear this up. Let me just make a phone call. You coming all the way out here was unnecessary."

The driver was already getting into her truck. "You left the car on a public street outside your house. It was well within my rights to take repossession. Have a great day, Ms. Dodson."

I stood there a whole minute before things slowly clicked into place, like I was completing a Rubik's cube. Putting my phone away, I went back to Ms. Stocking, who'd taken a seat on her porch like we were a matinee. Only thing missing was some popcorn. "I hope you got that Uber app," she said.

"You said Mrs. Dodson's had a woman visitor. You get her name?"

She shook her head. "Walked by her once. She didn't even bother to say hello."

"But you'd recognize her?"

"I don't see why not."

I showed her Erin's latest Instagram pic.

# TWENTY

I had four missed calls and three unanswered texts by the time the Uber got me to Chelsea. All from Erin.

Erin, who had changed her name from Karma Dodson. Erin, who had changed her *face* from Karma Dodson's. Erin, who my sister had found out was nothing more than a con artist with a good dye job and implants probably still under warranty. I had no clue exactly what was going on, but there was no doubt in my mind it had played a part in Desiree's death. Why else wouldn't Erin have come clean?

I had no idea why Karma had decided to reinvent herself as Erin Ambrose. I didn't need to know. Because if it wasn't something shady, she would've mentioned it the million and one times I'd brought up Karma's name. Instead, she'd let me go on a wild-goose chase.

When had Desiree first realized her "sister" was a fraud? When had she linked Erin Ambrose to Karma Dodson? When had she confronted her about it? Two weeks before her death? Two days? Two hours? Because there was no question that Desiree would have.

Maybe it was a leap from con woman to murderer, but I didn't know the real Erin at all. No one did. Which meant I had no idea *what* she was capable of.

Once again, I wanted to get my hands on Desiree's cell. But until the cops were ready to hand it over, I'd have to make do with what I could find on mine.

I spent the Uber ride cyberstalking and avoiding Erin's attempts to reach me. Maybe the leasing company had tipped her off they'd taken possession of the car. If they had, it meant she knew I knew. My immediate inclination was to call and confront her from two hours, two states, and seventy-eight miles away. But the Mel in me took over. Confronting someone over the phone wouldn't do. It needed to be face-to-face.

The dive into Erin's Instagram account took me so deep I needed a scuba tank and wet suit. Lots of selfies in exotic locations with infinity pools, aqua-blue oceans, and an endless supply of colorful fruit trays that came pre-filtered. I scrolled back and back and back, for once not caring if I accidentally clicked LIKE. It took a good five minutes to get to her first-ever pic. It was a mirror shot in the bathroom of a Beverly Hilton hotel room. She'd tagged the location so we'd *know*. The filter was the flower crown, which slimmed your nose, made your eyes larger and lighter. It was exclusive to Snapchat so she must've transferred it over.

Looking at it now, I wondered if this was the photo she'd taken straight to her plastic surgeon. I'd seen the unfiltered Karma courtesy of Ms. Stocking. She'd looked like Erin's fugly second cousin once removed. Flat chest. No ass. Brown eyes sandwiched between muddy brown hair and a nose a clown would don.

I went over her IG again, this time more slowly. The captions were straight from an influencer checklist. Cliché after cliché trailed by an onslaught of vague hashtags like #love and #fun. The photos were mostly solo shots, and when there were other people, they were never brothers, sisters, or parents—not even on Mother's Day, Thanksgiving, or Christmas. There was also no mention of where she grew up. Her last birthday was celebrated with friends on a beach in Cabo and filed under #friendshipgoals.

I cross-referenced her photos with the ones on Desiree's account. She'd started popping up about a year ago, their first joint pic on a girls' trip to Cannes. I wondered who'd paid.

The Uber pulled up to Erin's town house. No one had stuck a foreclosure sign on it, so I assumed the only thing the new-and-improved Karma wasn't paying was her car note. I flew out of the car, up the steps, and into even more of a rage when no one immediately answered the doorbell.

The door itself was black and solid enough to withstand a *Wizard of Oz*–level tornado, bookended by slivers of glass too thin to be considered windows. The type more for ambience than seeing inside. I didn't care, leaning so close to the glass my nose left a smudge. It didn't matter. Erin's housekeeper would make it go away.

I rang the bell again, laying on it like a taxi driver in rush hour. It took her another sixty seconds to appear from the second level. She'd changed since this morning—now opting for a long-sleeved brown shirt dress with a matching belt—but the blond hair I now knew was a dye job was still captured in a ponytail.

Having made visual contact, I backed away, stopping just short of falling down the concrete stairs. Not scared of her. More scared of myself and what I might do. I needed her to explain. She couldn't do that with my hands around her neck.

Erin finally made her way to the door. I watched as she opened it wide, then poked her head out.

It was the makeup artist.

"Can I help you?" Starr smiled at me like I was dropping off a package.

My introduction must not have left much of an impression. I smiled anyway. "Hi. I'm Lena. I met you the other day."

"Oh, right," she said but clearly still had no clue who I was. "What's up?"

"I was just looking for Erin. She here?"

Starr looked confused. "No. Is she supposed to come by?"

*Of course* this wasn't her house.

"Sorry," I said. "She said she was gonna stop by on her way home. She must've changed her mind." I leaned in, gave her my best Perky Black Girl. "Guess I can just catch her at her place."

"It's done being renovated? I thought she was still staying at the Omni."

I thanked God for trusting rich people. I knew where to go next in this scavenger hunt. But first I had a question. "How long have you been doing her makeup?"

* * *

Starr had known Erin for just short of eighteen months. They'd gotten close enough—Erin often hung out at Starr's house, including the day I'd picked her up to go to see Free. Starr was vague and unbothered about Erin's background, taking her poor little rich girl story at face value. But then so had I. I did ask about Erin and Desiree's relationship. Starr'd never seen them fight. I got her cell phone number and left.

My walk to the subway was quick. I snatched the last open seat from a jackass in a suit who should've given it to me anyway, then said a quick prayer Sherry would be at the Omni front desk when I got there.

She was, just not by herself.

"Hey, girl," I said.

The guy next to her answered. He could have inspired a '70s disco song—white and uptight, with specks of brown hair covering an otherwise bald head. He looked primed to talk to the manager, even if he *was* the manager. His name tag read BRENDAN.

"Welcome to the Omni. How may I help you?"

I glanced at Sherry and the smile pasted on her face, then looked back to Brendan. "Yes, I'm here to see Erin Ambrose."

His eyes jumped like Kris Kross but recovered quickly. "I'm sorry but we don't have a guest by that name."

He hadn't even checked, which meant he knew her. The question was if she really wasn't here or if she was just using an alias. Privacy and all that bullshit.

Sherry cleared her throat. "Brendan, I'm gonna take my break."

"What about a Karma Dodson? She in?" I said as Sherry came around the counter.

He just gave me a look. I shrugged. It was a long shot. Short of throwing out random name combinations Erin might have checked in under, I was out of ideas. "Clearly I got the hotel wrong," I said. "Sorry to bother you."

I was five feet out the front door when I heard my name. Sherry puffed a Newport right in front of a DON'T SMOKE WITHIN 20 FEET OF ENTRANCE sign. I walked over and strategically placed myself so any hand-me-down smoke wouldn't come my way. "What was that about?"

"He's uptight AF." She inhaled. "He's not lying, though. Erin's not checked in."

I sighed. "Someone said she was."

Sherry exhaled and checked her cell. "Still got five minutes on my break. Walk with me."

She took off. I kept up as we left a trail of smoke in our wake. Sherry waited until we were around the corner to speak again. "There's a rule in New York City. You stay at a hotel longer than thirty days, you're considered a tenant. And New York is a bitch when it comes to evictions. A lot of hotels don't let you stay more than a month. You gotta check out even just for a night, then you check back in."

Erin's thirty days must have been up. "When will she be able to come back? Tomorrow?"

Sherry blew out another cloud of smoke as we passed a Dunkin' Donuts. "When she pays the twelve thousand dollars she owes. Her card on file got declined. She's been promising to give us a new one for a month." She took another puff. "Brendan finally had enough. Told her not to come back. A shame. She's a great tipper."

I'm sure, especially since it was probably someone else's money.

"Brendan wasn't pleased when Erin was here for your sister's party, but there wasn't much he could do."

"Did Desiree know?" Maybe that's what tipped my sister off.

"She had to. She was there enough times when Brendan or Javi bugged Erin about a new card." She smiled. "At least she didn't use yours."

I rolled my eyes. "Erin's a fraud. Desiree found out."

"And?"

I'd always appreciated Sherry's bluntness. So I gave her some of my own. "And I think she might have helped Desiree 'accidentally' overdose."

If I was hoping for shock and awe, I didn't get it. Sherry just stubbed out her cigarette on a wall. "I don't know. Even if she is a fraud, I can't see her hurting anyone."

"Because she's pretty and blond and white? Society loves to have us believe pretty, blond white women are always victims. Never the threat. Erin has clearly taken advantage of that."

"Touché," Sherry said. "That would definitely explain the argument."

I stopped, wondering why it'd taken her so long to share that tidbit. "When?"

"Night Desiree died. Javi saw it on the security cam."

"You didn't tell me."

"I thought you knew. Your dad sent someone to get all the footage from that night."

It was the first I'd heard of it, but getting rid of evidence was part of Mel's MO. It was why no one knew if the window incident was just an urban legend. But it also made me hopeful. Maybe that was why Mel had been acting so strange. He actually did believe there was more to the story. It would explain why no one had told me. They didn't want me to know I was right. And if Mel knew, Tam and Veronika knew too.

"Can I see it?"

"It's long gone. Your dad made sure of that. Only people even saw it were my managers."

"Javi and Brendan." Brendan wouldn't even give me a name. I held out no hope of him giving me a video. "You think Javi would talk to me?"

Sherry smiled. "Give me thirty minutes. Brendan'll be off work."

I waited Brendan out at the Dunkin' Donuts, picking at a Boston cream until I felt mentally prepared enough to call Erin back. It was looking more and more like my surprise confrontation was a no-go. When she didn't answer, I sent her a quick WYA text, then stared at my phone for eons while envisioning her on the run in sunglasses and a headscarf, checking into a flight to Cuba on a fake passport. But this wasn't *Mission: Impossible*. She was probably getting a facial.

Exactly thirty minutes later, I again walked through the Omni hotel entrance. This time I noticed the cameras. There were more in the lobby than people. Small black lenses protected behind rounded glass.

Sherry stood at the front desk. "How are you with lying?" she said when I got to her.

That did not sound good. "What's the scale? Out of ten?"

She just stared.

"Maybe a seven," I finally said. "Nine if I'm really motivated."

"Great. Javi said he'd talk to you only after I told him your dad had sent you."

"Great." My inflection was nowhere near as excited as hers.

"They require one of us to be at the front desk so I'm stuck here. But he's in the office."

She gestured to a door less than ten feet behind her. It was half open, and I could barely make out legs, both desk and human. I prided myself on being a quick thinker, someone who could tell you what fifteen times fifteen is in a split second. But that didn't extend to lying, and I had ten feet to come up with a reason why Mel would send me back down here.

I knocked when I got there, and a voice told me to come in. They didn't spend any of their interior design budget on the manager's office. It was clearly meant for one person, though they'd stuffed two desks in there anyway. These were pushed up against opposite walls and looked straight out of an IKEA catalog. The one farthest from me was spotless, nothing but a desktop computer and a pen in a pen holder. The other one was a hot mess—Javi's.

He looked over when I came in, then popped up when he realized I wasn't Sherry. Surprisingly, he was about my age. Brown eyes. Tightly coiled black hair. Light brown skin. And either he'd lost weight recently or had never had much to begin with because his suit made him look like a kid playing in his dad's clothes. He shook my hand.

"Let me apologize if there were any further issues regarding your sister's stay." He sounded nervous. Mel must've laid into him about the video. "I hope you convey that to your father, Ms. Pierce."

"Scott," I said, then continued on before he could do the obligatory *What?* "Lena Scott. I legally took my mother's maiden name when I graduated high school. Mel didn't come to my graduation. The name change was eighteen-year-old me's way of saying I wanted nothing to do with him. Still don't think he's noticed."

Javi was too good at his job to smile. He just nodded. "Scott is a cool last name."

"I certainly think so," I said. Then, "Mel didn't send me here. He didn't even bother to tell me about the security footage. So I can go to him and ask to see it. Or you can tell me what happened."

He said nothing at first, then walked over to Brendan's desk and started rummaging through a drawer. "The other manager takes all the notes. He has better handwriting."

He found what he was looking for, then came back with the file and Brendan's chair. "Have a seat."

Javi sat back down too. "I remember most of it but just want to be sure." He glanced through the file and spoke without looking up. "It was in the hallway on fourteen. Time stamp was 8:04 p.m. Ms. Pierce and Ms. Ambrose appeared intoxicated. Ms. Pierce was trying to open the door to her room, but it was a struggle. Ms. Ambrose was on her phone. She said something to Ms. Pierce. We don't have audio so can't say what. Ms. Pierce snatched the phone from her. Ms. Ambrose attempted to get it back. Your sister pushed her. Someone must have been in the room because the door opened, and Ms. Pierce ran inside. Ms. Ambrose ran in after her. And that was it."

Sans water-glass throwing, it sounded like some drunken girl fight you'd find right before the commercial break of a reality TV show. "And you have no clue what it was about?" I said. Was this when Desiree had first confronted Erin?

He shook his head. "We didn't see them again until close to midnight.

Things still appeared frosty. They walked side by side but didn't seem to be speaking."

"They were alone?" I said since he'd mentioned someone had been inside the room.

"No, Zarah was with them." He smiled. Sheepish. He'd used her first name. No "Ms." It meant one thing: he watched her show.

"Sherry said you were having problems with Erin. That you banned her from the hotel?"

"Sherry has been spoken to about being so talkative," he said. "Look. I have friends at other hotels. Ms. Ambrose has developed a rep for forgetting to pay her bill. There's always an issue with a credit card, promises her accountant is wiring over money, mock surprise when it doesn't show up. Just when we're about to call the police, she appears with a cashier's check. Or a friend bails her out. So no, she wasn't banned, but we were going to suggest she not come back. But we haven't seen her since Ms. Pierce's things were picked up. She called us that same day to say someone was coming to pick up all *her* stuff. I didn't ask where they were taking it."

It looked like my scavenger hunt was over.

# TWENTY-ONE

After I left Javi, I circled the block, trying to figure out what to do next. My first thought was Zarah, so I blew her up any way I could think of. iMessage. Voice mail. Even WhatsApp. No dice. Probably still under doctor's orders.

On my second trip past an Equinox, it hit me that my only other connection to Erin was her ex Billy. I could take the subway up to Gravity Fitness to see if he knew any other hotels she'd stay at. It was a long shot, but I was still cocked and ready to shoot.

The 14th Street station was a block west. The humidity had followed me to the subway platform like a stalker, clinging in ways my favorite black T-shirt never did. The platform wasn't crowded. At least not yet. I'd beaten the work crowd by a good hour. A group of Black teenagers with a boom box stood on the uptown side. Their demeanor and outfits were a dead giveaway they had big plans to entertain the masses on the ride up. Kids like that were the sole reason I carried cash.

I dialed Zarah again. She finally picked up. "Terri?"

I paused. She clearly hadn't checked the ID. "It's Lena."

"Oh. Hey. Sorry, I thought you were the assistant at my doctor's office. I'm in desperate need of more meds."

I checked the digital display hanging from the ceiling. Two minutes until the next E uptown. My time with service was limited. "Sorry to hear that," I said, then jumped right in. "Desiree and Erin fought the night she died?"

There was a pause long enough for the countdown to change from two minutes to one. We weren't on FaceTime so I could only imagine her expression. "Yes…"

I waited for her to say more, then prodded her along when she didn't. "About?"

She said nothing, so I spoke again. "Maybe Desiree found something out about Erin?"

"I honestly don't know. Neither said anything. I was running late as usual so I was mostly in the bathroom getting my face together. I don't think either of them trusted me yet, and since Desiree and I still weren't back where we used to be, I sure as hell wasn't going to ask why they were being weird. I did see Erin snatch her phone out of Desiree's hand."

Understandable but no less frustrating. "How did they seem the rest of the night?"

"Erin seemed more put out than Desiree. But then Desiree had pregamed hard so there was nothing that'd keep her in a bad mood."

I glanced at the subway display. "Did Erin ever mention where she was from?"

She thought it over. "Now that I think about it, no. But she definitely name-dropped everything else like she was new money. What's up with all the questions?"

There wasn't enough time to explain. "Nothing. It's just she offered to take me on a trip to LA. Figured I should know who I'd be traveling with."

The display flashed zero and the uptown train pulled in. One of the Black kids picked up the boom box as the doors opened and the crowd spilled out.

"Don't do it," Zarah said. "Naut's still waiting for her to pay him back for putting a Costa Rica trip on his card. She booked the hotel. Said she'd pay for everything. Of course, her card was declined. A mistake, she said. Told him her accountant would take care of it as soon as we got back…"

"Did Desiree know?"

"Yep. She got defensive when I brought it up, like I was talking about *her*. Said Erin was good for it. That Erin'd paid her back for a trip they took a few months ago. You know, your sister even had that girl spend the night at my apartment. Something about needing to check out of her hotel. You know she stayed four days? Thought I got rid of her, but she'd left her credit card at my place. Came back and stayed two more nights."

And just like that I finally knew where to find Erin.

Home. Not alone either.

*Shitnuts.*

I thanked Zarah and hung up with a choice to make. Stay on the platform with guaranteed cell service to call Aunt E or get on the train. I checked the display again. Eight minutes until the next train. Too long to be idle, especially with a fifty-minute subway ride, double that time for an Uber.

The last of the commuters boarded just as the train beeped. The signal the doors were about to close.

Stay and warn Aunt E or get there as soon as I could.

I decided to do both. Calling Aunt E while jumping on the car. I wasn't the only straggler. Just as the doors half closed, an East Asian dude reached his hand out, causing the automatic doors to fly back open.

For once I was happy for the interruption. It gave me a few precious seconds to let the phone ring. And that it did. Over and over and over, until finally the mechanical voice from the old-school answering machine picked up. I was just about to leave a message when my phone cut off. Too many calls and not enough charging meant my battery had drained down to nothing. I'd never yell "Keep your phone charged, jackass" at a movie screen again. Now there was nothing I could do but pray we made good time and play out every possible scenario in my head, from Aunt E safe at Zumba to Erin, now knowing I knew, holding her hostage.

The train wasn't crowded, but I was too wired to sit. I stood by the doors, leaning back against the sign asking me not to.

"Yeah, I got caught up, but I'm on the E train uptown now. Be there in a bit."

The latecomer stood next to me, ending his leisurely conversation. He must've had Verizon. I was switching as soon as I confirmed Aunt E was okay.

He saw me looking and smiled. I gave him one too, all Perky Black Girl. "Hey," I said. "Can I use your phone real quick?"

He smiled wider, raising the large mole on his right cheek. "Why?"

Of course, he'd think I was flirting.

"I need to make sure my grandmother's okay and I don't have service."

"How do I know you aren't gonna run away with it?" But his voice was teasing.

"I think you'd be able to catch me...If you don't trust me, how about you call her?"

He thought it over. "What's the number?"

I recited it and he punched it in, smiling as he held it up to his ear. Like this was some big joke and the person on the line would tell him he'd won a million dollars. I could barely remember to breathe.

After what felt like an eternity, he spoke. "Want me to leave a message?"

*Shitnuts.* "I'm good, thanks."

I was tempted to ask him to place another call, this one to Detective Green. Or even 911. But I didn't. Partly because the last thing I needed was the cops busting down Aunt E's door. Those stories never ended well. Not for us. And partly because I had no concrete proof Erin knew I'd found out her secret. Her texts had been frequent, but they'd also been friendly. I had to believe Aunt E was safe for the time being.

I finally took a seat, zoning out until it was time to transfer to the shuttle and then the 6. By the time I got to my stop, I'd done a halfway decent job convincing myself Erin wasn't even there, that she was checking into some fancy hotel with an expired credit card. But as soon as the subway doors opened at 167th Street, I ran the entire way home.

"Aunt E!"

I stormed into her apartment. Erin was across the room, standing right next to Aunt E. I stopped abruptly. They were baking. Erin smiled over at me as she poured the mashed orange mixture into a pie shell. "My first sweet potato pie."

I said nothing, just took in short, heaving breaths.

"You okay, Lena?" Aunt E watched me with those intense eyes of hers. Thank God Erin seemed oblivious. "I tried to call you back, but I know you don't check your messages."

I looked back and forth between them. Once. Twice. Three times. Finally, I spoke. "Just surprised to see Erin still here, that's all."

"I've been trying to reach you all day," Erin said.

*Me too.* Aunt E kept staring, but I avoided her.

"How was Pennsylvania?" Erin said. "You see Karma Dodson?"

*Yeah, right in front of me.* She must've not known that I knew. She'd obviously sent her mother away so I couldn't talk to her. "It was a dead end." I smiled. Let Erin believe her plan had worked. "Let me run to the bathroom."

I picked up the cordless in Aunt E's bedroom and called 911 as soon as I closed the bathroom door. "Yes, we have someone in my house I think might be dangerous."

After I gave the operator my address, she promised to send a police car right away. "How soon can you get here?"

"Fifteen minutes."

I hung up and checked the time: 4:31. Every minute felt like ten. Perky Black Girl was long gone. Super Black Woman was at the ready. I could do this—keep Erin occupied until they got here. Then leave it to the police to figure out if she was a murderer or just a fraud.

I splashed water on my face, wiping my hands on towels that had been there since the dawn of time before heading back to the kitchen. The pies were now in the oven, and Erin was doing dishes. Aunt E sat at her kitchen table. She said nothing when I came in. Just watched me.

"I didn't hear the car pull up," Erin said.

I came over to help her dry. Last thing I wanted was for her to have easy access to steak knives. "Left it at your house. Remember?"

I watched to see how she'd react. She barely blinked. "You didn't text me."

"Figured you'd be home. I knocked on your door and everything." I stopped myself. It'd be silly to tip her off before the police got here. "Obviously you weren't. How was your meeting?"

"Great. Think they might invest." She handed me the final plate. "My turn to pee."

As soon as she left, Aunt E spoke. "What is going on?"

I waited until I heard the bathroom door close before I walked over to her. "She's a con artist. Desiree found out. I think she may have something to do with Desiree's death." I couldn't say *I think she killed her.* Not to Aunt E. Not until I knew Erin was out of the house. "The police should be here any minute."

Aunt E swallowed. "Let me get Kitty."

She always kept her hot-pink Hello Kitty aluminum bat next to her bed. I waited until she was well on her way before running to the front window to see if the police had arrived. There was no one outside.

When I walked back to the kitchen, I saw Erin's purse sitting on the table. I had it unzipped before I even realized what I was doing. Zarah had seen Erin snatch her phone back out of Desiree's hands, which meant Desiree had seen something Erin didn't want her to. I needed to see for myself. Unfortunately, the designer bag was filled to capacity. No doubt a by-product of not having anywhere to live.

I felt around, recognizing objects by touch. Lipstick. Wallet. Hairbrush.

I kept going until I felt a zipper. Something rectangular was inside. I unzipped it. Bingo. Hot-pink plastic.

The screen was black when I pulled it out. I tapped the home key to wake it up, praying she didn't have a passcode. The lock screen photo popped up.

My smiling face stared back at me, crowding in next to Mel and Desiree.

Desiree's phone. The one I'd been wanting to get my hands on since she died. The one I'd assumed had been stolen with the car. There was only one reason for Erin to have it.

She had been up there with Desiree that night.

I touched the home key again, bringing me to the Enter Passcode screen. I started to plug in my birthday.

"What the hell are you doing?" Erin said.

She was behind me. I took my time turning around, holding the phone up like she'd told me to freeze. We stared at each other from across the room before I spoke first. "Holding my dead sister's phone. The one I've been looking for."

I'd never been in a physical fight in my life. But I'd seen enough of them on TV. The real ones on Worldstar. The fake ones on soap operas. The even more fake ones on reality TV. I thought I knew how this would all go. I'd pull out my earrings, then pull out her weave. I'd hurl punches and improperly used synonyms for a female dog. Flashes of anger would result in flashes of nipples as we rolled round and round on the floor.

Turns out, I stayed exactly where I was. Didn't even think about throwing the phone at her head. Just held it more tightly. Because as much as I wanted to beat her ass right then and there, I wouldn't. I couldn't. Not with Aunt E in the house. Not with knowing what Erin had already done to Desiree.

"I can explain," she said.

I glanced at the time on Aunt E's cable box: 4:43. Three more minutes. I could stand here and listen to my sister's murderer explain why she'd killed her if it meant that in four minutes she'd be explaining it all to the cops. And then to cellmates and then to a jury of her peers who wouldn't believe a single word coming out of her mouth—just like I wasn't about to.

"It was a mistake." She sounded like she thought that would make me feel better. That my sister dying was only some miscalculated math problem on her SATs. "I'd done some coke, and there had to be something in it. I didn't know what I was doing when I—"

I finally let loose. "Killed her."

She stepped back as if I'd actually slapped her. "What? No. I was talking about why I have her phone. I was with someone when Desiree died. You know that."

I glanced at the clock. Two more minutes. "Yeah. Mr. One Night Stand Whose Name You Forgot."

"Why would I lie about that?"

"Why would you lie about having a town house in Chelsea? Why would you lie about your rich daddy screwing your nanny? Why would you lie about your name, Karma?"

Recognition hit her like the car she'd had repossessed. All my plans to wait for the police up and left too. "You took my sister to the Bronx so no one would know you up here. Shot her up with heroin, went back to her hotel room, and went to sleep."

She shook her head, faster and faster. "I'm a liar, yes—"

"Con artist."

"Con artist. But if I killed Desiree, why would I still be here? I want to know what happened to her just as much as you do." She took a step closer.

"No," I said. "Stay there."

"I loved her."

I looked away, not because I couldn't look at her but because I wouldn't. Super Black Woman. From my peripheral, she was still staring at me hard. As if willing me to look at her. To believe her.

"I helped her."

Bullshit. "Only thing you helped her do was die."

Aunt E came from the bedroom, bat in hand. Erin didn't see her. Erin moved, and I couldn't help it. I flinched, revealing the tough-girl talk was just that. In truth, I was scared shitless, praying the Super Black Woman cape was bulletproof. I'd never wanted to see a cop more in my twenty-eight years of being Black.

"I just…I just want to show you something." She held up her phone as if it was the smoking gun. "I wouldn't hurt you. I would never hurt you."

I finally met her gaze. She did actually look hurt. "Too late."

Erin opened her mouth, then just closed it again. Then she pulled up whatever she wanted to show me on her phone. I saw Aunt E grip Kitty even tighter. She needed to stay where she was. I shook my head, hoping she got the hint.

We were all silent. Me waiting for the cops. Aunt E waiting for my cue. Erin nervously tapping at her screen. She must've found what she wanted because she took another step in my direction. Luckily, Erin would have to get through two couches, a coffee table, Gram's recliner, and a dozen knickknacks to get to me.

"Can I just show you this?"

She didn't wait for an answer, just hit PLAY and held the thing up. I glanced at the clock again instead. One more minute. I could force myself to be interested for sixty seconds. I put on my best *I'm interested* face. The one I always wore during Quantitative Analysis. But I couldn't make out much. Then I heard it.

The sound was guttural, like someone choking. Had she filmed Desiree dying? Really?

"Throw it." I could sense her hesitation, so I repeated myself, barely containing the shake in my voice. "Throw. It."

There was a pause then and finally she did as told. Her lob was light but made it, dropping softly on the light blue carpet a few inches in front of me. I picked it up with my left hand. The right was still reserved for Desiree's. I watched the video, then recoiled. Erin was sucking dick like she'd planned to upload the video herself to Pornhub. I paused it, not sure if I should be relieved or disgusted.

"Check the date," she said as I averted my eyes.

I really didn't want to, but looking at the phone again, I tapped the screen with a right knuckle. Manhattan, New York. June 5, 2019, 4:08 a.m.

Leave it to Erin for even her alibi to be fucked up. Still, it didn't explain Desiree's phone. Didn't explain why she'd been lying for six days. I threw her phone back with nowhere near the same courtesy. She jumped as it hurled past her. "Great," I said. "You can show it to the police when they get here."

"I'm still here because I want to help you. I wasn't lying about that."

I rolled my eyes, thinking of her "help" this morning. There was no doubt she was the one who'd called the police to scare me away.

"I can help you," she said again. "Help you put Zarah away for killing Desiree."

The doorbell rang.

# TWENTY-TWO

T urned out the police came and went as quickly as a one-hit wonder. My story was half-baked—the person threatening me had left to threaten someone else. They were happy to follow suit without a single follow-up question. The one time I was happy the police could be so apathetic.

After they left, Erin was still staring at me like she wanted to cry. I wasn't sure if it was because she was sad about what she'd done or just that she'd gotten caught. We were still on opposite sides of the room. She sat on the couch. I sat in Gram's recliner. The one usually untouched, like a memorial. Instead of it feeling strange, I felt empowered. Like Gram was holding my hand. Aunt E was in a chair of her own midway between, like a referee. Her Hello Kitty bat lay across her lap.

My cell went off in the kitchen. All three of us ignored it. There were already too many phones in play.

"You have two minutes to give me the TL;DR version of why Zarah killed Desiree before I call them back," I said, and Erin leaned forward like she actually believed me.

"I loved Freck. Like a sister."

I was tired of the same old lines, the same old bullshit. "You don't get to say that. Not anymore. Not when you lied to her about who you were."

"What makes you think I lied to her?" She paused, like an actor waiting for her costar to deliver the next line. But my mind went blank. She kept on. "When Mel cut her off, your sister was dead broke. Anything she earned from that silly reality show she'd spent on clothes to wear on it."

She was right. Desiree had never had a reason to save, running through Mel's bank account like it was a treadmill. But still, I objected. "She had money coming in. I saw the #spon tags on her posts."

"Any sponsored posts were paid with more clothes, not money. And before you bring up the influencer trips, they're great when you're there but don't keep a roof over your head when you aren't. Your sister was broke, homeless, and had no one to turn to."

She paused just long enough, I knew the jab had been directed at me. I said nothing, just put Desiree's phone down so I could rub my wrist.

"She could have come to us," Aunt E said. "She knows we would have done anything for her."

You could tell by the smile Erin gave Aunt E that she liked her, didn't want to hurt her feelings. "And what? Stay in the spare bedroom? With all due respect, Aunt E, this place doesn't fit the Instagram aesthetic. Even if you're going for vintage." The smile was long gone by the time she turned back to me. "I was able to take care of us while we figured out how to get her some cash. First thing we did was use the credit card."

"*My* credit card," I said, even though we all knew damn well I hadn't paid for it.

"Credit cards are great for small things, but you can't slap a credit card down for office space. Especially one that didn't have either of our names on it. We needed a larger chunk of money. And that's where Free came in."

"We're supposed to be talking about Zarah."

Erin moved her bare leg slightly so it peeled off the plastic on the couch. "I'm getting there."

"This has to do with Desiree's pregnancy?"

"Pregnancy *test*. You can get a fake one on Amazon for $9.79. Gets here in two days if you have Prime."

My gasp started loud, but I caught myself midway, faltering into a strangled intake of breath. Desiree hadn't had a miscarriage. She hadn't had an abortion. She hadn't had a baby in any form.

"And you both thought this was okay?" I said. "Conning people for money?"

"He could afford it. All of them can." For the first time since I'd exposed her, she sounded defiant.

Desiree had been many things. Selfish. Narcissistic. Addicted to the spotlight as much as she was to any drug. But the Desiree I had known—loved—didn't steal credit cards and fake pregnancy tests. It made me scared for what else she'd done. What Erin was about to tell me. What had gotten her killed.

A phone rang again—Aunt E's house line. I waited until she went to answer it before I said anything else, pretended it was because I didn't want Aunt E to hear when I wasn't sure I wanted to hear myself. "How does Zarah play into this?"

"The accident. Two years ago. Freck wasn't driving."

"I know that." Now. It was why I had been desperate to find Zor-El. Then I realized what Erin was trying to say. "Desiree told you Zarah was driving the car?"

I'd assumed it was some man. Some stranger. Some random hookup. Not a girl Desiree had known her whole life. The one who'd been there her first day of school. First dance. First date.

Erin hesitated, then finally said, "No. Not outright."

"So you're lying. Again." I was ready to call the cops back.

"After the thing with Free, the money didn't last long. Desiree was ready to hit someone else. I told her to be patient, but she was anxious. I'm not sure if she liked the money or the power. We spoke about the accident, that she had blacked out but wasn't driving. It was something she mentioned in passing but didn't really want to talk about. Then a couple of months ago something happened. She suddenly got mad, was asking me how to get money out of the real driver. I told her it was a waste of time. We got into a fight, and she never brought it up again."

"Then why do you think it was Zarah?"

"She was there that night."

"A lot of people were there. It was a party." I conveniently ignored that I'd been just as adamant it was Erin with just as little proof moments before. "You think Desiree tried to blackmail Zarah and instead Zarah killed her."

More statement than question. She realized it too because she opened her mouth, then shut it again. Finally, she formed words. "She was there."

"Yes, but even if Zarah was driving, why lie about it? And why kill Desiree over the truth? Desiree got a slap on the wrist. Zarah would've had the same lawyers. Gotten the same sentence."

"That *slap* destroyed your sister's career. Zarah just hit ten million followers. She's not doing sponsored content. She's got actual endorsements. A makeup line."

She sounded convincing. But still. "If you're so sure it was Zarah, why haven't you told the police?" I said.

"Because I needed proof." Erin pointed to the phone in my lap. "That's why I kept Desiree's phone when I realized she'd accidentally left it at the hotel that night. Desiree started hanging with Zarah the same time she started talking about the accident again. And I heard them arguing the night she died. Zarah kept saying she was sorry. That it was her fault."

That was news. "Was this before or after your fight with Desiree?"

She didn't blink. "I was still hooking up with Billy. Freck'd caught me texting him right before we went out. She didn't like him any more than you do. Like I said, she was a good friend. She'd be happy to know I actually did hook up with someone else that night." She laughed, then caught herself when she saw my expression. "I'm telling you the phone is key," she said.

"Why not give the phone to the police? How do I know blackmail wasn't your idea? Still is your idea."

"I didn't give the police the phone for the same reason you haven't told them your suspicions. I don't trust them. There has to be something in that phone. Been driving myself up the wall trying to figure out the passcode. You can only put in five attempts before you get a one-minute time-out. You fuck up the sixth time? Five-minute time-out. Seventh time? Fifteen minutes. You get it wrong ten times? Erases the data completely. Needless to say it's been taking me a while."

It served her right.

"Maybe you'll have better luck," she said.

"I doubt it." If she could lie to me, I could most definitely lie to her. I glanced down and the phone woke up. Desiree's smiling face staring right at me. Knowing what was behind that smile made me feel the same as not knowing what was behind the lock screen—both feelings scared me.

Aunt E came back in, using Kitty like a cane. She wasn't aware of the turn the convo had taken. "That was Tam. The police closed Desiree's case. It's officially an accidental overdose."

Of course they did. I was surprised they'd waited this long. They'd had their minds made up from the moment they found her body.

Aunt E was still going. "We're free to get Desiree's car and things. She wanted to know if we could pick it up since we're so close to the police station."

I stood up. "Sure thing." The one silver lining was that I could finally get my hands on Desiree's belongings.

Erin stood too. "Guess I should probably go…"

She trailed off as if waiting for me to offer my spare bedroom complete with turn-down service. The only reason I wasn't calling the police back was because I knew she'd use the opportunity to trash Desiree. But there was no way I could let her stay in this house. I didn't care how apologetic she seemed. I didn't trust her. Not anymore.

But Aunt E spoke first. "If you nee—"

For once I cut her off. We could argue about it *after* Erin was long gone. "Great," I said. "I'm sure you have somewhere else to go."

I doubted she could afford a hotel room, which meant she probably couldn't afford a plane ticket. And it wasn't like she had her car.

"I can stay with Starr. I just need my stuff."

"You can wait outside. I'll bring it out."

"And my keys?"

"You don't need them. Your car's been repossessed."

I headed toward the front door, ignoring Erin's surprise and Aunt E's disappointment.

*  *  *

Erin had claimed she kept her Louis Vuitton weekend bag in her car so she could hop on a flight whenever she wanted. Lie number 4,376,371. Both she and her designer luggage would be Starr's problem tonight.

I placed Desiree's phone on my kitchen counter as I walked to the back of my apartment. Erin hadn't opened the curtains in the guest room so it was as dark as night. I didn't bother with the light switch. I was on a mission. I could make out shadows of all the stuff she'd spread out on my dresser. Looking at it now, even in the dark, it was clear she had been planning a lengthy stay.

There was a dark lump on a chair in the corner that had to be her Louis Vuitton. I tripped over what I was sure was a designer heel. I picked the bag up. Of course, it was practically empty. Its contents were spread all over the room.

I grabbed earrings. Jars of moisturizer. Even dirty panties I picked up with an eyeliner pencil. The whole lot thrown back into the bag. I didn't even check if the assorted bottles, palettes, and compacts were all the way closed. It'd serve her right to get foundation all over everything. I hoped her card got declined when she went for dry cleaning.

Once all traces of Erin were packed up, I went downstairs. She was waiting in the driveway, talking up Ms. Paterson of all people. I didn't say anything. Just left the bag on the front stoop and locked the door behind me. I set the alarm, even put on the chain.

Aunt E opened her door as I was heading up the stairs. "Is this all worth it? You haven't been sleeping. Haven't been eating. Haven't been acting like yourself."

My back was to her so I rolled my eyes. She sounded like Mel. If she accused me of acting like Desiree, I would rip out both my braids.

"I'm okay," I said.

"Are you?"

I didn't answer her—because I didn't know.

After a moment she kept on. "You didn't have to kick that girl out like that."

Aunt E had spent three decades working in a high school cafeteria, dishing out compassion along with lunch specials. She had cheered the ones who graduated. Cheered the ones who didn't. I wasn't surprised she felt bad for Erin.

I kept going up the stairs. "She's going to stay at the five-thousand-square-foot town house. The one she told me she owned. She'll sleep fine tonight."

"Lena, I just think you—"

But I cut her off for the second time in my life, my voice as gentle as I could make it. "And I just think you need to trust me when I say we can't believe anything she says. Please."

Aunt E didn't say anything. Didn't move either because I didn't hear her door close. She just stood there until I disappeared.

Back inside my apartment, I grabbed Desiree's phone as I went into my bedroom, ignored the pile of clean laundry I'd dumped on one side of the bed, and hid under my sheets like I'd just watched a scary movie. Except this time the bogeyman was my own sister, and I wasn't scared of what I'd see in the mirror. I was scared of what I'd see on her phone.

It didn't help that the phone woke up without any prompting. I silently cursed Erin for keeping it charged. Mel, Desiree, and I stared out. Even in pictures, Desiree was so alive I could practically hear her heart beating. It was something about her smile. In theory, it was the same as mine, worn like a too-big jacket. The same one Mel begrudgingly pulled out on special occasions. But there was just something about hers. I stared for too long, gripping the phone so tightly a film of sweat formed between the pink case and my hand.

Even though it would take only a flick of my thumb to pull up the passcode screen, I couldn't do it.

Her *phone*.

The lone thing separating me from knowing exactly what Desiree had been up to. And now I had it, I couldn't bring myself to unlock the damn thing.

Desiree hadn't been perfect. I knew that. I'd accepted it until the day I couldn't anymore. Her drug use had been bad, the accident worse. Even then, she'd hurt only herself. But this was different. This was lying and cheating and stealing from others. At least Robin Hood gave it to the poor.

I wasn't just mad at Erin; I was pissed at Desiree. Death was supposed to absolve you of your sins. Make you an angel worthy of heaven's pearly gates. It gave people who loved you—even from afar—amnesia. They forgot that you never mowed your grass. Played your music too loud. Drank too much. Held grudges. Told all their business. Never bothered to apologize for your temper. Death turned you into a great neighbor. A loving boyfriend. Someone who just liked to have a good time.

But death hadn't absolved Desiree. It had only made her worse.

And now I was staring at my own version of Pandora's box. Part of me hoped she'd changed the password from my birthday. That I'd plug in those six digits and nothing would happen. That I'd plug it in ten times and the phone would wipe, taking Desiree's sins with it.

Then I could convince myself that I'd tried.

But I knew better. Knew there would always be what ifs. Erin's voice constantly whispering in my ear, trailing me like a lost puppy. So I took a deep breath and did it, tapped the screen so the picture-perfect version of my sister disappeared and the real version could finally appear: 1–1–1–0–9–1.

The family pic was suddenly covered with row upon row of apps Desiree had meticulously searched for, downloaded, and deemed worthy of her first screen. The boring default apps had been banished. There was no Stocks or iBooks or Newsstand. Of course photos, camera, and messages still remained, joined by ones I assumed were requisite for anyone with more than a hundred thousand Instagram followers. Facetune.

Linktree. Something called Afterlight. I stared for a good two minutes, then forced myself to focus.

Texts seemed like the logical first step. The green square with the thinking bubble also had a red notification—628 unread. And I knew they all hadn't been sent post-death. I was an empty inbox type of girl. Desiree had been too but only because she'd barely used her email. Her texts were a completely different story.

And sure enough, one click confirmed this wouldn't be easy. Desiree had barely put anyone's name into her contacts. Just inputted their number, sending them a "Hi" or vice versa. It'd drive me bananas, but Desiree had been good with remembering people—especially ones who could've done something for her.

Zarah wasn't in her first page of texts. I scrolled but still didn't see her name. I recognized others: Naut. Erin. Tam.

I did a search, and at last their conversation popped up. A message from Desiree telling Zarah she'd gotten the box of her makeup. Couldn't wait to try it!! Zarah responded with three heart-eyes emojis, a promise that she couldn't wait for Desiree's birthday, and a link to info about the Omni bar. The iMessage showed a preview of the site. It'd been sent a week before Desiree's party.

No texts since.

I moved on to the call log. Maybe they'd been like they were as kids and spent hours on the phone. It was a repeat of the text situation: numbers mixed with names. None of them Zarah.

I had one last option. Instagram.

Her DMs were just as crowded, but at least everyone had names. Profile pictures too. Desiree had what I could only guess were thousands of messages. None of them from Zarah.

It was looking like Erin had lied. Again. And I'd just let her leave. Even packed for her. Not the best decision I'd ever made. I was tempted to send her a text along the "Hey, big head" variety but hit Starr up instead. It took her a full hour to respond. I spent the entire wait staring at *my* phone. Erin hadn't arrived. They hadn't spoken at all.

I caved and texted Erin. She left me on read.

*Shitnuts.*

I told myself I didn't need her, especially now that I had Desiree's phone. The answer to what got her killed was in here, whether through Zor-El, the video, or something else completely. I just had to find it.

For the first time in almost a week, I thought about her old dealer. Alfie was still in her contacts, but the call log showed no recent action. And when I clicked on their messages, the last one was years ago. Guess Erin hadn't lied about that. I didn't find Alfie's replacement either. At least not one naive enough to mention drugs in their texts.

So I went through all her contacts again, looking for anything that could help me figure out what had happened, this time checking all the messages, those deemed important enough to be added to the contact list and those not. I checked Erin's texts, but if they'd done anything illegal, they were too smart to put it in writing. It was all funny emojis and On my ways. The texts from Naut were filled with I'm sorrys and I love yous and Please pick ups, all in the gray bubbles. I was falling down the rabbit hole of Desiree's life. There were no threats and there were no videos. I didn't even find anyone who could be Zor-El.

The only thing I learned from Desiree's call log was that Apple kept only the last hundred calls. She had a good number post-death—either telemarketers or nosy friends. Of course, my name popped up. I took a moment to realize what that meant. I was still in her phone simply as "Sis." She hadn't deleted my contact info.

I'd called eighteen times the day after she died.

I kept scrolling back. She'd also had a good number of calls on her birthday. If she'd spoken to Zor-El, it was lost in the sea of well-wishes. I started clicking on each name or number to check incoming and outgoing calls, even dialed a few that had more than one exchange. I only reached answering machines for clothing shops, Starbucks, and the like.

I moved on to her camera roll, figuring maybe she'd saved the video Sherry had heard her mention. I was hit with pure chaos. I'd expected the selfies and the group shots that fed her Instagram account. But Instagram didn't have the hodgepodge of funny memes and inspirational quotes, the random screenshots of who knew what, the snaps of bags and shoes she no doubt intended to one day purchase or finagle her way to being gifted. If Gram had been an organized hoarder, her granddaughter had been a virtual one.

She hadn't deleted a single thing. I scrolled back two years to the night of the accident, but there were no videos. Just selfies. It felt strange to see her like this. The photos that hadn't made it to Instagram, the real look at her life. I was drawn to the ones that weren't picture-perfect. Spent too much time on one taken in front of a mirror shaped like a large puzzle piece. She'd smiled, but I could tell she'd been crying.

It wasn't her eyes. They were fine, Desiree having no doubt realized that as long as you don't rub them too hard, your eyes won't get red. No, it was the nose. When we both cried, our noses got red. I'd looked it up once. It was because of the extra blood rushing to your face. In my high school graduation pictures, my nose was redder than a *Game of Thrones* wedding. And even with the Fenty trying its best, I could see her slight tint peeking out. But she was still beautiful.

I stared at her for a good ten minutes, then I did what I'd been avoiding for hours now.

I searched her contacts for my own name.

I popped up.

I clicked. Stared at the messages for longer than I wanted to admit. Even though I'd blocked her, I'd spent the last two years hoping she would reach out. That she'd attempted to send an apology I never saw. Passed on a funny emoji months later as a peace offering. Reached out occasionally with a "Hi" to see if I was still being stubborn as hell and still had her blocked.

But there was nothing. The last message from me was the night of her accident. Asking if she was okay. There was still a blue dot next to it. She hadn't even opened it.

I locked the phone and went to bed.

## INSTAGRAM LIVE MARCH 1, 2017,
### 1:37 p.m. Eastern @RichiiiiieRich

Richard Santos's camera trails his best friend, Carl Softley, through a crowded, nice restaurant. Carl glances back at the screen. Nervous.

"Go." Richard's voice is encouraging.

Carl continues on, weaving through tables until he hesitates again.

A few feet away, Desiree Pierce and Zarah Turner sit by a window. It's just the two of them. Their conversation looks intense, but the restaurant is loud enough that the camera doesn't pick up what they're saying.

Carl glances back again, his eyes going wide as Richard calls out, "My friend loves you."

Both Zarah and Desiree pause and turn in their direction. Zarah immediately smiles as Desiree downs the rest of the yellow-colored drink in her martini glass. Carl turns his back to us again so we can't see his expression.

Zarah smiles at him. Instantly sweet. "Thank you. You want to take a pic?"

But it's Richard who speaks up again. "Oh. I meant *her*. I mean he loves you too, of course. But he *loves* Desiree."

Zarah's smile dims but still manages to stay on as Desiree now turns to Carl. "That's super sweet. Thank you. *Do* you want a pic?" She glances at Zarah. "All four of us."

"It's fine," Zarah says, but it's clearly not. "I'll just order you another drink."

"I'm okay for now."

"No. You need another drink."

Desiree stands while Zarah motions to the waitress. Carl shyly walks toward her.

# TWENTY-THREE

I finally caught a glimpse of her. She'd taken off as soon as she saw me, going full hundred-meter-dash despite wearing four-inch stilettos and the slinky black slip dress that was the last thing she'd worn. She weaved around and around the playground. She was giggling. I was quiet. Determined. But she stayed out of reach. And just when I was about to catch her, I woke up in a sweat to the sun shining through the window. I'd forgotten to close the curtains.

I was confused at first. My bedroom window didn't face east. Then I grabbed my phone and realized it wasn't morning at all. It was almost 4 p.m. I'd slept all day. Something I'd never done before in my life. That was Desiree's domain.

A text from Kat had showed up on my notifications, but I ignored it—too busy looking at the date. It said Tuesday. Exactly one week since Desiree's last day alive.

I did a search for her name on my cell. I was surprised at what I found. Practically nothing. Even the *Daily News* had run only a short paragraph mentioning that they had found her car and that the police didn't think it was involved in her death.

I should've been happy Desiree was no longer front-page news but instead it scared me. The news cycle had moved on, which meant the rest of the world would too. What if her killer was never found? I'd seen enough true-crime shows to know that the longer an investigation took, the less likely the murderer would ever be found. And though I'd learned more about Desiree than I ever wanted to know, I was still no closer to figuring out what had happened.

*Shitnuts.*

I forced myself to push away the panic coming up my throat and instead focused on what I could do. What I could control. I remembered I needed to pick up Desiree's stuff from the police precinct.

It wasn't much, but it was *something*. I jumped out of bed, putting on my Rosie the Riveter shirt and black jeans again because they were the closest thing to me that didn't need ironing. Then I bypassed the shower to brush my teeth and throw a lightweight beanie over the fuzz showing on my braids. My jeans felt looser than they had two days ago. I reasoned it was because I'd stretched them out.

Aunt E had let herself in again. She'd left a foil-wrapped plate on my kitchen counter. As soon as I unwrapped it, I knew she felt bad for trying to make me feel bad about kicking Erin out. It was lasagna. Another of my favorites that she hated making. I covered it back up. I'd go apologize myself—after I got Desiree's things.

I kept the bikes in the hallway on the first floor, past Aunt E's door and on the way to the basement. But I ignored my Schwinn, doubting a bike would fit in the back of Desiree's Tesla. I'd have to walk it. I'd never been to the 44th Precinct before. Luckily, Google Maps informed me it'd take just seven minutes.

When I got outside, Google told me to head straight, and I followed as if I'd heard it say Simon Says. I thought about what Erin had told me as soon as I hit the pavement, still not sure if I could believe her. There was no proof of an argument between Zarah and Desiree. Desiree treated her cell like her virtual office, and this wasn't 2001. The video wouldn't be on some mysterious jump drive or backup hard drive. It'd be on that phone. And it wasn't.

I got to a dead end. A literal one. The mechanical voice told me to go right and then left.

When Erin had realized the jig was up, it'd taken her a nanosecond to shift the blame to Zarah. Erin knew what *I* wanted: to find the person responsible for Desiree's death. I just wasn't sure of her endgame. She had sounded so sure that Desiree's phone would implicate Zarah. But she had to know it wouldn't. Was she willing to throw an innocent person under the bus? Did she think I was so desperate to pin the tail on Desiree's killer I'd rush to the police station?

I didn't realize I'd screwed up until the white van stopped fifty feet in front of me. I'd been so distracted I hadn't even noticed it passing by.

Suddenly I had no idea where I was. The street was deserted, just one oversize beige brick building to my right. The other side was lined with a fence protecting an abandoned lot. The only cars were on the cross street. It felt like they were miles away.

I instinctively reached for my pepper spray in my back pocket, then realized I'd left it at home along with my common sense. I knew better than to go down a street not teeming with people.

I envisioned the worst-case scenario. A man jumping out of the van. Dragging me kicking and screaming while his co-conspirator waited to drive off. The vision stopped there but only because it was always where the TV shows and movies cut to black. I braced myself, ready. But what happened next felt much, much worse.

Nothing.

The van just idled, the car engine a gentle hum. No one got out.

I stopped, not sure what to do. The police station wasn't within yelling distance, but it was close. Just not close enough. I could keep going, hoping I could run past the van to the precinct a mere tenth of a mile away. Or I could turn, go back the way I'd foolishly come. It was farther, but at least they'd have to give chase.

The van was white. New York plates. I stared at the Ford logo on the back as I made my decision. I'd go back. Make them work for it. But first, I'd take a pic. My hands shook as I struggled to open the camera app.

"Hey!"

Startled, I dropped my cell. The voice was male and didn't indicate friend or foe. I needed to call 911. I bent down to pick up my phone.

"Where you think you're going, girl?"

There was an accent, but I couldn't tell from where. A shadow joined the voice. It got bigger and bigger as I finally grabbed my cell, my mind no longer on calling for help and instead on just getting the hell out of there. I instinctively headed into the street, my feet moving at what would be 6.7 on a treadmill. It was what I did whenever I had to walk alone at night. The open road safer than any sidewalk. It was easier to see car headlights than people lurking in shadows.

I was almost midway onto the black pavement when the voice spoke again. "Lena! Aren't you heading to the precinct? You're going the wrong way."

Stuart.

I stopped. Fifty feet ahead, the van still lingered, but I felt better. Safer. I tore my eyes away to look at Stuart, smiling at me. My fear must've shown because he stopped a few feet away. "I scared you. It was my horrible fake accent, wasn't it?"

I shook my head but couldn't get words out. Not yet. Noticing, he got serious. "No, I did. Crap. I'm sorry. I keep screwing up. Didn't think of the optics. I was just so happy to see you. But you're alone. And I ran up on you."

"No, it wasn't you," I lied as I nodded in the direction of the van that still hadn't moved.

Stuart glanced at it before turning back to me. "Oh, the kidnap van." He gently took my shoulder, led me back toward the sidewalk. His hand felt warm, safe. "I can see why that would freak you out. There's probably some guy in there wanting you to put the lotion in the basket."

I just stared at him. He shook his head, mock disappointment on his face. "Don't tell me you've never seen *Silence of the Lambs*."

We walked past the van. Inside was a white guy, shaggy blond hair covering half the phone next to his ear. He spoke animatedly, so involved in his conversation he didn't even look in our direction. He had to be lost. My gram used to say lost white people were like sharks. Just as afraid of us as we were of them.

I felt silly. I turned to Stuart. "I have never seen *Silence of the Lambs*."

"We need to rectify that. Immediately."

"*We?*" I said, just to clarify he was implying what I thought.

"*We.* Believe the Webster's Dictionary definition would be you and me. We. Watching the movie. While eating food."

I still needed clarification. "Food you cooked?"

"That depends. You prefer your food to be edible?"

So he *was* flirting. My first inclination was to do what I always did. Change the subject. But he was nice and he was smart and he was definitely cute. There was no way I could even think about wasting time watching some movie about lotion until I knew exactly what had happened to Desiree. But maybe down the road. I liked that he already knew I'd had a sister.

I finally responded. "Sometimes. I eat eggplant, and that's barely edible."

"Great. I'll make eggplant. Pair it with some brussels sprouts."

"And bologna."

"I actually like bologna."

"What have you been up to?" I finally changed the subject, thought about there not being an article in today's paper.

"I actually got some good news that's been keeping me busy."

I didn't say anything more because we'd gotten to the end of the block, and the 44th Precinct was to our right, a massive two-story square covered in dirty red brick. Raised subway tracks served as a backdrop while a collection of white NYPD vans created their own parking spaces on the sidewalk. The ground sloped down so we had to lean back slightly as we made our way to the door.

Stuart noticed me eyeing it as we stopped at the entrance. "First time here?"

"And hopefully last," I said. "I have to pick up Desiree's stuff."

He nodded as if he understood what that meant, then was kind enough to try to keep things light. "Inside's not what you might expect. Nowhere near as fancy as some station you'd see on TV."

I nodded, though I had no expectations for the décor. Just like I had no expectations that anyone inside would help me. Especially not Green or Zizza. I turned to Stuart. Considered telling him what I'd discovered.

He smiled. "You know, I really would like to take you to dinner."

If I told him everything I'd learned, he'd help me make sense of it all. He'd just have to promise not to publish anything. At least until we figured it all out. "To celebrate your good news?" I said.

"A publisher wants me to write a book."

That tore me out of my own thoughts. I smiled, genuinely happy for him. "Dream unlocked. Amazing news."

"I'd like to think so. They want me to write about Desiree."

I don't know why that shocked me so much, but it did. "Like a true-crime book?" Suddenly I felt hopeful. "You think something happened to her when she died?"

But he just shook his head. "More like a biography."

I took my time responding, just scratched my wrist. He didn't rush to fill the empty space. "*What* about her life? I know they're not going to pay you just to focus on her hopes and dreams. Does Mel know?"

He stepped back. "I can practically see the smoke about to come out of your ears, but it doesn't have to be like that. People want to know about your sister, your family—especially now. And if I say no, they'll get someone else. Talk to me. Help me share the real Desiree. The sister who got your favorite singer to write you a love note back."

I reached for the door. "No."

He didn't follow me inside.

* * *

An hour later and I was sitting in Desiree's car, her belongings in a clear plastic garbage bag on the passenger seat. Neither Green nor Zizza had come out to see me, and I hadn't asked about them either. Hadn't even attempted any small talk with the nameless badge who'd had me sign the paperwork and confirm everything on the list they gave me was there. Stuart had disappeared, though he'd texted yet another long-winded apology. I ignored it, knowing I needed to figure out what had happened so Desiree's legacy wasn't some hit piece disguised as a biography.

I settled back in the driver's seat and took a deep breath. The car was a four-door Tesla. I didn't know the model or year, but it had to be new and expensive. The outside was red and shiny, the inside a stark white. You'd never know the car had been stolen, then found, then parked in some police lot in the middle of the Bronx.

It was surprisingly clean—the better to take any emergency IG-destined selfies. The thought crept into my head as I adjusted the seat: What if Desiree *had* actually gone old-school? Keeping the video from the night of her accident somewhere else. What if she'd kept it on a flash drive. Kept that in her car.

Of course, a car interior could hold just as many secrets as Desiree herself. Center consoles and cup holders. Sun visors and seat-back pockets. Glove boxes and map pockets that hadn't served their intended purpose for a good ten years. Desiree's Tesla was no exception. Just in a prettier package. I went through it all. Twice. And only yielded a hair tie and a Starbucks lid.

I was bent over the gearshift porn-star style, running my right hand under her passenger seat, when I found myself staring at the plastic bag. There had been no flash drive on the list the police had given me, but I decided to check anyway. Righting myself, I took her purse out. Or attempted to. It was heavy—no doubt the sole reason Desiree had developed such toned arms. I had to take a deep breath to lug it out and set it directly on the passenger seat, shoving the plastic bag with the rest of her stuff onto the mat on the floor. Inside the purse was a mess. She would always throw things in there and then dump them all out again if she had to find something. I figured she'd have been proud when I did the same, spilling it out across the white leather seat and surveying the contents. More hair ties. Dirty tissues. Tampons. No flash drive. I even checked all three tubes of lipstick.

In a fit of desperation, I moved on to her wallet. It was small and black, with some designer symbol I didn't recognize. She'd bypassed all the provided credit card and money slots to shove everything into the small gap in the middle. It practically overflowed with receipts. The two on top broke for freedom and fell onto my lap. I picked one up. An ATM receipt dated just twelve hours before Desiree died. She'd taken out $50, leaving a remaining balance of $250,080.

I blinked at the number. Erin had said Desiree was dead broke. That they'd spent the money they'd conned from Free. And I got that rich-people broke was different from regular-people broke, but Erin had still made it seem like they had been living off credit. Mine at that.

It made no sense.

I stuffed it back into the wallet and reached for the next receipt on my lap. It was also from an ATM. This time she'd taken out $60 two days before she died. Her balance had been $130.

My sister had somehow come upon $250,000 in a day. Suddenly Erin's ridiculous suggestion Desiree had blackmailed someone didn't sound ridiculous at all.

*Shitnuts.*

I'd planned to take Desiree's things straight to Mel's apartment, but that could wait. It was time to go home. The drive was mercifully quick. I pulled into our driveway, locked the Tesla, and went inside. Aunt E's apartment was unlocked as usual. As soon as I opened her door, I understood this afternoon's peace offering. It had been a preemptive apology.

Erin was on the couch, rooted to the same spot like it was her assigned seat and talking on her cell. I frowned. Pissed. Last night I'd been mad that I'd let her just leave, but now I was mad she was still here. She smiled at me, but the look I gave her must have reminded her that her absence had not made my heart grow fonder. We still weren't cool. The smile slid off her face.

Aunt E was nowhere to be found, though I heard faint shuffling in the bathroom. I made my way to the kitchen. My eyes stayed on Erin with each step as if she would grab one of Gram's knickknacks and make a run for it.

"Well, I appreciate anything you can do to help me," Erin said.

I shouldn't have been surprised she was still here. Aunt E was nothing but a big softie. There was more lasagna on the stove. I dished up a plate and stuck it into the microwave to have an excuse to eavesdrop.

For a minute, Erin listened to whoever was on the other end of the line. "And like I said, I can have the money wired this afternoon."

She hung up just as the microwave went off. By the time I'd gotten my plate out and had turned around, she was sitting at the kitchen table. Desiree's seat at that.

"Good news!" She smiled.

I finally smiled back. "Let me guess. You're getting your car back. Question, though. Who'd you trick into paying for it?"

We stayed like that for longer than necessary, both smiling so hard I thought my jaw would collapse. I was determined not to speak first and then I wished I had.

"You know, for someone so similar to me, you're very judgmental," she said.

"I've never had my car repossessed."

"Okay."

"Or not paid a bill."

"I'll give you that one too."

"Or pretended to be someone I'm not."

"Now, I'm not so sure about that one, Lena *Scott*. From the Bronx. I bet you pat yourself on the back every night before you go to sleep for living in the 'hood.'" She used air quotes. "Ignoring that you choose to live here because it's closer to the Ivy League college you're getting your *master's degree* at. You're lying to yourself that you're not as bad as the white people in Harlem you look down on."

I stabbed at my pasta. "You don't get to talk about race. Wherever the hell I live. Jersey. The Bronx. Or Mars. I'm still Black."

She shook her head. "You're not Black, you're green. And no amount of daddy issues is going to change you from the poor little rich girl you are. You live in the house your grandma gave you. Live *off* the house your mom left you." She nodded at the fork in my hand. "You don't even feed yourself. Aunt E might as well be your personal chef. You can ignore your own privilege just like you ignore that expensive-ass bike your daddy gave you. Doesn't mean it's not there."

My smile was pinned on. "Mel doesn't pay for my school."

"Right, because he probably paid for the house that pays for school. And the house that lets you not have to pay rent."

Mel had paid off Gram's house and given my mom the house in South Orange. I couldn't deny what she said, so I did the next best thing: deflected. "Don't you need to go get your car?"

"I don't want the car back. I was on the phone with Lava Lounge."

It was the bar Desiree'd partied at the night of her DUI.

She kept on. "The woman I spoke to didn't work there two years ago and didn't know who did. But she promised to ask around. Maybe we could talk to them. See if they remember Zarah leaving that night with Desiree."

It was actually a good idea. But still. "They're gonna be pissed when you don't give them that reward."

She looked away before I could see whether that one had hurt. If it didn't, the next one would. "I have good news too. I unlocked Desiree's phone."

She couldn't help it. She turned back, excited. "And?"

I finally took a bite. Took my time chewing, then swallowed. "And nothing. Literally. They were friendly. Happy to be back in each other's lives. Their last texts were a few weeks ago about Zarah's makeup line. Hadn't texted since."

There was no way I was telling her about the deposit or the MIA video.

"You went back to the night of her accident?" she said.

I nodded. "Just some drunk selfies, no videos. I even checked their DMs. There was nothing."

Erin jumped up. She got only two feet before I caught up, grabbing her nearest wrist. "Now you want to leave," I said.

"I'm just grabbing my phone."

Pulling her hand away, she continued into the living room, me following so close I would've slammed into her if she'd stopped short. She grabbed her phone from the couch just as we heard Aunt E's voice from the hall. "You two getting along?"

Erin's smile looked genuine. "Trying to." She turned to me. "Let's go to my room."

It wasn't her room. It never would be. I smiled at Aunt E as we passed, and she lightly grazed my arm. I stopped while Erin kept on. Aunt E waited until Erin had disappeared into the spare bedroom before she spoke. "Friends close. Enemies closer."

I nodded, relieved, then finally followed Erin. She hadn't bothered to make the bed. I stepped over both throw pillows and sat next to her. My eyes immediately went to the chip on the wood nightstand, left when I'd pushed Desiree during an unsanctioned game of indoor hide-and-seek. We'd both ended up hiding as soon as we heard Gram stomping down the hall.

Erin tapped a few times and handed me her phone. It was open to Instagram, an account I hadn't seen before, though I did recognize the person in the endless stream of silly selfies. "Zarah's finsta," she said.

"I know." At least in theory.

People created "fake Instagram" accounts to unironically show a more real side, a counterpoint to the pitch-perfect public persona they presented on their main account. Finstas were normally private and reserved for close friends. They were for the photos you couldn't share with your millions of followers, your parents, or your boss. Photos you didn't have to spend way too long Facetuning. Those photos were for other people. These were for you. It was a favorite of celebrities and teenagers alike.

"So you checked the DMs to this account too?" Erin said.

I hadn't, though I should've realized Zarah would have one. I'd heard of them but never actually seen one. Desiree had never had one, once telling me she didn't feel the need. It didn't count if it couldn't be liked by at least ten thousand people.

I didn't say anything, which was all the answer Erin needed.

"They weren't texting each other because they'd moved to DMs," Erin said. "Humor me. If I'm wrong, you can enjoy yourself by saying 'I told you so.'"

I stood. "Fine."

We moved in sync, traveling back past Aunt E as she watched *Judge Judy,* heading out of her apartment and up the stairs to mine. Desiree's phone was where I'd left it on my nightstand. Erin took my room in as I turned my back to her to put in the passcode and open the app. "What's the screen name again?"

She told me. I pulled it up, clicking on messages.

"You telling me so or not?" Erin said.

When I didn't respond, she moved to peer over my shoulder. We stared at the last DM. Desiree'd sent it to Zarah at 2:07 a.m. the night she died.

All it had was a video icon.

# TWENTY-FOUR

I pushed the icon. Nothing happened. I pushed again.

"It's gone," Erin said.

"That's impossible." I hit it again but still got nothing.

"No, that's Instagram. It doesn't keep a record of what you send someone."

I spent a lot of time on Instagram but with the sole purpose of keeping tabs on people I didn't want to talk to. I'd never sent—or received—a DM. "Why would they do that?"

"Blame Snapchat." She looked at me. "What's wrong?"

I let my hand drop. "I think there's a video from the night of Desiree's DUI."

Sherry had said so. Erin nodded. I waited, expecting her to get on me for holding out because that's sure as hell what I'd do. Instead, she stuck out her hand. "May I?"

I hesitated, then handed it over. Erin long pressed the video icon. A menu popped up, offering Reply, Details, and Unsend. She selected Details, opening yet another menu. It had the time when the video had been opened—a few minutes after it was sent.

"Damn. Zarah opened it twice," Erin said. "That's the max before it disappears forever. Makes me think the video isn't on Desiree's phone, though, because any videos you upload from your camera roll don't disappear. So it was something recorded elsewhere—probably from someone else's phone or a laptop or something."

It was like *CSI: Instagram,* except I clearly wasn't going to figure this out in sixty minutes. I sat on my bed. Something else wasn't adding up. "Did Desiree tell you about any large deposits to her bank account?"

She looked up. "No. How large?"

"Quarter of a million. She had an ATM receipt in her wallet."

"I told you. We need to talk to Zarah."

I thought of Zarah and Desiree, but not the perfectly made-up, Photoshopped, and filtered women the world knew. Instead, I remembered the first time I saw them together at Gram's house. I'd come over to find Desiree and Zarah on the couch, staring at Desiree's phone, giggling over some boy, finishing each other's sentences. Unlike with Erin, I hadn't felt jealous when I saw them. I'd felt like I was getting two sisters instead of one.

"Wouldn't the money mean Zarah paid her?" I said, hopeful.

But Erin wouldn't let up. "Weren't you supposed to meet up with her?"

"I did."

"And?"

"We didn't talk much because her doctor gave her something strong. She's been depressed since Desiree died."

"Or avoiding you."

Was she? Could Zarah have killed Desiree over a DUI? If Zarah'd paid Desiree's blackmail, had that left no reason for anything more extreme to happen? And yet Desiree had sent the video after she'd gotten the deposit. Hours before she'd met someone here in the Bronx and died. None of it made sense, and as much as I hated to admit it, Erin was right. The only person who could explain it all was Zarah.

I sent Zarah a quick text. Meet tonight?

I waited for the telltale bubbles to pop up, knowing they represented more than someone composing a text. They would be proof Zarah wasn't as involved in this as Erin was alleging.

While I'd been working my cell, Erin was doing the same. Desiree's phone sat between us. "I DMed Zarah's finsta," Erin said. "She read it. No response."

She showed me. The message was just a quick How you holding up? The word "Seen" appeared under it. I still had Zarah pulled up, so I tapped her name and hit AUDIO. I wasn't expecting her to answer, just to let it ring before going to voice mail. But she didn't even give me that courtesy. It barely rang once before the automated message kicked in. She'd hit IGNORE.

By the time I heard the beep, I was pissed. I hung up. While I was brooding, Erin was searching Desiree's phone again. I snatched it from her. Protective. "What are you doing?"

"We need proof before we talk to her. Hopefully someone from the bar will remember something but maybe not. There has to be something here."

"I checked," I said but still opened Desiree's camera roll. Last night the goal had been proving Erin wrong. Now I wanted to prove her right.

But there wasn't anything. Not in the finsta messages. Not on the camera roll. Not in their iMessages. The last messages were the same. The makeup and link to the Omni website.

"Click on it," Erin said.

"It's just a link to where the party was." iPhones show a preview. The address was right there.

She tapped it herself. I wanted to break her finger. Sure enough, the Omni webpage popped up. Staring Erin down, I X'd out. She looked away. Point proven, I was about to close Safari when I noticed the GoFundMe site. Safari keeps track of pages you visited, displaying each open in a new tab. Desiree had been looking at a post for help with funeral expenses for someone named Kevin House.

There was an old blurry photo. A Black guy with his arm around a little girl who looked just like him. They'd raised $25,845 of their $12,000 goal. Just below the DONATE NOW button was the creation date: June 15, 2017.

"That's the month after Desiree's DUI," I said, pulling it up to full screen. There weren't any details about how he'd died, just the donations. One hundred bucks from a Nadine Jenkinson. Twenty-five from a Dillon Rookers. A whopping fifteen thousand dollars from Anonymous.

"You recognize the name?" Erin said.

"No." Desiree'd never mentioned a Kevin House. But it could have been an old teacher. A friend's dad. Even just the wrong link.

So I searched online for "Kevin House" and "death."

The *Daily News* popped up, the story ironically written by Stuart. HOMELESS MAN FOUND DEAD IN HIT-AND-RUN.

Things clicked into place.

Desiree's car hadn't just hit a pole that night.

If someone else really had been driving, here was a very good reason to keep her quiet.

* * *

My wrist throbbed the entire forty-five-minute subway ride to Zarah's place in Tribeca. So much so, my body began to normalize the feeling. Go numb.

No one answered when we rang the buzzer. Zarah was hiding or not home. We camped out on the stoop of the closed art gallery next door, Erin calmly sipping coffee she'd picked up down the block. I hadn't gone with her, rooted to my spot, not even able to blink.

Kevin House had indeed died the night of Desiree's accident less than ten blocks from where her car hit that stoplight. Sometime in the early morning of Saturday, May 20. No one had seen—or heard—what happened. Someone had come across his body while walking their dog at dawn. None of the papers had given Kevin's passing more than a couple of sentences. Police had no suspects. There were no follow-ups.

The few details I did learn came from Kevin House's GoFundMe page. He'd been a father, though the phrasing—or lack thereof—made me think not a good one. There were no positive adjectives—"beloved," "adored," "cherished." Just facts. Their father had died and they needed money for a proper burial. Thanks to the fifteen-thousand-dollar anonymous donation, they'd reached their goal.

The lack of pomp didn't change that Kevin House had been killed, and there was a good chance my sister's car had done it. Any physical damage to the car was blamed on the stoplight.

Desiree had witnessed a murder. I just wasn't sure what had happened next. Had the deposit not been blackmail but hush money? And if they'd paid Desiree off, why take her life? As Erin loved to point out, Zarah was the only person we knew who was there that night. I still wasn't sure that automatically made her the driver. But it did make me more anxious than ever to talk to her. Neither Erin nor I spoke while we waited. Erin busying herself with her coffee and phone. Me watching the people who occasionally walked by, hoping and not hoping that one would be Zarah. It was after 10 p.m., but no one glanced in our direction. This wasn't Pennsylvania. People minded their business in New York.

At 10:18, my phone buzzed for the first time in hours.

Stuart.

I deleted the notification, but Erin saw it anyway.

"Is that the reporter? Thought he was back in your good graces."

I ignored that.

She didn't let my bad manners deter her. "How'd he screw things up this time?"

"I don't want to talk about it."

"No prob. I'm just glad you hate someone more than me. Maybe we could start a club. Him and me and—"

"I said I don't want to talk about it."

"Hopefully you didn't let *his* car get repo'd too."

"That's not funny," I said. Then, "He's writing a book about her. It's going to be a hit piece—sex, drugs, rap music. And that's if he just includes what people already know. He wants my help." I mimicked his deep voice. "Someone's going to write it, at least it's me."

I finally shut up, and she did nothing to fill the silence. Obviously thinking about what this meant—for her. Then she spoke. "Can Mel talk to the publisher? Get it killed?"

"Would he?"

"Maybe. He's probably still pissed about the article. He now knows he can't control what Stuart writes. You should talk to him."

I was about to tell her that wasn't happening when an Escalade pulled up. Zarah didn't wait for the driver to open the door. When she got out of the back seat, she was alone. She looked fine. Great even. Nothing like the shell I'd seen last time.

I jumped up. But Erin was faster. "Hey, chickee." Erin's voice was friendly.

Zarah paused long enough to take us in as we did the same. Up close was a completely different story, like a photo with the filter removed. The two layers of perfectly applied makeup probably not from her drugstore-bound line could not hide how exhausted she looked. Like she'd been on for so long she needed a citywide power outage.

"Hey," Zarah said. "Wasn't expecting you two."

"We were in the area," Erin said. "Stopped by Château. You know Desiree loved that store. Was hoping to get something for the funeral. Lena and I were just chatting about how hard you were taking things. We wanted to make sure you were okay. Can we come up?"

Zarah paused ever so slightly, then nodded. "Sure, but only for a few minutes."

We followed her inside, Erin and Zarah mindlessly chatting as we weaved through the hall and into the elevator. I had yet to say a word. Zarah had yet to notice.

She opened her front door, throwing her keys on the side table as we followed her in. "Have a seat." She motioned to the kitchen counter with the pair of tall plastic chairs that looked as uncomfortable as I felt.

I sat, placing my cell on the counter. Erin took the seat to my right, and we watched Zarah fuss around her kitchen, grabbing enough stuff to make a salad. "How is everything going with the funeral? I know it's not for a few weeks."

Zarah looked at me, but Erin answered. "As good as can be expected. It's invitation only so we're getting the guest list together. Do you know Kevin House?"

Zarah paused, but more like she was trying to remember who he was. "No. But I can ask around. They go to school together?"

I just shook my head as Erin hopped back in. "Yes…" She trailed off when she saw me. "Kinda. Her professor."

Zarah was too smart not to notice the discrepancy. "What's going on?"

Erin was about to open her mouth. I didn't let her. "Desiree DMed you a video right before she died. We know you saw it."

"Twice," Erin said.

"Okay…" Zarah said but didn't stop moving.

"What happened the night of her DUI?" I needed to know.

And that's what finally stopped her. She put the bowl she was holding down and gripped her counter so hard blood rushed to her perfectly manicured thumb. "It was my fault."

Erin threw me a look. *I told you so.*

This was it.

Zarah had done it.

Unlike with Erin, my first inclination wasn't to fight. Instead, I sat stock-still, my pounding heart the only thing moving. My brain willed my body to just get up and get out of there. It was the only thought my mind could form.

Yet I couldn't go. Not until I heard her say the words. Admit what she'd done.

"We were supposed to go together, but I was running late, so she went without me even though I told her to wait," Zarah said. "I didn't know why. It was just some lip-kit launch. When I got there, we were both mad at each other. I was ready to ignore her, pretend to have a good time. The place had two floors, and she spent most of the time upstairs, so I barely saw her. Guess the bartender was cute or something. He thought she was too. He was making her drinks strong. By the time she stumbled downstairs, she was even drunker than normal. Still mad, though. She didn't even say bye. I didn't know she'd left until Kara got me. Said Desiree was causing a scene outside like we were still taping the show. So I went out. She was a mess. Crying. Blubbering. And I just wanted her to leave. But she didn't. So I went back inside. Even though I knew she was so upset." She stopped talking.

"But you came back and…" I trailed off.

Zarah shook her head. "No, of course not. I let her stay out there, make a scene."

"So how was her accident your fault?" Erin sounded annoyed. I was just confused.

"Because I let her leave." Zarah would look only at me. "She was gone when I finally went back outside, like, an hour later. Like I said. My fault. Lena, I'm so sorry."

Maybe she was, but I could tell she wanted me to absolve her. My sister was dead, and here was Zarah, wanting us to comfort her for being a shitty friend. And though I understood, I didn't have it in me.

"And the video?" Erin said. I'd forgotten she was there. "Why would she DM you a video right before she died? A video you didn't say anything about."

"I did." Zarah looked at me. "I let the cops see it. They just said it showed she was clearly intoxicated. Desiree was a mess. Ranting and raving. I'm sure she only sent it to me because she and Erin were fighting that night. She needed someone to complain to. Said it wasn't my fault. It was *his* fault. He was supposed to take care of her. That she'd protected him. And he'd lied to her. I knew things were bad between them but not that bad."

"Who?" I said.

Zarah looked at me as if I already knew. "Mr. Pierce."

"Mel?" I didn't get what Zarah meant. "Because he cut her off?"

Zarah shook her head. "Because she saw him the night of her accident."

Mel in New York? No. He and Veronika had been in Maryland for his alma mater's graduation. He never missed it. "You must've heard her wrong," I said.

"No." She sounded confident. "That was why she was so upset. She wanted me to know she blamed him."

I stood up. "I have to go."

# TWENTY-FIVE

Gram and Aunt E had dropped Mel off at Morgan State less than a month after he graduated high school—eager to get him out of the Bronx. He was the first to go to college, but he didn't graduate. He stayed just long enough to pledge Omega Psi Phi and collect enough scholarship money to start his label with Free. Aunt E said Gram hadn't spoken to him for two straight weeks when he'd come back sans degree after junior year. Morgan offered him an honorary doctorate years later, but Gram was not impressed. It was why she'd been so overjoyed when I graduated from Penn—getting there early enough to nab a good seat. Mel hadn't come to that graduation either.

Despite the aborted education, Mel still considered himself a Morgan man—going back to Baltimore twice a year for Homecoming and graduation, often bringing along artists to perform at both events. They weren't nearly as upset about his dropout status as Gram was.

He hadn't missed a trip in twenty-five-plus years, which was why I was so confused how he could be in two places at once—seeing Desiree in New York and holding court in Maryland.

Zarah was as happy to show us out as we were to leave. Erin asked a few more questions, but Zarah didn't know anything else. Like why Mel had been in town. Or where Desiree had seen him.

When we got outside, it felt like the temperature had gone up at least 50 degrees.

"You believe her?" Erin said as I requested an Uber.

"I believe she believes herself. That Desiree saw Mel. But Desiree was so drunk that night. Maybe she was confused."

"Or maybe he really was there. You should ask him." When I didn't respond right away, she spoke again. "You gonna be okay?"

"Yep. Gonna go home. Take some melatonin. Figure crap out tomorrow."

I did just that. Went straight to Highbridge. Erin didn't come with me, and I didn't bother to ask where she was going to stay.

I hadn't made my bed, so it didn't take long to get back in, ignoring the clothes still piled high on the left side. The melatonin didn't help, though, even when I doubled the dose. So I got out my laptop.

I started with *The Baltimore Sun*. Their archives page had gone with form over function, a simple gray-and-blue interface highlighting screenshots of actual newspapers from years past. I started my search too broad—just Mel's full name. Over two thousand hits. So I narrowed it down. "Mel Pierce Morgan State Graduation 2017." Much better results, ones they made you pay to see. They wanted $7.95 a month for full access. Luckily, they also offered a free seven-day subscription. I started my free trial and found myself staring at a front-page photo of Mel, wearing a blue suit and orange tie and smiling next to the college's president. The paper had done an entire two-page graduation spread. Mel was in almost every photo.

I checked the date just to be sure: Saturday. Hours after Desiree's accident. Then I checked the time Morgan had held their ceremony. The processional had started at 9:30 a.m.—less than an hour after she and I had gotten into our final fight.

I leaned back on my headboard, desperately needing to process it all. He shouldn't have been there, and I didn't mean the night before. Mel shouldn't have been at Morgan that morning—not with his daughter laid up in a hospital. And yet there he was. Business as usual.

It was cold-blooded, but it was also an alibi—one he would need if he'd done the unthinkable. Did he meet up with her after she saw him that night? Take her keys to get her to calm down? Hit Kevin House while she was passed out in the passenger seat? And then abandon her at the scene of the second accident, when the car hit the pole, minutes later? Would he let his own daughter take the blame? And did he do much worse when she finally figured it out?

No.

It felt like too much of a leap.

Even if he was in town, it would've just been the impetus for her acting so irrationally. Maybe it made her run off with some random man she'd let drive her car.

I don't remember finally falling asleep, but when I did, Desiree was there for another round of hide-and-seek. I found her easily, but it didn't matter. I still couldn't tag her. We ran in circles. Round and round and round. And just when I was about to catch her, Mel stepped between us.

* * *

I woke up to my phone buzzing quick jolts like the world's weakest earthquake. It'd stop, then start again a few minutes later. The only reason I didn't throw it across the room was because it was already over there, sitting on my dresser. I finally got out of bed just to make it stop.

Erin.

"Morning," she said when I picked up. At least she didn't say it was good. "Just wanted to check in. Make sure you slept okay."

"I'm fine."

"Good. Because we still have to figure out what the hell was going on, especially if you don't want to talk to Mel…" She trailed off, hoping I'd correct her. Just hearing his name made my wrist itch. When I didn't say anything, she kept going. "I was thinking you should talk to Naut again.

He'd be the one person other than me who she'd talk to about this. He could confirm if Freck saw Mel that night."

I rubbed my forehead like it would help clear the cobwebs. Erin was right. Desiree had met Naut months after her accident, but I'm sure it came up. "Why don't you talk to him yourself?" I said.

"He's not my biggest fan."

She knew I wasn't either, but she hadn't let that stop her from talking to me. "I'll text him," I said. "See if I can stop by his apartment."

"Great. Let me know as soon as you leave."

With that she hung up. Erin was bossy as hell, but she was also right. And although I still didn't completely trust her, I appreciated she'd done what she'd said. Stuck around. It was like she still had her evil powers, but now she was using them for good. It made me believe at least a little bit that we both did still have the same goal: to find out what had happened to Desiree.

I texted Naut I was in the neighborhood, though I was still in my apartment. Asked if I could stop by. By the time I got out of the shower, he'd responded he was home.

I got my bike.

*　*　*

Getting upstairs to Naut's apartment wasn't a problem this time. I didn't even have to bring up a package. The only thing that greeted me on his floor was music. I followed it like the Pied Piper to his door, then knocked. No one answered, but I doubted he could hear me.

So I sent a text. Here.

The door opened a few seconds later, but it wasn't Naut. Just a white guy with his same slight build and height. He smiled at me.

"You're not Naut." I raised my voice to be heard over the beat.

"You're not the first person to be disappointed." We shook. His fingers were as long and delicate as a piano player's. "I'm Trevor. His assistant.

We're supposed to be getting the playlist together for his gig at the Apollo Friday night, but he's in the Zone."

I nodded like I knew what that meant, then followed him inside. "Apollo Theater? Fancy."

"He curates this monthly late-night producers' showcase. DJs between acts. It's like amateur night but with beats. You should stop by. It's free."

The music was louder in the apartment but somehow more enjoyable. The new MacBook Pro was being put to good use. Naut sat on his couch directly across from Desiree's mural, eyes closed. Guess this was the Zone. Trevor plopped next to him, head automatically nodding along. Someone else would be able to describe what I heard in detail. Throw out words like "breakbeat" and "bass lines." I just knew it sounded good.

I didn't know what to do. Sit. Dance. Go to his bar-like kitchen and raid his fridge. So I just stood there and tried to get in the Zone myself. Just as I was getting into the music, it stopped. The silence so abrupt I almost screamed. Naut's eyes popped open. Trevor dared to speak first. "That's fire, man."

Naut nodded, then looked at me. Expectant.

"Definitely fire," I said. "Your neighbors must love you."

"Especially when I get them tickets." He stood. "Want something to drink?"

"It's ten a.m.," I said.

Then I realized I was supposed to be in Strategic Management class. For once, I didn't give a shit.

"So mimosas." Naut walked to his kitchen as Trevor put on a pair of headphones. "I got the invite to the funeral."

"You going?" It felt weird to ask.

He didn't say anything until he'd gotten out his ingredients and was pouring champagne into three glasses. "Is it horrible to ask if it's open casket?"

I shook my head. I understood, too well. Desiree hadn't been old. She hadn't been sick. And even when you're not talking to someone, there's a comfort knowing they're out there somewhere. I understood if Naut still wanted to pretend the woman he loved—we all loved—wasn't in a steel box with a silver brush finish interior.

"It's not," I said. He stopped just as he was about to top me off with orange juice so I clarified. "It's not horrible to ask. We're Black. It's definitely going to be open casket."

He took a long sip. "You sleeping okay?"

"I've been taking melatonin like they're vitamins."

"I don't even bother. The dreams get me."

"I have those too. Hide-and-seek. I can never find her."

"I'm always in a bathroom washing my hands while she knocks on the door."

"You ever let her in?"

"No. Maybe tonight's the night, though."

"We'll have to keep each other updated."

He laughed. "What's going on? I know you didn't come here to analyze my dreams."

I hesitated, remembering how our last conversation had gone. "Did Desiree ever mention her DUI?"

He gave me a strange look.

"I know you think she killed herself, but she didn't," I said. "And it's not just me being in denial. Her death had something to do with her DUI. I just need to know what." When he still didn't say anything, I kept on. Sounding more desperate with each word. "I know you didn't know her then, but did it ever come up? Bedroom talk, maybe."

"It wasn't something she wanted to talk about. How do you think it's connected?"

I took in a breath. "She always insisted she wasn't driving that night. And—"

He broke in. "She told me that, but then she told E! that too. It was years ago, though." He downed his drink and prepped another, heavy on the champagne.

"I think she recently found someone who saw her car," I said. "Maybe even someone who took a video. We can't find it, though."

He caressed his glass as he stared at her mural. "Well, then she definitely didn't let me see it. I wasn't the one in her bedroom, remember?" Suddenly, he slammed his glass down with such force I was surprised it didn't shatter. "If she had told me, I could've helped her. Made sure she was okay."

He was silent for a bit. We both were. Then he calmly picked his glass back up. "Another round?"

* * *

Naut had been angry, but he'd also been right. He wasn't the one Desiree was talking with before she died. That person was in England, probably looking at naked pictures on the non-family phone.

I would have called Free as soon as I got into the Uber, but I didn't have his number. Either of them. I'd already forgotten he'd seen Desiree the day she died, that he'd mentioned she was in a rush to meet someone. I hadn't followed up at the time because I didn't know I needed to.

Aunt E had her door open when I got back, her whites piled high in a hamper serving as a doorstop. I peeked in, but she wasn't in her front room. I'd stop by after I made my call.

I grabbed Desiree's phone, sat on my couch, and said a quick prayer. *Please let me find his number.* I knew he wasn't in her contacts, but they'd definitely texted. It took me a half hour to find the exchange. I'd bypassed it before because it was one of dozens she'd replied to with three heart-eyes emojis. I'd assumed it was a standard birthday text.

I was wrong.

Here's the thing. Texts and replied-to emails are stories told in reverse. Like *Memento.* Or *How the Garcia Girls Lost Their Accents.* Or those scenes Virgil did in the *Aeneid.* And like any good story, heart-eyes emojis aside, my scroll up through Desiree and Free's ended with a single image, this one a screenshot of Desiree's Wells Fargo transactions. An expanded view of the $250,000 I'd seen in her bank balance. It was followed by a thank-you with exclamation points only outnumbered by the heart-eyes emojis and the eggplant thrown in for good measure.

I scrolled to his response, a mass of unpunctuated messages sent line by line that let me know he'd yet to master the talk-to-text function.

I was happy to give it

You know all you had to do was ask nicely ha ha

Glad I got to see you

Go enjoy your birthday

She'd responded with more red-hued emojis. Ooh a text back! I'm glad we did too. Though we woulda had a cute-ass baby. She'd ended with the three heart-eyes emojis in a row.

That answered one burning question. The $250K hadn't been a black-mail payoff or hush money. It'd been a birthday gift. She must've told him some sob story to have gotten *more* money out of him, since the baby money would have come through months before. I scrolled back up further, hoping to have missed a mention of a video and instead hit a succession of naked pictures. At least she'd been smart enough not to show her face.

I dialed the number on my cell, but he didn't pick up and hadn't bothered to set up his voice mail. The only thing that stopped me from calling back was not wanting to annoy him. Instead I texted, praying he was the type to check his Unknown Senders list.

He wasn't. Over the next six hours, I called twice with the same lack of response and left a couple more texts—caring less and less with each one about staying on his good side. The only time I stopped obsessively checking my phone was during hour two when Aunt E came upstairs to tell me lunch was ready, then it was right back to me and my iPhone in a staring contest. The texts I got were false alarms. I ignored both Omar and Erin, who asked for updates while sharing she was still looking for someone who had worked at the bar the night of the DUI. For shits and giggles, I looked up where Free had been when Desiree got her DUI. His world tour had been stopping in Toronto.

It was close to dinner when my desperation reached peak levels.

Beyond calling and letting it ring enough times to spell out "Pick up" in Morse code, I had just one other idea.

Desiree's phone.

Apparently getting a call from your dead lover's number was enough to make someone pick up.

"One sec…" His voice was calm, the quick answer the only indication he might've been freaked. It also wasn't the sole voice I heard. There was damn near a cacophony in the background, a buzz of people all speaking over each other. I was trying to make out where he could be when the voices abruptly disappeared. When Free spoke again, his was the only one I heard. "Who is this?"

"Lena."

He audibly exhaled.

"Been trying to reach you all day. Finally realized this was the only way I could get you to pick up."

"That's 'cause this one's mainly for pictures."

"I know." Even though I didn't want to. "When we met up, you mentioned you only saw Desiree for a few minutes on her birthday."

"Yeah. She left to meet someone."

Maybe she'd gone to see Zor-El. Maybe she'd gone to see…someone else. "She say who?"

"Nope. Didn't matter to me. Just know she had to pick something up. Figured it was a gift."

Or a video. "She didn't say where either?"

"No."

"I'll let you get back to…" I trailed off. It could be anything from the studio to an orgy. "Let me know if you think of anything. I texted you from my own number."

There was a long pause and then, "You okay?" Said like he meant it.

Of course I wasn't. There was a whole laundry list of things I could share, but I stuck with the one directly related to him. "Mel knows I came to see you. Don't know how he found out."

What's the saying? The enemy of my enemy is my friend.

"I told him," Free said.

Or in this case a snitch. Ironic, considering his profession. The popular narrative was Free and Mel hadn't spoken in years, that they hated each other so much the Grammys once beefed up security. But I guess them not talking—like so many things related to hip-hop—was BS.

"You two chat often?" I said when I was finally ready.

"Only when it's important."

"Snitching on me was important?"

"*You* were important, Melina. I called him because I was worried."

If this was some scripted '90s sitcom, this would be where teenaged me said, "I already have a father."

Grown me just wanted to hang up. Instead, I put the phone on speaker and dropped it on the counter. "I'm twenty-eight. Older than both you and Mel when you started Free Money. I'm not a kid."

"But you're his kid. Doesn't matter how old you are."

I guess because Free spoke to my family more than I did he felt he could explain it all away. "Oh, right," I said. "Mel needs a Father of the Year plaque next to the platinum records. You're acting like he's some sitcom dad when he wasn't even speaking to the one child he actually cared about."

"It's hard to be a father when you didn't have one yourself. It doesn't come with a manual. And as much as Mel wants to act otherwise, he's just human."

I rolled my eyes before I remembered he couldn't see my disgust.

"He was there when he needed to be," Free said. "How he needed to be."

I flashed on what Zarah had told me. Thought about Kevin House, who'd also had a daughter. "Like the night of Desiree's accident?"

"Desiree and I never spoke about that."

He wasn't getting off the hook. "And you and Mel?"

He paused just long enough to make me think maybe Zarah was right. I waited him out, staring at the clock on my microwave. It'd just flicked to forty after when he spoke again. "When's the last time you saw Mel cry?"

My wrist throbbed. "It wasn't the night of Desiree's accident. I can tell you that."

He kept on like he was defending a thesis. "At Ma Pierce's funeral?"

Free said it like he already knew the answer. Mel hadn't cried. Not at Gram's or my mom's, for that matter. The closest I'd seen were the red-rimmed eyes in his office.

"Just tell me what he said about the night of her accident," I said.

But he was still acting like he didn't hear me, used to talking over people without anyone pointing out just how damn rude it was. "'Tear It Up' was the hardest song I ever wrote." Free's subject change was abrupt. "I must've wrote twenty-five verses at least. None were good enough. I'd write. Crumple it up. Throw it on the ground. By, like, four a.m. you couldn't even walk in the studio without stepping on something. I'm in there alone; my boys had gone to sleep. The engineer is on break. Your dad is nowhere to be found. It's dead quiet. And I hear this noise."

I leaned against the counter. I wasn't one of the millions of people who would kill to hear this story.

"A wail, like a cat in heat," Free said. "I get up. Follow it down the hall. Closer I get to the bathroom, the louder it gets. I'm about to open the door when I realize it's your dad. Crying. Your mom'd found out about Veronika. She hadn't let him see you since."

I flashed on a memory of my own. Me young enough to sit on Mel's lap, too busy enjoying the cadence of Biggie's voice to even try to pay attention to the grown-up talk between my parents. Comfortable. Happy. Secure. Until my mom yanked me out of Mel's arms. She must've just found out her boyfriend was screwing her best friend. I remember I cried, reached back to where I had just been. Because I wanted my daddy.

There weren't any more memories of Mel at our house after that.

"My mother wasn't a bad person," I finally said.

"Your dad isn't either, Melina. He loves you. He may have loved you from a distance, but *you* were his first love. Not your mother. Not Veronika. Not even Desiree. You."

# TWENTY-SIX

The alarm beeped downstairs. We had a visitor, but I didn't care. It was probably Erin, and I was too busy trying to prove a point. Ignore a feeling. I focused on the anger, confusion, and guilt that had been driving me the past eight days. It helped me avoid the anger, confusion, and guilt that had been driving me my entire life. "He lied about being in Manhattan the night of Desiree's DUI."

"And?" Free spoke so quickly it made me think my theory was correct.

"He may even have been driving the car," I said, not ready to mention Kevin House.

"That's bullshit. Desiree would've told me."

"Maybe she didn't know. What if he let her take the blame for it? What if he had to cover his tracks?"

"What are you trying to say Mel did?"

I couldn't say it aloud so I said nothing at all.

"Mel isn't my favorite person in the world," Free said at last. "He's an asshole, but he loves his kids. He'd never do anything to hurt them." He paused as the voices came back, having found his hiding spot. "You know that too, Melina."

"Are you saying he wasn't in town?"

"I'm saying you need to finally talk to your father. I gotta go."

For a family that had made its money off music, we weren't good communicators. I'd never heard Gram or Aunt E refer to each other as their girlfriend. Just like I'd never heard them say a peep about what had happened between Mel and my mom. It was Grown Folks Business even when I'd become grown folks. And it wasn't all their fault. I'd never asked—about either relationship. I'd been happy to accept Aunt E and Gram for what they were and anxious to accept Mel and my mom for what they weren't.

And even though I probably should've finally had a heart-to-heart with Aunt E, I still just wanted to sit in my assigned seat at her kitchen table eating lasagna.

Luckily, Aunt E's door was open. I barged in, expecting to see her and Erin in the kitchen. But Stuart sat in my chair, charm on full display. Aunt E was even giggling. Stuart had his notebook out but not open. Not yet. Too busy twirling his pen and smiling. Just like he'd done when he interviewed me.

I stood waiting for them to notice me. Aunt E was first. "There she is. Stuart here came by to talk to you."

I glanced at the notebook. "Talk to me or about Desiree." Stuart didn't turn around, but the twirling stopped. I kept on. "Did you mention that you suckered some publisher into paying you to write about her?"

Aunt E kept the smile as she watched me. "He did. It's a great idea."

When I didn't say anything, Stuart finally turned around. "Lena—"

"Leave," I said.

"I'm not going to—"

"Leave."

"You have to trust me."

"No, you have to get out of my house. I will call the cops. Maybe they'll come quicker than normal since they're all your friends."

"Lena—" Aunt E was pissed, but then so was I.

"No, it's okay." Stuart stood up. "I'll go. There's this adage in journalism. Show, don't tell. I'll show you I'm not the bad guy here. I'm not going to cash some paycheck and spend eighty thousand words talking about how horrible a person your sister was. Then maybe you'll talk to me." He smiled. "Over dinner. *Silence of the Lambs*."

"Leave."

And he did, walking to the door with me behind him for every step. I stood in the hall and watched until he got into his MINI Cooper. Then I slammed the front door, went up to my apartment, and sat on my couch to call Tam.

"Mel Pierce's office."

"How long do you keep an archive of Mel's schedule?"

"Lena! How are you doing?"

I was too anxious for small talk. "Fine. Two years? Five years? Aunt E is trying to remember someplace they went."

She paused. "Date?"

"May 20th, 2017." I hoped it wasn't as ingrained in her brain as it was in mine.

She typed, then said, "Don't think Aunt E has the right date because Mel was at graduation. He flew private to Maryland Thursday morning."

"I'm pretty sure she said she saw him Friday night. Did he come back?"

More typing. "Nope. They were scheduled to come back Sunday afternoon, but I had to book a last-minute flight for Veronika..." She trailed off. When she spoke again, her voice was so quiet I pushed the phone closer to my ear. "Aunt E definitely has her dates wrong. May 20th was Desiree's accident."

I exhaled. If Mel'd come back Friday, Tam would have booked the flight, marking it in her carefully kept calendar. Mel didn't even know how to get his own MetroCard. Yet Desiree had insisted she'd seen him. Of course, she also was so drunk she'd passed out and didn't even wake up when her car was involved in a deadly hit-and-run.

"Were you able to pick up Desiree's stuff?" Tam said.

"Yeah."

"Think you'll be able to drop it off at the apartment?"

I hadn't planned on it, but I needed to talk to Mel. "I can do it today or tomorrow."

"Great. Mel and Veronika are in town. You want me to tell him you're coming?"

I started to say yes, then flashed on my convo with Free. I sucked in a breath. "No. I'll tell him. I just need his cell."

She'd given it to me several times. I'd just never bothered to write it down. And it wasn't like Mel ever called me.

"Great! I'll text it to you," she said.

Her text landed before we even got off the phone. It took me a lot longer to actually open the message. Instead, I paced the area between my living room and kitchen like I was completing a 5K. I was tempted to go for a marathon but instead finally reopened my phone.

Tam hadn't shared a contact, instead opting to send the number directly. I didn't have to even type it in. I could just press and Apple would dial. I could do this. I would do this. Dial the number. Say hello when he answered. Tell him I needed to stop by. I hesitated, then pushed the number so suddenly I almost gave myself a fracture.

I let the phone ring two times before I hung up and lobbed my cell toward the couch like it had caught fire. It rang in midair. I let it go to voice mail. There were ten blissful seconds of silence and it rang again.

At least I knew where I got my phone stalking from. It was as annoying as I'd always assumed. Knowing he wouldn't give up, I picked up the phone. Mel's number flashed on the screen, already seared in my memory. I'd be able to recite it when I was eighty. I hit the phone icon.

"Hello," Mel said.

"It's me," I said, then realized I'd need to clarify. "It's—"

"Everything okay, Melina?" He sounded concerned.

"Oh, yeah. Of course. I was calling about your car's extended warranty. Press zero to speak to a representative."

He laughed then. It wasn't something I heard a lot, certainly not in his interviews. His laugh was thick and hearty—like good soup. I let it peter out before I spoke again.

"I got Desiree's stuff." I took in a breath. "Wanted to know when you'd be home so I can drop it off."

"When do you want to come?"

"What about tomorrow morning? Nine-ish. You'll be there?"

"Yep. You coming hungry?"

I doubted it. "I'll eat before I come. See you tomorrow."

"Nine-ish."

"Oh." I forced myself to be casual. "I had a question about the night of Desiree's DUI. Something she said, but we can discuss it tomorrow."

He paused. "Okay. Tam will tell you where to park the car."

When we hung up, I plopped onto my couch like I had run that race. Exhausted. Mentally. Physically. Definitely emotionally. The call had gone well. Maybe Free was right. Mel would never hurt Desiree—or me. I felt like I'd come back down to Earth.

* * *

I managed to eat the next morning. Aunt E and I shared ham with fresh hash browns and biscuits. Aunt E's eyes were on me more than her plate. "I'm glad your appetite's back."

"I need sustenance. I'm dropping Desiree's stuff off this morning."

"You want company?" Aunt E said. "I always wanted to drive a Tesla."

"You don't even have a license."

"Don't need one. Car that expensive should drive itself."

I fiddled with a piece of ham. "Mel's gonna be there. I spoke to him last night."

To her credit, Aunt E didn't look surprised. She just calmly nodded. "Glad to hear that." She took a bite.

The question was out before I even realized I'd been thinking it. "What happened when they broke up?"

Aunt E's mouth was full so she used it to her advantage, taking time to chew and swallow. "Your Gram always thought it was your mom's fault. You know Black women and their sons."

I did, so I wasn't surprised. "And you?"

"I had my own thoughts."

"Which were?"

"You should talk to Mel about it. Let me know what he says. I'll tell you if my thoughts were right."

She smiled then, trying to keep it light. My whole body felt weighted down. Still, I managed to stand up. My appetite gone again. "Got it."

"Lena."

I paused at the trash can. Waited. Hopeful.

"You…" Her voice stalled out, then caught again. "Don't forget to wash your plate."

* * *

The drive to Mel's reminded me why I biked. I stared longingly at a Citi Bike breezing past as Desiree's air-conditioned Tesla sat in Fifth Avenue traffic. I'd never wanted more in my life to be sweaty. But by the time I got to the apartment, I wished traffic had been worse. I felt less nervous asking about Desiree's DUI than asking about my mom. At this point, I didn't believe Mel had been in town—not with the newspaper photos and Tam's records—but I needed to know why Desiree would've thought she saw him. See if she'd called. If they'd at least spoken. If Mel hadn't been the driver, I doubted he knew who it could've been. Murder Mel would've taken care of them long ago.

To say talking about *that* would be an easier conversation than asking him about my mother was probably all anyone needed to know about my parents' relationship. I'd heard her version of the breakup enough. When a Free Money song would come on the radio. When we'd see one of his artists on a magazine at the grocery store. When one would perform on late-night TV. Both before and after my visits to Gram, ones that always seemed to coincide with Mel being out of town. But he'd never offered his side, and I'd never asked.

The parking garage was around the corner from their place. I gave the keys to the valet, grabbed Desiree's things, and headed over. The door-man was polite. The ride to their floor was short. The door was already open when I got off the elevator. Veronika stood there, smiling like she was posing for the cover of *Architectural Digest*.

I clutched the plastic bag, sure Mel would just pop up behind her like the star of a horror movie. But he didn't.

"I'm so glad you came." Veronika pulled me in for a hug, ignoring the bag wedged between us.

She stepped back, and I didn't know what to do. So I just presented the bag. "Everything the police gave me."

She didn't take it. Just looked at it, and I understood. These were her daughter's final belongings and I was acting like it was a house-warming gift.

"You still have that expensive water?" I said, more to fill the space than my stomach.

Veronika defaulted to Stepford Wife. "Of course. I'll be right back."

I went into the living room and sat, putting the bag down beside me. The apartment was quiet, like the moment right before the bad guy pops out of the closet.

But my villain was still missing.

I was staring down the hall when Veronika came back with two glasses of water. She handed one to me. "Have you gone back to class yet?"

I shook my head, barely able to remember what class I was missing today. Any minute now, he'd show up. "You need any help with the funeral? I know I've been MIA."

"Everything's set." She took a sip. "We sent out the invites for the larger service, but we want to do something just for the family and some close friends. You'll come?"

"Of course."

Any minute.

"Tam said you were the one who had the idea about the dress. Desiree would have loved that. She was so lucky to have you as a sister."

"I was lucky to have her." I glanced at the hallway. "Where's Mel?"

"He's not here." She had the nerve to smile, like it was no biggie. "He had a last-minute meeting."

Of course he did. I set the glass down next to the coaster on her coffee table. All it had taken was him laughing on the phone and I'd fallen for it.

"He should be back by ten. He told me to tell you to wait. You're not leaving, are you?" Veronika would attach herself to my leg if it meant following through on Mel's wishes.

"Which door is Desiree's room?"

"Second on the left."

When I got there, I wanted to slam the bedroom door. The only thing stopping me was that Mel wasn't around to hear it. Instead, I closed it behind me and just took everything in. I could count on three fingers the number of times I'd been in here and could count on four more how long it had been since the last time. True to form, they'd redesigned it.

If Veronika's living room was tailor-made for a design mag, Desiree's bedroom was tailor-made for the @Bedrooms_of_Insta account. I beelined to the white marble vanity closest to me. Took in the makeup, chair, and mirror. All waiting for someone who'd never come back. It looked picture-perfect. Just like her. I opened the lone drawer. Inside was a mess. Just like her.

I tightened my Super Black Woman cape and noticed a clock: 9:22. Less than forty minutes to get what I needed before Mel got back. No time to get emotional.

I was looking for a laptop, iPad, or jump drive. I went through the vanity drawer, then did a sweep of the room. She'd packed a lot into the space, which meant a lot of places to hide things. Bed. Two dressers. An ottoman. The color scheme all pinks, grays, and whites. And it was spotless. The housekeeper more than earned her paycheck.

I started with her walk-in closet, then worked my way back toward the door. I searched everywhere. Peeked in shoes. Looked under mattresses. Inspected drawers. Though I found her "massager," I didn't find any video. Still I kept on. When I'd gone through everything, I finally checked the clock again: 10:21. I gave up. Desiree had grown up here. If she hadn't wanted something found, she would've known where to stash it. It was time to finally talk to Mel.

I didn't see him when I left Desiree's room. Veronika was on the couch,

Desiree's belongings spread out next to her. She stared at them. Motionless. Seeing her like that stopped me dead in my tracks. "You okay?"

She jumped, and the perfectly made-up mask slipped back into place like she was going to a masquerade. "Yep," she said. Automatic. "It's just, I don't know. Seeing her stuff like this."

I nodded, appreciating her honesty as she kept on. "Knowing she won't use it again. It makes it real. That she's gone."

That's when a tear escaped Veronika's eye. I should've gone over, comforted her. Instead, I just stared like she was the Mona Lisa.

"A mother isn't supposed to go through her child's things. She's supposed to go through mine. Finally get her hands on this necklace." She touched her diamonds. "It was her favorite. She'd put it on as a kid and parade around wearing my Manolo Blahniks."

I sat down on the other side of Desiree's things. My proximity must have made her feel vulnerable. The wall shot back up like a geyser. "Mel should be here any minute."

"He's still not back?"

"Not yet, but let me call him." Smiling at me, she waited until he picked up. "Hey! I'm here with Melina…We're waiting for you…" Her face fell as she listened. "No. It's fine. Let me ask."

She looked at me, phone still pressed to her ear. "Mel's going to be a bit longer."

An intermediary.

"How much?"

"He doesn't know, but you're welcome to stay until he gets back."

I stood. "No." I was about to say I had a meeting of my own, but I left it at that. No bullshit excuses. Veronika looked like she understood enough not to ask for one either. I turned.

"Wait."

But I didn't. I was opening the front door when she came up behind me.

"You left your credit card with Desiree's things."

I stopped, turned to find Veronika offering it to me. The Visa White Card.

---

A row house. Desiree Pierce knocks insistently on the door to the basement apartment, then backs up and pulls down the bouquet of balloons in her right hand, blocking the view of the door.

"Leeeennnnaaaa." Her voice is whiny and slightly slurred. "Open the door."

A few seconds later, the door opens but whoever opens it is hidden behind the balloons. Desiree starts singing "Happy Birthday." The Stevie Wonder version written for MLK, Jr. that's a staple at every Black birthday party. Her voice is awful.

When she finally gets to the final "to ya," she ends with a flourish. There's a pause, then the voice of Lena Scott. "Des, it's six thirty a.m.!"

Desiree doesn't notice Lena's discomfort. "On your birthday. I came right over to celebrate."

"Let me guess. From the club?"

"Perhaps. Are you gonna let me in? I can sing again. Make sure your neighbors really hate me."

Lena laughs. "Come on."

"Take these balloons. They were a bitch to get in the car."

Lena takes them, finally revealing her face. She's still in her bonnet and pajamas, lips dry and ashy. Her eyes bug out when she sees that Desiree's also recording her.

"Eek," Desiree says.

Lena's free hand instinctively goes to wipe her dry mouth as she pulls the balloons in front of her face. "Are you on Live?"

"Nope," Desiree lies. "I just wanted to get your reaction to the gift. It's cool. I'll just turn the camera to face me. We can hear it."

Another lie.

Desiree puts her hand out, balled in a fist, and Lena slowly pulls the balloons back down. "Ready for your gift?" Desiree says.

"Sure."

She flips her hand over and melodramatically opens it.

"What is that?" Lena sounds confused.

"It's a Visa White Card. From Mel. Invitation only. One of the perks is swag bags."

Lena's face falls.

# TWENTY-SEVEN

I clutched the credit card the entire Uber ride home, rubbing it so hard
I was surprised the numbers didn't come off. I jumped every time my
phone buzzed—hoping it was him. Wanting to apologize. Wanting to
know why I left. Wanting me to come back.

It never was. It was Omar or Erin or Gmail alerting me there were
"hot singles" in my area. My mood was shit by the time I walked in my
front door. Aunt E peeked her head out when I was halfway up the steps.
"How'd it go—" She stopped when I didn't. Finally spoke again just as I
got to my own door. "I'll be here when you want to talk."

I didn't want to. Not anymore. I beelined straight to my couch, throwing the credit card on the coffee table. I didn't turn on the television,
didn't ask Alexa to play Spotify.

I didn't move until there was a knock on my apartment door and
Erin came in. She smiled tightly. "I called to check on Aunt E and heard
you weren't in a good mood. Before you get mad, she told me not to
come. But I'm staying with a friend in Harlem so it didn't take long
to get here."

When I didn't make a crack about her friend's house, she took another
tentative step in. I braced myself, waiting for her to ask me what had

happened. Instead, she just sat on the sofa, put her head back, and stared at the ceiling, a look of utter peace on her face. It was the first time I'd ever seen her not checking her phone.

She didn't move when I finally got up, retrieved Desiree's phone. She didn't move when I sat back down and opened the phone app, scrolling to the day she died. Last time I'd picked numbers at random. This time I called back every single one.

The first was spam. So was the second. The third, the voicemail of some famous person on their third reality show. It went on like this. Call after call after call. Pressing each number without really thinking it through. I was clumsy with the few people who answered. Just saying I was her sister, wondering if they'd met the day she'd died. They all sounded perplexed as they answered no.

After an hour, I was done. Erin still hadn't said a word. Just watched as I threw the phone dismissively on the coffee table. It stopped a few inches from the credit card. It was only then Erin moved. She picked up the Visa, looked at the name, and finally smiled. "Freck and I had so many good times with this."

"So I heard. Lots of hotel stays."

"And dinners. And clothes. I got a thousand-dollar facial once. Broke out bad the next day. We used it for everything."

She threw it back down, leaning back again on the couch just as I sat up. "Everything?"

"At one point it was our sole spending money, so yes."'

"So Desiree probably used it the day she died."

"We used it for breakfast before she ran off to see Free."

"Ever check the account?"

Erin just gave me a look. "We didn't have to pay it off so there was no need. Why?"

"Good." That meant I could create an account log-in. It was technically my card. I grabbed my laptop from my bedroom.

Within five minutes we were looking at a log of Desiree's last purchases. I even printed them out.

It wasn't the aha moment you get in movies. Whoever she'd seen after meeting Free, she hadn't footed the bill. So I made Erin go back through each charge, highlighting any she didn't recognize. "Starbucks—2025 Broadway," I said to her. It was dated two weeks before her death.

She responded, "Wasn't there."

I highlighted it. The credit statement proved Desiree's soy chai latte addiction was just as bad as everything else. She'd gone to Starbucks. A lot. I flipped the page. Checked the highlights. That's when I noticed it. Desiree wasn't going to Starbucks a lot. She was going to *a* Starbucks a lot.

"Why would Desiree spend so much time on the Upper West Side?"

Erin shook her head. "No one we know lives up there."

I opened Google Maps, put in the address. "It's a block from where Kevin House died. A few blocks from her accident. And look: there are charges for the restaurant next door too."

The area was as residential as one could get in the city. If there was a witness to her accident, it wasn't because they were there clubbing it up. They were probably at home.

"She could've been meeting Zor-El." I checked the time on my cell. "It's only noon. Plenty of time to head over. Ask if they remember seeing her. Anyone with her." I jumped up.

"You want company?" Erin said, then noticed my hesitation. "We can divide and conquer."

She had a point. "Let's go."

Erin was smart enough not to say much on the Uber over. The neighborhood was like I'd thought. Residences. Restaurants. Retail. We had the driver drop us off right in front of the Starbucks. It sat between a consignment shop and the restaurant. Bella Napoli.

"I'll start at the Starbucks." I motioned to the restaurant. "You wanna hit up next door?"

"Sure," she said. Then, "Mind if I get something from Starbucks first?"

"A nonfat white mocha, no whip?" But I smiled when I said it, so she smiled too.

"Maybe."

The place wasn't as crowded as I thought it'd be. One barista took orders and another filled them. Erin got in line while I ran to the bathroom.

By the time I got back, Erin was at the front of the line. She motioned for me to cut, but I shook my head. I'd rather wait, not feel rushed when I talked to the cashier.

The cashier looked like he was eighteen tops. His name tag read GREG. He gasped when he saw Erin. "Erin Ambrose! I follow you on Instagram!!"

Erin seemed embarrassed. "Thank you! I'm actually thinking of taking a bit of a detox."

"No." He sounded genuinely disappointed. "What do you want? On the house."

"I can pay for it."

"Don't worry about it. It'd be an honor."

She hesitated, then whispered her order so I couldn't hear. Greg's voice was much louder. "Nonfat white mocha, no whip. Got it."

She took out her wallet, stuffed a twenty-dollar bill into the tip jar. His eyes lit up. Erin still didn't look at me, just shuffled to get her drink. It was actually kind of endearing. By the time the guy in front of me ordered, her drink was ready. Erin came over to me. "Gonna go next door."

I nodded, then stepped up, ready to order my own nonfat white mocha, no whip. I was probably the only person in the continental United States without a standing Starbucks order. But when I got to the counter, Greg's face fell. "Are you Desiree Pierce's sister?"

I nodded, then smiled, anxious to endear myself as I swiped my credit card. "The freckles?"

"Yeah, but also I know she and Erin were best friends. Process of elimination. I'm so sorry she died."

"Thank you." I was about to ask if she'd ever stopped by when he spoke first.

"She was here a couple of weeks ago."

I nodded, thinking of the credit card statement. "Ordering a soy chai latte, I'm sure. She meet anyone?"

He shook his head, and even though I knew it had been a long shot, I was still disappointed. Greg handed me my receipt. "She just wanted to talk to Alex."

I glanced at the man putting together my drink, then said a quick prayer before I finally spoke. "That Alex?"

"No," Greg said. "He's not scheduled until tomorrow."

* * *

I practically skipped out of that Starbucks. Alex's shift would start at 11 a.m. I'd hit pay dirt so quickly that Erin was probably still at the restaurant. I went inside to find her taking a selfie next to a large mirror. WHY NOT INSTAGRAM THIS HILARIOUS SIGN? was written in big block letters.

*What in the entire fuck?*

"You want me to take it?" My voice reeked of sarcasm. "You can post it ASAP on IG."

She jumped when she saw me. "Lena—"

"Greg will be happy to know you're still posting after all. How many likes you think you'll get?"

"I only took the pic because of Freck. It's one of the last pictures she sent me. I wanted to do a side by side. I'm not putting it online." She held the phone out. "If you swipe you can see the original."

But I didn't. I said nothing at first.

"Fine, I'll delete it," she said.

Then I practically snatched it out of her hand. "Sorry."

I enlarged the pic. There was a man standing in the window, hair covered with a Yankees cap, eyes hidden by sunglasses. But even with the incognito treatment, I recognized his mole. The East Asian guy I'd seen on the subway. The one who'd let me use his phone to call Aunt E.

We weren't near the Omni hotel. He had no reason to be staring at us through a window unless…

I panicked. My first inclination was to whip my head around, and it took everything not to do just that. Instead, I forced myself to casually turn. I didn't see him.

"Lena, what's going on? You're scaring me."

That's because I was scared. I said nothing, just walked outside, this time not bothering to play it cool, almost knocking over a trophy wife and her poodle as I smacked through the door.

He was gone.

I wanted to be too.

Erin came out a moment later. "Are you okay?"

"We need to get out of here. Now."

I hailed a cab.

* * *

I explained everything to Erin on the ride home. Recognizing Mole Man from the Omni. Even walking by the white van. I was so thorough that she was just as scared as I was by the time we pulled onto our block. Why would a man be following me? How long had he been doing it? And had he been inside my house?

I immediately thought of Aunt E.

I had just put the key in the lock when Ms. Paterson came out from next door, wearing gardening gloves. The rosebushes between our houses were her pride and joy—and her excuse to be nosy. On a normal day, I treated her like a man trying to say "Hey" on the street. I was polite, but I never stopped moving. This time I waved Erin inside and walked right up to the fence separating our driveways.

"Saw the police were over. Another break-in?" she said as she examined her favorite rosebush.

"Not this time."

"Oh. Thought maybe you called them about the van."

I started. "The white one?"

She finally looked up. "You saw it too?"

"Blond guy inside?"

"Sometimes. Sometimes it's an Asian guy."

*Shitnuts.* "You've seen it recently?"

Ms. Paterson shook her head. "Now they use that Camry over there."

I whirled around. It was parked a few doors down but with a perfect view of my front door. The windows were all pitch-black, which meant there was no way I could see who was watching me. My heart double-Dutched inside my chest.

"No one's in there," Ms. Paterson said. "They leave the car. Come and go as they please. I called the police. They said it's probably a neighbor who doesn't want to lose his spot."

Her eye roll told me what she thought about that. For once I agreed with her.

"Usually the van comes at six a.m. Drops someone off. They sit for a few hours. Lord knows how they pee. Told the police that too."

I was tempted to go over. Except I didn't know what I'd find. Or maybe I was just scared she was wrong. That someone *was,* in fact, inside. So I stayed put. "Can you let me know if you see someone come back before tomorrow?" I said.

"I would if you answered your phone." She'd spent all last winter bugging me about a tree so I still sent her calls to voice mail.

I promised I would, then turned to go inside. But once again I hesitated at the front door. I felt exposed. I felt scared. But I also felt determined. Being Black, especially a woman, I was used to being underestimated. The microaggressions massive in scope, like when my white male boss was surprised I'd gotten into Columbia. Or the classmate, who could've been his son, when he was shocked I'd done better on the economics exam. Or when these two men thought they could follow me for days and I wouldn't find out. Wouldn't do something about it.

I would, though.

But first I needed to get rid of Aunt E.

* * *

When I was twenty, I got an internship in Midtown. My mom and I hadn't been getting along, so I'd asked Gram if I could stay during the summer. She probably had the spare bedroom ready before we even got off the phone. It was bliss. They fed me. They loved me. They didn't bug me when I stayed out late, though I know they waited up.

But one weekend in August, Aunt E came into my room early in the morning. She'd sat on the edge of the bed, affectionately rubbing the mound that was my left leg as she spoke. "Lena, we need you to go to your mother's house. Just for the weekend."

I'd been half awake, but those words were as good as any shot of espresso. "Did I do something?"

"Of course not. It's just temporary."

"Why?"

But she was shaking her head. "Just trust me."

And I did. Gram dropped me off later that afternoon and was back Monday morning before 9 a.m. They never said what had happened, and though I'd thought about it a few times in the past eight years, I had never, ever asked.

"It won't be long. A week max."

"I'm not going to Mel's." Aunt E was in her usual place at the kitchen table, removing the skin from potatoes with a peeler she'd owned for decades.

I nodded. Not sure I wanted her at Mel's myself. I was in my usual spot too. Erin was still here but smart enough to be hiding in Aunt E's spare bedroom. "If you don't want to go to Mel's, you can go see your sister," I said.

"I hate my sister." She was on Long Island, and they got along about as well as Desiree and I these past two years.

"Or do one of those staycations at the shore."

"I hate water."

She was acting like a child.

"No one says you have to go in it."

"What is going on, Lena?"

I didn't respond.

"This has to do with Desiree, doesn't it?" she said. "I need to stay here. With you."

I placed my hand over hers, and she stopped peeling. "Just trust me."

Her face changed just enough, I knew she remembered that conversation too. After a moment, she nodded. "I'll call my sister."

Erin helped me get Aunt E's luggage from the basement, and I used the opportunity to update her on what Ms. Paterson had said. After all three of us got Aunt E packed, I requested an Uber. Erin eyed the Camry as Aunt E disappeared down the street. "They have to come back," Erin said.

"Apparently every morning by six a.m."

"Good. We'll follow them tomorrow."

"With? We don't have a car." I actually wished she'd gotten her Jaguar back.

"How quickly can you get one?"

The answer was an hour. Mr. Buck came through with his Cadillac.

I didn't sleep much that night, alternating between staring at my bedroom ceiling and staring out my front window at the Camry. So when my phone alarm went off at 5 a.m., I was ready.

Erin was awake, hoodied, and dressed in enough black to make me think she'd done this before. Her confidence was back in spades. I wasn't sure if this was Erin or Karma. Whoever it was, she looked at me and smiled. "I made coffee."

Outside was deserted when we left the house, but I was tempted to wave at Ms. Paterson's house anyway. She had to be watching. Mr. Buck's parking karma wasn't as good as the Camry's owners. He'd been forced to park the Cadillac up the block for us when he dropped it off, but Erin had insisted that was fine. Good, even. The van would drive right past us, and it'd be easy to follow.

We got in, Erin in the driver's seat. Me in the back like she was my

Uber driver. She said it was better like that, in case they did look in the car. Erin got so quiet I wondered if she'd gone to sleep. I'd only seen that level of calm from the guilty party on *The First 48*. I just sat back in the leather seat, anxious like I had been on long car rides as a child. I wanted to get there already.

The minutes ticked by so slowly it felt like my live playback speed was 0.25, the only thing moving fast my inhales and exhales. Finally, after a dozen lifetimes, I saw the headlights in the side mirror.

"Get down," Erin said, awake after all.

It took everything in me to listen when all I wanted to do was stare out the back window. I lay sideways, ear pressed against the leather, as Erin served as narrator. "Someone got out of the van. Into the Camry. Here comes the van."

A few seconds later, it passed us.

"Hit the lights."

I already had the Alexa app open. I selected Devices, then Plugs, turning on the one marked Living Room. Erin waited until the van turned right and disappeared from view. Then she started the Caddy and followed.

Tailing someone in real life was nothing like the movies. It wasn't sexy. It wasn't fun. And although my heart was pounding, it wasn't in a good way. Erin was still cool, even turning on the radio and switching it from Mr. Buck's favored WBLS to Z100. I stayed low but could see enough street signs to know we were heading into Manhattan, the sun slowly chasing us from the east. It was full-on day when we got to Fifth Avenue.

"Where do you think he's going?" I finally said.

"Hopefully back to the office. Maybe home. It's still early. I took a pic of his license plate, but that doesn't mean anything. It'll help to get an address or building name."

I knew we reached East Harlem because the streets got more crowded. "I'm gonna get up," I said, though I didn't move.

"It's fine. They're a few cars ahead."

I sat upright just as we hit a light. I refused to stare at the van in front of me. I looked out the side window instead. Everything seemed so…normal. People going about their day as oblivious to my shit as I normally was to theirs. A young mother practically dragged her uncooperative toddler down the street. I took in each step, the frustration on her face. The determination. The helplessness. They hadn't made much progress when the light turned green again.

I zoned out again until Erin spoke. "They're pulling over."

The van stopped, and someone got out of the front passenger seat. I wasn't close enough to see who it was, but I knew anyway. The guy with the mole. He didn't glance back as he walked quickly into a building.

It was Mel's co-op.

# TWENTY-EIGHT

E rin didn't stop, just cruised past Mel's building. She also ignored my tears, the ones I'd managed to hold back for nine days. The ones that now came with the ferocity of a Category 4 hurricane.

Mel.

She must've seen him the night of her accident. A flight from Maryland to New York would have been quick. He could've flown back for one night and still been smiling for the cameras at graduation the next day. He'd made sure to be seen during the ceremony. An alibi.

It would explain so much. Their falling-out. His willingness to not press the cops. And now this—having people follow me? He'd no-showed our breakfast. I'd assumed it was because he was the same old Mel. But had he been actively avoiding me because he knew I was still looking into what happened?

Could he have done it?

Could Murder Mel Pierce have killed his prized daughter, less than a mile from where he grew up, from where his mother had taken her last breath, from where his stepmother and other child still slept? It was too much to even consider, but it had been almost two weeks and every clue had led me here.

I zoned back in when the engine cut off. We'd somehow made it to Chelsea, to the block where I'd thought Erin lived just a few short days ago—before I realized my father was probably a monster.

"Let's go," Erin said, but I didn't move.

"What are you doing?"

"We can't go back to your house, and there's a low-key twenty-four-hour diner next block over."

"I don't want food."

"That's why I'm getting you liquor. The night manager likes me. He'll have you drunk AF in no time."

"It's, like, seven in the morning."

Erin opened the car door. "You've never been drunk at seven a.m. before? How sad."

She shut the door and didn't look back as she walked away. I waited until she was almost at the corner before I finally got out and ran to catch up. Even in the early morning, it was hot, and by the time we got to the diner, my tears were mingled with sweat.

Erin had been right about the manager. He had a crush. Within moments Erin and I were sitting across from each other in a dark booth drinking vodka and cranberry from the manager's private stash. He was kind enough to leave both bottles.

Erin waited until I polished off the second drink before she spoke. "I'm sorry."

And that's all it took. The tears came again, this time a Category 5. Now that I'd started crying, it felt like I couldn't stop.

She took my cup, mixed me another drink as she spoke. "Do you want to go to the cops?"

I shook my head. Not now. "He's on a first-name basis with the police commissioner. For all I know they covered up Kevin House too."

She nodded, then hesitated. "Stuart?"

There was no way in hell. If he wanted that for his book, he'd have to find it out himself.

"If your father did this, he can't get away with it."

She handed me my refill. I was just tipsy enough to notice she was abstaining but also tipsy enough not to care. I took a sip. It was much stronger than the first two. "The video." I jumped up. "The person Desiree had been stalking at Starbucks starts their shift at eleven. We need to go."

Erin gently pulled me down. "Let's get some food in your stomach first."

I ate, but for all I knew the meal could've been cardboard. I cleaned my plate without tasting a single morsel. The night manager got off at eight but stuck around for a good hour, distracting us with compliments and stories. When he finally left, we switched to water and stories about Desiree. I told Erin about the time we'd broken Gram's favorite vase while playing hide-and-seek and both chose the switch over ratting each other out. And how Desiree would watch patiently as I worked out card tricks when I wanted to be the Black girl version of Harry Houdini. How she always insisted the family who lived in her Barbie Dream House have two girls. And of course, how we held hands through Gram's funeral service and burial, and how she held me all night after my mom's. It was so much easier to think of my sister alive than dead.

By 10:00, I was sober-ish and hydrated and we were ready to go. Erin drove and I rode shotgun—still feeling groggy. It took twenty minutes to get to the Upper West Side, another fifteen to find a spot, and a final five for Erin to parallel park Mr. Buck's behemoth, but by 10:45 we were back at Starbucks. Greg waved when he saw us, then shook his head. I took it to mean Alex wasn't there. Yet.

The store had one long bench lining the wall, divided by four small two-seater tables. Erin and I nabbed the one by the window.

Alex turned out to be short, skinny, white, and on time, with blond hair he'd gone to the trouble of tinting the slightest bit pink. I stayed put when he walked in. And when Greg pointed us out to him. And when he looked scared shitless.

That was the last time Alex even looked in our direction, instead opting to hurry behind the counter, put on his green apron, and concentrate on making macchiatos like he was finding a cure for the common cold. I let him get through three customers before I finally got in line. Luckily, no one got behind me. Greg wasn't smiling as big when I went to place my order. "He's not happy to see you."

"I figured," I said. "What's the most complicated drink you have?"

Greg thought it over. "I had a customer order an iced ristretto ten-shot venti with breve, five pumps vanilla, seven pumps caramel, four Splenda, poured, not shaken once."

I had no clue what any of that meant. "I'll take four."

Alex didn't turn around when I walked over, but I knew he knew I was there. I waited until he'd finished the first drink before I said anything. "You knew my sister?" There was no one else in line. No one else within hearing distance if I kept my voice low.

He put the drink down.

"I think someone killed her." I didn't mention that person was Mel.

He hesitated before starting the second, and I used that to keep going. "I know you're scared. Because of whatever you saw that night. I'm scared too. But if you have a video, you can just give it to me. I won't say where I got it. I won't ask how you got it. I'll just take it and leave."

He walked away, and I deflated. He said something to Greg, probably about getting rid of me. But a second later, he was back. "He said I can take five minutes. I'll meet you in the bathroom. The code to the lock is 4322."

I didn't tell him I already knew it. Instead, I glanced at Erin, who gave me an encouraging nod, then I went down the hall. The bathroom was a single, probably forty square feet, but it began to shrink as soon as I shut the door. My heartbeat matched the tempo of a trance song. My wrist itched so bad I felt like I was being ripped apart from the inside out.

There was a knock, but I didn't move. I felt trapped, as much in this horrible idea as in the room itself. On the other side of that door stood the answer I'd been seeking since Desiree had died. The one I'd been sure I wanted. But now, when it was so close—when it was Mel—I wasn't sure at all. What was that video going to do except let him ruin my life even more?

Alex knocked again, and I cursed myself for not bringing my phone so I could text Erin to rescue me. I stood and waited and listened as Alex plugged in the code. I backed up until I ran out of space, and by the time he stepped inside, I was pressed against the sink. He closed the door, and we eyed each other, both realizing what a shitty idea this was.

After a minute, he spoke, holding his cell up like a barrier. "I don't live around here, but I've worked here for three years. I've gotten to know people in the neighborhood. I'd been hanging with a friend after work. I was leaving his place when I saw her car coming down the street. Swerving. Of course, I took a video. *Look at this fool*. Didn't think much of it until I saw an article a couple of weeks later about her arrest. I wanted to DM her right then. Tell her what I was reading wasn't what I saw."

I should have interrupted to ask it then: *Who did you see?* But I stayed silent. Let him take his own long, winding road to that final destination.

"I finally DMed her a couple of months ago. It had been on my mind with the two-year anniversary coming up. She didn't see the message. I spent the first week checking religiously. Then I took that as a sign. That I'd done all I could do."

As he spoke, he'd backed up too and was leaning on the closed door. "But then, like a month later, there she was in my DMs. I got scared so I didn't write her back, then she stopped by here. I told her the video was on my old phone. First she said it was fine. Then she asked if I could get the phone from my mom's in Delaware."

And that's when I finally got up enough nerve to ask. "What? What'd you see?"

"That it was a man driving."

Hearing it confirmed still felt like a shock. I wanted to tell Alex to stop talking. That I wanted to leave. But I couldn't get the words out, and he kept going.

"I had my mom send me the old cell. Desiree and I were supposed to meet in person so I could give it to her. But then the day came. And I got scared again and called in sick. Then she died. I deleted my Instagram completely."

I nodded, understanding. Even feeling relieved that I could walk away from this room. From Mel.

"But I still have my old phone. I never took it out of my work bag." Alex shoved the iPhone at me so hard that I had no choice but to take it. I could hear the video already playing. "My break's over."

And with that he left.

I should've just sat there in Mel's office last week, nodded along when Green said she'd overdosed. Thanked him for the update and then left to begin my life in a post-Desiree world.

But I hadn't. And now I had to watch.

I heard Alex before I could see anything. "This right here is why I hate being out after midnight. People like this shouldn't be on the road."

The video was dark since it was shot so late at night. The camera was moving, Alex clearly rushing to catch up to a pair of red brake lights.

"You see them?" Alex said on camera. "That car careening past me going at least sixty? Thank God there are no other cars. I thought they were gonna blow past the light, but he stopped. Almost. In the middle. Of. The. Intersection."

My heart sped up as the camera got closer to Desiree's car, as if I was the one running. Not Alex.

*Please don't let it be Mel. Please.*

It became my new mantra. I repeated it over and over in beat with each step Alex took.

He was within a few feet when the light turned green. And even though I knew better, there was a brief moment when I wanted the car to peel off. So we couldn't see who was behind the wheel.

But it didn't. And Alex caught up.

Just as he reached its bumper, the car shot off again. But he'd caught enough. An arm hanging out the driver's side window.

I continued staring at the screen long after the video had stopped.

The arm had been white.

# TWENTY-NINE

I went bungee jumping for my twenty-first birthday. It's scary as hell as soon as you fall back. That fear that your worst nightmare might come true at any second. But then you get over it, and there's this moment when you just let go. Surrender. Feel like the weight of the world is finally off you and you're free.

And just when you're about to reach full don't-give-a-shit mode, you get to the end of your rope and you're yanked back to reality.

I hadn't felt anything like it since—until I saw that video. Saw an arm not brown enough or tattooed enough to belong to Mel Pierce.

The free-fall euphoria lasted much longer with my feet on the ground, long enough for me to convince Alex to send me the video, grab Erin from her plum window seat, and get out of there. It wasn't until we got back to the Caddy that two questions made me recoil. "If Mel wasn't the driver, who was? And why does he have someone following me?"

"We can go back to your place." Erin buckled into the driver's seat. "The guy in the van should answer the second question."

She, of course, had taken the revelation in stride, donning the same stoic look she always wore when she wasn't pretending to be someone and something she was not. As with everything, she was both right and wrong. I needed to ask questions—just not of some stranger who'd been lurking outside my house. I needed to ask the stranger who'd been lurking outside my life.

Erin was about to start the car when I put my hand on her arm. "I need to go see Mel."

We drove south, then east. I gave myself the same pep talk as I had before. I could do this. I would do this. Have an actual conversation with my father. By the time Erin dropped me off and went to find a parking garage, I was ready. I hadn't called Tam to let her know I was coming. I didn't need anyone or anything getting in my way. The security guard let me go straight up. He didn't even call first. I was in the system.

The walk down Mel's Hall of Hits was quicker this time. When I got to the white receptionist, I smiled but didn't stop. Just kept going straight to the door. Barely paused long enough to ask my one question. "Can you buzz me in?"

She paused, unsure. "Is Mr. Pie—"

My smile went up two notches. "Why wouldn't he? I'm his daughter." I waited. After a second, I heard the buzz.

She didn't have time to alert the office Slack. I got double takes as I walked by, glances as quick as they were furtive. The group that'd previously set up shop across from Tam's desk had taken their road show to a random desk a few feet from the door. I turned as I walked by, smiled at them since I knew they saw me. "Afternoon," I said.

Tam was at her desk, playing her position in the defensive line. She had her ever-present mug of coffee, which she damn near spit-taked when she saw me. "Lena, did we know you were stopping by?"

I still didn't stop. "Nope."

Mel's double doors were closed, but not locked. I walked in, not having to glance back to know the shocked expression on Tam's face.

"I'm not meeting with him unless he gives us a guarantee." He was there at his desk, both his feet propped on it as he spoke on his landline. His sunglasses were off so I could see his eyes—my eyes. They looked in my direction and stayed there. His expression didn't change one bit. "Melina's here." He hung up before the person could respond. "Here to make a citizen's arrest?"

And that's what finally stopped me. Of course he knew.

I turned to close the door. Neither of us spoke until I took the seat across from him. And then he went first. "Yeah, I know. My child thinks I would kill my own children. Free told me."

"Free? Not one of the men you have following me?" I barely recognized my own voice, hadn't heard the sadness in it since I was a kid. "Yeah, I know too."

But he was shaking his head before I could put the period at the end of the sentence. "Those men are there to protect you."

"I'm twenty-eight years old. I don't need you to protect me, Mel." I left off the "anymore."

He finally took his feet off the desk. "Mel." He said his own name. "I'm Mel. You're Lena. Lena *Scott*."

It was the first time he'd acknowledged it. I'd wanted a reaction for ten years. It was nowhere near as satisfying as eighteen-year-old me had thought—had hoped—it would be. He grabbed his sunglasses from the desk, started to put them back on but stopped himself. Didn't say anything for a while.

"That hurt like hell," he said. "You changing your name like that."

It was as vulnerable as I'd ever seen him. "Yeah? Well, you missing my graduation hurt." An understatement but it was all I could get out.

"Your mother told me not to come."

That was news. Not surprising news, having lived with my mother, but news nonetheless.

"Since when did Mel Pier—" I stopped myself. "When did you ever listen when someone told you not to do something?"

"I sent a gift."

Tiffany solitaire diamond earrings in platinum. They were still in the box. "No one said you had to sit next to her, hold her hand, sing 'Isn't She Lovely.' You should've come. Instead, you went to brunch. I know because I fucking read about it in Page Six the next day."

The tears came then, and now that the dam had been broken, they threatened to fill the entire room. Drown us both. I didn't wipe them away. I'd cried about this man for hours. Days. A lifetime. And I finally wanted him to know. To his credit, he didn't look away. After a moment, he opened his mouth, and I waited for the next excuse.

"I'm sorry." It had come as fast as a pitch, but I didn't even try to catch it. Instead, I stared at the desk, as if I could see where his words had landed in front of me. He spoke again, softer, gentler, slower. "Thought I was doing the right thing. I didn't want you to see your parents arguing all the time, hating each other."

"So you decided it was better I didn't see you at all?"

But he kept going, as if it was the first time he was admitting it to himself as much as to me. "It got easier to stay away, to convince myself it was okay because I was paying for the house, the school, some magic trick your mother told my mother you wanted."

The Houdini box. I could still remember going down the stairs the Christmas I was ten and seeing it for the first time. And even though I'd abandoned the dream pretty quick, I'd kept the box. It was currently in my basement. Though I knew Santa hadn't really dropped it off, I never knew Mel was the one who'd bought it.

"Melina—Lena—I'd die for my kids. I'd kill for my kids. I just want you to be safe. It sounds melodramatic as hell, but it's the truth. Just like not coming to your graduation was one of the two biggest regrets of my life."

My first inclination was to make a joke about how the other was not signing some big-name rapper. "What was the second?" I said instead.

"Letting your sister drive off the night of her accident."

I folded my arms across my chest. "I thought you were at Morgan."

"Told Veronika I was having a boys' night with my frat brothers. Took a plane back."

Him having to fly back to New York wouldn't have been a big deal to Veronika. She might have come with him, but she wouldn't have thought it was weird. There was only one reason not to want her to come— or to know.

"What was her name?" I said. Unlike Free, Mel hadn't had a cheating scandal since my mom.

"Doesn't matter. I didn't want Veronika to know since it didn't work out so great the last time I got caught. Of course, I still lost my daughter. Again." He had to take a moment after that one. "Desiree saw me—us—coming out of some private club. Took off. I didn't find out about her accident until the next morning. When I called, she hung up, so I stayed in Maryland. Figured she'd tell her mother, but she didn't. She didn't come home either. Decided to shack up with that helmet guy."

I was still stuck on Desiree catching Mel cheating. It took me a second to get what else he had said. "Naut?"

I'd always assumed Desiree met Naut well after her accident since that's when he first started popping up on her Instagram.

"Naut," Mel said. "Ridiculous name. They met that night. She told her mother it was love at first sight or some shit. He was a bartender. Plied her with alcohol. Guess she was on her way to meet up with him when she hit that pole. Almost killed herself." He looked at me. "Why are you looking at me like that?"

I wasn't. He was just in my eyeline as I tried to work it all out. Two things were clear. Mel didn't know Desiree wasn't driving that night. And he sure as hell didn't know about Kevin House. I sure wasn't going to be the one to tell him either. Because I believed him when he said he'd kill for Desiree.

Mel thought she had never made it to see Naut. But what if she had? I flashed on Alex's video, the pale arm hanging out the window. Green had acted like Naut had an ironclad alibi—performing in front of thousands of people for thousands of dollars. But that alibi was hidden underneath his astronaut helmet. A robot could be under there pushing buttons on his Mac.

"Well?" Mel still stared at me.

"You're right," I said before I changed my mind and told him everything. "Desiree just overdosed. That's why I came by. What I wanted to tell you."

"You're done playing detective?"

I nodded, smiled, got up, for once glad he didn't know me well enough to know when I was lying. I made it to his door before he finally spoke.

"Your mother raised an amazing person."

When I stepped back into the sheer white of Pierce Productions, Tam was still at her desk and Erin was with her. They both smiled at me, tentative. "Everything go okay?" Erin said.

I nodded. "Naut."

\* \* \*

The Apollo marquee had long gone digital but still spelled its name out in iconic bright neon-orange letters. It was advertising the producers' showcase. Erin and I had spent hours camped outside Naut's building, but he hadn't been home. Finally, I remembered that I knew exactly where he was. And crashing his gig seemed like a much better plan than being alone with him—again—in his apartment. Staring at the picture he'd painted of my sister. When I'd first seen it, I'd assumed him painting over it was the worst thing he could do to her.

I was wrong.

After we parked the Cadillac, we walked over to the theater and followed the crowd inside, where Erin kept going until she found an AUTHORIZED PERSONNEL ONLY sign. She didn't even hesitate before going in.

No one stopped us then or as we wandered backstage, me gripping my pepper spray as our every move was accompanied by a soundtrack of today's biggest hits, thanks to whoever was doing crowd warm-up.

We stumbled upon the stage entrance next to a wall filled with autographs. The DJ onstage was sans helmet, but I wasn't surprised. Naut wasn't coming out early. This was the opening act. As I looked closer, I recognized his assistant, Trevor.

Seeing him out there made me realize he could've been the one actually performing the night Desiree died. All he would've needed was an astronaut helmet and a private place to plop it on his head.

We kept going, passing anxious producers sitting in a bland white room with outdated couches. The greenroom. But no Naut. So we knocked on any doors we thought could possibly hide a dressing room. We finally found him up a set of stairs and behind a door that said "2."

He responded to our knock, looking as if he'd been expecting someone else, and then became confused. Two separate worlds were colliding, like seeing your teacher at the grocery store. *Good.* I wanted him out of his element. Uncomfortable. Unsure.

He leaned in to hug me. "Lena…" The smell of alcohol on his breath was as faint as a damsel in distress.

I leaned back and he hesitated, unsure if he'd made a mistake. His smile when it came was awkward, and I wondered if that was how he'd smiled at Desiree when he'd taken her car keys two years ago. When he'd injected that heroin into her body nine days ago and left her to die.

"Everything okay?" he said.

"We need to talk."

He glanced at Erin, but she must've been giving him the same look. "Okay."

He stepped back to let us in. He was sans entourage so we were alone. The room was spare with the same French-vanilla-colored paint job as in the greenroom but way less seating. The few chairs were pushed against the counter that ran along one wall. A mirror was above them. It forced us to sit side by side. I took the middle. Naut slouched in the chair to my left. I placed my bag on the counter. The plan was for Erin to record our convo on her phone so we could deliver it to Detective Green.

It took everything in me to lean toward Naut instead of away in disgust as I pulled up Alex's video. Then I showed it to him, gripping my cell tight in one hand, my pepper spray tighter in the other.

Naut's expression was blank, then he smiled. It wasn't sadistic like the guy in that Jack Nicholson movie. It was one of relief.

"That's me." For once, he sat up straight, shoulders raised like a literal weight had been lifted.

But the weight had just transferred to me. I let my phone fall to my lap and used the suddenly free hand to rub my wrist. "Driving Desiree's car the night of her DUI?" I wanted to make it clear for the recording.

"Yes."

"Why?"

"Because my dad wasn't Mel Pierce." His voice was soft, but I heard him loud and clear. His eyes were on the counter like it was some reverse crystal ball that let you look at the past. "Desiree passed out as soon as she got in the car. Barely woke up when we had the accident. I got out. No one was there. So I just kept going. Didn't look back. I didn't sleep at all that night, expecting the police to come pounding on my door. They never did. And then the news reported she had been driving."

"When did she find out?" I said.

"She always knew I'd been driving. Don't know why she never said anything."

"About Kevin House."

And just like that, the weight was back. "That's his name, huh?"

It figured he'd never bothered to find out. "He had a daughter," I said.

"Kevin House with a daughter." He said it slowly, as if wanting to hear every word even though he was the one talking. "I don't know who told her about the hit-and-run, but she only found out a few weeks ago. She was pissed. Demanded money."

Erin finally said something. "When did you decide?"

"To pay her? Right away."

"To kill her," I said.

He jolted back to the here and now. "You can't be serious."

He looked at me, then Erin, and back again. Going back and forth between us like a tennis match. When he realized neither of us was going to correct him, he spoke again. "I loved her."

Everyone loved Desiree. Erin. Mel. Naut. But that love hadn't stopped them from lying to her, using her, doing worse. "People hurt people they love all the time," I said.

"Not me."

I raised an eyebrow. "You only kill strangers?" It was cold, but it should have been. Two people were dead because of him, and he was backstage at the Apollo.

"I had a gig."

"You or your assistant?"

Naut reached into his pocket, and I tensed. Tough Girl Act once again up and leaving like it was late for its next appointment. The pepper spray felt as heavy as a gun. But Naut pulled just his phone out. He showed me a photo. Him and Trevor at a bar. June 5, 4:54 a.m.

I should have been happy I'd eliminated another suspect. But unlike with Mel, there was no sense of relief. "Why the hell would you hang out with someone who was blackmailing you?" I said. "And don't give me that 'I was in love' bullshit."

"She stole my laptop."

"Big effing deal. You bought another one." I'd brought it up to him.

"There's a recording on there. Me talking about the accident. Drunk. A few months ago. Foolish to even talk about it, but the anniversary was coming. I didn't get rid of the recording. Guess I figured if something happened to me…"

"You'd have insurance?" Erin said.

"That then people would know what I'd done. It was my confession. It was only after she took it I realized how silly an idea it was. I wanted to convince her to give it back to me."

"When did she take it?" Erin said.

"First weekend in May. Right after my birthday. Still don't know where it is."

I hoped he never found it.

There was a knock and a woman came in, a fake smile plastered on like drywall mud. She didn't even pause when she saw the three of us. It probably wasn't the first time. At least we were all clothed. "Mr. Naut needs to get ready for his show."

Naut glanced at me, unsure of what to do. What I'd do. I just smiled, thinking of Erin's recording. "Break a leg."

He nodded, then stood up, never taking his eyes off me. As he trailed after the woman, I heard one final thing. "Can I get a drink?"

The lobby was loud when we got to it. The show was about to start. I leaned in to Erin's ear, anxious. "Did it record?"

She pulled out her phone. "I'm sure." But she glanced at the sign for the ladies' room. "Let's go in there and check."

The bathroom was deserted, everyone having rushed out to not miss the show. Erin pulled up her voice memo, hit PLAY. Nothing but static.

"No." I shook my head for emphasis. I wanted to cry. Again. "Fast-forward."

But it was still the same. She looked even more upset than I was. "No. It had to have worked." She hit her phone, like it was a TV in the '80s. "Shit. I'm so sorry, Lena. I swear it was working."

"It's fine," I said, having finally gotten better at lying. I placed my bag on the bathroom counter and pulled out my phone.

"What are you doing?" Erin said.

"Calling the police."

"Still? He'll just get an expensive lawyer. We have no proof other than an arm in a video. He's never gonna admit it."

"He already did."

"Because he was surprised. He'll think it over. Change his mind, and it'll be our word versus his. But we still can hit him where it really hurts. His bank account."

"He needs to go to jail. He killed somebody."

"Lena."

It wasn't her decision, wasn't her sister. I dialed Detective Green's cell phone. He actually picked up for once. "Ms. Scott," he said as a group of loud women barged in and surrounded the bathroom mirror like they were the cops. "Where are you? It's loud."

"Give me a second." I hurried into the stall farthest away, leaving Erin at the counter glaring at me.

I quietly gave Green the CliffsNotes version of what I'd found. Even with just the highlights, it took me a good five minutes. Green didn't say a word until I finished.

"Was he nervous? Like he might leave town?" Green said.

I leaned against the stall, thought about what Erin had said. "Don't know. If you want to talk to him, I'd do it now."

"And you have no idea where Desiree might have stashed his laptop? Maybe at your parents' apartment?"

"I checked her room and didn't see any computers. Doesn't mean it's not somewhere else. You want to talk to Mel?"

He sighed. "I can be there in ten minutes."

We hung up. I wasn't sure if he'd believed me. It was good he finally seemed willing to consider something I said. I exited the stall, ready to tell Erin that Green was on his way. That even if we didn't know who killed Desiree—yet—Naut would be going to jail for killing Kevin House.

But she was gone. So were my bag and pepper spray.

* * *

Green was wrong again. I spent the entire fifteen minutes he took to arrive alternating between looking around for Erin and texting her. As the number of unanswered texts increased, so did my anxiety. Had Naut done something to her too?

Trevor finished his set and Naut took over. Or at least *someone* in an astronaut helmet did. I went back to the dressing room. The chaperone stood watch. "Have you seen my friend? White girl? Blond hair."

By the look she gave me, she barely remembered me, much less Erin. I pressed. "Maybe she went to see Naut. If I can just go in there."

She moved in front of the door. "No one's allowed in but staff and performers."

"But—"

"You shouldn't even be back here."

*Fine.* I'd wait for Green. I stayed right next to her until he texted me, then I left to meet him in the lobby. "I can't find Erin," I said.

He looked nowhere near as alarmed as I felt. "When's the last time you saw her?"

"When I went to call you. She may have tried to speak with Naut again after I left. They won't let me check his dressing room."

He placed a hand on my arm to calm me. It worked. "We'll check. I'm sure she's fine."

I hoped he was right. He approached the door backstage. I was just about to follow him when my phone rang. Finally. But when I checked the ID, it wasn't Erin. Ms. Paterson's name flashed across the screen. I couldn't deal with her now. Not until I made sure Erin was okay. I hit IGNORE, but Ms. Paterson called back just as Green noticed I wasn't behind him.

"Go in. Be right there," I called out.

He nodded and turned as I hit the button to talk. "Everything okay, Ms. Paterson?"

"Why is that white girl breaking into your house?"

# THIRTY

S tay or go?

    While I thanked Ms. Paterson for the phone call, Green disappeared inside. The question was whether to follow him.

Stay or go?

If Naut didn't confess to Green, then it'd be my word against his. What if Green had to let him go and he disappeared? I waited a beat. Stared at my phone. Would the alarm company call? What had happened to make Erin take my bag, ignore my frantic messages, and head to the Bronx? Especially when the person she wanted to blackmail was still here? Naut couldn't have been with her. Ms. Paterson would have told me if Erin had brought company.

Stay or go?

She must have needed my keys. What did she want? Her bag? Desiree's phone? Something else entirely? If she'd wanted me to know, she would've waited. She had played me. Again. Trust and tears were a combination I didn't share with just anyone. The realization hurt—just like a sister.

I went.

I sent Green a quick text and headed for Mr. Buck's Caddy before I realized I didn't have the keys. It was almost 9 p.m. and at least the Uber ride home was short at that hour. I spent the entire seventeen minutes cursing. At jaywalkers. At other cars. At Erin.

I was happy Aunt E wasn't home, just like I was happy Kitty was. I'd use her if need be.

When we finally turned onto my street, it was deserted, and the lights were off in both Aunt E's and my apartments. Mr. Buck's car was parked haphazardly in front of my driveway. She hadn't even taken time to open the gate. My phone rang just as I closed the Uber's door. Ms. Paterson.

"She's still inside," she said as soon as I answered. "You want me to call the police?"

"I'll do it." Later. Besides, Green already knew. Kind of.

I hung up and stood there. What was she doing? The lack of lights confirmed what I already knew. She'd used me. After five minutes, it was clear that whatever she was after, she hadn't found it. She had to know I'd be home eventually, and she wouldn't have done all this if she'd wanted to be here when I arrived.

That meant I had to be covert. I opened the front gate just enough to slide through. As I walked by our blue recycling bin, I instinctively grabbed an empty vodka bottle. I tried my front door. She hadn't locked it behind her. I sure as hell did when I got inside.

It was strange, creeping into your own house. I didn't bother to turn on any lights. It was so black I couldn't even make out the basement door down the hall. I listened. But that was the thing with older houses. They were as sturdy as an offensive lineman. Erin could have been dancing to Beyoncé at full volume. I wouldn't have been able to hear shit. I paused on the ground-floor landing just outside Aunt E's apartment. Another quandary. Should I start with my place or hers? Desiree's phone was upstairs. Erin's stuff was down.

I chose Aunt E's door since it was literally within arm's reach and I could get Kitty. For the first time ever, it was locked. But was it Aunt E's or Erin's doing? I had a key to Aunt E's apartment. It was in my bag with everything else. So I went upstairs, tried a different door with the same result. Locked.

*Shitnuts.* I went back downstairs to wait Erin out. My phone lit up. In the darkness, it felt as bright as a spotlight. Ms. Paterson again. I ignored it, not because I didn't want to talk to her but because in the light I noticed the basement door. It was cracked open.

There was nothing down there but forgotten furniture and a washer and dryer. I crept down the hall, my eyes adjusting. When I got to the door, I slowly peered down the stairs. A beam of light as thin as she was slashed through the darkness. I could hear her moving stuff. I turned on the light abruptly and the noise stopped. She appeared at the bottom of the stairs, not looking surprised—or embarrassed—to see me.

"What are you doing, Erin?"

A clichéd question but also a valid one. She had the nerve to smile at me like I'd caught her searching for her Christmas gift.

"Looking for the video." Even from twenty feet away, she could tell I was confused. "Naut's laptop, Lena. Freck left it here."

"Right." I rolled my eyes. "When she stopped by for her weekly tea party?"

"During the first weekend in May." She repeated herself. "First weekend in May."

Then she disappeared back into the basement's abyss. First weekend in May? Then it hit me. That was when we'd had our break-in. Even at the time, it'd felt strange. Random. Someone had picked the front door lock but bypassed Aunt E's apartment to head straight for the basement. We'd only realized it'd happened the morning after.

Was that why Desiree'd been coming up here? I'd spent the last nine days feeling guilty my sister had needed me when she'd just wanted to break into my house—again—to pick up the blackmail she'd stowed for safekeeping. I didn't want to believe it. Maybe Erin was wrong. She was a liar, after all.

When I got downstairs, Erin was halfway in Gram's old china cabinet.

"Appreciate you turning on the light," she said.

"You have two minutes before I call the police."

Erin didn't stop moving. "We're doing that one again, Lena? You have any idea how much Naut would pay to get that laptop back?"

"I don't care."

"Right. I forgot—you're still doing the poor little rich girl act."

"We're doing that again, Erin? At least I know you were genuinely upset about your phone not recording his confession."

She finally stopped, turned around. Held her hands up in surrender. "I'm sorry. How about we do this? You still need to find the laptop. We can look together. Give it to the police."

"Or they can help us look." I meant to dial 911, but it was awkward trying to do it with one hand, holding the bottle in the other.

"Need help?" Erin stepped closer.

"No—"

She pushed past me, knocking me over, and headed up the stairs before I even realized what was going on. I didn't just lose my balance. I lost the phone and the vodka bottle too. It didn't help she'd turned the light out on her way. I didn't waste time looking for them, just ran back up too. By the time I got outside, the Caddy was turning the corner.

*Shitnuts.*

I needed to call the police, but my phone was still inside—somewhere. Hopefully my bag and keys too. I rushed back in, shutting the door behind me and heading down to the basement again. It was useless. I might as well have lost my phone in the Atlantic. The room was huge, the entire length of the house, and packed to the gills. I started in the direction I thought I'd heard it fall, where Gram and Aunt E had left a dining room table covered in Mel's old records. They were spread on every surface, including the floor. I started low and made my way up. I didn't find the phone—or what I really was looking for.

The laptop.

I continued through Mel's record collection, holding my breath, hoping not to find it. And I didn't. But I still had an entire basement to go. There were millions of places for Desiree to have hidden it. A cursory glance counted two dressers, yet another dining room table, and every toy Desiree had received in her lifetime.

She'd have to be able to remember where, so Gram's nondescript furniture was out. It'd have to be something we wouldn't stumble upon but she could get to easily, which meant it was nothing on the back wall. And it had to be something that could conceal a laptop, even one as slim and sleek as a MacBook.

I was betting on the Barbie Dream House. Technically it had been Desiree's, but we shared toys as kids. I loved playing with them all—except the Dream House. It was one of those three-story numbers you opened up like a cabinet door, fully furnished and with its own happy family. Barbie, Ken, and two kids living happily ever after—the picture of domestic bliss. I'd wanted to burn it with the rest of the Pierce family photos Gram had kept in her living room. The ones that didn't include me.

It was a few feet away from the record collection, weathered but looking better than a lot of houses in the neighborhood. If Desiree had evicted Ken and gotten rid of the master bedroom set, there'd be enough room in there for a laptop. I walked over, then bent down to pry it open, causing dust to fall like snow.

No laptop.

*Thank God.* I realized then that it was silly to even look. It probably wasn't here. I needed to find my phone and call the police. As I headed to the stairs, I saw Houdini's box, open and empty. Desiree had known how much I loved it, though she had never understood why. She'd never been one for sentimental value. She didn't even like vintage.

The box was big enough to hold a laptop. I bent down and pressed the button to open the secret compartment.

There it was.

Desiree *had* been the one to break in. And she'd left this here—for me to find.

She'd come to the Bronx because she *had* needed my help.

I sat on the stairs and opened it. There was a note inside. Desiree's handwriting. If I'd been expecting some final message from my sister, I would've been disappointed. The only thing I saw was a series of numbers and letters and the word "Objective."

When the laptop turned on, I realized the first part of the note was Naut's complicated password. His wallpaper was as clean as his place. Not a single app. I clicked the folder, and there everything was. File after file after file. It'd take me forever to find the video. I glanced at the paper again.

"Objective."

I typed it in. A folder popped up. When I clicked, there was just one file inside. The video's dimensions meant it had to have been taken with a laptop. It was too square for a phone. Naut was on camera but not looking at it. The angle was horrible, slanted upward like your uncle's first attempt at video chatting. All neck and nostrils. There was a glass in front of him with nothing but tinted ice blocking the left quarter of the frame. I had been expecting reality TV confessional, but he was actually talking to someone.

"I got you. Didn't I keep your name out of it before?" The voice that responded was muffled, as if from across the room. I saw the back of some couch, a wall, half a painting in the frame—it could have been someone's place. It could've been a hotel.

"Yes. But you don't get it. You don't…"

Naut trailed off. Took a drink.

"Get what?"

Muffled.

"I hit some homeless guy. Think he was Black. I didn't even see the light, didn't even see him. I heard him, though. Kept going. Straight down 64th Street… Why are you looking at me like that?"

The response was muffled. I couldn't make it out. But I could tell from Naut's expression, he didn't like what'd been said. "It *does* matter."

"It was just some homeless guy. It was years ago." This time the voice was stronger.

Naut grabbed the glass, nervously moving it so the ice clinked inside. It was so close to the speaker it blocked out the conversation. I strained to hear, only succeeding in picking out stray words. "Police." "Don't care." "Dead Black guy."

Even though I couldn't hear exactly what he was saying, I could see Naut's expression. He was believing whatever he was hearing. He only stopped shaking his glass when a new one slid into frame, this one filled practically to capacity with a deep brown liquid. He brought it to his mouth.

The second voice was much clearer now. "The police haven't linked that man's death to the accident. And if they do? So what? Let her rich ass continue to take the fall. Her daddy can get her out of it just like he got her out of the DUI. There's nothing to connect you to it."

My breath caught, and I fell back onto the dirty basement floor. Now that it was up close and not being drowned out by ice cubes, the voice was familiar. Too familiar. Deep and melodic even when discussing something as horrible as murder. To think I'd considered it comforting.

Naut hesitated.

The voice again. "You didn't get rid of the key fob like I told you to?"

Stuart's brown hand finally came into the frame, taking the quickly emptied glass away.

He'd known the truth the entire time. About Desiree. About Kevin House. About it all. And instead of reporting it to the police, he'd encouraged Naut to cover it up. But why?

There was a beep upstairs, the sound so faint I wouldn't have recognized it if I didn't already know what it was. My front door. Erin had picked a hell of a time to come back. I quickly paused the video, closed the laptop, and returned it to Desiree's hiding spot. I tried to cram the fifteen minutes I should've been looking for my phone into the fifteen seconds it took for Erin's footsteps to reach the basement door. I would've had better luck finding Waldo. I finally gave up. If I played it right, I'd have the element of surprise. Let her come down to me. Then I'd knock her out as soon as she hit the bottom stair.

I grabbed a lamp Erin had thrown on the floor. It was so heavy I needed both hands to pick it up. Not ideal, but what choice did I have? Erin was small. It wouldn't take much to hurt her. I bent down, waited next to the Houdini box. She opened the basement door too fast and it squeaked.

Clomp. She was on the first stair. Clomp. Second. She picked up speed as she continued down. Faster. Faster. Faster, until—

"Lena. You down here?"

Stuart.

# THIRTY-ONE

I jolted for only a second, but that was all he needed to see me crouching next to the stairs, lamp in both hands. His eyes were cold and lifeless. And I suddenly understood why he smiled so much. Because otherwise his face showed his true colors.

"You okay?" Good Old Stuart finally kicked in. Friendly Stuart. Flirty Stuart.

I scrambled up. "Yeah, you just scared me." It was easy to sound afraid when you were.

He was dressed in a black suit, no tie, top buttons of his black shirt artfully undone, revealing his pecs. I could barely look at him as he motioned to the lamp. "You gonna put that down?"

*No.* I gripped it tighter. He didn't come any closer. Just watched me, until he spoke again. "You sure you're okay?"

He not only had a good half a foot and eighty pounds on me, he was standing in front of the lone exit. I had one advantage: that he still thought I was clueless. Playing dumb was my best bet. If I could just get him to leave, I could call the police.

I finally let go of the lamp with one hand, let it fall loosely to my side. It felt heavy, but I wasn't letting it go. Instead, I returned the silly-ass smile still plastered on his face. "What are you doing here?"

"I came to apologize. Again. Then I saw your front door was open, and I got scared. Now here you are, ready to break some family heirloom over my head. Clearly something's going on." He motioned to the lamp. "Who was that for?"

"Erin." Might as well be honest. Sort of. "I think she…she…may have killed Desiree."

I wasn't the only one acting. He looked shocked. "Her best friend? Why?" He'd noticed when I hesitated. "Look, I'm not gonna write about it."

"I don't know all the details. Just that for some reason Desiree stole Naut's computer and left it here. That was why she was coming to the Bronx. To get it back. I don't know what's on it, but it made Erin do all this."

I motioned to the mess, but he kept his eyes on me. "She find it?"

I nodded again, a bit too quick. "Yep. Took it with her."

"Taking it to the police?"

"You clearly don't know Erin. More like Naut's apartment. Probably offering to sell it back to him."

"Great. Means we know where to find her." He motioned for me to head up. "Let's go, then."

I didn't move. "You want to go to Naut's apartment?"

Why? Had they spoken? Did he know that I knew?

He nodded, and I shook my head. If I could just get him to leave, I could break into Aunt E's, call the police from her landline. Tell them to meet him in Harlem. "You're the reporter. You go. I'll read about it tomorrow."

"No." There was a force to his voice that almost knocked me over. He must've realized it too because when he spoke again, it was more of a caress. "I'm not going to leave you alone. What if she comes back?"

"Okay," I said because at least it would get me upstairs and outside, where Ms. Paterson was no doubt lying in wait. If I could signal to her, *she* could call the police.

He watched as I slowly put the lamp down. "Ladies first." His voice was insistent.

I hesitated, then walked by him. As I did, I noticed his shirt wasn't unbuttoned by choice. The top buttons were missing. Freaked, I started to rush up the stairs, but he was close behind me. I glanced back and forced another smile. "I am glad you stopped by."

"That mean you accept my apology?"

*No.* "Maybe."

I could feel his breath as he trailed me out the front door. He closed it behind us, making sure to check it was locked. As he did, I looked around. For once, I cursed living on the quietest block in Highbridge. The lights were on in Ms. Paterson's first-floor window, but there was no telltale shadow. It didn't surprise me. She was too good at snooping for that.

I stared, hoping she could read my mind.

"My car's right there."

I finally turned away to see his MINI Cooper blocking my driveway.

"You okay?" he said again.

I nodded and began to walk toward the street. We were just a few feet from his car when I saw it. The brown hand splayed on the concrete. Her bare fingernails all that was visible, the rest of her hidden behind her beloved rosebushes.

Ms. Paterson.

I ran toward her. As I got closer, I could see something black and small a few inches from her hand. One of Stuart's missing buttons.

*Oh my God.* He'd killed her.

I got out half a scream before the hand covered my mouth. Something cold and hard pressed against my neck. A gun. "Shut up and get in the car, Lena."

I shook my head, scared but not foolish. Who knew what he'd do to me if he got me alone? I'd take my chances in public. Surely one of my neighbors would stop minding their business long enough to look out the window.

"Get. In. The. Car."

He used his body to push me across my driveway and to the waiting front passenger door. I slammed against it, then tried to go as slack as an obstinate toddler. I hadn't ever heard a gun cock before, but I still recognized the sound. "I will kill you like I killed your sister," he said.

I had finally gotten my confession.

And that was it. I went from pause to fast-forward, desperate to make it to the end of the story. I butted my head back, hoping to take him by surprise. It didn't work. I felt a searing pain on the right side of my head. Everything went black.

* * *

I woke up in the front passenger seat, hands bound together with jump rope and head throbbing where he'd hit me with his gun. The car was so quiet I could hear his breathing. Labored. Steady. Determined.

"You're awake," he said.

I glanced over. He hadn't bothered to put his seat belt on. Just mine. Another way to keep me restrained. I couldn't see the gun but knew it was there somewhere.

He had killed Desiree.

I forced myself not to think about it, not when I needed to stay alive myself.

"I really did like you," he said.

I ignored that, no desire to have some heart-to-heart. Instead, I looked out the window, tried to figure out where we were. Judging from the water, we'd just crossed the bridge into Manhattan. We were moving at a steady clip, but we'd have to slow down eventually, stop at some red light. If I could open the door, I could roll out. Get away.

"She didn't know, you know." And that's what got my attention. I finally turned as he kept going. "She thought I was going to help her get justice, as she called it. She'd agreed to give me the video so I'd write about what Naut did to that guy."

Kevin House. He had a daughter.

"Help his family get closure, she said. We agreed to meet up here, but then I realized she didn't give a shit that Naut's life would be ruined— my life would be ruined—if that video got out."

"Why?" I said, to keep him talking and because I needed to know.

"Why help Naut cover up what happened to begin with? Especially after you found out he'd killed someone."

"At the time, Naut was nobody. She was Desiree Pierce. Front-page news. And now? Now it'll all go into my book."

And that was it. I hit him with both hands since I didn't have much choice. The MINI Cooper lurched to the right. He righted it as I kept going. Once. Twice. I was going for a third when he lashed out with his right hand, nailed me right across the mouth. The force propelled me back, and the window cracked my head in the same spot his gun had hit before.

"Look, we can do this—"

He didn't finish his sentence. A car was on his tail, high beams on.

"New Yorkers are so damn impatient."

He sped up. But the car sped up too. We were both speeding toward a yellow light ahead. I looked back, hoping it was a cop but knowing it was probably a cabbie. I could see only bright lights.

I faced forward just in time to see the signal turn from yellow to red. Stuart didn't stop. Neither did the car behind us.

Stuart was going fast. Too fast for the city. He was so busy eyeing the high beams he didn't notice a car double-parked up ahead.

"Watch out!" I said.

He looked forward just in time to swerve into the left lane. High Beams followed suit. Stuart abruptly swung wide to turn right onto the next side street, and the car did too, cutting off a green cab.

As we turned, I could just make out the car.

A Cadillac.

Erin.

There were cars ahead but none coming from the opposite direction. Stuart careened onto the opposite side of the road, the Cadillac close behind him. Now a car was coming toward us. He swerved back into the right lane just in time. I turned around to make sure Erin also made it back. She did. Barely.

Stuart didn't slow down. That's when the fear left my body, wafting up and away like campfire smoke. I was going to die. And if that meant I was going to see Gram, my mom, and my sister, I was going to tell them I went out with a fucking fight.

I hit him again. And again. This time not letting up. Stuart tried to fend me off with his right hand while trying to still steer with his left. He slammed me forward, and my head hit the glove compartment. But as he did it, he instinctively eased his foot off the gas.

Erin slammed into us from behind. I remember what happened next only in bits and pieces. The car spinning, round and round like some demented Tea Cup ride. Stuart being next to me and then being gone. My seat belt stopping me from joining him.

When we stopped turning, the car had done a 180, and it was deadly silent.

\* \* \*

I opened my eyes, but it was too bright so I immediately closed them again. There was a voice. Male. Deep. Talking, but I couldn't make out what he was saying. I felt a moment of fear, but it was quickly replaced with fight. I was going to fuck him up.

But when I opened my eyes again, I realized this wasn't a car. And that wasn't Stuart. Mel stood with his back to me, facing the light. It was as angelic as I'd ever seen him.

I had to be hallucinating.

"He's the only reason I'm not suing your whole damn organization."

Or maybe not. I closed my eyes again. I was in the hospital, which meant I'd survived. Even though my head felt like I was having the worst hangover of my life.

Mel kept talking. "It sure as hell isn't because of that other one."

When I opened my eyes again, he'd turned around. "And now you made me wake up my daughter. Tell him he can come up now."

Conversation over, he pressed his earpiece to hang up the call. He walked right up to the standard-issue hospital table next to me and took me in. Smiled. I tried to speak, but my mouth felt like cotton.

"You need water." He put his phone down and grabbed the pitcher from the table.

He poured me a cup and handed it over. He'd gone a bit too hard with the ice chips, but it tasted good. Better than the four-hundred-dollar bottle at his apartment. I finished the whole thing, even though it hurt to swallow. Mel's phone rang again. He ignored it—too busy watching me. He moved only when someone knocked on the door. "Come in."

Detective Green. The concern on his face morphed into relief. Made me realize I needed to do my own self-evaluation. My left foot was in a cast and both wrists were bruised. My throat felt raw. I raised my right hand to take stock of my head. Found it was bandaged.

But at least my left wrist didn't itch.

Mel barely greeted Green, sharing not more than a nod before refilling my plastic cup.

"You look great, Lena," Green said. I'm sure it was a lie but one I appreciated nonetheless. "I just wanted to come check on you. Give you an update."

"And *thank* you," Mel said.

"Yes. And thank you."

I nodded, took a drink. I finally got one word out. "Stuart."

"Dead."

I'd gotten my wish, but it sure didn't feel like world peace. If anything, it just felt like more chaos. He'd played the Magical Nonthreatening Negro role to a tee. The suits. The smile. The "I'm on your side." Like Desiree, I had fallen for it. It would take a long time for me to get over that.

"We do consider Desiree's case closed. Now a homicide. Same with Denise Paterson."

I nodded. I couldn't think about that now, and wasn't sure I'd forgive myself later.

I thought of seeing her body, then being in that car. The chase and then: "Erin."

She had to be okay. The Caddy was as big as the MINI Cooper was small. She had to have braced herself. There had to have been an airbag.

"We think she's alive."

"Think?"

I tensed, and some machine in the room beeped faster. *She saved my life.* Mel touched my hand holding the cup, led it to my mouth. "Drink, Melina. Erin was okay enough to walk away from the accident."

Green nodded. "No one's seen her since. We'd like to talk to her if she does reach out to you."

I hoped she would. But despite this peace treaty, I doubted I'd tell them.

"We did arrest Neil Marks, so thank you for that."

I nodded. I'm sure Naut's arrest was front-page news, though I wondered who wrote the article. I hoped he got a shitty-ass headline.

Mel's phone went to his lock screen. The photo was the one of the three of us. I looked at it, at Desiree smiling at me. She wasn't perfect. She'd made mistakes, especially at the end of her life. But she'd died because she wanted to do the right thing—or at least her version of it. The guilt about not being there for her when she needed me would never go away, but I was happy that I was able to prove this for her—even if it had landed me in this hospital bed. I was exhausted, too tired to take in any more updates. Green got the hint too. "I should probably go."

His exit was swift, leaving just me and Mel. I pretended not to notice him staring at me, as if I'd up and disappear right in front of his eyes. Finally, I looked at him.

"Drink," he said again, and I did as told. "Aunt E was with us all night. Eventually I had someone take her home. We need to call her."

I nodded.

"And I still think you should move." But he'd smiled when he said it.

"No." But I smiled too. At least tried to.

"You're gonna be okay," he said.

"Of course I am," I said, my voice finally strong. "I'm a Pierce."

A close-up of Desiree Pierce looking flawless. A waiter in a dress shirt walks behind her holding a bottle of champagne.

"You guys, I have the most amazing news. Zarah's show got picked up. I'm gonna be on TV! Ahhhh." She fake screams, then turns the camera to her right and leans toward Lena Scott so they're both in the frame. "Say hi to my big sister. Lena."

But Lena's not paying attention. She casually holds a mimosa as she stares intently at someone next to her, ignoring the eggs and bacon on the expensive-looking plate in front of her.

"Lena!" Desiree's voice is louder.

Lena finally turns.

"Say hi!"

"Hi!" But she's already looking back at her neighbor.

Unbothered, Desiree pans more so we see who has Lena's attention: Mel Pierce. "That's my dad," she says to the camera. "What are you two talking about?"

Mel looks at Lena conspiratorially. "Nothing," he says.

She smiles. "Right. We're definitely not talking about anything to do with a window."

She laughs. Mel laughs. After a minute Desiree joins in. When things die down, Mel lifts his champagne glass. "Let's make a toast. To good memories."

They clink. Desiree's hand comes into frame. She speaks next. "To dreams coming true."

They clink again as Mel looks expectantly at Lena. "To happiness," she says.

"To happiness," they all say.

They finally drink, Desiree moving her phone so she can down the rest of her drink. When she's done, she slaps the glass on the table with such force we hear it echo.

"I want a pic."

Lena smiles at her. "Me too."

The camera shuts off.

# ACKNOWLEDGMENTS

There was a period where I never thought I'd ever get the chance to write acknowledgments again because I'd never *finish* a book again, so it's surreal to be doing this.

Though writing technically is a solitary endeavor, it's not something that I could ever do alone—it took a lot of people to turn an idea I got from a real *Daily News* headline into an actual book with a beginning, middle, and end.

To my agent, Michelle Richter: I've always told emerging authors that your agent shouldn't be your friend and yet you are one of my closest friends. You believed in me when literally no one else did—including myself. And there's no one else on the planet I'd want to have by my side for every up and down.

To my U.K. editor, Katherine Armstrong, thank you so much for believing in my work and bringing Lena across the pond. I also want to thank the entire Simon & Schuster UK Team including Laurie McShea, Genevieve Barrett, Mina Asaam, Sian Wilson, and folks I haven't met already yet but already am forever in their debt.

To my U.S. editor, Helen O'Hare: I always tell people at my day job that I have no ego when it comes to what I write there but I have all the ego when it comes to my books. So thank you so much for dealing with my adorable (right???) writer quirks and for bringing out the best in me—even though I know I don't always make it easy. I'm so proud of this book, and you are the reason for that. (And you were right that this only needed one Brazilian butt lift joke.) A huge thank you to the Mulholland/Little, Brown team as well.

One of the coolest things about being a writer is that you make writer friends who give you great feedback and encouragement. So thank you to Brenda, Chantelle, Cynthia, Ellen, Gigi, Gordon, Laura, Leslie, Lisa, Lizzie, Mariella, Mia, Nadine, Nikki, Quincy, Rachel, Roselle, Sarah, Shawn, Sonia, Stephanie, Valerie, Vanessa, Walter, and anyone whose name I don't have here but are so cool they won't hate me for not including them.

I also need to shout out my writing group, The Fab Four—Alex Segura, Amina Akhtar, and Liz Little. Though my thanks won't be as cool as the ones in Alex's acknowledgments (you'll need to read his book *Secret Identity* to see them!) or in Amina's (check out *Kismet* to see those), do know that you all came into my life at such a needed time. Being on this journey with you makes all the uncertainty of this business worth it. *Let's do this!*

I also need to shout out two amazing groups just because they are super cool and super needed: Sisters in Crime and Crime Writers of Color.

Because I would be disowned if I didn't thank them and because they're actually a really cool group of people, my family. Thank you for letting me borrow your names, stories, and even freckles for this book. I especially need to thank my mom Valerie, my niece Mallory and my nephew Julian because I know that they all will be looking for their names in this book. So here they are!

Finally, to my grandpa Bill. I will always regret that you weren't able to see this book published before you passed away.

# ABOUT THE AUTHOR

Kellye Garrett is the acclaimed author of *Hollywood Homicide,* which won the Agatha, Anthony, Lefty, and Independent Publisher "IPPY" awards for best first novel and was named one of BookBub's Top 100 Crime Novels of All Time, as well as *Hollywood Ending,* which was featured on the *Today* show's Best Summer Reads of 2019 and was nominated for both Anthony and Lefty awards. Before writing novels, Kellye spent eight years working in Hollywood, including a stint writing for *Cold Case.* The northern New Jersey resident currently serves on the board of directors for Sisters in Crime and is a cofounder of Crime Writers of Color.